MINE TO KEEP

PROTECTION SERIES BOOK 4

KENNEDY L. MITCHELL

© 2021 Kennedy L. Mitchell

All rights reserved. This book or any portion thereof may not be reproduced or used in any manner whatsoever without the express written permission of the publisher except for the use of brief quotations in a book review.

This book is a work of fiction. Any references to historical events, real people, or real places are used fictitiously. Other names, characters, places and events are products of the author's imagination, and any resemblances to actual events or places or persons, living or dead, is entirely coincidental.

Cover Design: Bookin It Designs

Editing: Hot Tree Editing

Proofreading: All Encompassing Books

❋ Created with Vellum

ABOUT THE AUTHOR

Kennedy L. Mitchell lives outside Dallas with her husband, son and two very large goldendoodles. She began writing in 2016 after a fight with her husband (You can read the fight almost verbatim in Falling for the Chance) and has no plans of stopping.

She would love to hear from you via any of the platforms below or her website www.kennedylmitchell.com You can also stay up to date on future releases through her newsletter or by joining her Facebook readers group - Kennedy's Book Boyfriend Support Group.

Thank you for reading.

PROLOGUE

The revolving door shifted with a soft *whoosh* from her timid push against the tinted glass, heated air from inside the hotel lobby immediately warming her frozen cheeks. In awe of the elaborate lobby, Jessica Hale paused just inside to take in the grandeur. Fingers stiff from the cold gripped the edges of her black wool coat, fluffing the trapped winter air away from her body and dispelling the few watery flakes adhered to the shoulders and sleeves.

Long delicate fingers trembled, though not only from the icy wind blowing off the nearby river, as she removed one snug leather glove followed by the other, shoving both deep into the coat's side pocket. Behind her, a gust of cold air sent her long dark hair whipping forward. A man in an expensive-looking suit entered the hotel and hurried past, clearly more confident in his night's plans than her.

"The first time will be the best and scariest. It is for everyone."

Jessica reminded herself of her new online friend's wise words and repeated them as a mantra, as she had the last few weeks to not back out of the illicit plan. Every time she considered calling the entire night off, the idea of returning home to Jett, instead of standing there in the lobby, forced to witness his indifferent stares and be ignored for the smartphone always clutched in his grasp, reestablished her resolve.

Jessica shook her head to dislodge the insistent nagging voice, urging her to back out now before she did something she could never take back.

Too much time, effort, and money went into arranging this night and ensuring she covered her tracks online and off. After this first encounter, it would be easier, even though the idea of the butterflies that took flight in her belly the moment she drove out of the driveway diminishing with every visit didn't sound nearly as thrilling.

Sucking in a confidence-boosting breath, Jessica forced her feet forward. The heels of her four-inch black stilettos clicked along the sparkling white marble tile. Her nervous eyes flicked from one side of the lobby to the other to make sure no one she knew lingered nearby. Though that chance was slim. No one in her normal suburban-housewife social circles knew about The Black Rose, much less could afford a single night in this luxury.

The massive crystal chandeliers that hung from the vaulted ceiling caught her wandering eye, their dangling teardrop crystals casting sprinkles of brilliant light along the black-and-gold-wallpapered walls and floors despite the dreary, dark night outside. As others who used this hotel as their rendezvous had noted, the hotel staff remained in the shadows until needed. To the right, a meek woman stood behind the reception desk, her eyes lowered to the black granite counter, never chancing a glance at the guest checking in.

Anonymity.

The Black Rose offered ultimate privacy in spades to their unique and cautious clientele. There wasn't another hotel like it in the Louisville, Kentucky, area that catered to those who needed to remain anonymous to those around them. It made The Black Rose perfect for clandestine affairs. A place where two relative strangers could find passion and lust in the arms of another, their spouses or partners none the wiser.

This wasn't her. Deep down, Jessica knew it was wrong, going against all her black-and-white morals. But the never-ending lifeless nights with her husband, Jett, feeling more alone with him ignoring her pleas for attention, drove her to this, turning her into the type of person she used to judge from the church pew.

Cheater.

Adulterer.

Whore.

Worry filled her stomach as she followed the signs toward the hotel bar. She had arrived early enough to park three blocks away in a cash-only lot, as instructed by others she'd met through the Affair Me app, and have a drink to calm her racing heart.

Inside, the dimly lit bar shielded other patrons. Muffled murmurs and bursts of sensual laughter from the shadowed booths alerted her that she wasn't alone. A clink of glass, the pop of champagne, tinkling laughter—it all flowed through one ear and out the other, easing the tension from her stiff shoulders.

This was just a regular bar, a routine drink on an ordinary night. That was what she had to tell herself to keep moving toward the glittering bar. Just tonight; then tomorrow things would go back to normal. Days filled with PTA meetings, soccer practices and games, and a husband who didn't care if she was there or not, as long as he was fed.

Her stomach sank just thinking about it.

Only one night was on the table for the first meeting. The promise of more wasn't to be discussed unless both parties agreed on the compatibility between the two. The app made it simple with the ability to select each person's predilection for the qualities they sought in a partner.

After nights of searching based on her location and preferences, Jessica selected a man the complete opposite of her husband in all the best ways. The man's profile had a five-star rating—the site had a rating system for safety, attractiveness, and, of course, pleasure—and the attached pictures made Jessica drool at first click with his wavy dark brown hair, smoldering hazel eyes, and a jaw even Gaston would swoon over.

The embodiment of perfection.

Jessica knew he wasn't perfect, but for one night, a few hours, maybe they could be perfect together.

Removing her thick coat, she draped it over the high brass barstool back and slid onto the neighboring stool's black leather cushioned seat. The short hem of the recently purchased black dress crept up her thighs, showing more skin than she found appropriate in public.

She snorted a quiet laugh at that. Nothing about tonight was appropriate.

With a few fidgeting tugs at the dress, she gathered her long hair in a single hand and held it in a makeshift ponytail, pulling it over her shoulder. Sighing through her pursed lips, she closed her eyes, trying to dampen her nervous energy.

"What can I get you, miss?"

She nibbled on her lower lip while scanning the rows of liquor bottles behind the bartender.

"Champagne, whatever you have by the glass."

Without another word, the bartender shifted down the polished mahogany top, reappearing moments later with a spotless champagne flute filled to the top with bubbling liquid. He placed a crisp white cocktail napkin down before resting the glass on top.

Her quivering fingers tugged the paper napkin closer before wrapping around the fragile glass stem. Crisp bubbles exploded on her tongue, gliding easily down her parched throat with each long sip, the glass only half full when she finally had enough and set the delicate glass back on the bar top. Licking her red lips, she casually glanced down the bar, curious to see if anyone else seemed as nervous as her.

At the end of the bar, a couple was cozied up on one barstool, not caring about anything going on around them. A single woman sat a little closer with just a few chairs separating them. When the woman's gaze met hers, Jessica snapped her attention to the champagne flute, nerves spiking, heat building beneath her cheeks. She quietly cursed herself for looking around. No doubt her curiosity made her break some kind of unspoken rule in this place.

Her pulse raced, sweat collecting along her clammy hands. What if they kicked her out after all she'd done to make this night happen? She'd come too far, done too much to not have her own blip of happiness for one night. Now instead of butterflies, dread weighed heavy in her gut.

"First time?"

Jessica's head snapped in the woman's direction. A warm, comforting smile and bright, though slightly bloodshot, eyes immediately put her at ease.

"Is it that obvious?" Jessica said with a resigned exhale.

The older woman's smile grew as she angled her head toward the bar, where Jessica's nervous fingers were busy shredding the corners of the cocktail napkin. She cursed herself once again and crumpled her growing mess into a tight fist. Reaching around, she shoved the trash into her coat pocket.

"Hey, it's okay," the woman said, her voice warm. "We've all been there at one point." Jessica whipped her head toward her, eyes wide. The woman laughed, revealing straight white teeth. Fine lines sunburst out from the corners of her eyes. "Surprised?"

"It's not that. It's just a surprise that all this is real life," Jessica admitted. "This hidden group of people, you know. I'm still shocked by its popularity when no one knows about it unless you go looking for it."

The woman hummed her agreement. "But those who look for it always find a way."

"Yes," Jessica said, her voice weak. Because that was her. She'd found it after another night desperate for passion, for life, even if that meant finding it outside her marriage vows.

"Sounds like you really need this. Things bad with your spouse?"

Jessica's shoulder rose and fell in a single-arm shrug. "It's just nothing. No passion, no long looks or touches. I can't tell you the last time we had sex—" She cut herself off and winced. "Sorry, I overshare when I'm nervous."

"It's okay. I'm here enough to have heard it all."

Though the woman was pretty for her age and seemed happy, deep down, Jessica hoped she wouldn't end up like this woman. There was a hard look to her that no makeup could hide. No, she wouldn't be a repeater like this woman. Tonight's events would only be this once, to relieve pent-up pressure from the past two years of being invisible to the man she'd committed her life to. This would not turn into a lifestyle for her—she wouldn't allow herself to turn into this woman.

Jessica took a long drink, finishing the remaining champagne. "I just want to feel again, even for just a night."

"Then you've found the right group of people."

Jessica went to reach for her phone to check the time, only to remember she'd turned it off for the night like the rules stated. No phone on meant no GPS, pictures, or audio. This meant nothing left the hotel, allowing the participants to return to their spouses with no evidence left behind. They even sent all the communications through the encrypted app, which the owners ensured could not be hacked.

"Do you know what time it is?" Jessica asked, just realizing she didn't even wear a watch. *Rookie mistake.*

"Eight thirty." The woman chuckled at Jessica's responding flinch. "You're *that* early, huh?"

Jessica dipped her chin in acknowledgment. "We're not meeting until nine."

"Did he get the room?" Jessica nodded. "Good, that leaves less of a paper trail for you to cover up."

"I even parked down the street like others suggested to keep from having my car associated with the hotel."

"You've done your homework," the woman said with a knowing smile. Taking a sip of her nearly empty highball glass, she finished the drink and slid it toward the other side of the bar. "I always like to have a few drinks first too. Loosens me up for the night's events. Have another. You have time." She motioned for the bartender, who appeared the next moment. Laying down a crisp hundred-dollar bill, she winked at Jessica. "For my drinks and hers."

Without a goodbye, the woman slid off the chair and walked toward the bar's only visible exit. Jessica's gaze followed her until she disappeared around the corner. Alone again, Jessica turned back to the ornate bar, her glass full and the cash gone.

Feeling a bit more confident about her decision to come tonight, Jessica took a sip of the bubbly liquid and smiled around the glass's smooth edge.

Now all she had to do was wait.

And then, hopefully, have the best night of the last few years with a sexy-as-sin man with no strings attached.

With an even wider smile, Jessica relaxed against the chair's brass back and raised her glass in the air, saluting her reflection in the gold-veined mirror on the opposite side of the bar.

She deserved this.

Deep down, she knew in her heart that she deserved everything that was to come.

1

CHARLIE

"Good morning, Special Agent Bekham."

I tipped the thin manila envelope toward the female agent, stepping into the elevator, too engrossed in the phone conversation to verbally respond. Out of the corner of my eye, I watched her reflection in the mirrored wall as she blatantly scanned a sensual once-over from my dress shoes all the way up, pausing on the tattoos adorning the top of the hand holding the folder. She sank her upper teeth into her lower lip, then lifted a hand and pressed it to her lower belly, the movement causing the diamonds adorning her engagement and wedding rings to sparkle in the artificial light.

"Yeah, I'm getting on the elevator now, so I might lose you," I said into the phone pressed against my ear. "I'll present what we have on the cases to my section chief, but there's not much to go on, you know that. I'll call you back with his answer, though don't hold your breath. I'm not his favorite agent in the world, if you can believe that."

The female agent shuffled, inching closer. Nostrils flaring in annoyance, I shifted too, moving closer to the control panel to prevent us from touching. The folder in my hand bent in my tightening grip. This kind of blatant behavior wasn't a one-off occurrence. Apparently, I was the fresh meat here at Quantico, and come to find out many of the female agents had a thing for tatted bad boys. Which wasn't a bad thing if I had time to turn their advances into something physical.

"I can see that." My friend chuckled on the other end of the line. "You're not one to blindly accept orders and authority."

"You say that like it's a bad thing."

"Let me know what he says. I could really use your help on these unusual cases."

"Sounds good, Bryson. Talk to you soon." I ended the call and slipped the phone into my slacks pocket, ignoring the woman literally licking her lips as she stared at my crotch.

"Rumor around the office says you're single," she said all breathy like she was already imagining herself pinned against the elevator wall.

Fake smile plastered across my face, I gave her left hand a pointed glance. "By that rock and band on your hand, it looks like you're not." Her face flushed red, that left hand immediately tucked behind her back. I tsked at the movement, allowing my disdain for blatant cheaters to show. "Though I appreciate the early morning eye fuck, I don't lick what's not mine, and I sure as hell don't share."

Guilt's steel claws gouged inside my chest when her overly sultry smile fell to that of embarrassment and shame before morphing to anger. With a huff, she shot a death glare my way and angled herself away from where I stood. Was it terrible that in the few months I'd been at Quantico as part of the BSU team, I'd made most of the women in the office believe I was a total dick? Sure, considering I always felt like shit after being an outright ass proved my attitude wasn't admirable.

I didn't do it to be an ass, though it saved me more times than I could count. It had to be something with the tattoos that made the women here not take no for an answer.

I glanced down at my covered hands, rotating them in the artificial light. Whether it was the tattoos or rumors of my previous antics, some women thought I was down for anything, even if I said no repeatedly. So now, instead of acting flattered at their advances, I acted like a cocky prick.

I left the womanizing and all-nighters back in Nashville when I took the new gig and moved to DC. Now was time to focus, to prove to my asshole boss and the higher-ups that they made a solid choice in adding me to the Behavioral Science Unit as a profiler. Starting fresh and focusing on advancing in my career meant no interoffice romances, even if the woman was single and willing. It hadn't been too much of a hardship, considering the new job literally sucked the life out of you mentally and physically. Any free time I'd had since starting six months ago was spent unpacking my minimal belongings or catching up on much-needed sleep.

The elevator slowed at the BSU division floor, followed by a sharp ding bouncing through the enclosed space. Not daring a glance back, I stepped off the elevator, visibly relaxing when the doors whispered shut behind me. Pinching the knot of my thin black tie, I adjusted the position as I confidently strode toward the glass door. The scanner beeped beneath my badge, allowing me access to our restricted area.

Multiple phones insistently ringing, the soft murmur of groups of agents chatting, and the scent of cheap burnt coffee assaulted my senses the moment I stepped into the bullpen. A genuine grin pulled at the corner of my lips as I surveyed the area and the few team members. The existing members of the profiling team welcomed me into the fold greedily, excited for the help, not caring about my hard exterior. At first I assumed it was my amazing people skills and profiling ability that made them immediately warm up to me, but a week into the job, I discovered it was more because they were overworked and stretched thin and just happy to have a new member to help lessen the load.

"Bekham." My attention swung toward the team's section chief's —aka asshole Carter—office. "Good of you to join us." I made a show of glancing at my watch, knowing I was thirty minutes early, like usual. "My office."

The muscle along my jaw flexed as I clamped my mouth shut to keep from saying something I would regret. A man like him wouldn't forget it if I embarrassed him in front of the watching team. With a clipped nod, I started toward the short set of stairs that would lead me to his office. As I passed a desk with three agents gathered around, Agent Peters caught my eye and nodded in greeting. The other agents around him offered warm smiles before turning their attention back to the grouping of pictures scattered along the desktop.

"How was the San Diego case?" Carter asked when I clicked the door closed behind me, not even glancing away from his laptop.

"Good. Caught the bastard. Doesn't get any better than that." Tapping the file against the chair back, I waited in front of his desk.

"There was mention of unnecessary roughness in the capture of the suspect per the report I received this morning."

Annoyance bloomed, causing heat to build beneath my skin. "The bastard had kidnapped and was about to rape his thirteenth victim, sir," I ground out. "He fled the scene, forcing us to pursue. The fact that he walked away with his life shows I restrained myself."

I was proud as fuck. I didn't kill the bastard with my bare hands.

Carter's dark eyes flicked over the top of the laptop screen. In one long calculating stare, I felt splayed open before him. "Don't let it happen again. I'm adding the complaint to your file." After almost a full minute of silence, he said, "The message you left this morning said you wanted to talk. Already quitting, I see. Can't take the hard work required to be a part of the BSU team, I'm assuming."

I held back a growl of annoyance. To say he and I didn't see eye to eye was an understatement. He was reluctant to hire me but was forced to by the section chief because of Agent Peters's reference and the urgent need for help. His disdain for my visible body art and the way the female agents paid close attention to me instead of him—who I'd recently learned through the office gossip was the most eligible bachelor until I arrived at Quantico—made working with him every day a fucking nightmare.

"No, sir. I'm loving the job, actually. Though I could be more help if allowed to use my computer skills with the same clearance and authority as the technical analysts."

"That's their job, not yours. Stick to profiling the way it's always been done and let them handle the back end."

Fucker. Dumb fucking fucker.

Shoving down my hatred, I swallowed hard and cleared my throat to redirect the conversation to why I called him in the first place.

"I called this morning to discuss a case an agent I know down in the Louisville, Kentucky, office would like our help on." Stepping around the chair, I tossed the file to the desk. It slid across the smooth surface, pausing right beside his laptop. Reluctantly, he opened it and flipped through the pictures and accompanying case notes.

"Five women," I said, pointing to the pictures of the women. "Ages ranging from late twenties to mid-forties, all found in the Ohio River over the course of eight months. The first four bodies were too decomposed to gather evidence or determine the exact cause of death, but the most recent victim was only in the water a few hours."

His brows narrowed as he studied the notes. "It says here the coroner listed them all as suicides. Why would the agent need our assistance?"

"Yes, the bone fractures indicate they jumped or fell from a high elevation into the water, but that's it. No other sign of foul play, except with the most recent victim. The coroner believes she had sex a few hours prior to being in the water."

"I still don't—"

"They're successful women, careers. Two even left behind a family. There were no indications of depression, none on medication or talks of suicide per the spouses and family. They just went out one night and didn't come back."

He hummed as he thumbed through the pictures. "Different ethnicities, different ages. Doesn't seem to be a pattern. Maybe Louisville just has a suicide spike in middle-aged women."

My hands curled into tight fists, and I tucked them behind my back before he could see my annoyance. This was the exact reason I wanted this division, why I'd worked my way to the BSU. If someone wouldn't have said they were just prostitutes or junkies, maybe my mom wouldn't have been murdered or the ten after her. But no one cared, like my asshole boss, to put the time into seeing the trend, the oddities of the reoccurring theme.

"Let me go down there and check." His hard eyes shifted to me, brows arched. "I'll even drive down there instead of taking the jet." Which was saying a lot, because the jet was fucking cool. "I'll review the recent body firsthand, talk to the coroner. The agent wouldn't have reached out if he didn't feel there was something to this. He knows his jurisdiction. He's an excellent agent."

"You're too new."

"Sir, I'm a seasoned FBI agent. I can handle the initial scouting of this case."

With an incredulous huff, he shoved the pictures and notes back into the manila file. With his middle finger pressed in the center, he pushed it back across the desk toward me. I caught it before it could tip over the edge.

"No." I bit my tongue to keep from ripping Carter a new one for being a shortsighted prick. "We have too many *real* cases to sort through. There are several on your desk at this very moment. We don't have the time or the personnel to waste on some non-profiler's hunch. Dismissed."

"Sir," I gritted out. "They need—"

"If you continue to press my authority over this team, I will have you reassigned, Agent. We're done here."

The heels of my shoes ground into the worn carpet as I twisted toward the door, eager to put distance between me and that fucker so I didn't enact my murderous thoughts. My steps thundered down the short hall and stairs, declaring my frustration to all those watching from the bullpen.

Not making eye contact with anyone, I weaved through the sea of desks until I reached my own. The wheels of my chair clattered when I jerked it back and slammed my ass down into the seat. Tossing the file to my desk, I leaned forward, pressing both elbows to the hard surface and raking my hands through the long top section of my black hair.

Too lost in mentally planning that fuckhead's murder, I didn't notice someone approach until a soft, attention-seeking throat clearing jerked me out of my inner turmoil.

The quiet red-headed profiler, who I'd met once, maybe twice, because of her always being out working a case, shoved her thick black-framed glasses up her pert nose from where they'd slipped as she stared down at me in my chair. I sucked in a breath, inhaling her soft scent. This close, I was reminded of how striking she was with her natural beauty.

"You all right?" she asked. I fully expected her to be meek, voice all soft and breathy, but a strong, confident, even tone caught me off guard. As she stood over me, I gave her tall, lean body a quick assessing once-over. With her long legs, I guessed she was only a few inches shorter than my six-foot-three frame, tall for a woman. Red hair highlighted with golds and blondes, flawless fair skin, and captivating jade-green eyes. With the sharp tailored black suit and the fact that she looked at me like a man and not a piece of meat, I instantly gave her my full attention.

"Sorry, I'm Rhyan Riggs. Not sure if you remember meeting me."

I grasped her extended hand, returning her firm shake.

"I do. We met when I first started, I believe."

She dipped her chin, eyes dancing around the room. "The first few months getting your feet under you can be challenging in this division." Leaning a thigh against the desk's edge, she turned her full focus to the file I'd tossed. "What's that?" she asked, tilting her head toward it.

Of course, as a profiler, she'd quickly identified the source of my frustration.

"The reason I'm fucking pissed," I gritted out. "An agent friend asked me to present a case to the boss, hoping for our help. He thinks something's going on in Louisville, Kentucky, but Carter doesn't feel the same way. He completely dismissed the idea and me."

Gnawing on her bare lower lip, she stared at the file instead of me. "Yeah, he's not open-minded about cases that aren't clear-cut for our division. Can I look, give you my opinion?" She held out her hand, palm up, and curled her fingers.

I handed it over and gave her the same spiel as I did earlier. Rhyan listened, reviewing the notes and pictures while I spoke, clearly paying more attention to the details than that upper-level asshole.

After I was done, she shut the file and handed it back. My shoulders slumped in defeat, believing she was yet another who dismissed oddities of the case. With another push to the middle of those thick frames, she twisted around and left. I watched in complete disbelief as she climbed the few stairs and knocked on our section chief's closed door.

"She's so odd." Without meaning to, I swiveled my chair an inch, leaning an ear toward the two newbie agents tasked with coordinating our travel and connections with local law enforcement. "Have you ever talked to her?"

"She's a know-it-all," the other woman said. "Been that way since she got here last year. Did you hear why she left the Seattle office? Such a scandal."

A chair squeaked, and the slow roll of wheels told me the other woman had inched closer to her coworker to hear the details. "Why?" she whispered.

"It was this enormous scandal. Her husband caught her running around on him with a coworker. They transferred her to—"

"We leave tomorrow. We only have a few days to determine if it's a BSU case or not." I swiveled around, blinking at Agent Riggs, who, while I was eavesdropping, came back and was now leaning against my desk. "Why did you offer to drive? The jet is so much better."

"Because I thought…. Wait, we?" I said, trying to articulate the overload of questions flashing through my head. "What's going on?"

She lifted a slim shoulder. "You seemed passionate about the case, and after reviewing the notes and hearing you present your reasoning behind us being needed, I believed you. I think you're right." I felt my dark brows inch up my forehead at her declaration. "Even though the suicide rate in America has continued to rise, there are consistencies in the data that don't fluctuate with the increase. Men die by suicide almost four times more often than women, a firearm is used in almost 50 percent of all suicides, and the most affected are middle-aged white men. Those are just a few of the consistent statistics. None pertain to the five cases you have, which go outside the data parameters."

"Wow," I breathed and leaned back in the chair. "That's—"

"Information overload," one agent who was gossiping earlier said just loud enough for me and Agent Riggs to hear.

Something in me flared brightly as I watched the agent before me go from confident to insecure in a blink. She nibbled on the corner of her lip, those green eyes staring straight through me, as if focusing would help her ignore the snide comment.

"Extremely informative to the case," I stated loudly to shut the women up behind me. Why I suddenly felt protective of the woman was beyond me, but it was there. "What time do you want to leave tomorrow?"

"It's almost a ten-hour drive—"

"Eight if I drive," I cut in with a smirk. "Seven and a half if I get to drive my car."

"Sports car?" I nodded. "Classic or modern?"

I leaned against the desk. "Classic."

"Ford or Chevy?"

"Ford."

She eyed me up and down, but not in an eye-fucking way like other women. No, this was a calculated data-gathering scan.

"Mustang," she said, nodding to herself. "Shelby."

"What year?" I rapped my fingers along the top of the desk, expecting her wrong answer. "If you get it right, I might let you drive her."

"1969."

My jaw dropped. Once, twice I tried to come up with words but couldn't.

"I'm a damn good profiler," she said, shoving off the desk and retreating a step. Her gaze quickly jumped over my shoulder before settling back on me. "And I saw you in the parking garage once. Eight tomorrow morning. Swing by and pick me up. Bring enough clothes for a few days. If we're both right, it will take some time to profile the unsub. There's little to go on."

Dumbstruck, I said nothing when she turned and walked away. I was still gaping at the turn of events, as the women's gossip at my back picked up with a feverish pitch. Something about being a home-wrecker and whore was tossed around. As I watched Agent Riggs settle back into her desk, picking up the top file on her stack and leaning back to inspect the contents, I realized her pile of case files was twice mine.

Which meant she didn't have time for this wild-goose chase I'd pitched and she'd defended me on.

So it begged the questions: Why did she intervene, and why offer to come along?

My suspicions rose, making my muscles tense.

Good thing I wouldn't have to wait long to find out her motive for helping.

Tomorrow would come soon enough, and we had a long drive ahead of us. Plenty of time to uncover answers and find out the truth about Supervisory Special Agent Rhyan Riggs.

2

RHYAN

My heels soundlessly stamped along the geometric hallway carpet as I strode down the hall, casting a glance behind me every other step to ensure no one followed. At the restroom door, I pressed a hip to the fake wood and hurried inside. The door whispered shut behind me, but I didn't move, just stood completely still, a shallow breath burning in my lungs as I listened.

Silence.

With a sigh of relief, I stepped deeper into the women's restroom. Being a complete over-diligent creeper, I moved down the row of stalls, checking the lower portion for feet.

Empty.

Not wasting a single second of this rare moment alone, I swiped a thumb across the phone clutched tight in my sweaty palm. After selecting the only number stored in the favorites list, I pressed the smooth, warm glass to my ear.

After the first ring, I paced the length of the three individual ceramic sinks, my restless energy demanding an exit as I waited for my friend to answer.

"If you're calling to be talked off the hypothetical ledge your anxiety created, I can't—"

"It's not that." I grimaced, catching my reflection in a mirror. My anxiety-induced panicked calls were worse lately, I'd give her that. Though this was a common occurrence nowadays with the never-ceasing stress of the job and my messed-up personal life. "I did it," I whispered into the mouthpiece, unable to stop my growing smile.

"You finally killed that fucker of a boss? Listen, babe. You're my bestie, but you know I can't defend you if I know you did it."

Her response made my smile grow, my cheeks burning as they bunched in a way I hadn't felt in months. Olivia Reynolds was hands down the best friend any woman would be lucky to have. I counted my blessings every time she picked up and listened to me talk in circles or worry about a future incident that would probably never happen. She was my rock, my emotional support. In turn, I offered her a spot of relief from her daily hectic routine of being a wife and mother to two sets of twins.

"No defense necessary. I didn't do *that* thing, though only because I've yet to devise the perfect murder."

"Which, I have to admit, Rhy, is concerning. You're smart as hell and work with serial killers all day. You should have a basic plan in place by now. It's been fourteen months."

"Been counting the days since I've been gone, have you?" I said with a huffed laugh.

"Um, yes. I miss my best friend. I have no one to make poor decisions with and then blame the consequences on after. It's a terrible imposition you've put me in by leaving Seattle and moving across the continent to DC."

"I talked to *him*." I sucked in a breath and bit my lip to keep from babbling.

"*Him* him?" she whispered, her excitement clear despite the distance between us.

"Yes," I squeaked.

"No shit. The hot tattooed one?" I nodded like she could see me. "Rhy, that's fucking outstanding."

The pride in her voice brought a well of tears to my lower lids. She knew what such a simple step to anyone else meant for someone like me. She knew it all, every detail about my life, good or bad, the anxiety that drove it, and the past I was still running from despite the distance.

"I need details." A commotion sounded in the background from her side, followed by a cry so loud I pulled the phone away from my ear to spare my eardrums. "I swear these kids are trying to drive me insane. They're doing it on purpose," she said, voice wobbly as if she were holding back tears.

"Olivia, you're an amazing mother. They're not doing it on purpose. You just feel that way at the moment—"

"Mommy's on the phone," she yelled away from the mouthpiece, but not far enough. Yawning my jaw, I tried to clear the tickling vibrations her loud, shrill voice caused. A child's muffled voice responded among the wails. "Then find a Band-Aid. You're fine enough to tattle on your brother. You're fine, Lucy." She sighed, then whined, "Rhyan."

"Take a minute. Step outside on the porch to give yourself a second to reset." Instead of hearing the screen door screech open, the familiar gurgle of wine being dumped into a glass had me shaking my head. "You grabbed a drink, didn't you?" A crack of the screen door slamming shut had me jumping in my heels. The creak of old wood, the grind of rusted metal, and I could envision her falling onto the old porch swing with a plastic cup of wine in hand.

"Maybe. Don't you dare judge me, Rhy. I'm trying to survive this tiny army of ungrateful humans the best I can without my bestie at my side."

"You know I'm not judging you. It's just...." I flicked my wrist to wake up my watch. "It's four here, which means it's one there. Do you have a plan for someone to pick up the other two after school if you have more than that one glass? I can call an Uber—"

"Go back to telling me how the tattooed hottie pinned you to your desk and had his way with you while everyone watched," she said.

"I said nothing about being pinned to a desk or others watching." I laughed, shaking my head.

"Oh, that must have been what I envisioned, then. It was great.

You should totally do that, then tell me all about it so I can get my daydream fantasy details correct. You know how we lawyers love the incriminating details."

Sighing, I leaned against the tiled wall and stared up at the fluorescent lights. "It happened this morning. I walked over when I noticed he was frustrated after meeting with Carter, and... Olivia, I was normal."

"Of course, you were normal, babe, because you are. You're not odd or awkward, no matter what that dipshit Brian—" I hissed at hearing his name, interrupting her. "Sorry, forgot. I know that dipshit He Who Shall Not Be Named made you believe that junk, but it's not true. You didn't believe that about yourself before he royally fucked with your head."

I huffed, knowing she was right. But knowing it and believing it were very different concepts. "That was a long time ago."

"And you're still the same smart, fun, generous, beautiful woman now as you were then."

"With saggier boobs."

"Yeah, well, yours still look better than mine. I have fucking black diamond ski slopes for tits after four kids."

"We're getting off topic."

"Right," she said. "So if you're calling, that means it went well and you have more to share. Though not about desk sex, which, I have to admit, I'm a little let down by."

"OMG, you're killing me with the desk sex—" A crash in the background cut me off. "Everything okay over there?"

"There's no smoke, but I should probably go back inside soon before they go all *Lord of the Flies* on me. Which means as much as I want every detail of your encounter with Agent Bad Boy, I'll need the short version."

"Right, short version. Here's the CliffsNotes. I backed him up on a case he thought we should investigate, though our boss disagreed. I got us a few days to check out the evidence, and now we're going on a road trip together to determine the validity of a BSU case."

"Holy shit."

"Right," I exclaimed. "We leave tomorrow."

"Keep me updated. Pack the good underwear, and please trim."

"Trim what?" I laughed. "It's work."

"Trim it all. Listen, don't overthink it like I know you so want to do right now. Well, except for the case details. Obviously overthink those."

I huffed in fake annoyance. "When do I ever overanalyze a situation till it consumes me whole with multiple outcomes that will probably never happen?" I asked in a mocking tone.

"Exactly. Call me if you need me for emotional support. But, Rhyan, just be you. The real you, not this version of jumbled confusion that dickhead turned you into. You're strong, you're beautiful, and you're smart. Repeat that to yourself when you feel yourself getting worked up and overwhelmed with anxious thoughts. You've overcome too much to let the past crush you now."

I sniffled and tilted my face up to the ceiling to keep the well of tears from spilling down my cheeks. "I will," I croaked around the emotions clogging my throat. "I love you, Olivia."

"Love you too, babe." A longing deepened her normally light tone, piquing my attention. But before I could ask what was going on, she hung up, the line going silent.

The edge of the phone thumped against my thigh as I tapped it, lost in thought.

Before I could spiral down into too many worst-case scenarios around my bestie's unusual tone, voices had my eyes snapping up to the slowly opening door. Instead of acting like a normal human, I dashed into the closest stall and quietly shut the metal door. If anyone saw me, they'd surely think I was up to something, but nope, just me being odd Rhyan Riggs.

"It's just not fair, you know? She doesn't even try, and she's a cheater."

My stomach dipped. I immediately knew who the woman was referencing. The rumor mill worked overtime to spin my reasoning for coming to this office with me, this terrible human being, which I never tried to correct. It was sad, but I'd rather be the villain in their gossip than the pathetic woman I was struggling to not be in this new life I was creating for myself in DC. "I've done everything to get his attention, and nothing. I even bought that pheromone stuff I found on Instagram that promised to attract every male in the vicinity. Which I guess worked, but I'm not interested in Carl the mail guy."

I rolled my eyes. Of course, she did.

"He keeps acting like this big asshole. I heard he laughed in one woman's face when she asked him for a lunchtime quickie. Can you believe that? She put herself out there, and he laughed at her." My brows rose a fraction at that tidbit. *Totally didn't get the asshole cocky prick vibe off him, but then why would he intentionally act rude?* "But what he doesn't know is that makes him even hotter. Bad boy *and* a jerk? Sign. Me. Up. All day, every day, I'll ride that huge thing he's hiding beneath his slacks. I swear one day I saw it near his knees. That's why I keep pushing to let him know I'm interested. He said no the first few times, but I know he'll come around."

Ah. I was pretty sure she'd just answered my question about why Charlie acted like an asshole to the women who approached him. Apparently, no meant no unless you were a guy; then it was merely a suggestion.

Poor guy.

"We could always offer us as a package."

I glanced over my shoulder, so wishing someone was in the stall with me to see me motion toward the door in an "Are you hearing this shit?" gesture.

"Yeah, that might work. We both know he'll still be available after their brief road trip. She's too damn awkward for someone like him. She'll scare him off, and he'll never look her way again."

The distinct sound of two stall doors closing and then them peeing had me suctioning both palms over my ears. Listening to them gossip was one thing, but hearing them pee felt like an invasion of privacy. Thankfully their voices still filtered through.

"Shit, this hurts. The doctor said the burn would be over by now."

Forgetting about my ears, I smacked a hand over my lips to keep a snicker suppressed.

The two continued talking, thankfully moving on to more personal matters than me as the chief topic. When their voices faded and the restroom was once again silent, I pushed the door open and stepped out, feeling a little heavier than when I'd dashed inside.

At the sink, I wrapped both hands around the smooth edge and stared at my reflection, my pale skin nearly translucent beneath the harsh lights. The dark circles dulled my normally bright green eyes. Skin dry in places, almost invisible reddish-brown brows, and raw lips from all the nervous gnawing.

Maybe they were right. My worn-down appearance alone would turn off someone as attractive and desired as Agent Charlie Bekham. He was probably attracted to the younger ones, just like....

I shook my head, locks of thick red hair swishing and slipping over my shoulders.

I shouldn't get my hopes up, but it was hard not to. For the first time in almost two years, something excited me besides profiling serial killers, and drew my attention away from my constant anxious thoughts. The butterflies that took flight when he was near or the way my heart raced when his deep voice filtered through the office was exciting. That was all I needed, nothing more.

This little crush was just that—an insignificant crush that he would never return.

He clearly had his choice of women, and I knew better than to want more with a man like that. Been there, did that, and had the broken heart as proof. I needed to stay in my lane. It was safer that way.

Stable, in control, and boring.

That was Agent Rhyan Riggs to a T. I needed my work persona to bleed into my personal life. That way my new solo life, all the lonely nights and single dinners, wouldn't feel as hollow and depressing.

Maybe Agent Rhyan Riggs could save regular me from myself.

Every muscle rebelled as I trudged up the stairs toward my small apartment. Sweat still slicked my exposed skin and collected in the band of my sports bra and leggings. Even so, I grinned through the ache. My nightly barre classes took everything away, the stress of the day, and calmed my circling thoughts. Once or twice, the details of a case pieced together during an intense session. Sometimes I just needed a blank mind, my focus somewhere else, to make the evidence make sense.

Tonight it was about something different, though. The text from He Who Shall Not Be Named ignited an inferno of worry and anxiety that needed to be extinguished immediately. That bastard didn't get to interrupt my life here, not after everything he put me through. Even though a part of me still desperately wanted to respond, still sought his approval and attention.

"Pathetic, Rhyan," I muttered under my breath as I shoved the key into the dead bolt and twisted it harder than necessary. After shouldering into the empty apartment, I set the laptop bag by the door for tomorrow morning's routine and moved on memory alone through the darkened space toward the laundry room.

After separating my work clothes and stripping off the sweaty workout gear, I divided them out between laundry and dry cleaning. I'd just pushed the start button on the washing machine when a chime from the other room caught my ears.

With all the blinds closed and lights off, I had zero worry about walking through the apartment naked. It wasn't like anyone was home or would stop by. That would require a partner or friends, neither of which I had here in DC.

Padding across the kitchen, I pulled a water bottle from the counter and went back to the front door. Somehow I knew who the text would be from even before I swiped the screen, but still I hit the side button, bringing the screen to life.

Brian: We really need to talk. Don't ignore me.

Just like I did earlier, I swiped the text and pressed the clear button. Avoidance was something I'd become very good at since I left his cheating ass. I needed a distraction, or I'd be up all night debating my life choices and obsessing over every turn that brought me to here.

So I turned to what I'd learned was a better use of my obsessive nature.

Pulling a file folder out of the side pocket of the laptop bag, I brought it to the couch and tossed it to the secondhand IKEA coffee table as I strode toward the single bedroom and connected bathroom.

Ripping back the shower curtain, I twisted the knob on the wall and held a few fingers beneath the cold spray, waiting for it to warm. I would shower, then plop on the couch to study the case details until falling asleep, only to wake before sunrise to begin the same routine all over again. This was how I kept my anxiety from squeezing in around me, forcing the breath from my lungs until a full-on panic attack drove me to my knees.

Routine was key to my mental survival.

So why in the hell did I agree to an impromptu road trip with the sexy new profiler I had an inappropriate crush on?

I knew that answer. I just didn't want to admit it to myself.

Even with the routine, the all-consuming workload, and fun calls with Olivia, I was fraying at the seams. My coping mechanisms to keep moving forward were slowly losing their effectiveness. Something needed to change or all I'd built for myself would unravel, leaving me floundering with no lifeline left to grasp.

This limited existence wasn't a life. It was survival.

And maybe, finally, it was time to take back the reins of my life and start living again.

After a long shower spent contemplating life beneath the warm spray, I settled into my one extravagant purchase—a comfortable couch. After grabbing the folder from the coffee table, I stared at the blank front. Every night about this time, I would promise myself tomorrow would be different, that I'd shove the shit Brian put me through for years into the past and move on with my life. Though tonight it was different because tomorrow was that break in routine, a first step toward a new beginning.

Yes, tomorrow will be different.
It has to be.

3

RHYAN

What the hell is wrong with me?
Another gust of chilled spring air had me tugging the sides of my suit jacket tighter to protect what little body warmth I had left. I stood outside the glass doors of my apartment building waiting, watching, but mostly second-guessing my life choices as I always did when left alone with my thoughts for too long.

Dotted along the sidewalk that led to the busier residential streets, several of the cherry trees were in full bloom. The pink-and-white petals fluttered and soared with the occasional early morning wind. Beside my black stilettos, a small pile gathered in the building's corner, those petals lacking their brethren's soft pink hue, now brown and wilted.

Turning my unfocused gaze from the heap of dying petals that were once beautiful and full of life but were now sad and wilting, feeling way too connected to their life cycle and comparing it to my past, I flicked my watch to check the time. *Ugh.* Fifteen more minutes until Agent Bekham was set to pick me up if he was on time, maybe longer if he was like the rest of the population, always running late.

Shifting my weight, I grumbled under my breath, my annoyance directed inward. Why must I be obnoxiously early for everything? Couldn't I be normal in this one thing and maybe just be on time for once in my life? But instead of being normal like everyone else in the world, I stood, now shivering from the chill slowly seeping through my trousers and jacket, waiting impatiently like a fool, as I had been for the past ten minutes.

Chewing on my lip, I thought back to when it all started, when my obsession with being on time pushed me to be rudely early to every occasion, work—heck, even my barre classes. During undergrad and law school, I was always on time for class but never obscenely early as I am nowadays. I didn't need to think too hard to correlate a certain timeframe and my complete shift in personality and behavior. I started the slow change the moment I met Brian and wanted to live up to his stupidly high expectations. It worsened after we moved in together and then took a nosedive the following years. In the midst of the abuse, he made me believe everyone changed for their partner to better the relationship. It never occurred to me that I was the one doing all the changing while he stayed the same.

What a damn fool I was.

Thank goodness I had Olivia in my life before meeting Brian. She stuck around when everyone else gave up on helping me realize what I'd gotten myself into. She tried to help me leave him, to see him for the narcissistic, manipulating asshole he was. Not that the long phone calls and nights of crying on her shoulder did any good. I continued to blind myself to the truth until that one day, when the blindfold was ripped off and his true nature was revealed. The day I finally grew some balls and left the bastard. Seeing the man who you'd smothered your real self for, who you thought loved you, cheating on you with his TA was the final straw.

In a way, it was a blessing seeing his face buried between her legs with her writhing on the desk. It made me snap, and now I was here, away from him, able to ignore his texts and calls to keep from being drawn back into his manipulating orbit.

"And I was worried I'd be here too early."

The familiar masculine voice snapped me out of my consuming inner thoughts. Brows furrowed, I narrowed my eyes to see the person behind the wheel of the black Suburban idling along the street in front of my apartment building steps.

"Where's the Mustang?" I asked as I bent over, grabbing my go bag in one hand and laptop bag in the other. I straightened but waited for a response before taking a step closer.

Charlie's blue eyes searched mine, no doubt trying to figure out what was wrong and why I wasn't moving.

Good luck, buddy. You and my therapist can compare notes, and hopefully one of you can figure out why I overanalyze everything.

"As much as I love driving her, I figured the Suburban would be more comfortable for you. Hope that's okay."

The bags' handles dug into my fingers, cutting off the circulation, but still I waited as I processed through his reasoning. What was his ulterior motive? Was this a ploy to do something nice, then make me try the rest of the trip to show him how appreciative I was for the thoughtful gesture? Why else would he do something kind if he didn't want to hold it over my head?

"Here, let me help you with those."

The driver door flew open, and Charlie gracefully unfolded his tall, lean body out onto the sidewalk. His questioning stare didn't drop as he approached, heels of his dress shoes clicking along the concrete and up the few steps to where I stood. At his gentle tug, I released my death grip on the bags. With a crooked smile, he inclined his head toward the SUV and turned, jogging down the three steps with my bags in tow.

I stood rooted in the same spot when he reappeared after tossing both bags into the back. He studied me, then the apartment building.

"Are there more bags?" I shook my head, sending locks of my red hair flying outward to catch the breeze. "Okay," he drawled. "If that's all you're bringing, you ready to go? I'm in desperate need of coffee on the way out of town. Hope that's okay."

"You didn't have to do that," I said, going back to the earlier conversation.

"Do what?" he asked, confusion clear in his tone.

I waved toward the Suburban. "I'm not your direct superior. We're equals in title, and you don't have to suck up—"

"Listen, Agent Riggs—"

I held up a hand, cutting him off. "Call me Rhyan, please."

Charlie dipped his chin and slid both hands into the pockets of his black slacks. "Then you should call me Charlie. Listen, I'm not sure where the lines got crossed, but I did the car switch just because… well… fuck, to be thoughtful, I guess. Sorry if that offended you."

Well, shit. He seemed genuine, but so did Brian all those times when I took the kind gesture with open arms, not realizing it would come back to bite me in the ass later.

"Why be thoughtful?" I asked with more force than polite. *What do you want in return?* Was what I wanted to ask, but I bit my lower lip to keep that question buried deep inside.

Both his wide shoulders rose in a noncommittal shrug. "I'm confused. Is the Suburban not okay? I can go back and get—"

"I just need to know why you would do this for me when you originally wanted to drive your own car."

"You did me a solid yesterday with that asshole Carter, making this trip to Louisville even happen. I thought I could repay you by not making you sit in my Mustang's small bucket seat, cramped with those long legs of yours smashed against your chest for nine hours."

"That's it?"

"Um, yeah. Should there be another reason?"

Ah hell, I was confusing the hell out of him. To be honest, I was confusing the hell out of myself with my insistent pushing to uncover his ulterior motives. Though it seemed he didn't have any; his body language and unfiltered confusion said he told the truth. *Isn't that a surprise? Wait, did he mention something about noticing my long legs?* Did that mean he was checking me out or just casually mentioning how lanky I was?

Chapter 3

I turned my gaze down to my cropped black slacks like they held the answer on how to dig myself out of this awkward hole. Wiping my clammy palms down the sides of my thighs, I swallowed, nodding. "Right, sorry, I just needed.... Never mind, forget I grilled you about this. It's not important. Let's just go."

Finally forcing my feet into action, I brushed past him, rounded the hood, and pulled open the passenger door. Tension mounted the moment we both slid into the front seats, Charlie settling behind the wheel without a word. We only made it two blocks from my building before it became too much. And because I was the most awkward, broken individual on this planet, I blurted the most random conversation starter ever said to another person.

"Did you know koalas can catch chlamydia?"

Someone should tattoo "What the hell is wrong with me?" along my forearm, considering how many times I say it to myself.

At the red light, Charlie slowly turned his head in my direction and blinked. "What was that?"

My cheeks warmed in embarrassment, and I pressed chilled fingers to the flaming skin to soothe the building flush. "Nothing," I grumbled. Looking at the door handle, I debated how weird it would be if I just got out and offered to walk the rest of the way.

"Oh, I don't think so, Rhyan. You just brought up koalas and chlamydia in the same sentence. You don't get to deflect and not follow through."

Groaning, I sealed both lids tightly shut and tapped the back of my head against the headrest. "I'm strangely obsessed with learning and regurgitating random irrelevant facts." I cracked one eye open to peer across the console, fully expecting annoyance to be written across his features, only to find a wide grin showing off his straight teeth. "Sorry," I said, waving him off. "I'll just stop talking for the next several hours."

The light had turned green, but he continued to study me from the driver seat. A car horn blared behind us. Lifting a middle finger in the air to the impatient driver, he turned his attention back out the windshield and inched the SUV through the intersection.

"Makes you wonder though, doesn't it?" he mused, that wide grin still firmly in place. I pressed my lips firmly together to maintain my needed vow of silence. "How did they catch an STD, and what kind of invasive exams are those Australian vets conducting on their wildlife to figure that shit out?"

My lips trembled with the need to part, allowing me to word vomit everything I knew about this oh-so-random subject. Why did I know so much about koalas and their reproductive health? Well, because I'd latched on to a random fact that piqued my interest, I became obsessed and would fall down the proverbial rabbit hole till I lost hours of my life like I did with most things in my life.

His quick glances my way and knowing smirk said Charlie noted my restraint and found it amusing for unknown reasons.

"If only I knew someone who could answer those pressing questions," he said while tapping a thumb along the top of the steering wheel. "Because I'd love to know more about pandas and chlamydia."

That was it. I couldn't take it a second longer.

"Koalas," I blurted. "Koalas, not pandas. There's nothing fascinating about pandas." I stopped myself and tilted my head, remembering something unique I read one night about them. "Well, that's not true. They have one cool fun fact. Pandas have a wrist bone that acts as a thumb to help them hold the bamboo while they eat."

"Really?" Charlie asked, like he actually found this interesting.

I studied him out of the corner of my eye. *Is that genuine interest in his tone, or is he simply humoring me like everyone else?* He lacked the normal dull tone, and there wasn't a sigh of annoyance at the end. He could be smirking because he was making fun of me in his mind. No doubt the scene I created earlier and now random STD facts stated my oddness loud and clear.

"Rhyan?"

"Huh?" I asked around the lip clamped between my teeth.

"The koalas? You can't drop a chlamydia fun fact and then leave me hanging. And I can't google the answer since I'm driving."

There was nothing mocking about his words, only real intrigue.

"You really want to know?" I asked, unsure.

He nodded and circled a hand between us in an urging gesture.

So I did. DC was a blip on the horizon as I answered all his pointed questions. With each mile, every inquiry, and off-topic discussion, my anxiety eased while my confidence built.

Maybe I wasn't so awkward to be around after all.

"Now you're just making shit up," Charlie remarked as he climbed into the Suburban.

I slammed my car door shut, dropping the full bag of snacks onto the floorboard between my feet. Stretching both legs out with a groan, I clicked the buckle in place and reached between my knees to rummage through the random selection of food I'd purchased inside the gas station while Charlie filled the tank.

"I'm not, I swear. The human head remains conscious for about ten seconds after being decapitated."

"How in the hell would someone know that? Did they ask the head questions?"

I shrugged, not knowing the answer, and held up the king-size Snickers bar in one hand and a single serving bag of Cheetos in the other. "Not sure about that one. I didn't want to know more, to be honest, so I stopped searching that fun fact. I see enough of that gruesome stuff on the job, you know? Which one do you want?"

He narrowed his eyes, glancing between the two snacks I held on display. "Did you purchase anything remotely healthy or just that processed stuff?"

I wiggled the candy bar between us. "The Snickers has peanuts. Peanuts are healthy, so Snickers are healthy."

His lips curled in a smirk. "Connect-the-dots nutrition," he said with a huffed laugh and then grabbed the candy bar. He ripped open a corner of the wrapper, took a massive bite, and started the Suburban. "You're an odd one, Rhyan."

"Yeah," I agreed with a resigned sigh, slumping back against the seat. "Tell me something I don't know."

"How about the fun fact that I like it?"

"What?" My brows rose on my forehead as I stared dumbfounded at his handsome profile. Ugh, why did he have to be so damn attractive? It made this whole crush thing that much more difficult to ignore. "You're joking. Please don't make fun of—"

"It's different," he cut in around a mouthful of chocolate and peanuts. "And different is a nice change of pace."

Cheetos forgotten, I shifted along the leather seat, angling my body toward the driver side. "You say that like our job isn't tossing us something different every day."

"Well, yeah, the job is always different, but I'm referring to the way you interact with me." He swallowed. I couldn't help but follow the motion as his throat worked, finding myself doing the same. "You're being you without all the pretense, and that's different. Welcomed, really."

It was on the tip of my tongue to agree that I felt the same. That it was nice being around someone who didn't make me feel less, or weird, or incompetent because of my nervous quirks.

"Want to talk about the case?" I asked after clearing my throat. I needed to direct the conversation away from the personal path we were headed down.

"Sure," he said, glancing at me out of the corner of his eye.

"I looked over the case file last night and wrote down a few questions that popped up." I pressed a thumb to the release button, and the seat belt retracted. Careful of the bag at my feet, I twisted to wedge my upper body between the two seats and over the center console, stretching to reach my laptop bag tucked in the back. The seat molded beneath my knees, my ass in the air. I reached as far as I could without falling into the back seat, my fingers brushing along the leather side. "Just a little farther," I muttered under my breath. "Oh come the fuck on."

My happy cheer filled the Suburban when I finally grasped the edge of the bag and hauled it closer. The soft material slipped

Chapter 3

beneath my palm as I dug around the side pocket for the spiral-bound notepad I'd written in last night. With the small pad in hand, I fell back into the seat and refastened the seat belt, silencing the insistent beeping alarm.

Adjusting my black frames back into position, I shot Charlie a victorious smile and held up the notebook, only for that smile to immediately fall. My heart stalled as I took in his white-knuckled grip on the steering wheel, the tightness pinching his features, and the twitching muscle along his clenched jaw.

Shit, what stupid thing did I unknowingly do now?

Clearing my throat, I inched closer to the door, hoping the additional space from me would ease his obvious annoyance. That always helped when Brian had enough of my awkwardness.

Charlie's blazing blue eyes cut my way, studying my now closed-off posture. With a soft curse, he shook out his hands and rolled his shoulders back as if physically shrugging off the earlier tension.

"Did you find what you were looking for?" he asked through gritted teeth.

Fumbling through the used pages, I flipped to my scribbled notes. "Yeah, sorry, I didn't mean to do that."

Those dark brows were so furrowed, a deep line formed between his eyes as he studied me. "Do what?"

"You know."

He held my wide-eyed gaze for several seconds before turning back to the road. "Read me your thoughts on the case."

I released a slow breath to calm my rattled nerves. Good, he'd moved past whatever I did to invoke his frustration instead of pointing it out. I preferred avoidance rather than listening to him berate me for all the ways I'd just screwed up.

"Rhyan."

"Hmm?" I mumbled in response as I stared at the notepad, not seeing the words I jotted down last night before crashing.

"Your thoughts?"

"Oh, right. The case, my notes. Sorry, just got lost in here." I tapped a finger against the side of my head. Adjusting my glasses, I focused on the notepad. "Anyway, moving on. We already discussed my opinions on the suicide angle the local police have used to label these deaths. So many suicides outside of the normal data parameters don't make sense, so we need to uncover what does."

"Interesting way to change directions."

"Well, if we can identify what these women have in common, besides living in the same town and being found in a river, we have something to go on. If we can't find their commonality in either their lives or cause of death, then we don't have BSU-needed cases."

His hands twisted back and forth along the steering wheel. "Based on what my buddy sent over and your data, my gut tells me we do."

I nodded in agreement. "It's why I urged SSA Jackass to reconsider. You've done good work since joining the team. If you feel we're needed, then I'm inclined to believe you based on your performance." He whipped his eyes from the road to shoot a surprised look across the console. "What? I'm the most senior member on the team because of my performance in another office before transferring to the BSU. Because of that, it's my job to monitor the results of the team in the field to ensure we're running efficiently despite being shorthanded."

"I thought Agent Peters was the official team lead," he said absentmindedly.

My smile turned sad, and guilt pressed into my chest. I turned to the window so he wouldn't profile the sudden shift in my mood. "I'm not a people person. Agent Peters helps me on the leadership aspect of my team lead role while I focus on reviewing the reports you file after each case. You have powerful instincts, and that shows in your performance in the field. It's hard hitting the ground running in this role, going out there alone, and you stepped up immediately, owning the profile role like you've been here for years instead of months."

He huffed. "Now your apprehension about taking my change in vehicles at face value makes sense. You assumed I was sucking up to you because of your role on the team."

Sure, I'd let him believe that instead of the truth that I'm forever mind-fucked by a narcissistic asshole who always expected tenfold back when he didn't do anything nice or thoughtful.

"So, back to the case," I said, directing the conversation back to a safe topic. "What fits? What did these women have in common that the lead detective didn't find or connect? Once we uncover that aspect, we have a case."

4

CHARLIE

Stop thinking about her perfect ass.
 And her long legs.
 And that silky red hair that I would wrap around my fist to hold her in place while I....

Fuck.

The leather groaned as I shifted in the seat, angling my twitching cock away from the subject of my dark fantasies. Why the hell did she have to be so... her? This adorable and hilarious personality, all wrapped up in a knockout body with legs for days that would fit perfectly around my waist as I slammed home repeatedly until she screamed my name.

"I'm wondering if they were raped."

And just like that, my cock went limp. Any lust-filled thoughts about the gorgeous Rhyan vanished in an instant.

I cleared my throat and took a swig from the water bottle I'd nursed for the last hour. "What makes you wonder that?"

"Based on the coroner's report, the most recent victim showed signs of having sex close to her time of death. But there's no way to determine if it was consensual or forced. Based on recent studies that claim that one in three women worldwide will be or have been subjected to sexually motivated violence, it makes me wonder if the sex was consensual or forced, and who it was with."

Red fiery anger burned in my chest at the horrendous statistic she'd just rattled off. "That begs the question: were they raped, then murdered, or were they raped, then committed suicide from the physical and mental trauma they endured? Which would turn our focus from a serial killer to a serial rapist."

"Interesting theory on the serial rapist," she mused. "I hadn't thought of that angle. Though I hope we're hunting a serial killer."

"Why's that?" I had my own opinions on why I'd rather hunt a serial killer than a serial rapist but wanted to know why she would too. Her mind, the way it worked, seeing differentiations of normal everyday elements, was fascinating. And a turn-on. Who knew I had a thing for brilliant, good-looking redheads?

"Well, from my perspective, asking a victim to come forward and reveal every detail of their trauma is the one aspect of this job that rips me apart. I sit there asking them to be brave and tell me everything about an event that they desperately want to forget, to share intimate details with a stranger. And it's always me, or another female agent, because it's easier for the survivor." I zeroed in on her using the word survivor instead of victim. "The dead don't have to relive it. I don't have to sit there and witness their devastation and anguish. We gather the evidence from their bodies, then put them to rest. That's selfish, isn't it?"

"I don't think so," I said, wiping a hand across my dry lips. "But still, five women committing suicide after being raped, it goes against the statistics you rattled off yesterday."

She grimaced. "Yeah, sorry about that. Sometimes I can't stop myself from unloading the random facts and statistics I have crammed in here." She pointed a finger at her head. "And you're right. So now we need to figure out if the most recent victim had consensual sex or was forced before she ended up in the river. That small caveat will affect the profile. I also want to talk to the victims' spouses. I know the lead detective already did during his initial investigation, but we can read them better, get a feel for if they're hiding something. I noticed four of the spouses are on board with changing the COD to murder."

"You think the husbands were involved?"

She shook her head, then shrugged. "We can't rule anything out, but I was thinking more like they have more to gain if it's ruled a murder than a suicide. Which is why they might hide things from the investigation."

I slammed the heel of my palm against the steering wheel when I connected the dots of what she was saying. "Life insurance doesn't pay out on suicide. If we change the COD to murder, they get the cash."

"Exactly." Opening a bag of Skittles, she poured a handful into her palm and tossed them all into her open mouth. "How much longer till we get to Louisville?"

At least I thought that was what she said.

"Another hour, maybe longer depending on rush hour traffic once we get closer."

She nodded and swiveled to stare out the window. A calm silence filled the SUV, as it had several times in the long drive. My ass hurt from sitting for so long, but nothing near what it would've felt like if I had driven my Shelby like I originally planned.

Speaking of which....

"Yesterday, you seemed interested in my ride. You into classic cars?"

Her full lips pulled at the corners in a genuine grin. "I had a 1967 Chevy Camaro." I whistled low in appreciation. *Fuck, that's hot. Is there anything about this woman I don't find attractive?* "I sold it a few years back, needed something more practical. My dad and I restored it during high school. It was my graduation present when I left for college."

The sadness in her voice was like a punch to the heart.

"And where was that?"

"Home or college?"

"Both," I countered.

Her lips pressed into a line, and those light brows dipped. "Kansas and Seattle." The way she shifted along her seat and the tension on her face spoke loud and clear to her being uncomfortable with the personal questions. So far this entire trip, she diverted the topic any time the conversation veered toward her personal life.

Interesting.

"Chiefs or Seahawks?" I asked to hopefully chase away whatever dark memories were now a thick cloud over her mood.

Instantly, her demeanor changed, visibly relaxing into the seat. "Chiefs all the way. Do you want to know why?" Her brows jumped along her perfect, fair skin, begging for my response.

"Why?" I asked, loving that she'd lowered her defenses and this version of Rhyan Riggs was back out to play.

"The Chiefs' stadium has better hot dogs."

A small chuckle built in my chest, growing into a full laugh that rumbled through the SUV. Rhyan's cheeks bunched, skin glowing a slight shade of red as I sniggered at the most ridiculous reason to like one football team over the other.

Still laughing, I adjusted my hands on the steering wheel, my focus out the windshield. A soft tap on my shoulder drew my attention back into the SUV. I glanced at my shoulder, then at her, completely confused at what was going on.

"I can't with the personal questions, okay?" She chewed on the corner of her lower lip, a strip of crimson already visible from earlier gnawing. "Just the case, my random facts, and other nonsense."

"Can I ask why?" Those rumors about her drifted to the forefront of my mind, but I couldn't see how it could be true. This funny, quirky, dedicated agent sitting across from me seemed at odds with the woman everyone whispered about.

Movements stiff, she wiped her palms down the front of her slacks. "I have a period of my past that I've packed away. If I open myself up to those memories...." She shook her head, sending those long red locks glinting in the afternoon sun pouring through the windows. "I have to look forward, not back. It keeps me sane." She huffed, before correcting herself. "Sane-ish."

I thought about her declaration for a minute. The boundaries were clear—nothing personal, only business—but it wouldn't do. I wanted to know this woman beyond the talented profiler. Every minute that ticked by with us in the damn SUV made me need more of her. Sure, there was a sexual component, because she was sexy as fuck and smart as hell, but there was more to it than that. Maybe it was the profiler in me, but I wanted to know what made her tick, why she was reluctant to talk about her past, even something as simple as discussing certain cities.

What the hell happened to Rhyan Riggs?

"What if I counter that?" I proposed. "If we're both right about this case, we'll be working together until we catch this bastard." She nodded in agreement, the worry on her face clear as fucking day. "So how about you reserve the right to pass on any question or conversation if it hits an uncomfortable memory? You were smiling when you mentioned your dad and restoring the car." That same smile crept back up her cheeks. "But Seattle seemed to trigger you to shut down."

And it did again.

"Why?" she asked, apprehension in her weary tone. "Why would you care about me?"

"Because I want to know you," I said with a shrug as I adjusted my hold on the steering wheel. "Maybe move toward being friends. I don't have many, or any actually, in the DC area. It would be nice to have at least one." I released a resigned sigh. Not sure why in the hell I was opening up when she wouldn't, but maybe she just needed me to go first. "Before I landed with the BSU, I'd been in the agent role for several years. I knew what they expected out of me, and I was good at it. Then I up and moved to DC, was placed on an established team. It just...."

"Kicked you down a notch?"

"Well, that's one way to put it, but yeah. Peters is the one who referenced for me, and his advice was to learn the ropes, work the cases, and keep my head down. So that's what I'm doing, but it doesn't seem to help me in the friends department."

"Or in the girlfriends," she muttered under her breath as she turned to the window.

"What was that?" I asked, arching a single dark brow. Interesting that she noticed the attention I'd avoided since arriving at Quantico.

"Nothing. Well, it just seems every woman, married or not—heck, even some guys—are trying to get their piece of you."

"So I'm a piece of meat," I grumbled. She blushed and shook her head, clearly uncomfortable from what she said. "It's okay. I don't hate it in the right situation, anyway. But I don't eat where I work or munch on someone else's juicy meal." Just to make her face flush an even brighter red, I rolled the ball of my tongue ring along my lower lip.

I wasn't sure if she was breathing as she stared, lips slightly parted, chest heaving with her quick breaths.

"I get a pass on any question or topic?" she clarified after a minute.

"Yep."

"And you won't push me to tell you more?"

"Not if you don't want to."

"I won't sleep with you," she blurted.

"Didn't know that was even on the table, Rhyan, but good to know."

"I'm a mess," she stated, as if telling me more about herself would alter my decision to be her friend. "An anxiety-ridden, sometimes obsessive mess."

"I'm a control freak who thinks if I work a little harder, push myself a little more, I'll be able to save the world, or someone's world."

"That's not a bad thing," she chastised.

"And who said yours were?"

She opened her mouth twice like she wanted to counter my statement but couldn't come up with a decent argument. Finally, she just smirked and held out her hand for me to shake.

Heat from my hand clashed with her ice-cold palm and fingers. A zing of excitement traveled up my arm straight to my heart. The moment my fingers engulfed hers, I never wanted to let go.

"Touché, friend. Touché. Let's start this friendship from the top.

I'm Rhyan Belinda Riggs, and if you say a word about my middle name, this friendship is officially off the table."

My smile grew. "Charlie Kyle Bekham. You can ask anything you want about my name."

Settling back into my seat, I couldn't smother my wide grin. Covering it with my hand, I watched the landscape turn from country to urban as we entered the Louisville city limits.

Friends. That's a pretty damn good place to start.

A DULL ACHE radiated along my overused cheeks from all the smiling and laughing of the last hour in the SUV as we rolled up to the police station. Shifting it into Park, I leaned forward to take in the small building.

"Ready to see if we're right?" Rhyan asked, already reaching for the door handle.

With a clipped nod, I shoved my door open and stepped out into the late-afternoon heat. The spring air was heavy with humidity and significantly warmer than the weather we left behind in DC. I turned to face Rhyan as I stretched both arms high overhead and immediately burst out laughing at the thin film of condensation that coated the front of her black-frame glasses. Unable to see my exact location, she shot me a middle finger in my general direction.

"It was a meat locker in the Suburban," she grumbled, tugging off the glasses to wipe them on the purple silk shirt she wore beneath her suit jacket. "I'll let you know when I gain feeling in my toes and fingers again." She flexed and tightened her fingers as if working the blood flow back into the tips.

My chuckle silenced, and my smile vanished. "Are you serious? Why didn't you say something if you were uncomfortable? I would've—"

"You were comfortable." After wiping off the lenses, she situated the frames back on her face and angled her head toward the front door. Her blank stare after that statement had me balking.

"Yeah, but you clearly weren't if I froze your toes and fingers solid."

"So?"

"So," I snapped, not sure why this bothered me so damn much, "next time tell me, and I'll fix it."

Okay, what is her deal? She made it seem like whatever she wanted, or felt, didn't matter, just mine. Again, that question of what in the hell happened in her past that turned her this submissive had me scowling at the sidewalk. I said I wouldn't pry, but eventually I would. Someone needed to straighten out her overly selfless ways. It wasn't just about what others wanted; she mattered too.

I questioned how she managed a solo case as we ascended the stairs side by side, assuming she allowed herself to be walked all over by lead detectives and supporting agents, but that concern fell flat the moment we stepped into the Louisville police headquarters.

The happy, funny, nervous woman faded, and Supervisory Special Agent Riggs, the confident, brilliant version of Rhyan, stepped forward. Shoulders back, features determined, she strode ahead of me for the front desk. After explaining who we were and who we were there to see, she turned and started toward the elevator bank.

I stretched for the Call button, but she beat me to it. I cut my gaze her way as she stood tall, eyes forward. Several of the uniformed officers watched from various places around the lobby, their gazes locked on her. If it wouldn't be too obvious, I would stare too. A strong, confident woman in a sharp business suit was my kryptonite.

"Well, okay, then," I murmured for only her to hear as I shot the other men watching her death glares.

A corner of her lips twitched, but she smoothed it down. "Intimidated?" she asked, not turning away from the still closed elevator door.

Intimidated? Hell no. Turned the fuck on? Yes.

"Nah," I said instead of the truth. "It fits you." That got a raised eyebrow response.

A dull ding echoed when the elevator arrived, followed by a groan of metal when the doors slid open. After allowing the three passengers to depart, we stepped inside. She jammed the pad of her thumb on the button for the third floor.

I leaned back against the railing, twirling the key ring around one finger as I watched her. Rhyan caught me studying her from the corner.

"Do not profile me," she said, though there was a lightness to her expression.

"I wasn't," I lied.

"Right." Chewing on her raw lower lip, she watched the floor numbers illuminate above the door. "This version of me has always been the easiest. I don't have to fake confidence," she admitted, still watching those numbers. "I'm good at what I do, and I take pride in that."

"I'm usually the dominant, cocky one on these things," I mused, the words swallowed by the arrival ding of the elevator when we reached the third floor. Before the doors opened, she whipped her face my way, eyes wide. "What, like you didn't already hear? I can be a cocky asshole. But I can take the back seat on this one. You're the more senior agent. Plus, I'll enjoy watching you." Reaching out, I slammed a hand against the elevator door to keep it from shutting with us still inside. "Sorry, that came out wrong. Watching you work the case."

"So you'll be the submissive?" she offered, lips twitching like she was fighting a smile.

"The observer," I corrected. Though if she wanted to be in control, I'd be more than happy to let her dominate me for a while. Especially if her commands required my face buried between her thighs.

A stiff nod dislodged her glasses, slipping them farther down the bridge of her tiny nose. After resituating them, she walked out of the elevator with me a step behind.

The detectives' bullpen ground to a halt the moment they laid eyes on her. A mix of animosity and appreciation merged in their blatant stares as we moved down the hall. She stopped short halfway down, causing me to almost collide with her back.

"How about partners?" she said, spinning around to face me. Those almond-shaped, jade-green eyes tilted up to meet mine, though with her heels, we were almost the same height. "We work this case together. Which means I'm trusting you not to...."

"Railroad you in front of a room full of alpha males."

"Exactly."

The fact that she had to say it out loud made my protective side flare to life. How many times had some asshole agent walked all over her in front of a bunch of detectives to make her so cautious with me?

"Not a problem, Rhyan. Never done that to a woman, friend or coworker, and would kick my own ass if I ever did."

Her eyes narrowed ever so slightly as she scanned my face. "You're very blunt."

"Is that a bad thing?"

"No, just different. Come on. The lead detective and the agent who reached out to you are waiting. I asked them to set up a room for us to work in until we figure out if we have a case or not."

Without waiting for my reply, she swiveled back in the direction we were heading and started forward. This time I matched her long strides, walking beside her, shielding her from the hostile stares.

Being there, at her side, protecting and supporting this amazing woman felt right.

More right than anything had felt in a long while.

5

RHYAN

The memory of Charlie absentmindedly toying with his tongue ring the entire trip had somehow short-circuited my overactive mind. It was all I could think about now. The case, a potential serial killer, Brian—nothing else consumed my thoughts except that damn tongue ring sliding along Charlie's lips.

Standing back from the group of men, I observed him as he greeted his friend, Agent Bryson Bennett, and the lead detective, Steven Hicks. Bryson seemed genuinely relieved at our presence while the detective looked ready to commit a murder instead of investigating one.

After a brief exchange between the two, Bryson swiveled his focus my way. "Charlie here mentioned you're the reason these cases are being considered by the BSU." He smacked an open palm between Charlie's shoulder blades, which he shrugged off with an exaggerated snarl.

"Damnit, Bennett, you're still a handsy fucker."

"SSA Rhyan Riggs," I said, taking his offered hand.

A wide smile lit up Bryson's face. "Thank you for fighting for this. I truly appreciate it."

"Did Bekham also mention this savior agent would look like *that*?" Hicks said, condescension dripping from every word.

The two men froze, their smiles falling into tight-lipped scowls as they turned their attention to Hicks, who now looked like the cat who murdered the canary. Slowly I rotated on the balls of my heels, looking down to meet the arrogant gaze of the detective.

"I'm positive my associate didn't comment on my appearance as it does not pertain to the assessment of the cases."

"Potential case," Hicks corrected. Crossing both lanky arms, he widened his stance. *An arrogant male detective with an overinflated ego and something to prove—how original.* I forced my eyes not to roll. "Bryson here—"

"Agent Bennett," Bryson growled.

"Yeah. Bennett is the one who asked you down here to review a bunch of suicide files."

"You don't think they're connected," I said, stating the obvious. Clasping both hands behind my back, I shifted my attention from the arrogant fuck back to the empty board that would soon hold the pictures and details of each victim. "I'm not saying you're wrong, but there are sufficient anomalies that warrant our particular skills to review the evidence and case notes. I apologize if our presence here increases your insecurity in your ability to label the cases correctly. In the future, we will tread carefully to protect your thin ego."

I could almost feel the heat from his anger at my back, but I didn't turn. Instead, I kept my hard glare on the empty board, showing him I didn't give a rat's ass about him liking or disliking us being here. This wasn't the first time I'd met resistance when arriving to work a case. Even if they reached out for our division's help, most men in high-ranking roles didn't enjoy being directed by a woman.

"I'm calling your boss," he said, voice trembling with restrained anger. "You don't have the fucking jurisdiction—"

"Hicks," Agent Bennett snapped.

I held up a hand, stopping Bryson from stepping in, and glanced over my shoulder at the flushed detective. "Actually, we *do* have fucking jurisdiction, considering one body washed up on the Indiana

Chapter 5

side of the Ohio River. That means it's our case if we want it to be, no matter who you call or how much you hate it." Turning, I inclined my head to Bryson. "I'd like to see the bodies and talk to the coroner now that everyone is done marking their territory."

Bryson's responding grin crept up his cleanly shaven cheeks, making his tough exterior soften. With an exaggerated wink at the detective, he swept out a hand, gesturing toward the door Charlie and I walked through only minutes before.

"After you, SSA Riggs. The coroner is waiting like you requested in your email last night, as are the recent body and pictures of the previous victims."

"Great. Thank you." I didn't even chance a glance toward Hicks as I marched past him for the door.

The click of dress shoes against the stained concrete floor said the two agents followed close behind as I headed for the elevator. The sting of stares crept along my skin from every angle, but I kept my eyes trained forward, just as I did when we first arrived.

My knuckle popped beneath the force as I slammed my thumb against the down button several times, then a few more, needing even this small outlet for my pent-up anger.

"Damn, SSA Riggs, that was badass."

Smile forced, all the joy from the hours in the SUV with Charlie gone, I turned to Agent Bennett. "Please, drop the formalities when it's just us. Call me Rhyan."

He nodded, that grin of his fading a fraction.

"You got it. But call me Bryson, then, though you can call me that no matter who we're around."

The brittleness of my smile fell away at his genuine response. "It will still be Agent Bennett when we're around others. Helps keep lines clear for those who look for a way to overstep boundaries."

"How much trouble do you think I'd get in with the BSU if I killed that fucker?" Charlie mused as we stepped inside the elevator.

Bryson maneuvered to the side closest to the panel and jabbed the button for the basement.

"Probably fired, but maybe not if you have the right lawyer," I said absentmindedly, watching the floor levels illuminate as the elevator descended. "I know a great one if you ever find yourself in that predicament."

"What?" both questioned in unison.

I caught their exchanged confused glance in the fuzzy reflection of the metal door.

"She's my best friend," I added, my smile softening at the mention of Olivia. "She's one hell of a defense attorney."

"So you're saying because she's your friend, I could finagle a friends-and-family discount on the lawyer fees?" Charlie said, the crack of his knuckles echoing in the small space as he massaged one fist, then the other. "Tempting. Very tempting."

I shot him a smirk over my shoulder. "Though if the murder is of that asshole detective upstairs, I'll defend you for free."

Charlie's blue eyes widened. "You're telling me you're an attorney *and* an FBI agent?"

I nodded, sealing my lips to keep my growing grin contained. "It's nothing, really. I don't practice, just have the degree."

"I don't think a law degree is a 'just a degree' type of accomplishment. Where did you go to law school?"

Ice flooded my veins at Charlie's innocent question. Thankfully the elevator slowed to a stop, my stomach flipping at the sensation, the doors opening keeping me from having to opt out of answering.

"This way?" I asked instead, stepping out of the elevator and away from Charlie's questioning stare. He could look at me that way all he wanted. Didn't mean I'd fork over the memories I'd worked months to keep locked away.

"Yep." Bryson falls into step beside me. "Listen, we can have all this transferred to the local FBI office if that fucker upstairs makes you uncomfortable. I just thought until we list this as an actual case, well, keeping it here would be better." He ran a hand through his short hair. "I didn't know he'd be so fucking territorial."

I patted Bryson's wide shoulder. "I've had to play nice in the jurisdiction sandbox with detectives and agents worse than that idiot upstairs. We're fine here."

The stench of chemicals and bleach assaulted my nose the closer we drew to the swinging metal doors at the very end of the hall. A few of the techs running various machines inside a closed-off room we passed peeked our way before returning to their work.

"Okay, but let me know if you change your mind."

Bryson reached the metal door ahead of us, pressing a massive hand to the center and pushing it open for me. "I've worked with this coroner, Jacobson, before. He's one of the good ones. He alerted me initially to the string of what he at first thought were suicides until the bodies kept piling up."

"Love that he was so observant with the trend," I remarked as we maneuvered through the small opening between the two doors.

A soft whirring and the clack of keys were the only noises in the large, pristine space. To the left sat three empty autopsy tables surrounded by various machines and wheeled trays with an array of implements on top. Opposite us on the far wall were rows of large square drawers where the bodies were held between autopsy and burial, and to the right sat a man behind a computer. At Bryson's attention-drawing cough, the older ME swiveled in his chair, long white hair floating around his shoulders with the quick movement.

Leaving the other two behind, I strode forward, my hand out. "Supervisory Special Agent Riggs."

The coroner took my hand and gave it a firm shake. "Jacobson. Pleasure to meet you SSA Riggs." After introducing Charlie, I turned toward the row of lockers.

"I hear you're the one who caught the trend and alerted Agent Bennett. Can I see the body of the recent victim and pictures of the previous that you took during your examination?"

Jacobson nodded. "I took the liberty of laying out the pictures as if the body were on the table. Thought that might help as you're looking over all five at the same time."

"Brilliant," I praised and meant it. Not having to flip through the pictures but seeing them positioned as if the body were still here was a tremendous help.

He paused in front of a drawer and pulled the sliding table

outward. "This is victim number one. Body was discovered eight months ago in the river, badly decomposed. There had been a missing persons report filed by the husband."

He continued rattling off the basic information I'd already memorized from the original autopsy report as he moved down the row, pulling open four more drawers, the last one holding an actual body, not pictures. Skipping over the other three, I paused at the body, still covered with a thin white sheet.

Lifting the cheap fabric, I slowly inspected every inch of victim number five's body, starting at the wrists and working my way up the arms. Slight bruising around the wrists, but nothing that I would claim was caused by typical restraints. No slicing of the skin or slender deep bruising. I shifted my focus to the feet and moved up her legs.

"And there was no sign of her being weighed down?" I asked. The ME, Jacobson, shook his head and ran an age-spot-dotted hand through his thinning hair. "What about the bones in the neck?"

"All intact."

A warm presence hovered at my back before stepping to my side. Portions of Charlie's black hair fell across his forehead as he leaned forward, inspecting the neck with narrowed eyes.

"There is a type of choke hold that allows the attacker to strangle someone without leaving a mark or breaking any of the delicate bones of the neck. Though that's highly specialized and incredibly difficult. Usually passion gets in the way, making the unsub sloppy."

I nodded in agreement. "That would point toward military training. Specialized military training maybe. Though with what people can google these days, we won't want to add that to the profile. What about water in the lungs, Doctor?"

"None."

"Interesting and a bit confusing," I murmured to myself, then moved around the two men to review the pictures laid out in the next drawer. "No water in the lungs on just her or all the victims?"

"All of them."

Still bent at the waist, I peeked up over the top of my glasses. "So that would mean all five women snapped their necks the instant they hit the water after leaping to their death, if the suicide theory were to hold."

I shifted my gaze to Charlie, who looked deep in thought as he raked a hand through his hair. I caught Jacobson studying Charlie in odd fascination.

What the hell is that about?

"Is it just me, or is that a near improbability?" Bryson said from where he stood several feet away. "One, sure. Two, breaking the laws of probability. Three, four, and five?" He leaned a hip against the clean autopsy table. "Something else killed them before they hit the water."

Lips pursed in a thin line, I turned my focus back to the pictures of victim number three.

What happened to you?

I turned to Jacobson. "The most recent body was the only one where you could determine sexual activity prior to death, correct?"

"Yes, the other bodies were too degraded and bloated to officially make that claim on the autopsy report."

My ears perked at his choice of wording.

"What about *not* on the official report?" Jacobson sealed his lips together, clearly uncomfortable with the question. "It would help if we had a general idea of what these women did prior to ending up in the river."

With a resigned sigh, he pulled off his round wire-frame glasses and rubbed at his eyes. "No semen was present, but there was evidence of inflammation. Now, could that have been from the time in the water or intercourse prior to death?" He shrugged.

"The most recent one, the one where it was clear she had sex prior to death. Tell me about that."

"Again, no semen, but evidence of trauma along the vaginal canal and cervix."

"Then why not state she was raped if there was trauma?" Charlie asked, voice tense.

"Because," I cut in before Jacobson could respond, "there are minor differences between someone who had rough, consensual sex and forced intercourse. With the various toys meant to blend pleasure and pain—" I stopped when the weight of the silence settled on my shoulders. I glanced from the pictures of a bloated body to find all three men staring at me with strange looks on their faces. "What?"

"Nothing," Charlie commented with a cough. "Unless the bodies can revive and talk us through the night's events, we can't determine if the sex was consensual or not."

"From *these* bodies, no," said Jacobson.

That hovered in the room, weighing us all down with the truth. If this was the work of a single unsub, then there would be more bodies, and hopefully we'd get to them before the water erased all the trace evidence.

"Drug panel?" I asked, breaking through the tense silence.

"Clear."

"Stomach contents of the recent victim?"

"Alcohol and nothing else."

"Damn," I heard Charlie grumble from somewhere behind me. "It's not much to go on, Agent Riggs."

One by one, I inspected every inch of the pictures, checking for clues. I lost track of time, my sole focus on these women and determining what really happened to them. It wasn't until the last one, the actual body on the stainless-steel slab, that I noticed one consistency.

"What do you make of these?" I stood up straight and pointed toward the woman's shins.

Jacobson and the other two shuffled closer to huddle around the extended drawer. After situating his glasses and slipping on a fresh pair of gloves, he prodded at the area I showed.

"Swollen," he muttered. Hurrying over to his computer, he ripped off the gloves and began speed typing. Leaning close to the screen, he studied whatever he pulled up. "Based on the X-rays, there are hairline fractures along the bone just below that bruising."

"And did the others have similar fractures in the same location?" I questioned. Anticipation bloomed in my chest, quickening my pulse. This could be what we needed to tie all the cases together.

The click-clack of keys filled the space. Charlie shot me an inquisitive look over the body.

"All of them had some level of fractures along their shins. I documented each injury but just assumed—"

"That they were from the fall or hitting rocks in the water."

He hung his head, that thin white hair falling in front of his face.

"Hey," I said with force. His face snapped up to meet mine. "I have the opportunity to see this with fresh eyes, with all the bodies laid out at once. You missed nothing obvious and documented the details so we could refer to them later."

Jacobson sat up straighter in his rolling chair, some of that earlier shame of missing a key detail between the victims vanishing.

"What made you look there?" Bryson asked.

Turning back around to Charlie and Bryson, I waved a hand over the victim's lower legs. "Well, I was thinking, if it wasn't a suicide, what does that leave us with?"

"They were pushed," Charlie commented.

"Or tossed," I modified. "And to create the minor fractures along the rest of the body from what we suspect was a steep fall into the water, the bridge must be tall. And what do all high bridges have to ensure someone doesn't randomly topple over the edge?"

"Holy shit," Bryson said like a curse. "They all have some sort of railing,"

"Exactly. And no matter how strong or tall this unsub is, they would need leverage to haul dead weight over that railing. I figured it would lead to some kind of bruising or breaks. From the bodies, it appears our unsub put pressure on the lower part of the victims' legs while he hauled the upper half over the railing and then pushed the rest over."

"This is enough indication of murder, not suicide," Jacobson stated.

I replaced the sheet over the victim's legs and turned to face Bryson.

"I'm official labeling this as a BSU case. Five bodies, no matter how different or the timeframe between, with identical disposal sites is a trend made by one unsub." I turned to face Charlie. "I'll call our supervisory agent to let him know we'll both need to work this case. There are too many unknowns for me to feel comfortable leaving you to handle this alone. No offense."

"None taken," he responded. His blue eyes tracked down the row of opened cooler drawers. "This is unlike anything I've seen. I would appreciate any help."

Twisting my wrist to wake up the watch screen, I checked the time. "Let's call it a day and pick it back up tomorrow after I get the paperwork in line. Agent Bennett, I'd like to meet with the victims' significant others or close family members tomorrow morning. Please arrange for spaced-out interview times and have them meet us here."

I should have been exhausted from the lengthy drive while also on edge the entire time, being so close to Charlie, but excitement flowed through my veins, making my fingers twitch along my thigh. I needed to work out, relieve this built-up restlessness, or I'd be up all night worrying about the case, Charlie, Brian, future natural disasters that would never happen....

6

CHARLIE

Cold water ran down my bare chest, creating small rivers to dip and curve around my pecs and abs. The metal rings screeched along the bar, dragging the soaked fabric shower curtain aside. Stepping out of the shitty hotel shower, I left the scratchy towel resting on top of the toilet and moved into the frigid hotel room. The initial shock sucked the breath from my lungs, but I relished the crippling sensation. This was exactly what I needed to keep my shit together around the sexy-as-hell Rhyan Riggs for the unforeseeable future.

Every move she made today in those tailored slacks that hugged her firm ass ignited a new flame of attraction. Then there was that way she shut that fucker Hicks down, class with a dash of asshole. It was a shock that she didn't see the tent I was sporting in the elevator on the way to the coroner's office.

Just thinking about Rhyan had my cock twitching for the hundredth time today, eager for a piece of her. A frustrated groan rattled in my chest. *Icy shower, cold room—fuck, what else can I use to calm my dick the fuck down?* Gritting my teeth, I walked to where the arctic air pumped from the unit below the window. The cold shower and sudden freeze while drenched should have been enough to calm my dick. Hell, my balls should have been tucked up into my stomach for safety. I was so damn cold. Instead, my blood still sizzled beneath my skin and shot straight to my dick any time my thoughts drifted to Rhyan.

Palms sealed against the wall, I dangled my semi-hard cock over the blowing air, cursing under my breath at the cold, sharp bite against my sensitive skin. I had to get my shit together. She was crystal clear in the SUV that this was professional stepping toward friends, not toward fucking her with my tongue.

Despite the near icicles dangling off my cock and balls, my dick hardened at the image of my face buried between those lean thighs, showing her all the ways I'd mastered using the bar piercing in my tongue.

Shoving off the wall, I stormed to my duffel bag and ripped the zipper open, the bag tumbling off the luggage rack to the floor with the force. If I couldn't freeze my dick into submission, then I'd have to wear my mind and body out to keep these urges in check. Maybe exhaustion was key to calming my rampant dirty thoughts. Tugging a pair of snug boxer briefs up my thighs, I tucked my dick down the front, that simple touch sending a tingle straight to my toes.

"I'm in so much fucking trouble," I complained to the thick outline beneath the soft gray material. Hurrying to get the excited dick situation... well, situated, I pulled on a pair of Dri-Fit shorts, grabbed a sleeveless shirt, and stormed out the door, my mind on nothing but running until I only had energy left to breathe.

Two steps down the hall, something didn't feel right. With a curse, I twisted around, lunging for the door that was half a second from closing.

Its hard slam echoed down the empty hall.

"Fuck," I snapped, banging a fist on the door like that would magically make it open so I could grab my shoes and key.

Rookie fucking mistake. Anyone watching would think this was my first time out on a case alone.

I bunched the Dri-Fit material in my tight grip as I stalked down the hall toward the elevators. As I passed by Rhyan's room, a raised voice had me backtracking and lingering outside the closed door. The words were too muffled to make out, so I creepily stared at the door, debating if I should knock and interrupt the heated conversation she was having on the other side. That internal debate of the pros and cons ended when a string of shouted, rather creative curses came through loud and clear despite the door separating us.

Apprehension and a twinge of jealousy merged as I raised a fist and pounded the side of the fake wood door, making it rattle on its cheap-ass hinges. My toes pressed into the worn carpet as I bounced, eager to get a glimpse of Rhyan and kick the ass of whoever was pissing her off.

The snap of a lock disengaging had me stepping back to keep from crowding her the moment she opened the door. If it was Agent Riggs who answered, my proximity wouldn't matter, but if the woman who rode in the Suburban with me for almost nine hours was the one who pulled the door open, my close presence could intimidate. The two personalities, though both inside and wholly part of Rhyan, were vastly different.

A sliver of an opening appeared between the door and frame, followed by a single green eye peeking through.

"Charlie?" she said, confusion clouding her tone. The door opened wider, but she kept a tight hold on the edge, blocking me from entering. "Did you—"

I knew the moment she noticed my lack of clothing. Her words cut off abruptly as if she lost her train of thought, jaw slack, lips parted. Those striking green eyes devoured every inked inch of my shoulders, trailing from the designs decorating my chest down to my stomach. I noted that she didn't linger at the two nipple piercings; either she expected them or couldn't decipher that small of a detail because of her not wearing those thick glasses that made me want to bend her over a stack of books and spank her naughty librarian ass. A pink flush brightened her cheekbones and colored the long column of her neck.

Gritting my teeth, I willed myself to think of anything but the appreciative gleam in her glassy gaze.

Fuck, this was the exact opposite of what I needed to keep my eager cock in check.

"I was headed to the lobby," I said to break the vibrating sexual tension building between us. "And I heard you yelling as I passed by and wanted to make sure everything was okay."

"Yeah, I—" She hooked a thumb over her shoulder into her room. Suit jacket gone, no glasses, and hair down, she looked more relaxed than I'd seen her all day. "The phone. Talking. You know."

I bit the corner of my lip to keep from smirking at her stammering. *Ah, so it's Rhyan standing in front of me, not the more confident Agent Riggs.* It was strange dividing them up like she had multiple personalities, but she did. How she turned one off and the other on made little sense. Or maybe her confident side was really her, and the other, this self-conscious and suspicious version, was what she'd been conformed into by her past.

By someone in particular from her past.

My mood soured at the thought.

"Everything okay in there?" I asked. And because I was a dick and was fucking loving the way she ate me alive with her still-roaming eyes, I leaned against the doorframe, erasing the minimal distance between us.

Her nostrils flared, and a hand fluttered to her flushed neck, wrapping the fingers around the sides. I stalked the movement. My jealous fingers itched to dominate her in the same type of hold.

"The jackass isn't happy about my decision to label this as a BSU case, but I handled it. We need to stay in communication with him more so on this case than any other. Pretty much he expects us to prove our needed help every single day we spend down here. Fucking prick," she grumbled the last part with sheer disdain.

"I hate that fucker. Wish he'd die of shingles to the dick. How in the hell is he in that role anyway? Wasn't there someone—hell, anyone—better than him to lead the team?"

The moment the words left my mouth, her demeanor shifted. My stomach sank as she wrapped both arms around her chest and squeezed in a self-comforting hold. The earlier passion vanished from her now-downturned eyes, and those flawless teeth worried at her raw lower lip.

"I know, I'm sorry. It's my fault he's—"

"Hell, Rhyan. I didn't mean to accuse you of anything." I shoved off the doorframe and stretched to cover her hands with my own. I swiped a thumb along her wrists, desperate for her to look up at me. "It's not your fault he's a terrible leader and a bureaucratic asshole."

"But it *is* my fault that he's our section chief." When she peered up through those nearly see-through lashes, the guilt in her eyes gutted me. "It should've been me in that role, but I couldn't." She shook out of my hold. Sealing her eyes shut, she inhaled deep, those small nostrils flaring. A hardness replaced the earlier vulnerability when she peeled her eyes open. "Was there something you needed?"

It would be easy to walk away, leave her alone with her inner turmoil. Though the idea of leaving her to deal with whatever mess my words stirred up felt wrong. She was pushing me away, turning the focus from personal to professional as a defense mechanism.

"I was headed to work out. Want to join me?"

My words seemed to smack her out of whatever was going on in that brilliant mind of hers. She inhaled sharply and eyed me with distrust.

"What exactly did you have in mind?"

My pride exploded in my chest that I'd somehow piqued her interest and shoved aside her earlier mood.

"Running, either outside or in the tiny-ass gym they have somewhere in this building." With a raised brow, she gave a pointed look at my bare feet. "Yeah, I know. I walked out of my room without my shoes and key."

"And half dressed," she said a little breathlessly as she once again swept a quick look over my ink-covered skin. Fuck, what would it be like for her to trace that pink tongue along the outline of my many designs? Hell, just her fingertip caressing the various dips and lines along my back would be fucking amazing. "I already booked a barre class in an hour. There's a studio just down the street. Would you want to join me at the barre instead of the run?"

I tilted my head an inch. "I'm confused. Are you wanting to work out or drink?"

Internally, I high-fived myself when the corners of her lips twitched and a knowing grin spread across her face. "It's a workout class, a mix of Pilates and yoga." Her eyes glittered with what I assumed was humor. "It's mostly women, though you'll be a hit, no doubt."

"Pilates. Yoga. I'll be fucking terrible. I should stick to putting one foot in front of the other. Thanks for the offer, though." She nodded, though her shoulders slumped in clear defeat, making me rethink my decision. "But you know what? New city, new case. Maybe doing something new for a workout would be a nice change of pace. Let's do this Pil-oga shit. As long as you promise not to laugh at me the whole time."

She gestured to my chest and swept down my rippled stomach. "Looking like this, I highly doubt you've been made fun of, Charlie."

I shuffled on my bare feet. This time it was me growing uncomfortable with the sudden personal shift in conversation, bringing up memories I didn't care to remember at the moment. "Yeah, well, you'd be surprised. I didn't always look like this."

"Oh shit." She slapped that extended hand over her mouth with a loud pop. "I'm just as bad as them." The words were muffled behind the hand sealed to her lips.

"Them?" I questioned, now really lost. "Are we still talking about the cocktail workout?"

"Barre. Barre workout, not cocktail, and no. I'm referring to the two younger agents back at Quantico who want to tag-team you. Though, just a heads-up, be careful if you take them up on their offer or you'll be on a two-week antibiotics packet."

Too much was just said for me to quickly process. "What?"

"Fun fact, did you know women are more susceptible to STDs than men?"

I shook my head and ran a few fingers through my still-damp hair. "You know way too much about STDs, you know that?"

"Yeah, well, that fun fact about koalas sent me down a whole STD rabbit hole. I learned more than I ever wanted to know."

"So not from some pamphlet your doctor suggested you read." My lips twitched as I stifled my smile.

"What?" she squeaked. "No, I don't…. Just no. I don't sleep with random…. I mean, I'm practically virginal…." She stuttered to a stop and sealed her lips shut.

"I'm joking, Rhyan," I said, finally letting my smile free.

"Yay," she fake cheered, dancing the tips of her fingers in the air. "One more thing to keep me up tossing and turning tonight about how I almost told you about my lack of sex life."

"Pretty sure you can leave the 'almost' out of that now." Her eyes widened, realizing her mistake. "But why would that keep you up?"

Using her foot to keep the door propped open, she leaned her head against the sharp edge. "I'm an anxious person. Not sure if you've picked up on that fun fact about me yet or not. My version of anxiety causes me to overthink—everything. So at night I do this really fun thing of running any mistakes from the day, or any in the last decade, over in my mind, reliving the embarrassing moment like I can change the outcome with the sheer energy I pour into obsessing over it."

I nodded along as she spoke. "That doesn't help though, right? Worrying about it won't change the outcome."

Her dimmed smile was sad when she dipped her chin. "That's the fun part of anxiety. As many times as you tell yourself to let it go, to move on or forget about whatever is circling in your mind, you can't. You know it's draining, know nothing good will come from it, but you can't stop."

What the hell? That sounded terrible. How could she deal with that kind of mental exhaustion and still be this amazing woman in front of me?

"Sounds exhausting," I said, unsure of what else to say.

"You have no idea." Flicking her wrist, she held the watch's face an inch from her squinting eyes. Noticing the issue, I gripped her wrist and angled the watch my way.

"It's ten till seven." My soft grip flexed around her tiny wrist. I wasn't ready to stop touching her just yet.

"Great, thanks. I'm basically blind without my glasses, which I threw off when that jackass Carter attempted to make all this about you and me, not the case."

"Are you fucking serious?" I exclaimed, the boom of my voice carrying down the hall. The sound of a door opening had me leaning back to see what was going on. A bald head stuck out of the room next to Rhyan's. His annoyed glare found me, and the scowl on his wrinkled face deepened. "Hey," I said out the corner of my mouth, not dropping the angry neighbor's stare. "Mind if we finish this conversation in your room? I'm getting some hate stares out here that might morph into death threats if we keep talking about Carter."

"Shit, didn't think about that. But, um, do you mind?" she said while shoving the door open with her hip. "Putting that shirt on? Not that I mind the view. It's that I like the view."

Her eyes widened as she realized what she'd said, fair skin turning as red as a tomato.

"Forget I said that," she grumbled and turned away, pressing the tips of her fingers to her blazing cheeks.

Smirking at her slip, I flexed and stretched as I tugged the rumpled shirt over my head before stepping over the threshold.

Inside her room, I eyed the bed. My cock twitched in my briefs. Nope, not the bed, then, unless I wanted to make this conversation even more uncomfortable for us both.

"Why would he make us changing the COD from suicides to murder about us?" Maneuvering around the bed, I fell into the uncomfortable desk chair and leaned back, resting both arms along the cushioned armrests.

"Because he assumes that's why *I* made this a BSU case." My leering gaze fell to her round ass, no longer hidden by her suit jacket as she stretched across the bed for the black frames sitting atop the basic white comforter. She perched on the edge and situated the frames on her petite face. "He can't see that the case is legit, only thinking we're using it as a front to spend more time together. He really doesn't like you."

I huffed while twisting back and forth, contemplating how much to share about my rocky relationship with the asshole. "He hasn't liked me since the day I walked into Quantico. He was fully on board with me joining the team until my first day." The soft padding of the armrest molded beneath my tightening grip. "One look at me and bam, I was on his fucking bad side, doing nothing right."

"Well, I know that's not true because I review your reports, remember? But the him not liking you part is probably because he's a narcissist who can't deal with the fact that he's no longer the hot commodity on campus that he assumed he was." She shook her head and pulled a fistful of golden red hair over her shoulder, playing with the ends. "Before I made the move to DC, they offered me that role, to oversee the entire team. But I just couldn't. Even though he's difficult, and an asshole, and most of the time terrible at his job, there's no doubt in my mind I'd be worse."

"And you know that because you've tried managing a large team of profilers and failed?"

Her sharp green eyes cut my way at my sarcasm. "Well, no. I just know because of me being me. You've seen how I am, an anxious blubbering mess."

"What I've witnessed is the exact opposite," I retorted with passion. Who the hell did this woman think she was, putting herself down when it was a bunch of lies? Fuck, someone in this amazing woman's life really messed her up, and now my mission was to correct her unfitting views. "Not sure if you remember the scene earlier, but you being your badass self today put a certain dick detective in his place, eased the guilt of the coroner for missing some key evidence, and delegated all the needed tasks for tomorrow with no problem. And to top all that off, you did it on an empty stomach while I was sitting back hangry as fuck, about to rip apart the world for some damn food. Not sure what you mean by you not being a good SSA, because after what I've witnessed, you're wrong."

"Well, you've known me all of sixteen hours, Charlie. You don't know me." Her hands curled into loose fists, gathering the comforter between her fingers. Clearly I'd hit a nerve by pointing out her accomplishments throughout the day and praising her for them.

"So this person in here with me now," I said, waving toward her on the bed, "is really you, and the badass agent at the station is a front?" I knew it wasn't, because she said so earlier at the station when we first walked in. The confident Rhyan was her true self; this jumbled version where she thought so little of herself and what she offered was the fraud.

"No, of course not. I'm just—" She sliced a hand through the air, clearly done with the direction of the conversation. "I'm just not meant to lead. Let's leave it at that. Yesterday I didn't want the jackass's clear dislike for you to impede justice for the victims. That's what we're here for after all, right?"

"Right." Swiveling in the chair to dispel some of the restless energy, I noticed her laptop open, the screen black. "What in the hell is that thing?" I angled my head toward the ancient beast sitting on the desk. It was a surprise the desk didn't collapse beneath the weight. "I thought dinosaurs were extinct."

Instantly her features shifted back to relaxed and open. She crossed her arms in a fake pout. "Watch what you say. I like my laptop."

Jabbing a finger at the side, I grimaced like the touch physically hurt me. "This might be the first laptop ever invented. It belongs in a museum, Rhyan. How can the security team load the required software?"

A single shoulder lifted in a shrug. "Not sure. That's way out of my technical know-how. They *do* keep trying to take it away, but I plead my case to the IT department to just upgrade this one each time instead of investing in a brand-new laptop. Those guys are always so nice and willing to help."

I covered my chuckle with a fist pressed to my lips. "I'm sure they are very helpful when you stop by. Can I ask why you want to keep it when we have access to the best technology? This one has to be slow as hell."

"Well, it's familiar, even though, yes, it's agonizingly slow. I'm terrible at learning new tech. Hell, I can barely open my phone." My lips parted, ready to tell her I'd be willing to play teacher, when she held up a hand. "I've read your file. I know you're a brainiac with computers and all things technology. But really, I'm no good at any of it, and if you were trying to teach me, you'd just get frustrated when I wasn't learning fast enough and give up on me. Let's skip all the frustration on your part and get to where we both agree that I'm a helpless technology case."

"You say that like it's happened before," I stated, keeping a close eye on her reaction.

"What part?"

"The part where I'd get frustrated and give up on you. I'm not sure who tried to help you before, but this stuff isn't easy to learn. Patience and time are key when teaching the ins and outs of complex software."

That raw lower lip sealed to the top, pressing into a thin line. Her intense stare jerked away to now searching anywhere other than where I sat.

With a clap, she popped off the bed and hurried over to the small black bag resting atop the other double bed.

"Give me a few minutes to get changed, and then we can leave for the barre class. I like being early to get a front-row spot along the mirrors."

"Cool, I'll wait for you downstairs." The sticky carpet—why the hell it was sticky was a question I didn't want to know the answer to —pressed against my bare feet when I rose from the chair, reminding me I was still shoeless and keyless. "It might take me a little longer than you. I need to get a new key made to grab shoes."

She paused from rummaging around in her go bag, peeking up with a strange look across her face. "Don't think I'm a creeper or anything, but I may already have one for your room." Her features pinched in a grimace.

"You what?" That wasn't protocol, though I loved the idea that she could sneak into my room any time she wanted.

She groaned and sealed her eyes shut, tapping a finger to her temple. "Another fun fact about anxiety. I run through various irrational outcomes that will never happen so I'm prepared for all situations just in case. One of those scenarios I completely made up in my head was you needing help with me unable to get to you because your door was locked, and then you dying with me beating on the door. So, putting my mind at ease, I requested a key to your room." Focused on her wiggling toes, she gnawed on the edge of her lower lip. "I'm sorry if that bothers you. It's a gross overstep and unprofessional—"

"No harm, no foul, Rhyan." The fact that she worried about me shouldn't have made me happy, but it sure fucking did. "And right now, I'm glad you took that extra step to get one made for my room. You've now saved me a trip and possibly athlete's foot or something worse."

Ducking her head to hide her grin, she pointed to the laptop bag next to the desk. "The key is in there, the side pocket. It's the one with a star on the corner so I wouldn't get it confused with mine."

While I dug through the side pocket, searching for the key card, a door shut behind me. Checking over my shoulder, I found myself alone in her room, the shuffle of clothing coming from the other side of the bathroom door.

Turning back around, I eyed the sleeping computer. It called to me, begged me to turn it on and dig through her secrets. It was wrong, an invasion of privacy, but I was possessed by the need to know more about this Rhyan Riggs. To uncover what—or who, more likely—had twisted her into thinking so many untrue qualities about herself.

Was me searching through her search history and files an invasion of privacy? Well, yeah, but she started it by making a copy of my hotel room key.

Hopefully that argument would stand if she ever found out I snooped just a little.

Another cautious glance over my shoulder, ensuring Rhyan wasn't behind me. Ignoring the rush of guilt, I slipped the room key into my shorts pocket and clicked on the keyboard, snapping the laptop screen to life.

I cursed under my breath at the blinking password box, as if mocking me for even trying to sneak a peek inside. *Asshole.* If I had a few minutes, I could hack into the ancient machine, but I didn't have that kind of time before losing this small window of snooping opportunity.

Time to change tactics.

Gripping the sides of her smartphone, I flipped it over and tapped the screen.

Two texts unread.

Thank the computer gods she had an older phone model that allowed the full texts to be visible instead of hidden until a password was entered. The name listed as the sender for the first one made me snort. No doubt who that text was from.

Fucking Pencil Dick: I will hold you responsible for this case if it ends up being nothing. Think through the consequences and if he's worth it.

My lips tugged in a snarl, turning feral when I read the next text.

Brian: This avoidance you've always done when things get tough won't work. Time or distance changes nothing. I'm willing to give you a second chance. Be grateful for that and come home.

Setting the phone screen side down, I stormed out of the room, quietly closing the door behind me. Chest heaving, hands trembling from the restraint needed to keep myself from punching through the wallpapered wall, I stepped into my room and slumped back against the door.

Anger brewed in my veins, demanding I find this Brian fucker and help him into a shallow grave.

With this glimpse into her life, one that was taken, not given, I had to decide.

Do what I do best and dig for more details to help her cut ties with those who don't have her best interest at heart, or leave it alone until she comes to me for help?

But this wasn't my call to make. It was hers.

Which meant I had to wait for her to trust me enough to unveil the bruises on her soul, the dark spots we all had in our past. Only then could I offer my help.

All I could do now was wait.

And do everything in my power to make sure she knew I was on her side, the one fighting in her corner, no matter what.

7

RHYAN

Watching the elevator doors like a hungry hawk, I shot out of the uncomfortable chair in the hotel lobby, steadying my hands to keep the two coffees from spilling over, at the first glimpse of the man who terrorized my dreams all night. Who knew he was so damn flexible? There were several times during the barre class that I found myself out of breath, and it had nothing to do with the exercise. It was all him. Those tattoos were everywhere, and I was lucky—or unlucky, depending how you looked at it—enough to have seen the detailed artwork over his defined chest and rock-hard abs.

I didn't know men even came like that. I just figured all those pictures online or in magazines were photoshopped. But last night, outside my hotel room, Charlie stood there in all his muscular glory, clearly not photoshopped and looking better than a professional male model.

He rounded the front desk, the two women working behind it following his every step, those tattooed hands fanning open his deep blue jacket to adjust the collar. My fingers tightened around the paper cups as my belly twisted.

Workout gear or trendy suits, the man was sexy as sin.

Add his tongue ring and he was sin personified. The best kind, not like murdering and decapitating. Sexy sin, the sin of lust and passion.

I squeezed my thighs together to slow the steady throb that hadn't gone away since I woke up. After dreaming of Charlie making all my dirty fantasies come true all night, I wasn't sure there were enough batteries in the world to quell this insistent need. And of course, I left my vibrator at home, not thinking I'd need to bring it on a work trip.

Rookie mistake. But in my defense, I'd never worked alongside an agent who looked and smelled and sounded like Charlie before, so how was I to know I'd need nightly relief from this pent-up tension between my thighs?

His electric blue eyes flicked around the lobby, no doubt feeling my stare. His hands paused, and a small smirk tugged at his sensual lips when he found me waiting. My focus slipped to those lips that were made for performing indecent acts. No doubt if they pressed against my own, I'd spill every secret he wanted to know and beg him for more.

"You beat me again," he said, finishing adjusting his suit coat as he approached.

"Here, I got you one too." Some of the steaming dark liquid sloshed on the white lid when I thrust it forward. "Black, like you ordered it yesterday morning. Hope that's what you normally get. I had to guess. Or you could have mine. It's full of sugar, though. Or did you want something with milk—"

"Black's perfect." He took the offered cup. "Thank you. I was jonesing for a good cup." Those lips wrapped around the white lid, his eyes never breaking away from my own. His soft hum of approval had me swallowing a mouthful of scalding coffee to keep my groan contained. "Am I late? Thought we agreed to meet at eight."

"We did, and you're actually early. I was just earlier. I wanted to get a head start on something with the case."

"Anything I can help with?" he asked. Checking his watch, he shifted around me to sit in the chair beside the one I was standing next to. He grimaced, using the armrest to lower himself to the seat. "I thought last night's class was a joke until I woke up this morning barely able to fucking move. I even thought about calling in sick for the first time ever."

"I wondered how you'd feel today. It's obvious you're in excellent shape, but barre works a unique set of muscles until they fatigue. It's a tough workout."

"No shit. But oddly enough, I really enjoyed it. Nice change from my normal workout routine. Maybe I'll find a studio back in DC and add it into the rotation." He shifted, face pinching in a grimace. "Or not."

My smile beamed behind the disposable coffee cup. I took a quick sip and sat down beside him. When I swiped open my phone, he physically tensed, glancing away when I turned the screen around for him to see what I was working on. "What? You act like I'm about to show you a naked selfie or something. It's just the search I've been working on this morning for the bridges in and around the Louisville area."

He visibly relaxed as he released a slow breath.

"Sorry, wasn't sure what to expect."

"Get a lot of naked selfies, do you?"

"Can you please stop saying naked selfies?" he said with a half groan, half laugh, scrubbing a hand along his clean-shaven jaw. "And you'd be surprised."

"I saw the way the women last night were wiping up more drool than sweat, so probably not as surprised as you'd think." Shaking off that thought and the ball of jealousy weighing in my stomach, I shook the phone in my hand, drawing his attention to the screen. "I'm not getting anywhere with Google. It just keeps pulling up the same bridges. I've reached out to our dedicated technical analyst at Quantico, but...."

Charlie leaned closer, tossing an arm along the back of my chair as he scrutinized the screen, his fingers now a hairbreadth away from my bare shoulder.

"Yeah, I know. He takes forever to get back to you. I've asked Carter to let me have free rein, but he won't grant me the approval. But," he said, taking my phone, "just searching this way won't get you anywhere. Give me the search parameters you want the bridges narrowed down to, such as a certain height and location on the river. I'll get you a solid list by the end of the day."

"Really?" The hope in my voice was clear. Not meaning to, I leaned closer toward his chair.

"Or I could always teach you how to—"

I cut him off with a quick shake of my head. Taking a sip of coffee, I set it on top of the glass table by my feet. "I told you, it will just end up with you getting frustrated and me feeling bad about asking. Let's skip all that. You just run the search, and I'll go visit the bridges once you've pulled a few possibilities."

"Or," he countered, leaning farther into my personal space. I swallowed, hoping my breath didn't reek of sugary coffee. "I run the search, and then we go view the bridges together. That seems like a better scenario to me."

Huh. That was... odd. He made it sound like he wanted to be around me, not beaten down by the continued time together like Brian always did.

Pulling a thick section of hair past my cheek, I played with the ends, my unfocused gaze sitting right above his shoulder.

"If that's okay," he added. Reaching forward, he stilled the twist and flick of my nervous fingers. "If you prefer to do that kind of stuff alone, I won't push you."

"It's not that," I said in a rush, not even thinking how my response would make him think I didn't want to be around *him*. No sane woman would not want to spend as much time with him as possible. I was anxious, not insane. "I just keep finding myself asking why."

"Why these women were chosen?"

"Why you'd want to spend more time with me. Haven't you had enough?" His dark brows spiked up his forehead at my confession. "Sorry, forget I said anything."

"Listen," he said, setting his coffee cup beside mine with enough force that a spray of dark liquid erupted from the small drinking hole, spilling out onto the glass. His hands wrapped around my own, the tight grip startling me away from the mess. My pulse raced at the fierceness in his searching eyes. "Based on a few of your offhanded comments, I feel like I need to put this out there so there are zero questions on your end regarding how I think or feel about your amazing self. You, Rhyan Riggs, are not who you've convinced yourself you are. The woman I've had the fucking pleasure of being around the last day is confident, funny, wicked smart, witty, and—I might cross a line here, but fuck it—sexy as hell. Stop assuming I'm doing any of this under duress, or being shocked that I want to spend more time around you. I'm finding myself unable to stop, which is an anomaly for me. And I'll be honest." His grip tightened around my trembling hands. "I'm tired of hearing you degrade yourself like you're less than the woman, the agent, I see. Not sure how much more I can hear before I'm forced to take action."

With all he said, it was his last word that froze all brain function. "Action?" My voice trembled, but not from fear. "What do you mean, action?" I knew what I wanted that word to mean, but maybe he meant making me do fifty push-ups or something.

Those blue eyes blazed with a heat that threatened to burn me alive. "I've found certain—" He tilted his head back and forth as he mused over his next words. "—discipline helps correct unacceptable behavior."

Holy fuck. So *not* push-ups, but more pleasurable action, like my dirty mind hoped for.

"You'd hit me?" I said in a rush, more excited than terrified.

The corners of his devilish lips twisted upward in a sexy, cruel smile. "I don't consider turning an ass red with my palm prints as hitting. Do you?"

"Never... never really thought about it."

"Hmm, that's too bad." His spicy cologne wafted up my nose, my eyes almost rolling into the back of my head as his lips pressed along the shell of my ear. "Because I sure as hell have."

I was going to combust. Blood heated to the point of boiling rolled beneath my skin, and sweat slicked the back of my neck, making my hair stick along the sizzling skin. Unable to get a single word out, I watched in pure shock as he slowly pulled away. He shot me a knowing wink and pushed off the armrests to stand. After adjusting his jacket to cover the enormous bulge tenting the front of his slacks, he grabbed the two coffee cups off the table and gestured toward the front doors.

"Ready to head to the station?"

The sounds of the lobby came roaring back into focus.

"Um, sure. Just, uh...." I licked my lips and pressed a hand to my chest, hoping to keep my heart from escaping. "I just need a quick second."

His smile spread. That damn tongue ring poked out to roll along his lower lip. The fucker knew what he was doing and seemed to enjoy every second. Of course, I couldn't say I minded, even though I was almost certain I needed to change panties after all that.

"I'll bring the Suburban around. Take all the time you need."

Relief and disappointment washed over me when he turned and strode away, whistling like he didn't have a care in the world while I sat falling apart in the best way possible, all because of him. His dirty, fantasy-inducing words.

Only once he was gone did I release the breath burning in my lungs. Lunging for my laptop bag, I dug around the designated pocket and ripped out my cell, already dialing Olivia's number by memory alone.

"It's too fucking early, Rhy. This better be good," she muttered into the phone.

"He wants to spank me," I blurted.

A hotel guest getting her free coffee from the cylinder dispenser shot me a scathing look.

"Give me a second." A grumbled male voice sounded in the background, Olivia whispering for him to go back to sleep, that this was a Rhyan emergency. "Repeat that again for me, because I could've sworn you just woke me up with the words 'he wants to spank me.'"

"That's what I said. Holy shit, what does that mean?"

"Means I need to meet Agent Hottie with a kink. Now tell me the context. Repeat the conversation word for word. I need to know how spanking was on the table at this unholy hour."

Chapter 7

So I did. I told her everything Charlie said in his long speech, not leaving a single word out.

"Rhy," she said, and I stilled at her strange tone. "Do you trust this guy?"

"I do. I don't know what it is about him, but I do. He makes me feel like me being me is more than okay. That I'm desirable, which makes no sense."

"You *are* desirable, babe. I have to be honest, I really thought the hottie agent would just be a delightful diversion, but I'm thinking he might be more than that. He's right, everything he said, and if he thinks smacking your ass around will help what he said sink in, then I'm giving him the green light to do so until you can't sit for a week."

"Hey, it's my ass," I said defensively. Not sure why, because I was down to giving him the green light too. The memory of the conversation with Carter from last night sprang forward, tossing a bucket of cold water over my spanking dreams. "But it can't happen. We're already under too much scrutiny with Carter."

"You listen to me, and you listen good, Rhy." I sat up straighter as if she were sitting right in front of me, giving me that stern eye she reserved for me and her kids. "Your section chief does not own your body. The FBI does not get to tell you who you can or cannot fuck."

"But the case—"

"Has nothing to do with whatever craziness is going on between you and Agent Hottie. I know you won't let it distract you from doing your job. Would he?"

"I don't think so, but what about—"

"Then stop worrying about what happens when you get back to DC. Just do your job when you're working the case, and do him when you're not."

"Olivia," I chastised. "He doesn't know what he's getting into. The baggage that comes with me."

"Baggage that's drowning you slowly. Brian was an arrogant prick who manipulated you and fucked you over. That has nothing to do with you now and your glorious future. Move forward, Rhy, please.

Please move forward, and if this agent is that first step, then do it. Or him, however you want to put it."

"I can't do that to him. Or me."

Her groan of frustration was like a dagger to the heart. I expected this years ago, for me to finally push her away with my annoying habits and anxious thoughts. It was a wonder she stuck around this long, actually.

"Rhy, I love you. You know I love you, but I'm done with this conversation that we've had repeatedly. I've said my piece about this, and, to be honest, I'm done being your crutch. I think… I think me listening and being sympathetic about what you're still holding on to from Brian is hurting you more than doing you good." My heart squeezed. There was so much truth in her words, but it still hurt like a dull spoon digging my heart out. This was it, the moment when my best friend left me because she couldn't handle me being me another second. "Maybe this Charlie guy has the right idea. Maybe you need a more physical push to move on."

"Olivia," I whispered. "I'm sorry. I'll stop calling and…. Please don't leave me."

"Babe, I'm not. That's your anxiety speaking. You know in your heart we're ride-or-die friends. I'm just doing what I think is best to help you move on at this moment. I'm here for you, but in the future, the instant you bring up Brian or anything negative about yourself, I'll force you to do something terrible."

"And what's that?" I wiped at the tears threatening to escape. How did I go from wet between my thighs to unshed tears in the matter of five minutes?

"I don't know," she said with an exaggerated sigh. "I'll force you to eat kale or something just as disgusting. Just be yourself with this guy, and remember, no one owns you or your body. Do what feels right, and figure it out from there."

After quick goodbyes, I ended the call and tapped the edge of the cell phone against my thigh.

My anxiety wanted to capture these thoughts and hold them

hostage for hours, make me think of every way each action could go wrong. But I didn't have time for that, not today.

Standing, I shrugged the laptop bag over my shoulder and stood tall.

Olivia's ultimatum and Charlie's spanking were something for personal Rhyan to figure out. Right now, five victims needed Agent Riggs to focus on the case to find a serial killer.

But as I walked out the sliding glass doors, a single nagging thought wouldn't relent.

Could they both be right?

"THANK you for meeting with me, Mr. Bass." I paused by the door and gestured into the small interview room.

Mr. Kenny Bass, the first victim's husband, was the final interview of the day. As he passed, hands shoved into his jeans pockets, my stomach growled as a reminder that we didn't eat breakfast and it was well beyond lunchtime.

The prickle from eyes on me had me glancing over my shoulder. In the back corner, surrounded by two other uniformed officers, Detective Hicks glared with sheer hatred from across the room.

Outstanding.

Not giving him the satisfaction of acknowledging his clear disdain, I turned back around to Mr. Bass, fixing my fake smile back on my face. Charlie maneuvered between me and the doorframe, keeping a professional distance between us as he passed.

"I don't understand why I'm here," Mr. Bass said as he sat down on the black leather couch. It groaned under his heavy weight. Once, twice, then a third time, he flattened and straightened his tie against his solid barreled chest. His bloodshot eyes shifted around the interview room as he nervously fidgeted with the button on his suit jacket. "I told the detective everything I knew months ago, and he labeled it as a suicide. What do you people want from me now? I thought all this was done."

Sitting in the chair opposite him, I crossed one leg over the other and cupped both hands over my knee. When it was clear his frustrated rant was done, I offered him a glass of water, which he declined.

"I understand you're upset. Having to relive this must be traumatic. But I promise you we're only trying to find justice for Stacey."

That fidgeting stopped. "What do you mean, justice? She killed herself, end of story."

"Is it, though?" Charlie said, sitting on the armrest of the couch. "Our notes show you were supportive of the detective's findings that your wife, Stacey, killed herself from the very beginning. Even pushed to have her cremated before the autopsy."

"Stop saying her name," he snapped and then quickly recovered, once again smoothing down his tie. "It's too painful. I'm ready to move on with my life."

Charlie and I shared a quick, knowing glance.

"Why is that?" Charlie prodded. "Because you don't want us to dig deeper into the actual cause of death or because she killed herself to get away from you? That would be difficult for any husband to digest."

His flabby cheeks bloomed red. "She didn't do it to get away from me. She did it to get away from herself." I flinched, almost like his words were a physical slap to the face. "She was depressed—"

"There was no evidence of Stacey being on medication for depression," Charlie mused, studying the file in his hand.

I mentally shot Charlie a high five for knowing to keep using Stacey's name despite the shady husband's demand. Something was up with his adamant declaration of suicide, almost as if he knew we might uncover the truth if we kept digging.

"She was dealing with it on her own, or that's what she told me." He fell back against the stiff couch and crossed his arms over his chest. "Attending various support groups and shit like that. Obviously they didn't help like she said they were."

"Obviously?" I asked. "Why do you phrase it like that?"

"Well, she was headed to one that night, the last night I saw her."

"And what did you do that night, Mr. Bass, after your wife left for the support group?"

The man's cold eyes narrowed in suspicion. "What is all this? Am I a suspect or something in my wife's suicide?"

"Why would you ask that?" I questioned, keeping my voice calm and even.

"Because it sounds like you're asking for an alibi from that night."

"Do you need an alibi?" Charlie stood and went to lean against the door.

"I didn't kill my wife," he gritted, jaw tight. "She took care of that for me."

"So you thought about it?" I scooted closer to the edge of the seat, closing the small distance.

He shifted on the couch, angling his body in the opposite direction, and huffed like I'd said something funny. "We were married for seventeen years. Of course, I thought about it."

Charlie again flicked the manila folder in his hand and thumbed through the pages. "Says here if Stacey's death was declared a murder, you'd get a $250,000 life insurance payout. That's life-changing money, considering. Yet you're adamant that we not dig deeper into the cause of death."

"Considering what?" he growled, his hands flexed into fists.

"Considering how in debt you are." Mr. Bass visibly shook with restrained anger at Charlie's statement. "The bank says you're about to lose your home."

"Stay the hell out of my finances," Mr. Bass seethed. Standing abruptly, he took a menacing step toward Charlie, who stood up straighter as if preparing for a fight. "This bullshit interview is over. You want to talk to me again? Call my attorney."

As he exited, he slammed his broad shoulder to the center of Charlie's chest, who didn't shift an inch or, much to my surprise, retaliate. I joined him at the doorway, both of us watching as the man stormed through the detective bullpen. His shouts of FBI incompetence echoed in the hall long after he was out of sight.

Frustrated at the whole confusing case, and at myself for not having this unsub's profile down, I moved past Charlie and out the door. The quick click of my black heels against the stained concrete floor followed me as I strode for the murder board Bryson put together while Charlie and I were busy conducting the interviews.

Shifting my suit jacket out of the way, I gripped my hips and stared at the cluster of pictures.

"He's hiding something,"

I nodded, agreeing with Charlie, who'd followed. "But *what* is the question," I mused. Twisting, I searched his face, hoping to find answers to the thousand unanswered questions we still had regarding the case. "One thing that was clear after meeting him, anger management classes might do him some good. I could almost feel it pulsing off him when we kept pushing his buttons. But it's the anger that marks him off the suspect list. He wouldn't be able to kill his wife, then four others, without leaving a mark. Hell, he wasn't here five minutes, and he took his anger out on you physically. Speaking of which, you okay?"

Charlie smirked and rubbed a palm against his pec. "Didn't hurt."

I rolled my eyes to the ceiling and turned back to the board. "I'm not challenging your masculinity, Agent Bekham, just saying if Mr. Bass was our unsub, there would be more physical trauma to the bodies. So what does that leave us?"

Charlie stepped beside me, mimicking my stance. "What about the husband of victim number three, Jessica Hale? He was a strange one. The fact that he didn't report his wife missing for three days is suspect. Though the way he was excited about us possibly changing the COD to murder, I don't think it's him. He just wants the easy insurance money."

Frustrated, I tossed both hands in the air and interlaced them behind my head, weaving my fingers through my hair. "We have zero ideas on what connects these women. The victimology doesn't match up." I pointed to the first victim. "Early forties Caucasian." I shifted my finger to point to the next picture. "Thirty-three African American. Then a few months later, a late thirties three-times-divorced Caucasian. And the next two are just as different. Add in the odd cooling-off periods...." Dropping my hand, I fell back, sitting on the edge of a desk. "My gut and the data say this is the work of a single unsub, but what if we're wrong?"

I waved off Charlie, who looked ready to defend the case. Digging through my bag, I grabbed my wallet and muttered something about going to get something to eat. Hopefully getting some food in my stomach would help all the pieces fall together.

The murmurs of the station, the ringing of phones, and boisterous laughter roared in my ears, all meshing into muffled white noise as I wove through the sea of desks for the break room on the other end of the floor. Mind spinning over the possibilities and ticking off the multiple inconsistencies, I failed to hear the muted steps that followed me into the break room or the soft click of the door shutting until a male voice spoke, making me whirl around from the plexiglass protecting the rows of snacks and candy held hostage.

Fucking Hicks.

8

RHYAN

"You and that gangbanger need to leave this case alone," Detective Hicks said as he leaned a shoulder against the only exit from the tiny break room. A small round table with four cheap plastic chairs separated us. "They're suicides, just like I originally listed. There is no need for the FBI to be poking their noses around my closed cases."

Standing tall, I squared both shoulders and crossed my arms, mimicking his defensive stance. "What if you're wrong?"

"I'm not," he ground out.

"How can you be so sure?"

Hicks worked his jaw side to side, clearly not liking me questioning him. "Because that's what the coroner declared before that Bryson fucker stepped in, making him change everything. It's clear all the women were unhappy in their marriages and were looking for a way out."

"That makes little sense," I stated, tossing my arms out wide. I was too damn frustrated and hungry to play nice with this joker. "Statistics can't lie, and this, what you have going on in your city, does not fit." My voice rose as I shouted at him. "And why can't we find a cause of death?"

He rattled off a response about the cause of death being from their falls, but I let it flow in one ear and out the other, too lost in my own thoughts to give a shit about him defending his theory.

"The cause of death," I whispered to myself. "That's what we need to tie all these together."

"What the hell are you mumbling about?" he snapped. "Listen." He pushed off the door, moved around the table, and stopped too close for comfort. Nerves tingled, my stomach flipping as my fight-or-flight adrenaline seeped into my cells. "These cases, the families, they don't need you changing things around when they've already moved on. Tell that guy Bryson—"

"Agent Bennett," I said through clenched teeth. *What is with this guy and hating calling us by our titles?*

"Whatever. Tell him you're wrong, that he's wrong, and leave my city."

I held his hate-filled glare, not moving an inch when he shifted even closer, putting us toe to toe.

"We're not leaving until we uncover the truth. The actual truth of what happened to these *five* victims," I said, voice trembling. "I'd think that's what any good detective would want too."

"Listen, you fucking cunt. I will not let you ruin this for me. I've worked too hard to get to this point. Leave, or I swear I'll give you a reason to."

The machine at my back groaned beneath his palm when he slammed it against the plastic inches from my head. Still, I didn't move, not even as he leaned in closer, his rank breath wafting up my nose. My stomach churned at the mix of breakfast burrito and stale cigarette smoke.

Behind him, the door flew open, bouncing off the wall from the force.

"What in the fuck do you think you're doing, Hicks?"

Not daring to move, I slid my attention over Hicks's shoulder to the fuming man filling the doorway.

"Just having a chat with the pretty agent." Reaching up, Hicks flicked a lock of my hair and shot a conniving smirk over his shoulder. "She's rethinking the case, aren't you, doll?"

"Son of a bitch," Charlie growled and stormed over, knocking a chair to the floor in his wake. His long fingers gripped Hicks's collar in a tight fist and ripped him back from where I stood sealed against the vending machine.

"Agent Bekham," I rasped. Clearing my throat, I swallowed to keep Hicks from knowing just how intimidated I was by his little show of force. "He's right."

Both men turned, Hicks still in Charlie's tight grasp, grinning like the cat who ate the canary.

"*I am* rethinking the case, at least in the way we're approaching it. We're going about this all wrong." I pushed off the vending machine, my knees wobbly as I made my way to the small table and chairs. Falling into the seat, I stared at the circular coffee stains dotting the chipped surface. "Detective Hicks here pointed out that they were all unhappy in their marriages. Agent Bekham and I picked up on that today in the interviews. That's what they have in common."

"That's nothing to go off. Most women are unhappy," Hicks huffed and yanked out of Charlie's loosened hold.

"But what if they're not connected because of that, but them being unhappy with their spouses pushed them toward our unsub?"

Charlie's expression flashed from confused to intrigued. "They all went looking for passion that was lacking in their marriage. Which means they weren't attacked at random, but the victims possibly sought him out."

"Passion." Hicks chuckled. "You clearly don't know women or marriage."

Charlie's eyes glittered with danger. "Enlighten me."

"Married women at that age don't want passion. They want stability, routine. It's men who step out looking for a good fuck that their celibate wives won't give."

"Are you married?" Charlie asked. The way his grin grew malicious, I knew whatever was coming next would be at Hicks's expense.

"Yes," he snapped. "Fourteen years this past March."

"I see," Charlie said, rubbing at his jaw. "Well, I'll look up your address later, then."

"Why the fuck would you do that?"

"To send my condolences to your wife on her lack of sex life," Charlie said with a shrug, like he was commenting on the weather. "She clearly needs it based on your declaration."

"You son of a fucking bitch," Hicks yelled and launched himself at Charlie.

Charlie reacted quickly, as if he knew his words would set off the easily angered detective. Shifting aside, he snatched Hicks's outstretched hand, then twisted and tugged his arm between his shoulder blades.

Hicks snarled and thrashed but couldn't break out of Charlie's hold. "Stay the hell away from my wife."

"I'd save that threat for the man your wife is seeing behind your back." I would have felt bad for the guy when the sad puppy dog look flashed over his face, but he was a dick, so I didn't—that much. "Clearly you don't know women, or you'd know that older women want sex more than younger women. They crave intimacy that stems from passion and vulnerability with their partner." Blue eyes flicked to me. "And from my experience, their responsiveness to even the lightest touch is uncanny. If your wife stopped asking for sex, I can guarantee she found it somewhere else."

And... my ovaries exploded.

Okay, well, maybe not, but something sure broke inside me, sending a flood of moisture between my thighs. How did he know so much about women? And not just their bodies but what made them tick and why? Holy hell, there was no doubt—not that there ever had been—that Charlie would be a fantastic lover.

Too bad for me, I was his superior and shouldn't ever cross that line.

"Get the fuck off me." Twisting around, Hicks maneuvered out of Charlie's loosened hold. Pointing a finger between my brows, he snarled. "I warned you." With that threat, he threw open the door and stormed out of the break room.

"Rhyan." The vibration in Charlie's strained voice drew my focus away from the open door. A quick breath stuck in my lungs at the intensity of his tight features. "What the hell happened in here before I walked in?"

"Nothing," I muttered, waving him off like Hicks's accosting me wasn't as big of a deal as it actually was. I was never in any real danger. "He felt the need to put me in my place, I guess. But instead of convincing me to drop the case, he gave me a different angle into the victimology and what connected them." Peeking up from beneath my fair lashes, I forced a small smile. "I'm fine, really. Not that big of a deal."

"Then why are your hands doing that?" He jabbed a finger at my trembling hands like they had personally offended him.

I slid them off the stained table top and pressed both palms to the tops of my thighs.

"That, um...." The hard plastic shifted beneath me as I turned to the vending machines at my back. "I need to eat. Sometimes I get shaky when my blood sugar is low. It's why I came in here." I stopped, no longer caring about food or my health, just digging into this new angle to see if it had any validity. "But that can wait. We need to dig into their electronic footprints for the weeks leading up to the night the victims went missing and the night before they were reported missing."

"No."

I whipped around, gaping at the hard, commanding tone directed at me. Charlie righted the chair he'd knocked over and moved past me. I followed him, unsure what in the hell he was up to and why he looked so damned determined. He held the back of his phone to the vending machine and pushed a series of buttons. Neither of us spoke, the break room quiet except for the whirl of the machine and the clunk of food falling in rapid succession. The squeak of the metal hinges pierced through the silence, followed by a crinkle of plastic as Charlie scooped the various bags and candy bars out of the tray.

Dumping two handfuls of junk food on the table directly in front of where I sat, Charlie pointed to the center.

"There. Eat something, and then we work on this new angle."

"Charlie," I said, suddenly too tired to fight him on this. "We need to find their connection—"

"Fine." Fingers wrapped around the back of a chair, he twisted it around midair, slammed it back down, and wrapped his long legs around the back, resting a single forearm along the top. His dark hair shifted as he tilted his head toward the food. "You eat, and I'll talk."

I pressed my dry lips into a tight line, attempting to keep my shy smile suppressed. Besides my mother, no one had ever been this concerned about my health and eating habits. It was overbearing but sweet, and somehow endearing.

Conceding to his demands, I picked through the pile, selecting a Snickers and a snack-size bag of Goldfish. Charlie watched, not saying a word as I ripped both open.

"Talk," I said.

"Eat."

Blowing out a frustrated breath at his cocky dominance, I dumped half the Goldfish into my palm and shoved them all into my open mouth, my defiant gaze never leaving his.

"Happy?" I said around the mouthful, a few bits of crumbs spilling out.

"Not even close, but better." He studied my lips with an intensity I couldn't read for several seconds before he shook his head, as if breaking himself out of a trance. "Do you want to file a harassment claim?"

"You weren't that bossy about the food." I held the small bag higher, covering my smirk.

"This isn't a joke."

"Though if you tried to feed me, I would've drawn the line at that."

"Riggs," he growled, knuckles of the hand wrapped around the chair back going white.

Clearly I was pushing my limits with his restraint. "No, I don't want to press any charges. Hicks is an egotistical asshole, and yeah, he confronted me in a way I wasn't comfortable with, but I wasn't in any danger. During his rant, he let something slip that might explain his obsessive need for the cases to remain suicides. It has more to do with him not wanting to be wrong than anything, which is typical for a man like him."

"I want to bash his face in," Charlie muttered under his breath. He raked a few fingers through the long section of his hair, making several dark locks fall across his forehead.

"That won't solve anything and would interfere with the case, plus end up with you in jail. Not sure how much you think I make, but coming up with bail money would be a stretch."

Some of that anger faded, the tightness around his eyes and lips softening. "But it would make me feel better."

"True." I sank my teeth into the chocolate goodness, biting off an unladylike thick chunk. "He called you a gangbanger." I studied the artwork decorating the tops of his hand and the few tattoos peeking out from beneath his collar. "That was uncalled for. He knows nothing about you."

"I walked in on you scared with that motherfucker pinning you to the vending machine, and *that's* your takeaway?"

"How can he be a good detective when he lets his own assumptions get in the way? It's super judgey."

Charlie huffed, tipping his face up to the ceiling like he was praying for patience. Maybe he was. Maybe I was finally exhausting him with my presence. My gut twisted, the candy bar now like thick mud in my mouth.

"I'm used to it. I don't worry about what others think of me, and neither should you. Surrounded by straitlaced agents and officers every day, I've gotten used to the stares and comments."

"Why did you get them in such visible places?" And hidden ones, but if I started thinking about his bare chest, I'd get no work done. "Did you not know you wanted to be in law enforcement when you grew up?"

Charlie flexed and straightened his long fingers, staring at the designs. "I knew I wanted to be in a role where I could make a difference. It was a goal of mine since childhood, but that's a story for a different day. The tattoos, well, my obsession started small, with one across my chest, and then I just kept going back for more. After being invisible for so long, the visible tattoos drew people's attention, good and bad."

The wrapper in my hand crinkled as I crumpled it in my tightening fist. "And by people, you mean women specifically."

He peeked up through those dark lashes and smirked. "Maybe."

"How in the hell could you be invisible?" I said, covering my mouth as I talked and chewed. "The dark hair, captivating blue eyes, those lips—"

"What about my lips?" A knowing, cocky smile spread across his face as a flush heated mine.

"Nothing," I grumbled. Needing a distraction from his attention, I shoved away from the table, gathered my trash, and tossed it in the large gray trash can by the door. "But you know how you look. Even without the tattoos you'd attract attention." The chair's feet scraped against the concrete as I sat and scooted closer. The food was already helping, my mind clearing and anger easing. "Thanks for the food, by the way."

Elbow to the chair's edge, he rested his chin on a raised fist. "Remember last night when I mentioned I didn't always look like this? I was a skinny fuck throughout school. It wasn't until college that I put any actual weight on. Tall, scrawny, and pissed off didn't draw in the women or friends."

Well, that sounded lonely.

"Why were you pissed off?" I asked, picking up on that one tidbit of the conversation that seemed heavy with resentment.

His focus shifted to just over my shoulder. "My mother was murdered when I was a teenager." Without thinking, I leaned across the table and grabbed his tight fist, squeezing in what I hoped was a comforting gesture. "And no one cared. It wasn't until the killer moved on to women who mattered that the police even began connecting the cases."

"We all matter," I said with so much force that Charlie's unfocused gaze shifted back, eyes wide.

Chapter 8

For several seconds, we just stared at the other, maybe really seeing each other with none of the pretense or masks for the first time. Or maybe that was just me. Instead of the gorgeous, somewhat cocky, tattooed badass, I saw the real him, the one he kept hidden beneath the dark ink and sharp smiles.

"Fun fact," I said, clearing my throat to break the growing intensity between us. "Did you know only female mosquitoes bite?"

And just like that, the spell was broken. A wide, carefree smile split his face, and his shoulders relaxed. "Well, then, Agent Riggs. I clearly am not a mosquito."

I arched a brow. "Because you're not a tiny, annoying bloodsucker who spreads malaria?"

"Because I'm all male, and I bite. Often."

I swallowed hard, suddenly very thirsty.

Charlie observed my working throat. Popping out of the chair, he once again held his phone to the machine and pressed a series of buttons, followed by a loud thunk. A chilled bottle of water slammed down onto the table.

"Okay, so let's assume the victims were out looking for a fun night," Charlie mused as he paced the short length of the wall of windows. "A one-night stand, maybe. Where would they find that?"

Tapping a short nail against the plastic bottle, I considered all the options. "You'd go out with your girlfriends if you intended to find a random hookup at a bar, though none of the victims' friends said they were with them the night they went missing."

"Which means they went out alone."

"Most women wouldn't feel comfortable picking up a stranger alone, especially one who'd been married for a while. She'd feel out of practice in a way."

Charlie nodded. Stopping at the table's edge, he rummaged through the remaining food, selecting the bag of tiny chocolate chip cookies, and ripped it open. "When I get fat, I'm blaming you."

And you'd still be hot was what I wanted to add, but I kept my words down with several gulps of water.

"So if they wouldn't go out alone," he continued, "each victim went out to meet a specific someone. Someone they had talked to, built a trust of sorts with."

"How do people meet each other if it's not random at a bar?" I asked, picking at the plastic label.

"Really?" I lifted a shoulder in a shrug. "There are dozens of apps out there they could use. I'll run a few searches when we get back to the hotel."

"Nothing too in-depth," I said with a pointed look. "We're under too much scrutiny right now to add unauthorized searches to the list. But that's a good thought."

"I'll request their phones from the families and go through those too. Do you want to head back now? I can grab the Suburban."

My lips parted to tell him no, that we needed to stick around here to flush the details out and just run the searches later, when his last word resonated.

"If they went out alone, then where are their cars?"

He blinked. "Let's go find out."

Back in the makeshift office, I handed two case files over to Charlie. Not bothering with sitting, I flipped open the file of victim number three. Palms pressed to the top of the table, I leaned over the file, skimming the lines of notes.

"They found this woman's car in an impound lot," Charlie muttered, "but it doesn't say where the company towed it from."

"I'm willing to bet the others are the same. So that means the victims went out on their own to, let's say, meet the unsub, and then they never returned to their cars. Where are the vehicles now?"

"Returned to the families," Charlie said like a curse. "Any evidence would be lost. Too much time has passed."

"And if they were left behind, I doubt there would be any anyway. Seems like the unsub lured them to a location and never stepped foot in the victim's car. But we should ask the family if we could search through the most recent victim's car just in case. Who knows, maybe a receipt or something can help narrow down a location."

"I can handle that," Bryson chimed in. I glanced over my shoulder and nodded at him. "Hey, there's some talk going around that Hicks tried to shake you down. That true?"

I hooked a thumb at Charlie. "He has dibs on handling the situation."

"So there *was* a situation," he said, clearly upset at the thought.

"Yeah, well, he's an asshole who thinks he can throw his weight around. Which, do you know if he's up for promotion?"

"Not sure, but I can ask around." I shot him a thumbs-up and went back to scanning the files. "You sure you're okay?" he asked.

"Unfortunately, that wasn't my first time holding my ground against someone like him, and I'm sure it won't be the last. Men like Detective Hicks think intimidation works because I'm a woman, but he clearly doesn't understand the depth of this redhead's stubborn streak."

"How are we profiling this guy?" Charlie asked, eyeing me.

Moving to the front of the whiteboard, I surveyed the pictures.

"White male would fit with the statistics, even though he crossed racial lines. Based on the ages of women—" I tilted my head from side to side, "—they could be attracted to him because he's younger than them."

"Can I disagree with that?" Charlie spoke up, making me turn. "I would say older. If they're breaking away from their husbands for a night, they don't want an amateur. They'll look for someone who's attractive and looks like they can handle them in the way they're wanting."

"And what are they wanting?" I questioned.

"To forget," Charlie said. "To have a night where they don't exist except for that moment. An older man would draw their eye because he'll look like—"

"He can rock their world, then let them return to the nine-to-five," I finished for him.

He grimaced and nodded.

I cocked my head to the side, studying the sexy agent. Was that what he was used to? Being that person women would use as an escape, then leave once they had what they wanted—a night to never forget?

The idea of someone using him, not giving anything back, had a frown tugging at my lips. Clearly, he was lonely if he bargained for *my* friendship yesterday. How many times did Charlie give a woman what she wanted before she left, taking any possible connection with them?

"Okay, mid-forties white male. Medical background, maybe even a doctor."

"Because all women love a doctor?" Bryson questioned. Plopping into a chair, he leaned back, resting a foot atop the table.

I shook my head. "The unsub has medical knowledge to some extent. He's killing these women without leaving a mark. That takes understanding of the human body and extreme patience. A knife to the throat or head trauma would be quicker and end with the same result." I pointed to the most recent victim's picture. "There's a reason he kills them this way. Until we find out their COD, we won't know his signature, which could lead us to him. This means something to him.

"We need to know where those cars were found before being towed. That will give us a basic geographic profile. Agent Bennett, you locate the vehicle's last known locations. Agent Bekham, you dig into their electronic footprint for the two weeks leading up to the night they went missing and really drill down to that night. Anything could be significant: a bar receipt, a gas station purchase."

Charlie nodded. "I'll also look into their out-of-the-ordinary purchases at lingerie stores. If they were planning a night with the unsub, they no doubt bought something new for the occasion."

"Yes, great." Grabbing the water bottle, I started toward the doors. "I'm going down to talk to the ME. We need a cause of death. Let's reconvene here in a few hours."

9

CHARLIE

Hours after we split up, each working on our own assignment designated by the bossy Agent Riggs, I found her in the morgue. Instead of storming in, I watched her through the small window. She sat on an autopsy table, lips moving a mile a minute with the ME nodding along.

With their attention on each other, engrossed in whatever they were discussing, I took the moment to observe Rhyan in her element. Cheeks flushed with excitement instead of arousal, unlike this morning, eyes shining with intelligence and fire, she was beautiful.

Rhyan Riggs was a knockout, and it had nothing to do with her outer shell. Sure, her body was every man's wet dream, and those eyes shining with innocence and strength could gut you in one look, but it went deeper than all that.

The need to uncover the scars that lurked beneath the surface, to learn who hurt her and then hurt them in return, burned deep in my veins. Earlier she said, "We all matter," but why did I get the impression she didn't feel that statement included her?

Soft vibrations along my thigh had me reaching into the depths of my pocket, retrieving my cell phone. My brows furrowed at the unknown number calling. After tapping the green circle, I pressed the phone to my ear.

"Bekham," I stated while continuing to watch Rhyan through the small square window.

"Agent Charlie Bekham," the feminine voice asked breathlessly.

"You got him, but I'm afraid your friend steered you wrong. You can't use my number as your personal 1-900—"

"What? Oh hell, you are cocky. I'm not calling for a little afternoon delight."

"Who is this?" I grunted, already annoyed. Sleep was scarce last night with the case and Rhyan on the mind. Add the scene earlier with Hicks and I was one wrong comment away from exploding.

"Olivia," the woman said like I should know who she was just based on a first name. "Oh hell, she hasn't even spoken about me, has she? Well, that's just rude."

Rubbing my brows, I fought for control over the rising annoyance. "Clearly not."

"Olivia Reynolds, Rhyan's best friend." My breath froze in my throat. "Now I have your attention, don't I?"

"What can I help you with, Ms. Reynolds?"

"Chandler gave me your cell. He said you're a good guy, so I'm trusting that. Is she around?"

"In the morgue. Want me to get—"

"No," she shouted. "She can't know I'm calling. I called Chandler because something happened, and he thought you should know since you're with her."

Every alarm rang in my mind. "Is she in danger?"

The long, tense pause did nothing for my growing unease. "Her ex stopped by this morning after I took the first set to school." *First set? What in the hell is she talking about?* "He's looking for her, and it will only be a matter of time before he tracks her down in DC. Hell, maybe wherever you are depending on who he asks."

"Is. She. In. Danger?" I gritted out with more urgency than before.

Olivia sighed. "I'm assuming she didn't tell you anything about Brian, so I'll give you the CliffsNotes version. They were together for a while—against my urging, mind you. I wanted her to leave that manipulating piece of shit years ago, but she wouldn't, or couldn't. I stood on the sidelines, watching my friend fade before my eyes. Do you know what that's like?"

"Can't say I do," I choked out.

"He never hit her. That's what she'd always say. He wasn't physically abusive."

"But mentally he tore her apart. Made her feel less than him, like she couldn't live up to his standards, demeaning her in small ways that ripped her confidence to shreds."

"Exactly. How do you know all that if she didn't tell you?"

Because I profile narcissists all day, every day, and those are their key moves to keep someone vulnerable and dependent. My heart ached for the beauty just beyond the door.

"What do you need from me?" It was all I could get out through the roar clogged in my throat.

"You really care, don't you?"

"She's a special woman."

"The best friend a woman could ask for, really. So I'll tell you this. He can't get near her. He has something on her, something I can't break, and I have no clue where it stems from." Her abrupt pause spoke otherwise.

"You have an idea, though."

"Never repeat this, please. I'm just trying to keep my girl safe, you understand. She doesn't even know I think this, but... I think what happened between them was coerced from the very beginning. Then bam, she was under his spell, trapped in his cage of verbal jabs and controlling tendencies, unwilling to listen to me or anyone else. We were roommates our first year in law school, so I know the Rhyan she was before he dug his claws into her."

My knees threatened to give out. Surely, she didn't mean what I thought she was saying.

"Are you suggesting," I whispered, "that the start of their relationship, maybe even the physical piece, wasn't consensual?"

"I'm saying if anyone could figure out a way to manipulate sex from someone, it would be that asshole. He's a psychology professor at a nearby college, her professor when she took a few courses she thought might help her later in her career with the FBI."

"Son of a bitch," I hissed. He knew what he was doing and was in an authority type role where women like Rhyan, sweet and innocent, felt they could trust him. The fucker used that, used his authority and proximity, to trap her in whatever game he was playing. Closing my eyes, I counted to ten to calm down. Immediately, my stomach sank. "Shit, this morning I…. Fuck."

"Brought up the idea of spanking to get her to change her mind about herself." All I could manage was a confirming grunt.

"Yeah, she called me right after." *Fuck, I'm going to be sick. If I made her uncomfortable by being the cocky jackass I am, I'll beg for her forgiveness.*

"But don't worry," she continued. "She sounded interested in the idea, or at least not put off by it. Goodness knows that girl needs something more than the vanilla shit she had before."

Well, okay, then.

"But why tell me instead of letting her know this fuck might come around?"

"I'm assuming you've seen evidence of her anxiety. If she knew Brian was coming after her, it would toss her into a tailspin. I don't know why he's looking now. It's been over a year since she walked out on him."

"I do. A narcissist like that can't stand the idea that she left him and is doing okay on her own. It has nothing to do with her, or how he feels about her. It's all about him and his ego. I'd venture to assume the woman he recently had enraptured with him left or he just got bored."

She let out a low whistle. "Rhy *said* you were good at your job." That had me standing up a little straighter. "Listen, I just wanted to give someone a heads-up. She's a confident, strong woman and working really hard at moving on. In fact, her talking to you, opening up, is a gigantic step for her. Can I offer you some advice?"

"Sure."

"She's strong. Don't treat her like she's some fragile thing now because you know about her ex. Keep treating her however you have been, because I haven't heard her this happy, and so Rhyan, in a long, long time. For whatever my opinion's worth."

"Good to know." I thought about that for a second. "Are you the lawyer friend?"

"Yeah," she responded cautiously.

"Well, glad I have your number, then, because if that fucker comes around her when I am, I'll need it." Rhyan's green eyes flicked around the room and landed on mine. She lifted her hand in a small wave, freezing halfway through. "I gotta go. Let me know if you hear anything else, and I'll do the same."

I slammed my palm onto the cool metal door, popping it open.

"Everything okay?" Rhyan asked as I stalked into the room.

Shoving the phone back into my pocket, I began pacing in front of where she sat reviewing the autopsy notes.

"No. A friend is in trouble, and I'm trying not to lose my shit."

"That's terrible," she said, following my quick movements. "Do you need to go—"

"No," I barked. Sealing my lids shut, I turned my face to the ceiling. "I'm right where I need to be. Did you two find anything helpful?"

When I finally willed myself to look her way, there was a flicker of suspicion there. "No. And the good doctor here just ruled out nutmeg poisoning."

I froze mid-step. Turning to face her, I pressed both palms against the rounded edge of the metal table, leaning in close. The small distance between us was too much; an overpowering possessiveness was riding hard through my veins after that phone call. "Nutmeg." She nodded, features not giving anything away. "Now you're just making shit up."

Her long red ponytail swished from side to side. "Nope. Fun fact. Nutmeg is extremely poisonous if injected intravenously."

"What about cinnamon?" I countered.

Her lips twitched with an almost smile. "That I don't know. Wasn't on my fun fact sheet. But we've ruled out almost everything else. We're at a loss. They died before they hit the water, but how?"

A low grumble sounded from her stomach. With a sheepish look, she pressed a fist to her belly and glanced away.

"You need to eat. Real food."

"I'm fine," she replied. "I'm not leaving until I find something to go on."

Leaning closer to keep our conversation private, I curled a single finger, urging her to meet me in the middle. A flare sparked deep in my chest when she willingly obeyed my small command.

"Remember that conversation on discipline this morning?" The widening of her eyes and quick look to the ME signaled she absolutely did. "If I have to resort to that to get you to take care of yourself, friend, then I will."

"Friends don't spank friends," she whispered.

I shot her a wink. "Then you don't have the right friends. Come on, we're getting some food. I'm fucking starving."

AFTER A HEATED DEBATE, from my side, we compromised, eating an actual meal and continuing to work from the comfort of her hotel room. Seeing her relaxed, laughing, and spouting the most random facts while we worked the various avenues made me want to freeze time. Her smile gutted me every time. It was innocent, shy, even with a touch of hope. After talking to her best friend earlier, I now understood how rare the smiles she shared with me were.

And call me greedy, but I wanted more. Which was why I kept asking her for more fun facts instead of focusing on the case.

"You're kidding me," I said around a mouthful of Pad Thai noodles.

"Nope, and that's why you should recycle. One glass jar saves enough energy to watch three hours of TV." Setting the white to-go carton down, she padded over to the desk on bare feet and grabbed the stack of files, signaling the end of our break. "What are your thoughts on the profile so far?"

My fork scraped the bottom of the cardboard box, shoving what little remained of my meal into the corner. "I think it's on point. We won't know his motive until we understand the COD, though, which sucks ass. But based on what we've learned today, I'd add in that he hates women—married women to be specific—and tosses them over a bridge like trash. Not full of rage, patient, and smart as fuck."

She nodded along, agreeing with everything I said. As she flipped through the pages, her earlier smile faded, and she began worrying on that lower lip.

"What?"

Her mouth opened, eyes flicking to me before snapping shut. "Nothing."

"Rhyan," I drawled. "We catch this guy by asking questions, working together."

With a frustrated huff, which I suspected was directed more internally than at me, she tossed the files to the bed and sat on the edge. Fiddling with the string on her light gray joggers, she kept her eyes trained on the ugly carpet.

"Is what you said about women wanting an older man true?"

Ah, so that was what was bothering her. And I had a clue that it wasn't because of the case but more of a curious personal question.

"From my experience, yeah." Slurping the remaining noodles, I tossed the box across the room. It dropped into the middle of the trash can with a quiet *swish*.

"But you're not old," she said, turning. Bending her knee, she rested a leg on the bed to face me directly.

"I'm older than you think." Wiping my face, I chucked the crumpled napkin at the trash can. It hit the edge before tumbling inside the plastic bag.

"How old are you?" she asked in a rush, brows high on her forehead.

I didn't respond immediately, the anticipation making her lean closer and closer the longer I waited.

"Thirty-seven."

"Oh," she said with a relieved sigh. "See? Not old."

"How old are you?"

"A little younger." She chuckled. "Thirty-five."

"Just a baby," I said, gently pushing her shoulder with my hand. "So, does it apply to you?"

"Does what apply to me?"

"Are you attracted to older men because you think they'd know what they're doing in bed rather than going for a younger guy?"

I knew I said something wrong when her features froze. Internally, I cursed myself for asking the dumbass personal question, for pushing her on this kind of topic. She was clear on her boundaries, and I was the ass just stepping right over them.

"I don't know," she said with a pushed breath. "I've never really thought about it that way. The last guy... my ex-boyfriend mentioned a few times that *that* part of our relationship wasn't my strong suit." She shrugged like her words meant nothing, but the sadness leaking off her spoke volumes. "So since we broke up, I haven't really thought about it that much."

"'It' as in sex?" I asked cautiously.

"I didn't want to be reminded of how... of my shortcomings, you know? So it's easier to just not think about it and take care of the issue myself." Tapping the files, she shot me a sad smile. "Instead, I focus on serial killers and dead bodies."

"What did your boyfriends before him think?" *Holy fuck, that bastard put so much shit into her head. No wonder she's high strung.* "You with your love for statistics and data points, how can you take the opinion of just one guy as truth? You'd need a sampling of opinions to form a scientific conclusion."

Yeah, I was talking out of my ass.

"It's just him."

"See? So the others you've been with, they thought—"

"No, Charlie. I mean, it's just him, just my ex. I didn't... I haven't slept with anyone else. Just Brian."

Those green eyes bored into mine, begging me for something I didn't understand.

"Well, then, you need a wider focus group, don't you?" Pretty sure I remembered that term from my junior year statistics class.

Though as soon as I said it, I wanted to retract the statement. Wider focus group? Fuck that. I would be her focus group, just me. No other fuckers were getting anywhere close to her.

She tipped her head back, that long thick ponytail slipping halfway down her back, and groaned. "You sound like my best friend, Olivia. She says the same thing all the time, but it's not like I haven't tried, believe me. But I repel men just by being my strange, quirky self."

"Now that is hard to believe. You're amazing, Rhyan."

Fuck, why did my voice just catch?

"I do," she exclaimed. "I went on a date last month with a trainer I met at Quantico, and it was a complete disaster. I was so nervous I talked about—" She cringed and buried her face in her hands.

"Please don't tell me you talked about the poor koalas and their chlamydia problem."

Still hiding behind her hands, she bobbed her head.

I couldn't help it. I burst out laughing. My laugh rumbled through the room, making her peek through two spread fingers. "Okay, yeah, that's not the best opening topic if you want to take the date from the restaurant to the bedroom."

"I know." She dropped her hands, hitting her thighs. "I just get so nervous, and then shit spills out of my mouth and I can't stop. Then I get more awkward. One hour and ten minutes. That's the longest date I've been on in fourteen months."

"Damn," I said and whistled low.

"I'm a hopeless case. I'll end up in this job until they force me to retire, and I'll live out the rest of my life alone with my forty cats. I don't even like cats. I'm a dog person, but I'll get cats because that's what you do. Then I'll be the old cranky cat lady who gives out apples and dental floss for Halloween. Don't even get me started on Christmas—"

"Rhyan," I said, grabbing her by the shoulders. "Take a breath." She sealed her lips shut but obeyed, nostrils flaring with each inhale. Only once she'd taken several deep breaths did I continue. "It will be okay. And you know how I know that?"

She shook her head. "You can't know that. I'll die alone because I'm too awkward, and even if a guy gets past that, there's no reward in the end because I'm no good in bed."

"Stop. You won't die alone."

"How do you know that?" Tears accumulated in her lower lids. "I'll die alone and leave anything I have left to my cats. Who will no doubt just be waiting for me to die so they can gorge themselves on the expensive cat food that I never bought them because I was—"

"I know you won't turn into the crazy cat lady because you have me. We're friends, right?" She dipped her chin in a reluctant nod. "Well, friends don't let their friends start with one cat. I'll intervene, swooping in with a puppy in hand. And the cranky old lady who gives out shit at Halloween, well, that's an odd one to be concerned about, but we'll work through it when the time comes. Maybe we can compromise, and they can be caramel apples. And Christmases, you can spend them with me."

She huffed. "You'll have a family. All married and happy with two-point-five kids and a dog."

My grip on her shoulders tightened. "I doubt it." Inhaling a deep breath, I drew in courage to open up about what I normally keep locked down tight. "I'm alone too, Rhyan. I have no family left. Sure, I might have better luck on dates, but it's nothing serious. They always leave. I give them what they want for the night, and then they're gone. I've done that fucking routine, no pun intended, more times than I can count, and I'm exhausted. I'm not sure how much longer I can keep repeating the same pattern before I just give up, tired of giving a piece of me and feeling more alone than ever after."

A single tear leaked from the corner of her right eye. Reaching up,

I cupped her cheek, wiping the stray tear away with a swipe of my thumb.

"I want someone to call my own, who will be there for me when I have nothing left to give. A friend and a lover who can make me laugh one moment and lure me in with a simple look the next. But for men like me, that's not in the cards, no matter how badly I wish life dealt me a different hand."

10

RHYAN

The continuous hum from the air conditioning unit below the window and my labored breaths were the only sounds as I lay in bed, wide eyes stuck on the locked hotel room door. The nine-millimeter's coarse grip dug into my clammy palm. Nervous energy had sweat coating the back of my neck despite the chill in the room.

Three hours.

Three long, tedious hours. That was how long I'd lain there, wide awake, watching the door after Charlie left just before midnight. Now here I was unable to fall asleep because my mind wouldn't let me. Detective Hicks's threat today didn't rattle me then, but now that my mind had time to come up with at least thirty different worst-case scenarios, I was royally freaked out. Add in the constant texts from Brian, and I was on the edge of sanity with no hope of relief.

A contained, frustrated sob rattled my chest.

Damn, I'm just so tired—of it all. I desperately needed sleep, but the anxiety just wouldn't release its hold. I hated this, hated that I couldn't stop or turn it off no matter what I did. I didn't want to be this way.

A doctor last year had suggested medicine to help ease some of my symptoms, which worked for millions, but I just couldn't make that leap yet. A part of me was afraid if I calmed down my anxiety and my overactive brain, I wouldn't be as good at my job as I was now. What if fixing one part of my mind dampened another?

Anxiety was so fucking fun.

Knowing what I needed if I wanted a moment of rest, I climbed off the bed, sliding the gun out from under the pillow with me. Keeping it at my side, I tiptoed to the door, swiping the two keys off the dresser as I passed, and sealed an ear to the cold wood. Holding a breath, I counted to three before convincing myself the hall was safe.

The metal bar thump when I flipped it back, the click of the lock disengaging upping my anticipation. Only eerie quiet greeted me when I poked my head into the hall. Like I was about to cross the street, I glanced left, then right, then back again, just to be sure Hicks wasn't hovering in the shadows. Back sealed to the wall, I inched down the dim hall, finger hovering just above the trigger, ready for anything.

Four doors down, I pressed against it, checking the room number three times before rapping a knuckle against the center of the door. Breathing rapidly, I kept checking down the hall.

The door at my back swung open, sending me stumbling inside a step. Whirling around, I maneuvered past the stunned Charlie and hurried into his dark room.

"What's wrong?" he asked, still holding the door open. Through the faint light pouring in from the hall, I watched his features change from confusion to anger when his eyes caught the gun in my hand. "Fuck," he cursed and stretched for the gun sitting on the entry table while using his foot to keep the door propped open. "Did he find you? Is he here? I swear I'll kill that manipulating motherfucker."

Shit. I was right. Charlie thought the same thing. Hicks was a threat.

I wrapped the hand not holding the gun around my throat, my pulse thumping against my fingers in a staccato beat.

"I didn't think he'd actually come here or I wouldn't have left you alone. How in the hell did he find you?"

I inched back deeper into the room. Charlie stood guard at the door, muscles flexed as he held the gun between two hands. "I don't know. Maybe he followed us from the police station," I whispered and palmed my gun, adjusting my slippery grip. "Or asked the other officers where we were staying."

"How in the hell would he have influence over the officers here?"

That snapped my thoughts to a grinding halt. "Huh? He's a detective. Of course he has sway with them."

Charlie's back muscles tensed. Slowly stepping out from the hall, he quietly closed the door behind him and leaned against it.

"Who are you talking about?" he asked.

"Hicks," I said cautiously. "Because of his aggressiveness and warning today, I have this whole thing built up in my mind that he'll come after me. Who are you talking about?"

His silence stretched between us.

"Charlie," I said, hating the dread building in my gut. "Who were you talking about?"

Still, he didn't say a word. Stomping over to the lamp, I flicked on the light and turned to him, but all my thoughts fled. "You're naked," I squeaked and whirled around to face the blackout curtains.

"I sleep naked, Rhyan. I was asleep when you knocked on my door at three thirty in the morning."

Well, he had me there.

There was some shuffling at my back, but I didn't dare turn until he told me it was safe. Holy hell, I didn't know guys came in that size. No wonder women flocked to him. Maybe they had some kind of big dick radar and they just knew with one look that Charlie was one of the blessed.

"Rhyan," he shouted.

"What?"

"You can turn around now."

But when I did, it was worse.

"Sweatpants," I said, pointing the end of my gun in his direction of the thick dick outline still clear as fucking day. He immediately leapt away with a barked curse. "Not that. Find something else."

"Rhyan, what the hell is going on?"

Still staring at his amazing body and the way the pants hung low on his hips, I fought to regain control of my mind and the conversation. "Who did you think it was, out in the hall? You said you'd kill the fucker."

"What's wrong, Rhyan?" My eyes slid up his defined stomach and chest, meeting his weary gaze. "You came down here with a gun, scared. Why?"

"Like I said, I worked myself up, and I knew I couldn't sleep. I was hoping...." I pointed the gun at the one double bed that was still made.

"Please stop using your gun like a laser pointer." Scrubbing a hand down his face, he motioned to the bed. "You want to stay in here, fine. But I sleep naked."

Setting my gun on the desk, I tossed both hands out in exasperation and widened my stance. Apparently, Charlie thought that was hilarious based on the smile he fought to smother. Though that smirk died the moment he noticed my long naked legs. I didn't sleep naked, but sleep shorts weren't made for the leg blessed. I could tell half my ass hung out the back from the way the air kept brushing along my exposed skin.

Fuck, I didn't even put a bra on. He noticed it the same moment I remembered, those blue eyes flashing at my nipples threatening to slice through my shirt.

Shit. This was looking more like an excuse for a hookup than me being legit scared.

"Who, Charlie? If not Hicks, then who did you think was after me? Who else should I be scared of?"

His features softened, turning apprehensive. That couldn't be good. "Don't be mad."

"That's never a good start to a conversation."

"Your friend Olivia reached out to me today."

I stumbled backward and fell into the stiff armchair. There was only one reason Olivia would go behind my back like that. Break the firm line between personal and my career.

"I see."

Chapter 10

"Rhyan—"

I held up a hand. "Did she warn you about me?" I hissed. "About all my issues."

"About you? No, fuck no." After setting the gun back in its place, he sat on the edge of the bed and leaned forward, pressing his forearms against his thighs. "She called about your ex. Said he paid her a visit, and she was worried he'd find a way to you here."

My eyes shifted left, like I could see through the three rooms separating us from my cell phone that held the dozens of unreturned texts from Brian.

"And she didn't think I could handle it." I filled in the blanks.

"I think it was more about a friend looking out for a friend than thinking you couldn't handle the information."

I huffed. "Some friend. Calling the guy I have a crush on to tell him about my fucked-up past. I can't believe she did that to me. We're colleagues. She knows how hard I work to keep that dumpster fire of a relationship away from my job."

"Is that why you let everyone think the worst about you at the office?" he asked tentatively.

"I'd rather them think I'm a cheating whore than the pathetic woman I am."

"Rhyan." The angry undertone in that single word had my gaze locking on him. His hands wrapped around his knees in a death grip, as if he was holding himself back. "It's three thirty. You're in my room with nothing on under that tank top"—as if liking the mention, my nipples hardened to tight peaks—"and you just admitted to having a crush on me." *Wait, I did?* "I'm doing what I can to hold myself back from bending you over my knee and wearing your ass out for once again degrading the woman I find utterly amazing in every way. So either get under the covers right now, or this visit will turn out very differently from what you had planned."

My entire body trembled with want and excitement.

"Rhyan," he pleaded. "Please. I'm trying to do the right thing here, but you're making it nearly impossible looking at me like that."

"Like what?"

"Like you want me to show you all the ways your bitch of an ex was wrong. Prove it wasn't you who was bad in bed but him, because he didn't give two shits about your pleasure, just his own. And show you what you've been missing out on all these years, believing the twisted words he poured into your ear. To be the one you can lose control with, knowing I'll catch you when you fall, and be ready to do it all over again, and again, and again."

"Oh my."

"So which is it? Your own bed or crawling into mine?"

"I'm still mad at you," I whispered. Half of my mind wanted to dive into his bed, stripping as I sailed through the air. But the other half, the practical half, knew that would be a terrible mistake. Tomorrow would be here soon, and what then? Sure, I had a crush. Sure, I wanted to see if he could prove Brian wrong, but did that mean it had to happen tonight? "I'll sleep alone."

He hung his head and gave a brief nod. "Get in bed. I'll turn off the light."

"No stripping until it's dark," I warned. "I'm not saying no to what you proposed, just not now. Not tonight."

"So you're telling me there's a chance." I giggled a little at the forced, cocky tone.

When I crawled in the bed, I lay down on my back. "I don't want to be like them," I admitted, watching as that tattooed arm reached for the light.

"Like who?"

"I don't want to just take from you, Charlie. If this is more than just friends, I want it to be more than just a one-night stand, you know?"

"You have no idea, do you?"

"What?" I whispered as the room was doused in darkness.

"To me, you already are."

Chapter 10

THE SMELL of sugary goodness and coffee roused me from a deep sleep. Sniffing before my lids even opened, I rolled over, following the delicious scent. A low chuckle had me blinking, fighting back the onslaught of the sun's rays on my sensitive eyes.

"What time is it?" I croaked. A thick fog coated my brain, making it hard to fully wake. Shielding my eyes, I looked over my shoulder to the wide windows.

When was the last time I slept so hard that the sun woke up before me?

"Eight thirty," Charlie said from where he sat typing on his laptop, already fully dressed for the day in a sharp blue suit and crisp white dress shirt. With a curse, I kicked off the covers to untangle myself and scooted to the edge. "Calm down—"

"Calm down?" I exclaimed. "We're late. I'm never late. Shit, what if I get written up for this? What if you get written up for this? That might be the final straw for that asshole to fire you. We both know he already hates you. The end of your promising career will be my fault—"

"Holy fuck, that escalated quickly. Here," he said and held out a coffee cup. "Drink this. You'll feel better after. And we're not late. I reached out to Bryson and let him know we were going to walk the street in the geographic profile zone we defined last night."

"Oh." Plopping back on the bed, I grabbed the cup, our fingers brushing. That contact brought last night's conversation roaring forward. "I'm still mad at you, and Olivia."

"The coffee helps though, right?" He turned back to his computer and his own coffee. "The donuts are on the nightstand between the beds. I wasn't sure if you were a regular or cake fan, so I got an assortment."

"Bribery?"

"Most definitely," he said with a chuckle. "I'm guessing you normally don't sleep that hard."

Stretching across the bed, I scooted the box closer until I could grab the side. "Never. I'm always early. I can't tell you the last time I slept that hard, or that long, without waking up worrying about something." Choosing a glazed donut with white icing and sprinkles, I took a bite and moaned.

"That was my guess." His blue eyes twinkled with pride as he watched me over his shoulder. "You could take medication, you know. For the sleep and anxiety."

"I know," I said around a mouthful of donut. "But I'm managing it on my own." He hummed a noncommittal response. "What? I am."

Swiveling in the chair, he pinned me with a knowing stare. "Really? Remind me again why you escaped to my room last night."

To avoid answering, I shoved the rest of the donut into my mouth and smiled.

"No comment. Well played."

"I thought so too." Chasing the half donut with a few hot sips of coffee, I stood and walked to the window. The warm glass heated my skin as I leaned against it. The click-clack of keys had me turning from watching the crowded downtown streets to Charlie.

Brows pulled close, he rolled the silver ball from one side of his lower lip to the other as he focused solely on the screen. His nearly black hair was styled back, emphasizing his chiseled features. Disappointment bloomed within me at the white dress shirt covering the chest full of ink that I desperately wanted to trace with my fingertips. Or tongue.

"I don't want people to feel sorry for me," I said out of the blue. His fingers paused, hovering over the keys. "It's why I don't talk about it... him."

Turning in the chair, he spread his legs and interlaced his fingers behind his head, giving me his full attention. "What is there to feel sorry for? You left. I can't imagine how hard that was. I don't know the details, but knowing what I do about narcissists, I can only imagine how difficult a decision it was to break free."

"I ran," I whispered. "One day I just had enough, and I knew." Tears welled. Not able to maintain eye contact, I turned back to the window and watched the people along the sidewalks. "I knew I was with someone who would never give me what I gave to him. That was a tough pill to swallow. I wasted almost six years of my life with a man who only really loved himself. I did everything I could to make it work, put up with the backhanded comments and ways he'd carefully put me down when we were alone. It was so sneaky the way he'd do it without me realizing until later. Like the time after we'd had sex, he said I was lucky I was so pretty because that was really all I offered." Wiping at my eyes, I chewed on my lip, not knowing where to go from there.

"The good times were good though, right?" I nodded. "He made you believe in the beginning that you were his entire world."

"Yes," I croaked. "Looking back, I see all the manipulating moves clear as day, but then, then it was just him asking me to stay after class. Laughing at my jokes, the subtle touches, flirting banter. Even then, though, he'd put me down in certain ways to make me think I would never find better than him. He made fun of me wanting to wait until I was married to have sex, kept telling me it wasn't that big of a deal and he'd be willing to help me. That no other guy would teach a virgin." I laughed. Suddenly, all the sadness and grief bloomed into burning anger.

"I'm a smart woman," I said through gritted teeth. "I'm strong, independent. I was on track to be an FBI profiler, for fuck's sake. So why didn't I see it?" Whipping around, I found Charlie standing, his hands in his slacks pockets. "Why? Why didn't I tell him to shove it up his ass and tell the dean what he was doing? Manipulating me into falling in love with him, making me think I was honored that he would even look at me." Coffee sloshed out of the cup when I threw my arms out wide. "Now I'm this, this pathetic excuse—"

Charlie's hands sealed to my cheeks the same instant as his lips met mine. All the anger drained away, leaving a gaping hole that I desperately wanted filled. The cup tumbled to the floor, coffee splashing across my feet. Gripping his shirt, I tugged him even closer. With a rumbled groan, he slipped both hands into my hair and curled his fingers. The soft tug sparked a flare of pain, making me gasp. Taking full advantage of the opening, his tongue slid inside, testing and teasing.

With little effort, he walked me backward until my back sealed to the window. Moving even closer, Charlie wedged a thigh between both of mine and pressed forward. Heat blazed beneath my skin. My heart thundered in my chest as I became lost in his kiss. The feel of his hold on me, the protective way his body shielded me from the world, and his tongue that flicked and caressed with the odd sensation of the metal bar.

Tentatively, I played with the small ball atop the bar, growing bolder when his fingers flexed and his body pressed harder against mine.

A knock froze us on the spot. Pulling back, I searched his hooded gaze for an answer to what the hell just happened. At the next knock, Charlie offered a tentative smile, kissed me hard, and turned.

He cursed when he looked through the peephole. Glancing back to me, he motioned me to the right and opened the door a foot.

"Hey, Bryson. Thought we were meeting you at the station later?"

"I tried calling but couldn't get you. They found another body." At that, I inched closer to the door to not miss a single word. "That fuckhead Hicks didn't bother to call me last night when the 911 call came in."

"Fuck," Charlie growled. "Okay, let me finish up here, and I'll meet you downstairs."

"You know where Rhyan is?"

"Probably out walking the streets to find a connection between the lots we found the victims' cars in. They were all within a ten-block radius. That has to mean something."

"You let her go out there alone?" Bryson said with some heat in his tone.

"Give me ten. I'll call Rhyan and have her meet us too."

"Yeah, okay."

Charlie closed the door and turned, running a hand through his styled hair, disheveling the strands.

"I need fifteen minutes," I said, moving to the door.

Charlie grabbed my upper arm and turned me to face him.

"We're good, right? I'm sorry if I overstepped the friendship line—"

Chapter 10

"Oh, you did for sure, but yeah, we're good. Better than good." Not sure if it was his kiss or my confession, but I felt lighter, better. "Fifteen minutes."

"I'm sorry for overstepping with your friend too. Forgive me?" There was a vulnerability shining through that softened the thought of staying mad, punishing him for just trying to look out for me.

Now Olivia, that was a whole different story. Best of intentions or not, she still crossed a line. But that was between me and her.

"Okay," I whispered.

After the ding of the elevator faded into the empty hall, I counted to five to ensure Bryson was gone and then pulled the door open.

"Hey, Charlie," I said, halfway in the hall, half still in his room. "Thank you."

"Never been thanked for a kiss before."

I rolled my eyes at his cocky ass. "You know what I mean."

That facade he allowed everyone to see, to expect of him because of his exterior, faded, and a kind smirk pulled at his lips.

"I know. See you in fifteen, Rhyan."

11

RHYAN

Racing down the hall, I stumbled, catching myself on the wall when I held up the phone screen to check the time, ensuring I was still within the fifteen-minute timeframe I gave Charlie fourteen minutes ago.

An unread text from Olivia caught my eye, renewing my annoyance with my friend, but her worry and concern, despite the terrible way she went about it, made my heart go all mushy. She loved me and just wanted to keep me safe from Brian and maybe myself too. Walking away from him, moving across the country, was difficult to say the least, and she no doubt didn't want the last fourteen months of my struggling to move on to all be for nothing. If Brian showed up, it would set me back to where I started in my narcissist deprograming.

Jamming the down arrow with my thumb, I whisper-begged for the elevator to hurry. Not sure how we would explain my arrival at the impromptu meeting from my room instead of the streets, but hopefully Charlie already thought of a plausible white lie.

Before the doors were fully opened, I stepped into the elevator, held down the Door Close button, and simultaneously tapped the text from Olivia.

Olivia: Okay, your bad-boy fed said he let it slip that I called him. #Sorrynotsorry I won't ever apologize for doing everything I can to keep you away from that bastard.

Olivia: Which is why I'm texting this damn early. Apparently I'm not the only one.

Frowning at my phone, I sent a quick reply.

Me: What are you talking about?

Olivia: Ask your hacker boyfriend.

Olivia: I, for one, am on the "fuck Charlie" train. Choo-choo. Hop on board and ride, my friend. He's "call your expensive babysitter" date-worthy.

Me: That means nothing to me, you realize that.

Olivia: It means he's worth the hassle, the money, the time. And I have a feeling he feels the same way about you.

The elevator dinged, and the doors slowly slid open despite my cursing them to speed up. I sent a quick response before stepping into the busy lobby.

Me: He kissed me this morning. And I liked it. A lot. I hope to do it again soon.

I grinned ear to ear at the reminder of Charlie's lips pressed to mine, of the feel of his tongue caressing and stroking with expert finesse. A pleasure-driven shiver raced down my spine, making goose bumps sprout along my arms.

I shoved the phone into the designated pocket of my laptop bag and started toward Charlie and Bryson, where they stood in the far corner near the free coffee and wall of windows. As if he were watching the elevator, Charlie's blue eyes slipped over Bryson's shoulder and locked on me. Bryson turned, no doubt wondering what held Charlie's attention.

"Thought you were out walking the streets," Bryson questioned when I drew close, his tone a mix of suspicion and accusation.

"Had to pee." I hooked a thumb toward the bank of elevators. "Charlie texted me, said we have a new body?"

He nodded, still staring me down with a furrowed brow.

Shit. Shit. Shit. He knew, or at least suspected, something was up.

Chapter 11

Play it cool, Rhyan. Play it cool.

"Fun fact." *Oh hell, what is wrong with me?* "A koala's fingerprints are so similar to humans that they could taint a crime scene." Both men blinked at me, clearly unsure of what to say next. "Hopefully there are no koalas in the area," I said on the most forced, fakest laugh in history.

Bryson looked shell-shocked. Well, high five to me. I got him to stop wondering why I was upstairs. But Charlie, his entire body trembled. Fist pressed to his lips, hiding his smile, tears collected along the lower rims.

Sometimes being me was the worst.

"How long was the body in the water?" I asked, turning my complete focus away from Charlie to Bryson. If he was going to laugh, then I was going to ignore him.

He shook his head, still with a strange look on his face. "This one never made it to the water."

"What?" I said, all embarrassing koala talk gone from my worries. "Why do we think it's the same unsub?"

"Because he made a mistake. He didn't look for anyone or anything beneath the bridge when he tossed this victim over. She landed on a boat, the owner out doing some illegal night fishing."

I chewed on my lower lip, working through the millions of things that needed to be done now that we had a new victim.

"Have you two discussed a plan of attack?" I asked Charlie, who shook his head. "Okay, this is what we'll do. Bryson, I want you to interview the man who caught the body." I paused. "That is very odd to say out loud. Anyway, we need to know the exact time it happened. What he remembers, such as any out-of-place sounds, seeing anything out of the ordinary, things like that."

"Anything out of the ordinary besides a dead body falling onto his boat?" Charlie commented, humor brightening his voice.

"Yeah, smartass. Bryson, I'd also like for you to be with Detective Hicks when he informs the family. We need to know from them what this new victim was doing last night, and anything they can remember from the last week. Also, work on getting an APB out on her vehicle. Please make sure the ME goes over that body with a fine-tooth comb. I'll be by later this afternoon to review his findings and view the body myself. This could be the break we needed."

Despite the dead body, a thrill of excitement coursed through me, waking me up better than any coffee. This would be how we caught the unsub, I could feel it in my gut. He made a mistake, and now we needed to capitalize on it to save future lives.

"What will you two be doing?" Bryson asked, looking at us.

Charlie just smiled, biting that damn tongue ring when Bryson's attention was on me.

This could be a very long and torturous day for my libido.

Tucking a lock of hair behind my ear, I adjusted my thick frames and stared out the windows at the beautiful morning outside.

"We'll search for what's around the geographic profile area. There must be something specific that's drawing all the women to that ten-block section of the city on the night they were murdered." Bryson's lips parted, forehead wrinkled in confusion when I realized my mistake. "I didn't get far this morning in my search. Also, please get me the exact location of last night's body dump, and ensure officers keep the scene secure until we get there."

"You got it. What else?" Bryson rocked back on his heels, cracking one hand's knuckles, then another.

"We need to compare the data I gathered last night on the victims' spending trends the two weeks leading up to their disappearances."

I nodded, agreeing with Charlie. Shit, we had a lot to do, plus add more detail to the profile. Hopefully today would prove productive. "We can do that this afternoon at the station after I've seen the body and talked to the ME. I have a feeling this new victim will tell us a lot about our unsub."

After hashing out the finer details of Bryson's assignments, he left with a goodbye smack to Charlie's back, leaving us standing in the middle of the lobby, faces buried in his phone, mapping out where to start.

"I say here." Charlie tapped a finger over an intersection slightly east of the center. "We can roam around until we make it to the center. That way we miss nothing."

"Good idea." Eyeing the line for the free coffee, I started that way, but Charlie grabbed my hand, pulling me to a stop. "What?" I almost pouted. "I need coffee. Mine ended up on your floor this morning." My cheeks heated at the reminder of why I dropped said coffee.

"I need more too. I left mine upstairs on the desk. But we're not drinking that shit. There's a decent coffee shop around the corner. They also happen to sell breakfast food."

Smothering my shy grin, I fell into pace beside him as we exited the hotel. Men and women in suits and business-casual dress hurried down the sidewalks, weaving around us as we strolled along, still hand in hand. The warm sun peeked over the tall buildings, bringing a welcomed warmth to fight the morning's chilly breeze.

"Olivia texted me this morning." I said when he shuffled close, avoiding being knocked over by a flustered woman tightly gripping a map.

His hand slipped from mine, my heart falling at the loss of contact, only to flutter to life when it sealed to my lower back, guiding me around the corner. "Oh yeah? What did she have to say?" He continued surveying the streets and sidewalks as if scouting for danger.

"She was kind of cryptic, honestly, which is odd for her. She said I should ask you."

Squinting against the sun, he hummed a noncommittal response. "Not sure what she meant by that."

"Charlie," I warned and stepped away from his touch. Instantly, he stopped and reached for me, drawing me back to his side. A soft sigh brushed past my lips at the overwhelming sense of safety in his arms. "You're on thin ice already. Tell me what you did."

"Thin ice?" he said in an incredulous huff. "I bribed you with delicious donuts and coffee. I even got a thank-you for the best kiss of your life less than an hour ago."

Sniggering, I shoved at his bicep, which kind of hurt and didn't make him move an inch. "I never said it was the best kiss of my life."

His calloused palm scraped along my cheek, grip firm as he held me in place. "Are you saying I need to try again?"

Throat dry, all liquid now gathered between my thighs, I swallowed hard. Everything around us faded with his intent gaze on me, as if I were his entire world, as he waited for my response.

"I'm saying," I rasped, "tell me what you did. I have a feeling it had something to do with He Who Shall Not Be Named."

A spark lit behind his eyes. "All you need to know is I took care of the situation."

My jaw dropped, and icy fear crept through my veins. My back slammed against a brick building when I retreated, needing more space between us to think clearly. "You put a hit out on Brian?"

A wide smile broke across his face before he burst out laughing. A few women slowed as they passed by, eyeing him with a sexual hunger in the eyes. Couldn't blame them. A carefree, laughing Charlie was a sight to behold. Plus, I was still worked up from the kiss, the one that really was the best kiss of my life. Not that I would tell him that.

"Charlie, this isn't funny," I pleaded. Heat scorched beneath my skin as all the terrible outcomes from his actions ran through my mind on overdrive. "You could go to prison if anyone finds out. And we're the FBI. We know people find out even if you're some amazing hacker who could cover his tracks. I don't want you to end up on death row for me—"

His large hands rested on my shoulders, cutting off my rambling with a gentle shake. "Rhyan, calm down. Breathe for me. In and out." He didn't continue until my breaths were no longer coming in short pants. "I didn't put a hit out on him. I just ensured he couldn't get here to harass you. Though I will say if anyone was death row worthy, it would be you." He cringed. "That didn't come out right."

"What did you do, then?" I blurted. I needed way more detail than that to shut down my worries. "Because I've created about a hundred different terrible scenarios—"

"The fucker's name *might* have been added to Homeland Security's no-fly list as of this morning. Hypothetically, of course."

Breath frozen in my lungs, all I could do was stare up at him. With the flats I wore knowing walking was in our future, he was slightly taller than me, throwing off our normal equal height.

As I stood dumbfounded, being knocked around by the tourists with their faces buried in their phones, Charlie's cocky confidence faded and uncertainty took its place. Running a hand through his hair, he looked up and down the street, lips parting like he didn't know what to say.

"Charlie," I said on a forceful exhale, finally finding my words.

"I overstepped again, didn't I—"

"No, you.... That's not what has me speechless. I don't know how you did it, or even want to know what laws you broke, but thank you. Knowing he can't just hop on a plane to remind me how I'm better off with him than on my own is...." I relaxed, allowing the stress to seep from my tight shoulders. "It's amazing. Thank you."

That wide smile returned. "You're welcome. Though now that I've dipped my toe in the dark web, how about I dig deeper into our victims' lives—"

"No." I sliced a hand through the air for emphasis. "Not for the case. We can't risk the section chief finding out. He has clear-cut rules for the different roles of profilers and analysts. They have carte blanche access to all things on the web no matter the privacy laws. We do not." He grumbled something about bureaucratic assholes ruining his fun. "Have you gotten anywhere with the victims' cell phones?"

Turning, we started down the sidewalk once again. "That's the thing. The cell phones were never logged into evidence, or their identification."

I slipped off my glasses and rubbed at the bridge of my nose. "Fuck, this guy is smart. He probably dumped their purses into the river just like he did their bodies to cover his tracks." As we approached the coffee shop, a handsome man in a trendy suit and bow tie stepped out, holding the door open with a smile. "Thank you."

"Anytime, beautiful."

At his odd tone, I glanced over my shoulder, finding his eyes trained on my ass.

Shaking my head, I stepped up to the counter, ignoring the sudden commotion behind me as I studied the menu board along the back wall. "What are you—" I started to say over my shoulder to Charlie, but the words died when I found him still outside, the man's trendy suit held tight in Charlie's fists. I blinked, not moving, trying to understand the scene. With a hard shove, Charlie released the man and stormed for the glass door, yanking it open.

Features tight, lips pursed, he maneuvered around the other gawkers, coming to stand beside me.

"What was that?" I whispered, leaning around him to see if that guy was outside planning a revenge attack.

"He started it."

"What are you, four?"

"Have you ordered?"

With an annoyed, yet not so annoyed, huff, I swiveled back around to the young cashier, whose jaw was slack as she stared at Charlie.

"What do you like? I mean, what do you want from me? To drink?" the cashier squeaked.

"Ladies first," Charlie said, tossing an arm over my shoulder, clearly staking his claim, or maybe allowing me to stake my claim without moving? This was getting confusing. I still hadn't fully come up with all the ways that kiss earlier was a terrible decision. There were hours of tossing and turning and cringing to come before I could move on to my next fixation.

"Coffee, two sugars and cream, please," I said, still confused by what the hell was going on.

Charlie followed with his coffee order and added two breakfast sandwiches. I dug through my bag, searching for my wallet to pay, but he beat me to it. Phone hovering over the reader, it chirped, and a "payment processing" message appeared.

With a hand sealed to my lower back, Charlie guided me to the corner to wait for our coffee and food away from the few staring patrons.

"I need to get on that trend," I muttered. Chewing on my lower lip, I watched the door, just knowing the guy Charlie accosted was about to barge through with the Louisville cops in tow. "Does my phone even do that?"

"Yep. It's more secure than using a credit card. I could help you set it up."

"I told you I'm terrible at that stuff. You'll just get frustrated, and I'll feel bad for even asking for your help."

My name and then his rang over the murmuring crowd. With a smile, I took my disposable cup from the barista and weaved through the tiny coffee shop. When we stepped outside, I checked every which way, only breathing easily when the man from earlier was nowhere to be found. Charlie stopped at one of the tiny outdoor tables, setting his drink down to rummage through the bag holding our food.

Closing my eyes, I relished the spring heat warming my skin and the brisk breeze soothing the intensity.

"Here." Blinking, I refocused on the here and now, taking the offered McMuffin-type sandwich from his hand. But he held on, our fingers brushing when I tried to pull my hand back.

"Listen, can we come to an agreement on something?" Charlie asked.

"Depends," I responded cautiously. Holding a hand over the rim of my glasses, I squinted up at him, trying to get a read on whatever was running through his head. "What is it?"

"Hear me out, okay?" Releasing the sandwich, he gestured down the sidewalk and started walking. "I want you to forget it all, to start with a clean slate. Whatever that prick made you believe you weren't good at doing, or didn't meet the mark on, I want you to forget it." His low, growly voice laced with annoyance made my stomach tense.

"The computer thing," I said, connecting his train of thought to what I asked in the coffee shop.

"Among other things, yeah. He manipulated you to ensure you remained dependent on him—"

"Ugh, it's clear as day now that I'm out of that shit show." Tucking the coffee cup in the crook of my elbow, I peeled back the wrapper on the sandwich. "This looks good. Thank you. For this and the coffee. Not sure if I said that earlier."

"Don't let that keep you up at night. It's hard to see the destruction in a storm's wake when you're stuck in the middle of it."

"That's deep," I said, shooting him a side-eye look.

"Don't let these tattoos and piercings fool you." He waggled those dark brows, letting me know he was joking.

"Smart and sexy, and a hell of a kisser. You're a deadly combination." The moment the words escaped, I wanted to grab them from the air and shove them back down my throat. "Sorry, that was so uncalled for."

His answering pleased hum and wide smile eased some of the embarrassment and worry. "I'm glad to hear you think that about me, because I feel the same, Rhyan Riggs." Why did I love it so much when he said my full name? It was a little dirty, like he was the principal, and I was the naughty student. "Except I think you have me beat in the brains and beauty."

The scalding sip of coffee I'd just taken slipped down the wrong pipe. Coughing like a lifetime smoker, I shook my head, unable to speak.

"You don't get to disagree with my opinion," Charlie said, patting my upper back until I could breathe normally. "All right, we're here." At the corner of a busy intersection, we took in a 360-degree view. "Hopefully the nice weather holds out for our adventure."

I snorted at his choice of words. "Looks like mostly businesses lining these streets," I mused. I took a large bite of the sandwich. "Want to split up?"

Watching me attempt to chew the mouthful, the corner of his lips tilted up. "Nah. It would be more efficient, sure, but two sets of eyes are better than one. You could spot something I wouldn't or vice versa. Let's stick together and make sure we do it right the first time."

Chapter 11

"True. Okay, then, let's do this."

Pressing the crosswalk button, I alternated between the delicious sandwich and yummy coffee, allowing a comfortable silence to fall between us. And for the first time in too long, my mind was at peace. Just his protective, anxiety-distracting presence put me at ease, unlike anyone else. Sneaking a peek through my lashes, I found his blue eyes already on me. Gone were the worry lines and tension along his jaw, his features soft.

Just like me.

Perfectly content.

Because we had each other.

THREE HOURS and what felt like a billion steps later, the cool morning breeze had vanished, the bottoms of my feet throbbed, and a layer of sweat coated every inch of skin, drops slipping along my spine, causing my silk blouse to adhere to my back. Thank all the various deities that I wore black on black, the dark material hopefully camouflaging the growing sweat stains. Though Charlie wasn't fairing any better. After an hour of walking in the growing heavy heat, he ditched his jacket, then rolled up his sleeves, shoving them over his elbows, and now looked edgy enough to use the gun on his hip on anyone who looked at him wrong.

The heat, swollen feet, and sweat all sucked, but what inched up my irritation with every block was the eye-fucking directed at Charlie. It seemed every woman in the downtown Louisville area got the memo that a tattooed hottie was out on the street and felt it was completely okay to undress him with their eyes. One younger woman who'd slowed her jogging to a quick walk actually smacked into a lamppost, she was staring so hard.

I didn't feel bad laughing. It helped that Charlie seemed more annoyed at the entire situation instead of flattered.

With a loud groan, I shuffled to the side of a building, using its long shadow as a brief reprieve from the afternoon sun.

"We're getting nowhere slowly," I complained. Charlie grumbled his agreement and followed me to the shade. He released a quick puff of air when he fell back, reclining against the warm brick. "Where are we in relation to what we suspect is the center of the unsub's hunting zone?"

Switching his jacket from one arm to the other, he dug around his pockets, cursing about the material sticking to his thighs. Phone in hand, he wiped a few beads of sweat from his brow and held the device between us. "We're right around the center of the geographic profile. And fucking hell, does this state not know it's spring, for fuck's sake? I swear you can wring the air out."

"It seems unusually hot this early for them. Not sure the why behind the sudden heat wave."

He quirked a brow. "No fun facts about global warming you'd like to share?"

"I don't think fun and global warming go together in the same sentence."

"But fun and chlamydia do?"

I shook my head, unable to suppress my grin. "Okay, maybe I'll change it to 'interesting facts' instead of 'fun facts' when STDs are involved."

"Sounds like a solid plan."

"What are we even looking for?" I whined. Closing my eyes, I gathered my hair in a makeshift ponytail and fanned the back of my neck. "It's not like there will be a blinking sign that says 'Killer picks up women here.'"

"Would make our jobs easier." Charlie chuckled. "I'd say be on the lookout for a restaurant or bar. Where is somewhere a woman, out alone, would feel comfortable meeting up with a stranger and either staying or getting in his car?"

The clack-clack of rolling wheels along the cracked sidewalk had us both turning toward the sound. A woman dressed in an impeccably snug black dress and matching heels, sashayed toward a black town car, a small suitcase wheeled behind her. A man in a suit hopped out of the car, took her luggage, and helped her into the back.

Chapter 11

The coarse lines of the brick bit into my palms as I shoved off. *Break time over.* Standing in the middle of the sidewalk, I squinted to save my eyes from the bright sun, searching the building we were just leaning against.

"This building looks like all the others," I observed. "But where was she coming from looking like that?"

"It looks like a normal office building, but look at the revolving door. What office building has blackout limo tint over their front doors?"

"One that doesn't want anyone to see what's going on inside. Let's check it out." Ascending the short set of stairs, I checked over my shoulder to ensure Charlie was close behind.

Artic air assaulted me the moment I stepped into the immaculate lobby, immediately cooling my overheated skin. A pleasant aroma relaxed me with every inhale. Moving deeper inside what I now assumed was a boutique hotel, I took in the immaculate white marble floors and the enormous crystal chandeliers dangling high above us, skimming over the ornate wall décor, art and textured wallpaper.

Charlie's low impressed whistle sounded sharp and loud in the pristine, deserted space.

"What is this place?" he whispered. His thumbs flew across the phone screen, brows furrowed in concentration. "There isn't a hotel listed on this street."

"That's odd. Even exclusive hotels market to the public." Twisting around, I spotted the reception desk. The empty reception desk. "Does no one work here?" I spun on my heels, searching for any sign of life. Not a single employee in sight, but the tingling sensation of someone watching said they were around, just not visible.

Charlie and I exchanged a curious look before walking to the reception desk.

Lips parted, deep inhale filling my lungs. I was ready to call out for help when a beautiful young blonde woman appeared out of nowhere, a bright smile on her face. But there was something off. It was her eyes, or more so where her eyes were trained—on the counter.

"That's fucking creepy." Charlie dipped low, attempting to meet the woman's gaze, but she kept shifting it away.

"Good afternoon, and welcome to The Black Rose. How may I help you two today?"

"Yeah," I drawled, feeling a little freaked out by the whole thing. I slid my badge out of my bag, Charlie doing the same, and flipped it open, laying it on the granite counter. When she didn't react the way most people did when presented with two FBI badges, I tapped it a little closer to her side with a single finger. "Agents Riggs and Bekham with the FBI. We're investigating a string of murders and could use your help."

The woman's bright smile faltered slightly before righting the fake mask back in place.

Charlie set his phone on the counter beside our badges and swiped through to the pictures of the victims. "Have you seen any of these women here, maybe with a man? The same man, maybe."

The woman shook her head, long curls bouncing and swishing with the movement before Charlie finished showing the pictures.

"I'm sorry. I can't help you with identifying any previous or current guest of The Black Rose. Is there anything else I can offer my assistance with?"

"You didn't even look at the pictures," I chastised, annoyance roaring past the awkwardness of the place. "These women were murdered, and we're trying to find where they met their killer. Any information—"

"I do apologize, but I truly cannot help you." Pursing her lips, her gaze flicked from side to side. "The Black Rose prides itself in confidentiality and anonymity for its guests. I cannot help you. Every employee signs an NDA at orientation."

Well, shit.

"What about allowing us to review security footage—"

"Thank you, Cynthia," came an older female voice from behind us. "I'll take it from here with these two." Charlie and I whipped around, both instinctively reaching for our guns. The woman in cropped black pants, a pressed light blue dress shirt, and hair pulled in a tight bun frowned at the movement. "Can you please follow me?"

The click of the woman's modest heels was the only sound as Charlie and I followed. We passed by a single gold elevator and silent bar before heading down a narrow hallway. If Charlie wasn't with me, I'd be running through all the ways this could turn out badly, but his presence reassured me we could handle whatever happened.

At a nondescript door, she inserted a key into the lock and pushed it open, motioning for us to go inside.

"Ladies first," Charlie said with a cutting smile that held more menace than kindness.

The woman eyed him before stepping into the small office.

Before he let the door close behind him, Charlie tested the handle, ensuring we'd be able to leave when we were ready. "Some setup here," he remarked, satisfied with whatever he'd uncovered with the door and lock. Leaning against the closed door, he tossed his crumpled suit coat over the back of a chair and crossed his arms. "Now, start talking, because it seems to me your hotel has something to hide."

"There is nothing to say," she said, settling in behind the desk. The chair creaked as she leaned back. "The Black Rose is a posh, highly exclusive hotel that caters to a select clientele."

"So, zero marketing?" I asked, maneuvering around the basic office chair and easing into the seat. I almost sighed in relief.

"Correct, no marketing of any kind. Only word of mouth and other avenues."

"Such as?" Charlie drawled.

"I brought you back here to explain, in private, that we hold our clients' confidentiality above everything else—"

"Above their safety?" I snapped. "Because we're here investigating a string of murders in the area."

She tilted her head as if considering my words. "Were they killed here?"

I bit my tongue so hard it bled. "No."

"Well, then, if you want to accost my employees, access our security feeds, or scour through our records, I'll need a search warrant. We will hand over anything specifically laid out in the proper paperwork." Her snarky tone had me bristling, sitting up straight in the chair.

Fuck.

"Can you just tell me if you recognize these women? We're trying to figure out where our killer is meeting his victims." A phone appeared over my shoulder. I gripped the sides, flipping the device around to show the snooty manager.

"Not unless you have a warrant that supersedes the very detailed NDA I, and the other employees here at The Black Rose, have signed. Now, if you'll kindly leave without incident."

"The man responsible for these women's deaths could be a guest, a frequent guest. Six women, six bodies pulled from the water."

"I'm sorry I can't help, but my hands are tied." Standing, she smoothed down nonexistent wrinkles along the front of her pants and gestured to the door at Charlie's back. "Come back with a warrant if you'd like our cooperation."

12

CHARLIE

Frustrated Rhyan was adorable.

I continued to watch her pacing from afar, smirking at her grumblings as she moved between the lengths of crime scene tape, red hair whipping in the wind coming off the Ohio River.

"You're watching, not helping, Agent Bekham," she called.

Aw, it's even adorable when that frustration is directed at me. Like an angry kitten showing its claws. It would be interesting to see if that fire transferred to the bedroom. I swept the metal ball along my lower lip as I pictured her ordering me around, describing exactly what she wanted, where my hands and tongue should venture to next along that glorious body.

In most cases, I was the dominant, playing on my visitor's daddy issues, but Rhyan would be different. With her just now getting her feet under her, finding her inner strength after that dickwad cut her down for years, she might not want to be ordered around or praised.

Or maybe she would. Her friend Olivia said Rhyan was interested in the spanking conversation from yesterday morning. Sometimes women in leadership roles, surrounded by alpha men all day in their jobs, craved the reprieve of needing to be in control. Either way, if I needed to top from the bottom or be on top from the start, as long as it was Rhyan in my bed, I would count myself lucky.

My cock jerked at the bunch and bounce of her firm ass with every long stride. The straight-legged cropped pants she wore today should have been banned in most countries, for her at least. Every man we passed during our earlier excursion through downtown couldn't keep their eyes off the way they accentuated those long legs and hugged her round backside. Pissed me the fuck off.

"Charlie," she shouted, dragging my focus back to the case. "Any insight you could provide would be amazing right about now." Hands on her hips, she did her best to glare me down.

It was super cute. Mostly because there was no heat behind it. The way she looked at Hicks like he was the most inconsequential being on the planet when she dressed him down that first day, now *that* was slightly frightening and hot. The look she gave now said, "I'm tired, hungry, and really need to get laid."

Okay, maybe I tacked on that last one, hoping if I thought it enough, it would come true.

I blew out a slow breath to calm my fucking balls. Taking things slow would be a challenge, but 100 percent worth it for her.

"I'm thinking over here."

"Yeah, about my ass," she mumbled, checking to ensure the officers were too far away to hear her.

I waggled my brows, confirming her accusation. "Do you think her belongings went over the side like we're assuming the unsub did with the other victim's phones and purses?" I mused, channeling all my focus into ripping my gaze from her to scan the length of the pedestrian bridge. "I think the boater would've said something about a cell phone falling from the sky along with the body."

Rhyan's arms went slack at her side. "Good question." Twisting around, she pressed her hips to the railing and leaned over. With a barked curse, I hurried to grab her to keep her from going all the way over, plunging the considerable distance into the choppy water. Her soft flesh molded beneath my fingers, my hands almost encompassing the width of her hips.

"See anything?" I flexed my grip, stepping an inch closer to feel more of her body against mine. "You can stay like this all day, by the way. I don't mind."

"You're incorrigible, you know that?" she murmured. Hair flipped forward, head dangling, she craned her neck to shoot me a knowing look. "I see nothing. Was hoping we'd catch a break and the purse or phone landed on a support beam or concrete footer."

Slowly, she eased back upright. I held her tight until she regained her balance.

"Thanks," she said with a smile over her shoulder.

"No, thank *you*." With a huff, she pushed at my shoulder, turning to face down the pedestrian bridge. "So nothing here. Let's walk toward the Kentucky side of the bridge and see if we see anything."

The uniformed officer protecting the crime scene lifted the yellow plastic tape for us to duck under. Despite my eagerness to get Rhyan in bed, I shut down my second head to focus solely on scanning the wide bridge for any evidence.

People. Strollers. Debris that should've been tossed in one of the many trash cans along the bridge, but some lazy motherfuck—

Trash cans.

A light bulb went off, the words clanging around my brain. Not wanting to get her hopes up, I strode over to the nearest trash can along the side of the bridge the body went over. My sharp, loud whistle gained the attention of a few officers, who I waved over.

"Grab a pair of gloves and start digging through all the trash cans." They balked, grimacing at my order. "It's not a request, gents. We're looking for anything that could've belonged to the victim—"

"Or a murder weapon," Rhyan chipped in, moving to stand beside me while pulling on a pair of black latex gloves. The pop of elastic against her wrist made my cock twitch along my thigh. "Mind out of the gutter, hands in the trash," she chastised, clearly noticing where my thoughts went. "Look for anything that doesn't fit. Nothing is too small to set aside."

A loud clang drew onlookers' attention when the metal domed lid hit the concrete. The smooth latex tugged at my sweaty skin as I pulled a glove over each hand.

"What made you think to look in the trash?"

A waft of rotten food and dog shit rose from inside the can, the heat cooking the disgusting concoction within the black plastic bag. Chin on my shoulder, I inhaled a fresh breath to keep from gagging. "The unsub was thrown off because of the body hitting something solid instead of the water. I'm hoping that means he panicked and made a mistake. There's no doubt in my mind that he knew the second that body hit the boat instead of water. Hopefully his panic is our gain."

Black glove covering her nose and mouth, she stepped back, putting more distance between her and the stench. "Great idea. Looks like you've got this under control."

"Really? You're bailing on me?"

"Not bailing, just going to look somewhere less disgusting."

I smirked. "Chicken."

"I'll take that if it means I don't have to dig through that. I'll go check around the parking lot. Maybe he tossed it in the bushes or under another car."

Just as she turned to leave me to the dirty job, a ring sounded from my slacks pocket. Holding up both gloved hands already covered in... fuck, I didn't want to know what slime shit was dripping between my fingers, I tilted my head toward the sounds. "Can you grab that for me?"

Rhyan pursed her lips, clearly not happy with my request, but yanked off the glove covering her right hand before digging into my side pocket.

The wrong side pocket. Not that I told her that.

"You're an ass," she grumbled, moving to the other pocket. The volume of the ring intensified when she lifted the phone up high. "People are watching."

"Watching a friend help another friend," I said, faking innocence, batting my eyes, hoping to really sell it.

Chapter 12

After checking the screen, seeing it was Bryson calling, she swiped a thumb across the glass and held it to my ear.

"Bekham," I said, grinning ear to ear at the exasperated beauty at my side.

"The victim's husband will be at the station in an hour to deliver his statement. You two want to be here, right?"

"Yes. Any word on the vehicle?"

"Just got word a patrol car spotted it in a cash only parking lot close to where the others were found."

"Great, that makes the place Rhyan and I found today that much more likely as the unsub's hunting ground. You ever heard of a place called The Black Rose?"

"No, what is it?"

"A hotel. An upscale one."

"Then that's why I haven't heard of it. Between diapers and rent, I have little money to spare each month."

"Diapers?" I questioned incredulously.

"Surprised?"

"Yeah, I am. Didn't know you were that old to have an incontinence issue."

Bryson barked a laugh, the loud abrupt sound vibrating in my ear. "Meet me at the station when you can. I'll hold off on the interview until you and your girlfriend get here."

"You are observant, aren't you?" I cut a look out of the corner of my eyes, gauging if Rhyan heard Bryson. She cocked her head to the side and mouthed, "What?" The tension coiling in my gut released.

"Just a guy who's seen it enough on the job, and also had a work relationship before that had to remain hidden from others."

"It's a recent development," I offered cryptically.

"Take it from me," he said, tone turning more somber. "Don't let work get in the way. Your career isn't worth losing a woman like her over."

"Noted. Though I'll need more explanation on that at some point. See you soon."

Rhyan pulled the phone away, inspecting the blank screen behind her thick frames. "That was the oddest one-sided conversation I've ever tried to follow."

"They've identified the victim. The husband was notified and will meet us at the station in an hour for an interview."

She nodded, but the way she gnawed at that lower lip told me she wanted to ask more. Surprise rushed through me when she slipped the phone into the breast pocket of my dress shirt and patted my chest.

"Then I guess we need to get back to it. But later I do want to hear how diapers entered the conversation."

I chuckled while going back to shift through the cups and Styrofoam containers. "Honestly, I don't even have a fucking clue, and I heard the other side of the conversation."

Seemed I didn't know Agent Bryson Bennett as well as I thought.

"Agents," a male voice called.

Dropping the soggy half-eaten sandwich back into the bin, I joined Rhyan, jogging toward the uniformed officer with his hand in the air.

"What did you find?" Rhyan asked when we were close enough that she didn't have to shout.

"It might be nothing, but"—he held up a tiny black purse, one you would see every woman carrying at a nice restaurant or fancy party—"this looked out of place. It was stuffed down toward the bottom."

Exchanging her old gloves for a new pair, Rhyan took the offered clutch and popped it open. Several twenties, a driver's license, and a slim smartphone sat inside.

"This is everything," I said in praise to the officer. That phone, with my skills, could unlock this entire case. "We need to get all this down to the station for evidence cataloging, and then I can work my magic. I'll grab an evidence bag from—"

"I found something too," called a different officer, this one closer to the end of the bridge that opened up to downtown.

Rhyan and I exchanged an excited look, her lips parted and eyes shining. In a slight jog, we hurried farther down the bridge.

Chapter 12

When I saw the object in the officer's extended hand, I drew up short, slowing to a quick walk.

"A syringe," I stated, surprise clear in my voice. "What the hell?"

"It might not be the unsub's," Rhyan mused. "We didn't find drugs in the victim's system. The ME ran every test he could think of—"

"Including nutmeg poisoning," I said offhandedly.

Rhyan shifted on her feet, completely ignoring me.

"He didn't find a single trace of anything out of the ordinary, so what in the hell could've been in—" Rhyan cut herself off as she pressed closer, squinting at the syringe. "The tube and plunger look dry, like there was nothing in there. Oh fucking hell," she snapped, tossing her hands in the air. "Why didn't I think of that before? There was nothing in there to begin with. No drugs in their system, no visible signs of COD."

"Care to share your thoughts with the class?" I drawled, eager to know what her quick mind just pieced together.

"Air," she stated. Just the word, like I should know what the hell that meant. "There was only air in the syringe."

"I don't understand," the officer said, pulling the evidence closer, as if that could explain it all.

"Air injected directly into a vein is lethal. No visible marks or trace evidence except the injection site." Rhyan's excitement faded. "It sounds simple, but it's extremely painful. The victim feels like their heart is exploding for several long seconds." Chewing on the edge of her lower lip, she nodded to the evidence. "Bag that up too. Let's get both the syringe and bag to the station ASAP. We might have enough to identify this asshole before he takes another innocent life."

Inspecting the phone, assuming it was dead, I held down the power button to try it anyway. When it immediately powered up, I held the screen out to a watching Rhyan. The keypad flashed, making me groan.

"Hopefully the husband knows her password, or we're shit out of luck. Unless..." I said suggestively.

Rhyan's red-and-gold strands swayed with the shake of her head. "No hacking allowed." Puffing out my lower lip, I faked a pout. "No.

Do not give me that sad look. We do this by the book. I won't risk our careers." She hesitated before continuing. "Unless it's absolutely necessary to catch this guy."

"For now," I breathed, and dropped the purse and phone into the evidence bag an officer held open. "I can agree with that."

But if we hit a dead end that I knew I could blast through with a few unsanctioned searches, I'd do it. Screw my career. Sure, I was living my best life in the job I'd worked for years toward, but I couldn't let more women die at this fucker's hand if I could stop him.

Maybe it wouldn't come to that. But I had to admit, I felt handcuffed without my computer. Times like this, I missed being the smartest one in the room with technology and being allowed to use that knowledge to solve a case. But there wasn't a happy medium between a profiler and a hacker.

Or was there?

13

RHYAN

Another sob echoed around the police station's small interview room. Keeping my features schooled into a blank mask, I pulled yet another tissue from the box sitting on the coffee table between us and thrust it between me and the recent victim's husband. He pulled it from my pinched fingers carefully, like he'd done the previous few, and wiped at his damp cheeks before blowing his red nose.

"I don't understand," he cried between hiccups. "What does this mean? Tossed over a bridge. Who would do that to my wife?"

Bryson stepped forward. The man's bloodshot eyes tracked the movement, narrowing slightly. "It means we believe she's the victim of a serial killer."

A new well of tears slipped from the corner of his swollen eyes. "I did this," he whispered, more to himself than to us.

The three of us shared a confused look before turning our attention back to the man falling apart at the seams. Though I couldn't blame him. He thought his wife was missing when he called the police this morning. Then Hicks and Bryson showed up on his doorstep saying her body was in our morgue and we needed a statement for his whereabouts last night.

"What do you mean by 'I did this'?" I asked. With the tip of my finger, I inched the flat tissue box closer to his side so I didn't have to keep urging him to wipe his snot bubbles.

"I couldn't give her what she wanted, so she went looking for it. That had to be it, right? Having an affair, going out to meet other men. I picked up on the signs."

"What signs?" Charlie asked, spinning the victim's cell phone between two fingers.

The husband's demeanor shifted. Interesting that any time the men spoke up, the mourning man seemed to turn angrier, hostile even.

"Being more secretive about her phone, not letting me see incoming messages. Then last night she said she was going out and wouldn't be back until late. No details, just 'out.' I knew." His bloodshot eyes met mine. "I stayed up waiting for her. I thought... I thought when she didn't come home, that meant she'd left me for good for someone else."

"What do you mean, give her what she wanted?" Charlie pried.

The husband's gaze hardened when he looked in Charlie's direction. Jaw clenched, eyes narrowed, it was clear how the husband felt about the type of man Charlie represented.

Dominant. Alpha. Sexy.

Oh wait, that last one was how *I* saw Charlie. Surely the man in front of me didn't see the tattoos and exposed forearms as foreplay.

"Agent Bekham," I said softly, snagging Charlie's full attention. "Can you and Agent Bennett grab our grieving guest a glass of water?"

A beat of silence filled the space as Charlie studied me. I inclined my head a fraction toward the door.

"Come on, Bennett. You're with me, it seems." Charlie's hawk-like stare stayed on me until the glass door closed. I even felt it as the click of their shoes faded into the station's background noise.

Once both were gone, the husband slumped back, chin resting on his chest. Based on his soft features, reddened cheeks, and round belly, he probably felt intimidated by the two attractive agents. Not that I felt even a sliver of attraction toward Bryson, but he was attractive with his large frame, kind eyes, and commanding presence. And Charlie, well, he just oozed sex appeal. So yeah, those two had a negative effect on males with self-esteem issues.

"Can you answer the earlier question? It would help us narrow down who to look for in our search. What was your wife looking for?"

The husband swallowed and nodded solemnly. "She wanted more out of our...." He paused, face flushing an even deeper red.

"Sex life?" I finished for him. "Wanting more how?"

He shifted along the cheap black leather, eyes bouncing around the room, never meeting mine. "Rough stuff. I couldn't do that to her. I love my wife. But I knew when she stopped asking me to do that kind of kinky stuff with her, we were in trouble. She's a beautiful woman. All she'd need to do is ask another man, and he'd be willing to do it."

"What kind of rough stuff?" I asked softly. "I know this feels like me prying, but any information could help the investigation. If all the victims were looking for the same thing, we could narrow the profile."

His narrow fingers reached up and wrapped around his own throat. Rolls of thick flesh squeezed between his fingers. "Choking, dominating stuff that I just couldn't.... And"—he leaned in closer, eyes shifting back and forth—"butt stuff." This time, his face paled, but there was a steely look in his eyes. "I blame those romance books she reads. Made her want more than me, her husband. I am enough, damnit. What I offer, as basic as it is, is enough."

The sudden shift in his demeanor and accusations, putting the blame on his dead wife, piqued my interest.

"Do you know how she planned to find those who'd give her what you couldn't?"

To anyone else, my words were harsh, but I needed to push him, poke that fire clearly simmering behind his eyes. To what extent would he go to keep her from finding what she longed for elsewhere?

"No," he hissed through his teeth. His hands clenched into tight fists. When he noticed my attention, he forced them to relax along the top of his wide thighs.

"Was she recently talking to anyone you didn't know? Late-night phone calls or—"

"Just texts and messages." He paused. "But not on the normal texting app on our phones. I glimpsed her screen once. It looked different, almost more like a chat room."

"We need to get into her phone. Do you know the password?"

Wiping the back of his hand across his lips, he fell back against the couch. "It was one, one, two, two, three, three. But the last time I tried, it wouldn't take."

She'd probably changed the code when she started searching for someone to sate her sexual needs.

His humorless laugh caught me off guard. "It wasn't my fault at all. She shouldn't have gone looking for more. If she would've been at home with me, she'd still be alive."

I bit the tip of my tongue to keep from responding, but I couldn't help it. "Are you suggesting the fault, her ending up murdered, was on her?"

"I'm saying if she would've just been satisfied with what she had instead of wanting more, then she wouldn't have ended up like she did."

"Murdered."

His nod was clipped, full of indignation.

Fucking asswipe. Just because a woman wanted a little anal didn't mean she deserved the death penalty. My lip curled in disgust before I could smother it.

The door swung open, breaking our stare-off. Bryson and Charlie paused at the tension pulsing around the room.

"What did we miss?" Charlie questioned, voice tense. The plastic water bottle crackled in his clenching fist. "Here's that water."

It sailed through the air toward the jackwagon's face, who batted it away like an insect instead of catching it. It plopped on the couch before rolling to the floor. My lips twitched at Charlie's obvious animosity toward the man.

Chapter 13

"Thank you for your time today." I stood and smoothed down the black fabric along my thighs, which had *finally* stopped sticking to my skin now that I'd cooled down. "We'll be in touch when we have further questions."

He swiped the water off the floor and stormed out. Once the husband was gone from the room, Bryson escorting him to the elevator, I slouched back with a relieved sigh.

"He flipped from blaming himself, a mess of tears and snot, to putting the blame on his murdered wife." I shook my head, not understanding the quick change. "He blamed the romance books she read. Can you believe that?"

"A woman wanting more in their sex life intimidates some insecure men. He no doubt felt weak knowing she died trying to find a man who could satisfy her needs. And as far as the romance books go...." He paused, waiting until I met his sparkling eyes. "They're wonderful inspiration for the adventurous."

I swallowed hard, the now familiar flutter in my lower belly taking flight.

"I don't think he's our killer though." I groaned, closing my eyes. "He doesn't fit our profile at all and doesn't explain the previous victims."

A light tap on my shoulder had me peeking an eye open. Charlie gestured toward the open door. "Come compare the victims' history with me. Then we'll head down to the morgue. The crime scene techs need more time with the evidence we brought in before I can dive into the phone."

"Yeah, sure." Standing, I stretched both arms high over my head and interlaced my fingers. With a deep exhale, I elongated my spine, working the tension from my back and shoulders.

"Those pants should be illegal," Charlie grumbled under his breath.

"Funny, I thought the same thing about your forearms."

His thick, dark brows dipped in confusion, a line forming between them. Holding out those sexy, ink-covered forearms I wanted to nibble my way up, he rotated them one way and then the other, making the muscles flex.

"You're making it worse." I sighed, dropping my arms. "You should cover them back up."

"My forearms."

"Yeah, I just said that."

"I'm usually good at keeping up with sexual innuendos, but I'm fucking lost."

My cheeks bunched with a wide smile. "You have no idea, do you?"

"None."

"Forearms and gray sweatpants. They're most women's kryptonite. Add in you looking like an even sexier version of Adam Levine, and no one stands a chance when you're flashing so much skin."

He held up his forearms like a weapon. Rotating his wrists, he studied the flexing muscles. "So you're turned on right now because of these?"

"Honestly, I have been since this morning when you attacked me."

"Give me a chance and I'll show you attacked—"

"You two ready?" Bryson asked as he popped his head into the room. Charlie snapped his mouth shut, but that grin widened as he turned to face Bryson. "What did I miss?"

"Nothing. Let's do this." Raising both hands, Charlie flexed those delicious forearms while pointing in the direction of the murder board. "Let's go that way."

"You're impossible." I laughed as I walked by, pinching his taut forearm to emphasize my point.

At the small table we used to hold the evidence boxes and files, I pulled out a chair and plopped down. "My feet are killing me from all the walking earlier. But at least we have a lead on a location. We think he's picking them up or at least meeting his victims at The Black Rose."

Chapter 13

Bryson pulled out the chair across the table from me and rested both arms along the top. "Did they recognize any of the victims?"

"They stonewalled us, stating they all signed an NDA," Charlie said, sitting on the edge of the table facing the murder board, crossing one foot over the other. "The manager stated they wouldn't cooperate without a warrant. And I have a feeling that warrant will need to be very specific on what they need to allow us access in their system and with the employees."

"I'll take care of that." We all twisted to find Hicks hovering just outside the door. "Hey, Riggs." He shoved both hands into his slacks pockets. "I was wrong about the case, about it all. I'm sorry—"

I held up a hand, stopping him. "If you're willing to pull your connections to get us a warrant for The Black Rose, all is forgiven."

His shoulders slumped, posture relaxing. "You got it. Let me know if I and the others can be of any other help during the investigation."

As he walked away, Bryson leaned across the table. "I looked into it like you asked. Hicks is up for a promotion. Lieutenant."

"Which was why he was against me being right. It makes him look bad that five of his cases are reclassified as murders instead of suicides like he initially labeled them."

Charlie nudged me with his knee, pulling my focus up to him. "He's still dangerous, though. You should be very concerned at night alone in your hotel room." His words said one thing, but the mischievous grin and wink said another.

"Really?" Bryson said, doubt clouding his tone. "I don't think—"

"Charlie is kidding. Now focus on the case, Agent Bekham." I rolled my eyes when he flicked that tongue ring out. "What did you notice about the victims' habits prior to the nights they went missing?"

His professional mask slid into place, making me miss Charlie's playful side. "Cash withdrawals all around two to three hundred dollars at a time, expensive clothing purchases from high-end boutiques where they hadn't shopped previously, hair and waxing at salons. They all did some version of all those things, making me think they were altering their appearance for someone other than their husbands."

I grabbed a pen and wrote everything down on my notepad. "What about the night they disappeared?"

"Nothing."

I peered up, staring over my rims at a blurry Charlie. "Nothing?"

"No toll expenses, no credit card charges. I don't know about their cell activity since we don't have a warrant for that yet. I'm hoping this new victim's phone will give me some insight. "

My fingers twitched, nervously rapping the end of the pen against the top of the table. "That's concerning. Why would they do that?"

"They were all married, right?" Bryson said as he rubbed at the dark scruff along his square jaw. "And were stepping out on their spouses. It sounds like they didn't want to be found that night, or traced. Cash can't be traced, and with the cash only lots, there aren't any cameras or credit cards needed. They made that night undetectable."

"And they all did that," Charlie said, standing and walking down the whiteboard while inspecting the pictures. "So that means our unsub gave specific instructions to ensure his victims couldn't be traced back to where they met up or the activities of that night." He hung his head and ran a few fingers through his dark hair. "Brilliant, actually. He probably lured these women with promises of fulfilling their fantasies—"

"How is he finding them, though? How does he know their fantasies?" Frustration at the lack of answers and new questions made my words come out more as a snap. "Did he meet them at the grocery store and just strike up a conversation about their sucky sex lives and offer to remedy their issues?"

Both men remained silent, neither able to answer that one burning question.

How?

How was he selecting his victims? How was he gaining their trust that these women would obey his commands and meet up alone?

Chapter 13

"Could be as easy as an app," Charlie mused. Turning, he looked over his shoulder to me and Bryson.

"In this day and age, sure, but maybe not something mainstream," Bryson offered.

"Married and lonely," I mused, half kidding.

Charlie snapped his fingers and pointed to me.

"There's that one app. It's shady as fuck. It's for married people who want to step out on their spouses. It's made for affairs only."

"That's disgusting," I said. Bryson grunted his agreement.

"I agree, but it's a thing. A profitable one." His dark brows dipped, forming a deep line between them. "It'll be impossible to get a warrant for their accounts, and that's if they're all members of that specific app. There could be more. I've never really looked into it."

Standing, I snatched my notepad off the table and pointed the end of the pen to the elevator doors.

"Let's go get a look at her phone and talk to the ME. Maybe that will open the floodgates to the answers we need."

14

RHYAN

Palms suctioned to the cream square tile, a steady stream of steamy water cascaded through my clean hair, running down my back and casting me in a somewhat trance as I processed the day's revelations on the case. The cell phone, which Charlie was working on now in his room, provided zilch since we couldn't figure out her password, and the facial identification wouldn't work due to the swelling from the body's fall.

Nothing in her purse pointed us toward an identification for the unsub, and the syringe plunger and needle were still processing. Victim number six, unlike the others, had slight bruising around her neck and wrists, but nothing the ME considered trauma, more like rough sex. It correlated with the other evidence he found on her body, which pointed toward the unsub seducing the victims away from their homes, having consensual sex, not forced, then killing them.

With an air-filled syringe.

Beyond odd.

I'd never run across a case like this in my years with the FBI. Usually men were violent in the way they killed: stabbing, choking to the point of breaking the fragile bones of the throat, torture. But this was clean, simple. Smart.

Serial killers had above-average IQs, but that normally applied to how they took their victims and stayed off the authorities' radar.

Half the evidence made sense, but the other half didn't. So how would we process that? What could we add to the profile to help the Louisville police catch this guy before we found another body in the river?

The ring of my cell phone pulled me out of my deep focus. Shutting off the hot water, I pulled the curtain open and grabbed the small white cotton towel from the sink, wiping off my hand and arm first. I groaned when I saw it was Carter.

"Riggs," I said after answering the call and flipping it to speaker.

"I read your report." Sighing through my nose, I stepped out of the shower and began wiping the rivers of water from my torso and legs. "I'm still not convinced this is a BSU case."

"The sixth body in the Louisville morgue says otherwise." My own brows shot up at the snark in my tone and words. I never pushed back like that with Carter.

"How is Agent Bekham performing?"

Um, okay. Odd transition.

"Great. He's offered insight to the profile, pointed out things I would've missed. The detective here was difficult at first, as I listed in the report, but was helpful today. We're working on getting a warrant for the location where we believe the unsub is meeting his victims."

"Do you feel uncomfortable around him?"

I blinked at the phone. "The detective?"

"Agent Bekham. Keep up, Riggs. I've heard he's difficult to work with."

"Sir?"

"Answer the question, Rhyan."

I clenched my jaw, back teeth grinding at the condescending tone. "Where did you hear that, sir? Agent Bekham has been professional, insightful, and worked well with the local agent. Not sure who would say otherwise."

Well, professional minus that amazing kiss earlier, and the way his hand flexed around my hips on the bridge, or him putting my ex on a no-fly list. Oh, and then there was me sneaking down to his room because my anxiety got the better of me, then me admitting I had a crush on him, and my best friend giving him a call to discuss my past.

Yep, totally professional minus *all* that.

I swallowed as the list kept growing.

The responding silence would usually inch up my anxiety, wondering if I was about to be caught in a lie, be called on the floor, or worse. But standing there, naked in the small bathroom glaring at the phone, all I felt was anger and resentment at my so-called boss. How dare he check in on us, or worse, make shit up to see how I would respond about Charlie. The asshole didn't deserve to manage our team.

I did.

My hands paused where I was drying off my stomach.

Okay, first the snarky comment and now internally admitting to myself that I deserved the leadership role. Something was off with me. Placing a hand to my forehead, I checked for a temperature, studying my reflection for any signs of illness. *Shit, what if I'm having a mental breakdown?* Maybe being turned on all day plus the stress had pushed me past that breaking point I had teetered on the last year.

Or maybe this confident, passionate woman was more in line with the real Rhyan Riggs.

After patting my hair dry, I tossed the towel to the sink and tugged on the basic panties and shorts I'd set aside before jumping in the shower.

"See that it continues that way. He's on thin ice as it is."

"And why is that? I've reviewed his cases since he started with the team, and his close rate is fantastic. Have there been complaints from the local authorities?"

"Three days."

"Excuse me?"

"You two have three days to compile a solid profile and deliver it to the local authorities before I order you both back to Quantico."

"That's not enough time to catch this—"

"The cases needing your attention are stacking up. Our job is to profile the unsub, deliver it to the local police force, and then allow them to catch the suspect."

That was true, but we'd stayed until the unsub was identified and captured for several years now.

"Sir—"

"Three days, Agent Riggs. Update me tomorrow on your progress."

The screen flashed before going dark, showing he ended the call.

"Fucking jackass," I shouted at the phone before swatting it off the vanity. It tumbled to the ground onto a growing pile of dirty clothes. The screen flashed when it landed, drawing my attention to the several missed texts from Brian. "I'm surrounded by manipulating, egotistical, pencil-dick jackasses."

Yanking the low-support sports bra over my head, I situated the band beneath my boobs before pulling the light pink tank over my head.

My grumbled curses about irrational men and stupid-smart serial killers filled the bathroom while I stared at my reflection, combing out my thick, long red hair. Twisting up the wet mass, I secured it into a tight bun with two hair ties. I would need to dry it in the morning if I slept with it like this, but I didn't have an hour to waste doing that now.

Grabbing the ancient laptop Charlie got a kick out of and my room key, I headed for his room. Earlier when we parted, we both agreed we wanted to wash away the day's sweat and grime before eating dinner and continuing to hash out the details of the case.

Charlie answered after the first soft knock. The moment my eyes traveled down his body, I frowned, nostrils flaring in... hell, all the feelings.

"What?" he asked innocently. "You said you loved sweatpants."

Indeed, I did. Especially on a body like his. But I'd just put on a fresh pair of underwear, and if he didn't put something else on, I'd have to change into my last clean pair within the hour. The snug black T-shirt that hugged his biceps and highlighted every ripple along his stomach didn't help my surging hormones either. The two barbells pierced between his nipples poked at the soft fabric, taunting me to take a step closer.

"Three days," I said instead of leaning in to nip at those piercings, clearing my throat of the sudden dryness.

"That might be a challenge even for me."

Furrowing my brow, I glanced up. "What are you talking about?"

"A three-day sex marathon. What are you talking about?" he countered. Opening the door, he ushered me inside with a soft grip on my shoulder.

"Carter called, said we have three days to solidify the profile and deliver it to the local police before he orders us back to DC."

That humor-filled smirk vanished. A look of annoyance now pulled at his tense features.

"Did he now?" I nodded. "How can that asshole put others' lives in danger all because he can't stand me?"

"I wondered that too. It's all so odd. Why now? What changed?"

He studied me for a second. "You stood up for me. Pointed out his assessment was shortsighted, and now that we have proof that it's a series of murders and not suicides, we've proved him wrong. Maybe he's feeling heat from the top because we're not the only ones who think he fucking blows at his job."

The savory scent of melted cheese wafted up my nose, making it twitch and my stomach growl. Following the delicious scent, I paused in front of the four pizza boxes resting atop the bed I slept in last night.

"Four?"

"I didn't know what kind you liked, so I ordered a smorgasbord." He leaned a shoulder against the wall like the gesture wasn't a big deal. But to me, it absolutely was. He did that often, put what I might want or like into consideration when making a choice instead of just focusing on his own. After walking on eggshells for years, going with

Brian's choices to keep the peace, I'd forgotten what it was like to be seen even in something as small as this.

"Thank you," I rasped. "For thinking of me too."

"Rhyan, even if I didn't find you insanely beautiful and funny and want to strip you out of your clothes to lick every inch of your skin, I'd consider your choices too." My heart shuddered, and my lungs froze at his nonchalant confession. "That's a basic rule to being a considerate friend and human. It's not all about me. Anyone who makes you feel that way doesn't deserve your friendship or time."

Well, hell. Where was Charlie's voice of reason and profound proclamations of how I should expect to be treated during those expensive therapy sessions when I first moved to DC? He just punched through a thick wall of misconceptions with a few words, making a bigger impact than the professional.

"Hey." I startled when a hand slipped along the back of my neck, calluses scraping the skin and catching a few rogue hairs. With minimal pressure, he turned my face to meet his. Those beautiful, intelligent blue eyes searched my face, his lips dipping in a slight frown. "You deserve better than the second-class citizen you see yourself as. You deserve it all."

I slowly released the breath I didn't realize I was holding when his lips brushed against to my temple.

"You're right," I admitted.

"Usually am." He shot me a wink and flung open the first pizza box. "Now, for the big decisions. Cheese, pepperoni, hamburger, or veggie?"

It didn't pass my notice that he still had his hand wrapped around the back of my neck or the way his thumb brushed along my skin in slow, even strokes. Instead of calling him out, I leaned into the hold, savoring the feeling of safety it invoked.

Safety and arousal.

Now all I could picture was his palm sliding around gently, grasping the front of my throat and squeezing while he held me against the wall or pinned me to the bed. That black ink decorating his bronze hand would be a complete contrast to my smooth, fair skin.

One minute in the missionary position was the only way Brian would want sex, so this danger fetish I was developing was new and out of nowhere. But I had a feeling that with Charlie, new wants and desires might add to the growing list of things I'd like to try.

And I couldn't be happier, or more willing, to discover them all with him.

Covering a wide yawn, I typed with one hand, the screen blurring from my exhausted eyes.

"We can pick this back up tomorrow," Charlie said over his shoulder, fingers flying across the keyboard at a million words a minute. I studied his muscular back for a moment before responding.

"Were you always this talented with computers?" I crawled down the bed, stretching out my tight muscles as I went, and sat on the end.

"Yes and no. Learning new coding languages, figuring out the ins and outs of software comes easier than it might for others, but I've had to work at it too. We didn't have a computer growing up, so when I needed one for homework, I'd go to the library." Swiveling in the chair, he faced me and leaned back, interlacing his fingers behind his head and spreading his knees. It took all my willpower to not stare at the way his sweatpants draped over an impressive bulge between his legs. "My mom wasn't around much. She worked several jobs to keep the lights on and food on the table. She stripped at a club across town, sometimes worked the streets if she had to. She was on her way home from work when she was murdered."

His normally vibrant eyes went distant, as if he was recalling memories from that time in his life.

"Did you take apart the library's computer or something?" I joked, hoping to remove that ashen look from his face. "And that's how you became a master hacker?"

Gaze still unfocused, a corner of his lips twitched upward. "No.

Something snagged my attention at the library. Honestly, I don't even remember what it was, but I checked out a book on computer programing one night. I enjoyed reading that over the literary shit they tried to shove down my throat. So I kept reading and learning, teaching myself how to code. After my mom passed, I went to live with my dad." A silver ball slipped between his lips and rolled back and forth, back and forth. I became entranced as filthy visions played out in my mind. "He was fine, just a deadbeat, so I knew it was up to me to make sure we didn't end up homeless after his unemployment checks stopped coming. That's when I picked up hacking. It was wrong, but it paid the bills and helped me save us from being out on the streets."

He dropped his arms and studied the ink designs atop his hands.

"And the tattoos? Is that when those started?"

"I fell into a rough crowd at the community college I attended, all of us studying computer engineering but hacking on the side. It was the pain, the buzz of the needle that kept bringing me back to the artist's chair, which is why I got so many early on. Those few hours, I'd be numb, and considering I hadn't properly mourned my mom and was busy either evading the feds or going to school, that numbness was welcomed. In a way, it was my sanctuary from the outside world."

"You were running… from the people you wanted to be one day?" I asked, completely absorbed in his fascinating story. My elbows pressed to the insides of my thighs when I crossed them on top of the bed and leaned forward.

"Never said I had a squeaky-clean path to the FBI," he said with a forced smile.

"Do they know?"

"It's how I ended up in a windowless interrogation room. They finally tracked me down, which I'll admit I wanted, and offered me a deal. If I gave up my clients, the worst ones I was working for, they would offer me a lesser sentence."

"And?" I inched toward the corner of the bed to shorten the

distance between us. "Wait, did you spend time in prison? I'm crushing on a felon!"

Like I'd hoped, all traces of the earlier sadness vanished as his smile grew wider. Shaking his head, he leaned forward, clasping his hands between his spread knees.

"Would that change anything?"

Biting my lower lip, I shook my head. "I knew from the start you'd be a terrible influence."

"You have no idea," he practically purred. He dropped my gaze to stare at my lips. "But no. I offered to help, told them I wanted a job. At that point, I'd graduated with my BS and had applied to the academy. Most were against the idea, but an important guy at Quantico pushed my application through under the condition that I'd start out in Cyber Crimes. Which I did for a few years before working my way through different divisions, still helping more on the technical side. But the BSU division was always my end goal."

Something flashed across his face that I couldn't read.

"What?"

"It's not that I don't like the department, or the type of cases we work. It's just that I'm finding myself missing the technical side. It's where I excel, and when I'm out in the field, I'm restricted."

I nodded, even though I didn't fully understand.

"Are you frustrated with me for holding you back on this case? Keeping you from flexing your computer genius brains?"

He released a slow breath, and I braced myself for his frustration. But it never came.

"You're just trying to protect me from myself. How can I be mad at that? Though I will admit I miss it. It's a different aspect of profiling, and I sometimes think I'm not being used to my full potential. We have stacks of files, hundreds of victims who deserve justice, but red tape keeps me from helping us track down the killers faster. That is incredibly frustrating."

A heavy silence settled between the small gap that separated us, both of us unable to look away from the other. I wanted to tell him then that I was ready, that I wanted more with him even if it was just for the next three days, but a series of three beeps shattered the moment. Charlie's nostrils flared with his deep inhale. Body still facing me, he twisted to glance at his laptop. He did a double take before swiveling around completely and leaning in close to the screen.

"I'm in." A flash of pure excitement overtook his face.

"In?"

"The victim's cell phone."

"How? I thought you couldn't figure out her password." Unfolding my legs, I stepped closer to the desk and bent forward to see what held his undivided attention.

"I couldn't on my own, but the software program I built for times like this did. It runs through all the dates and other numbers associated with the file I uploaded and configures the top numerical codes she would've chosen. And boom, we're in."

I chewed on my lip while staring at the screen. The urge to ask him if this was legal pressed on me, but I honestly didn't want to know. This phone, however we could unlock the data inside, could be the key to our entire investigation. I couldn't let some red tape stop me from finding the unsub, especially now that we had a deadline, and I knew Charlie's feelings behind his desire to use his expertise.

Charlie unplugged the phone from his computer and swiped across the screen. Page after page of apps flipped by, too many and too fast for me to even try to identify them all.

"It will take me a while to sort through all the apps she's downloaded," he muttered, brows pinched. "And I thought my phone was full. This woman downloaded every available app in the Apple store."

Another yawn crept up. Turning away from Charlie, I nonchalantly covered my mouth, hoping he didn't notice.

"Get some sleep," he said over his shoulder, not looking away from the screen.

I checked my watch, frowning when I found it dead. "What time is it?"

"Almost midnight. Seriously, get some sleep. We have another long day ahead of us tomorrow."

What he said was true, but even though my body said I was tired, my mind was running a mile a minute.

"There's something off about the profile that's bugging the shit out of me," I said as I reached across his laptop to grab a cold slice of pizza. "But I can't figure out what."

Charlie glared at the pizza when it hovered above his laptop.

"How about you talk it through while I search through the phone? Maybe I can point out some holes or inconsistencies."

Taking my midnight snack over to the bed, I propped the pillows up and settled back against the headboard, pulling the stack of case files onto my lap.

"Okay," I mumbled around a bite of pizza. "I'll start with the basics, then work my way through the questions that haven't been answered yet with evidence."

Looked like it would be another long night working. But with Charlie just a few feet away, being able to talk through what was swirling in my overactive mind, it wasn't as daunting, or lonely, as it had been in the past.

In fact—and this was sad to say—I enjoyed it.

All because of him.

15

CHARLIE

Dry eyes burning, I continued to study the phone's bright screen, pushing past the discomfort. Almost done, then I could get some rest, like Sleeping Beauty curled up among the papers and photos.

Longing mixed with satisfaction swelled when I peeked over the phone's edge. *Beautiful in sleep and awake, and she thinks I'm a deadly combination. I have nothing on her ability to whip me under her spell with a simple look or hilarious comment.*

Pushing exhaustion aside, I turned back to the phone and swiped the screen for what felt like the thousandth time in the last hour.

I wrote down two apps that looked suspicious and needed a deeper dive, and thankfully this was the last screen full. Prior to falling asleep, Rhyan talked through the case, analyzing the specifics of the profile for almost two hours while I listened, speaking up when I could offer unique insight or a question about the direction of her thinking.

By the time she fell asleep, we had more questions than answers.

White male, forty to fifty, medical training, white-collar job, lived alone but was married at one point, probably divorced or going through a divorce because of his spouse cheating on him. Now had a hatred for all cheaters, targeting women who were searching for an affair. Lived or worked around the downtown area. Drove a vehicle that could move around a body with ease and was physically strong enough to carry dead weight along the bridge without leaving a mark on the body.

The odd way he killed his victims was the snag in the profile we couldn't figure out. That and how he would incapacitate the women to inject the air into their veins without leaving an obvious mark.

Officially done with the phone and working for the night—early morning, if I were being technical—I set it on the desk beside the laptop and rose from the chair. My back cracked, muscles straining as I stretched my arms up high toward the ceiling. Twisting one way, then the other, I held in a groan to not wake Rhyan. My bed called my name, begging me to slip beneath the covers to at least get a few hours of sleep, but I moved toward her.

I stood over her curled form, memorizing every detail like a fucking creeper. Lips parted, features soft with sleep with her hands tucked beneath her cheek, Rhyan appeared serene. Before I realized what I was doing, two fingers trailed through her thick red hair splayed across the white pillow. I nearly came undone earlier when she shook out her wet hair, freeing the wavy, damp locks. She had no clue what images that minor action stirred in my dirty-ass mind.

I wanted that hair pulled tight in my fist, using my grip to hold her in place while I devoured her lips or eased my throbbing cock into her open, willing mouth. Memories of this morning's all-consuming kiss sent a bolt of desire straight to my balls.

Breath picking up, I took a step away from the woman who I wanted more than any other before her. Perching on the edge of the bed, I leaned forward and covered my face with both hands. Pressing the heels to my eye sockets, I forced the bombarding thoughts of a naked Rhyan out of my mind. Fuck, I had to get my shit together around her. The last thing I wanted was to push her away because she thought I was a fucking creep.

"Hey."

My head snapped up at the soft, sleepy voice. Face still pressed against her hands, her green eyes met mine, blinking slowly as if she fought the urge to fall back asleep.

"Hey. Go back to sleep. I just wrapped up. I'm about to do the same."

The mattress shifted and dipped as she pushed up, licking her lips and lazily surveying the room. "I fell asleep?"

"About an hour ago."

Scooting to the edge of the bed, she collected the scatter of papers and her laptop onto her lap. "So sorry about that. What a superb partner I am, sleeping on the job while you kept on working. I'll head back to my room."

"Or you could stay."

"You want me to stay the night again?"

"Of course I do."

It was on the tip of my tongue to beg her to stay. Even if nothing happened between us, I liked her close. I needed her close. I felt more like myself and more like a man who deserved more from life when she was around. But I didn't, just nodded and stood when she did.

"I can't," she said, shifting on her feet.

Hand pressed to her lower back, I walked with her to the closed door. My grip tightened around the handle, but I couldn't make myself open it. Not when I knew it would result in her walking through it and leaving me feeling lonelier than ever.

"Good night," she whispered, and my attention perked up. Her cheeks were flushed, and her voice was breathy in a way that I, and my cock, immediately understood. "I should go." Her choice in words didn't fail my notice.

"You don't have to leave," I said, tipping her face up to mine with a knuckle pressed beneath her chin.

"I do, though. I'm sorry, I really am. I'm just not... I'm not ready." Those green eyes begged for me to understand.

Desire swirled within me as her chest heaved up and down with every quick breath. It seemed she didn't want to leave but felt she needed to.

It took all my willpower to shove the handle down and pull open the door. If she wasn't ready, that was fine. I'd wait. No way in hell would I push her past what she was comfortable with.

Patience and understanding were the way to her heart. Not jumping her, ripping off every scrap of clothing, and eating her whole, starting at her pussy.

Though I seriously wish it were, because fuck, I needed a taste.

As she slipped through the small gap, her heated gaze stayed locked with mine. Not okay with the idea of her being alone at this time of night, I grabbed my key and went to walk her to her room like the gentleman I normally was not. Seemed Rhyan was changing me in all the best ways possible.

"Don't," she said in an almost panic, clutching the files and ancient laptop to her chest. "I need you to stay there, in your room. Please."

With a stiff nod, I used my foot as a doorstop and motioned down the hall. "I'm not leaving until you're safely inside. That's not negotiable."

She chewed on her lower lip, clearly conflicted. She practically sprinted down the hall and fumbled with her key, though before Rhyan slipped into her room, she turned back my way.

"I had fun tonight," she said with a hesitant smile.

"Me too."

My grip on the doorframe tightened, knuckles draining of their bronze color, to keep me from marching down the hall and kissing those parted lips senseless. It was there, the same need and desire flowing through us both, but she held back.

Why?

I had no fucking clue, but I didn't need to understand. If that was what she wanted, then space was what I would give her.

Only once she disappeared and the click of her door closing whispered down the silent hall did I step back into my room. Back pressed against the door, I groaned and relaxed my head, the door vibrating when it collided with the solid wood. Squeezing both lids shut, I

Chapter 15

slipped a hand down the front of my sweatpants, beneath my boxer briefs, and fisted my swollen, stiff cock.

A sharp breath hissed through my clenched teeth.

Fucking hell. I couldn't remember the last time I was this hard without even touching a woman. Lately, it took a lot of foreplay and kink to get me this turned on. Now here I was, my dick ready to punch through a damn wall without a soft, warm body to sink into.

Tightening my snug grip around the base, I yanked the sweatpants and briefs down to my hips, the door's cool surface tingling my bare ass. The bite of cold air against my dick lodged a groan in my throat. I pumped slowly, tugging my fist to the tip, twisting back to the base as I pictured Rhyan splayed out naked on the bed, red hair fanned out around her, legs spread, sweet weeping pussy begging for me to sink inside.

Her fair skin flushed, breasts moving with each of her heavy pants.

Lips parted, ready to suck me dry.

Oh, how she would scream when I flicked her swollen clit over and over, teasing her to the edge until I fucked her deep with my tongue.

Desire and lust thrummed in my veins. Sweat slicked my skin despite the cold air pumping from the AC unit, beading along my forehead as I continued to work my palm up and down my straining cock.

I was so fucking close to exploding.

Sweats and briefs left piled on the floor, I stormed to the bathroom, ripped back the sheer fabric curtain, and twisted the chrome knob. Freezing water sputtered from the showerhead. Shirt still clinging to my damp skin, I moved under the spray. My barked curse and the pound of my clenched fist against the shitty square tile boomed through the small space.

Chest heaving, I willed my desperate clutch to ease, my hand falling to my side. My swollen dick bobbed in the frigid spray. Squeezing both eyes shut, I interlaced both hands behind my head to keep them from wrapping around my dick and finishing what I stupidly started.

I was a fucking idiot. She deserved better than me fucking my hand to the fantasy of her and me together.

A minute passed, then another, with me inhaling deep breaths through my nose and blowing out harshly through my lips, willing my cock to calm the fuck down. Little by little, the blood flow ebbed, calming my angry dick. I pushed the image of a naked Rhyan from my mind and the imaginary taste of her off my tongue when a sound snapped me from my lust cloud to full alert.

After I shut off the valve, water trickled from above, splashing to the collected water along the tile floor. I held a breath, waiting for the noise that snagged my attention to happen again. Or maybe I was going mad from blue balls. That was a real diagnosis. If it wasn't, I might be the first case ever.

A light rapping came from the bedroom.

A knock.

I stripped off the soaking wet T-shirt, tossing it to the shower floor, and secured a too-small white towel around my waist. At the door, I paused, eyeing my gun, but didn't reach for the weapon. There was no doubt in my mind that I could take down anyone with my bare hands with ease, or use my cock as a weapon, if the person at the door came to harm me.

Not bothering with the peephole, I pulled the door open.

The world froze.

I sucked in a deep breath, only able to blink. Any words vanished.

Rhyan's tiny pale hand was still raised as if to knock again. Chewing on the corner of her lip, she slipped those wide, bright green eyes down my naked chest, pausing at the towel. I cringed. There was no way she missed the tent my back-in-action cock created beneath the scratchy fabric, but without a pair of boxer briefs to somewhat hide the fucker desperately attempting to reach her, there was nothing I could do to cover my obvious boner.

"Rhyan." The one word was a mix of a command and moan.

Chapter 15

Pure innocence and vulnerability shone through her hooded eyes as she continued to stare at the now-shifting towel.

Fuck, what is wrong with my dick? The fucker needed to calm the hell down or he'd ruin this for both of us.

"I wanted to.... Does the offer still stand to not leave, to stay with you?"

Unable to verbalize a response, I shuffled back and opened the door wide.

Those damn pajama shorts, the ones that showed the sweet curve of her perfect ass, had a groan rumbling in my chest. "Rhyan, please have some fucking mercy on me. I won't pressure you to do anything you don't want to do. Either put some different clothes on if you're not ready for—"

"I am," she blurted, rubbing the palms of both hands down the sides of her bare thighs as her nervous gaze bounced around the room.

I crossed my arms, gripping my biceps in a bruising hold to keep from reaching for her. Words. I needed clear rules on what she meant by that amazing proclamation.

"What changed?"

Her features pulled in a wince. She lowered herself to the edge of my bed. "You have to understand. I... I've never done anything like this."

"This?"

"What I feel, what I want," she whispered. "I can't stop thinking about you, about us. And I wanted to stay earlier, but I couldn't. I had to.... You wouldn't understand."

"Rhyan, nothing will happen between us until you're open and honest with me. That's how this works. That's how we make this"—I motioned between us—"work."

Her hooded gaze lazily moved from my bare feet up my still-wet legs. Her pink tongue slipped out, sliding along her lower lip. Images of that tongue licking up and down my cock before I thrust it deep between those lips had a groan catching in my throat.

Fuck, I'm on edge. Maybe I should've jacked off to save myself the embarrassment of only lasting a few seconds if I get the privilege of touching her tonight.

"I haven't been with anyone but Brian." Some of that thrumming lust obvious in her flushed cheeks and quick breaths dimmed. "And I haven't been around anyone but myself since then, and I had to prepare." That last part was said into her hands, hiding her ruby-red face.

"Prepare?" Did she mean a butt plug or something? I highly doubted it, but I sure as hell would be fucking down for it if that were the case.

Moving one hand from her face, she circled a flattened hand over her pussy. "I had things to take care of. Olivia told me to do it before I left, but I didn't, and then when you suggested I stay the night, I freaked out. I didn't want you to see that mess."

Finally all the pieces fell into place.

"You needed to shave."

"Yes," she squeaked. "Can we move on now?"

"I have a razor," I said, taking a step toward her, unable to stop myself from closing the distance. "All you had to do was ask."

That other hand covering her face fell to the bedspread. "I would not shave in your room." She gasped. "No, just no."

In two long strides, I was in front of her, standing between her spread knees, my cock right at her eye level. I cupped her face and tipped it up. "I said nothing about you doing the work."

Her green eyes widened. "How do you make everything sound sexy?"

Tracing a finger along her jaw, I slipped a hand into her loose hair. "I could ask you the same. I need you to be specific about what you're okay with tonight. I won't push your limits, but I will toe that line unless we set ground rules."

"I don't know what I want," she whispered. Trembling hands rose, hovering between us. I hissed through clenched teeth when her hot palms pressed to my stomach, abs flexing beneath her curled fingers. "Can that be my answer?" Ever so slowly, she slid her hands up to my chest. "I just want this, want you. I want to touch you, feel your skin against mine. I want... I want you to touch me."

Closing my eyes, I tipped my face up to the ceiling, relishing the feel of her touch and reining myself in before I tossed her to the bed and buried my cock in her pussy.

"You'll tell me if I go too far." It wasn't a question but a desperate plea.

"What do you want to do?"

If I were a lesser man, I might have blown my load at the innocence in those words, her soft tone nearly my undoing.

I fisted the hand deep in her hair, and she gasped. I held her steady, face tilted up to the ceiling as I inched lower, brushing my lips against hers.

"Everything you're willing to give."

Her lids shuttered closed. The low desperate groan that escaped her parted lips snapped the remaining limits of my control. I closed the small distance, slamming our lips together. Hers parted, allowing me to dive in to take everything I wanted.

All of her.

Slipping a hand beneath her tank, I brushed the tips of two fingers along her soft skin. A delicious moan flowed from her lips to mine. Short nails dug into my skin, no doubt leaving crescent-shaped indentations along my pecs. Savoring every inch, I crept up her taut stomach, over her ribs. She sucked in a breath when my knuckle brushed along the underside of her breast—her bare breast.

Ripping my mouth from hers, desperation riding high, I gripped the hem of her tank and raised it to rest atop her heaving tits. Stunned, all I could do was stare hungrily at her perfect peaked nipples begging for my mouth.

My knees slammed into the thin cheap carpet, and her legs widened to accommodate my torso. Keeping a tight hold on her hair, I angled her head to the side, giving me open access to nibble my way down, sucking on that throbbing pulse. Soft moans filled the room.

Watching her reaction, I palmed her breast, squeezing until she gasped. I swiped a thumbnail along her hard nipple, and her back arched, shoving those delicious breasts closer toward my mouth. Fucking gladly, my lips sealed around her tight bud, sucking, flicking with my greedy tongue. Tip pinched between my teeth, I rubbed the metal ball of my piercing back and forth in hard, quick passes. Slim fingers engulfed the sides of my head, urging me closer, filling my mouth with more of her plump breast.

The rough cotton of the towel rubbed against my twitching dick, almost sending me over the edge. Gripping the side, I ripped it from my hips, dropping it to the floor and leaving me completely naked between her thighs.

"Rhyan," I breathed before nipping at the other breast, leaving tiny teeth marks along the swell. Forcing myself back, I cupped her breast and pinched the beaded tip between two fingers. Crying out, head back, waves of red hair cascading down, she was a fucking vision. Breathing hard, I fought to maintain control.

"More," she begged, her hips flexing, pushing her center closer to the edge of the bed.

I licked my lips. "I want to taste you." Licking along the exposed skin of her inner thigh, I gave another hard pinch to her abused nipple and bit hard enough to sting.

Her head snapped forward, as far as my grip would allow. Chest flushed red, eyes glassy, she panted.

"You don't have to. I know it's gross—"

Hmm. Seemed my sweet Rhyan needed a reminder of forgetting all that shit her ex put in her head.

With a wicked grin, I pinched and twisted that peaked bud to snap her mouth shut. Her demand for me to stop morphed into a groan of pleasure.

"If by gross you mean fucking amazing, then sure. I'd stay on my knees all damn day to eat your sweet, tempting pussy." She sucked in a breath, eyes searching mine. "I've dreamed of licking your slick slit clean, fucking you deep with my tongue. Please, baby." The term of endearment slipped out, but nothing ever felt so damn right. "Please let me eat you whole, devour every drop your beautiful cunt gives me."

Chapter 15

"Holy fuck," she breathed, eyes wide behind her glasses.

Sealing a kiss to her inner thigh, I pressed my nose against her damp center, inhaling her delicious musty scent deep into my lungs. I released her breast to fist the comforter. Several threads snapped beneath my curled fingers as I held myself back from ripping her shorts right off her body.

"Please let me taste you," I begged against her damp pussy, kissing her center after each word for emphasis. The bed bounced when she fell backward, my hold on her hair slipping. Eager to see the pussy that had starred in my wet dreams, I dipped a finger beneath the elastic band of her shorts, on either side of her hips, then paused.

"Rhyan, I need your permission." My hands trembled with restraint, but I couldn't allow myself to venture any further without a verbal response.

"Yes," she replied, voice a mere rasp. "Have all of me."

Shoving deeper beneath her shorts, I swore as I cupped her mound, groaning in pleasure at the slickness I found. Kissing the inside of one knee, then the other, I slipped a finger between her lips, teasing her swollen bundle of nerves.

Pulling the slick finger out of her shorts, I coated my lower lip, flicking the tip of my tongue out for my first intoxicating taste. Unable to be gentle, I ripped her shorts over her hips and down her thighs, tossing them over my shoulder without looking away from her perfect, fully shaved mound.

"Holy fuck," I groaned. Reaching down, I squeezed my overzealous cock in a near stranglehold. "You shaved it all. Fucking hell, I might come just from staring at you."

She said something in response, but all I could focus on was her swollen clit pushing between her shaved lips, begging for me to give it a lick. Palms to the inside of her creamy thighs, I pushed them wider, my muscles straining as I bowed as if ready to worship her blessed cunt.

Pulling back her lips, I surged forward, done holding myself back from what she offered. Flattening out my tongue, I licked her from bottom to top, pulling that swollen, needy nub between my lips.

Hollowing out my cheeks, I sucked, flicking and licking as she screamed, thrashing on the bed.

Blunt nails scraped against my scalp as she attempted to force my face harder against her greedy pussy. With a fingertip, I teased her opening below my lips, tracing the outside before dipping in an inch.

"Fuck," Rhyan cried. "I'm close. Please, Charlie. Please."

"Please what?" I asked, smirking as I peered over her mound to watch her breasts bounce with her labored breaths.

"Touch me," she begged.

"I am touching you, baby."

"No, no." Her head thrashed along the white duvet, that red hair wildly splayed. "Inside. Touch me inside. I need it. I need you."

"With pleasure," I purred.

Leaning back on my heels, mouth coated with her juices, I thrust two fingers deep into her channel, watching as her face pinched and relaxed in quick succession.

"That's it, baby," I praised. "You taste so good. So fucking wet, all for me. Tell me it's all for me."

"All for you," she whimpered.

"Tell me I'm the only one who gets to see this shaved kitty."

"Only you, Charlie. I only want you to touch me, to see me."

With a near feral growl, I dipped my face between her thighs, sucking on her clit with renewed fervor, adding in another finger to fuck her tight pussy. Her thighs clenched around my head, sealing against my ears, muffling her pleas for more.

I was consumed, nothing mattering except tipping her over that edge, feeling her squeeze my digits as she found her release. Driving my long, thick fingers deeper, I sucked her clit, flicking the hood with my tongue ring.

She quivered, everything tightening, then screamed my name.

A rush of slick liquid seeped between my fingers, my tongue dipping low to lick up every delicious drop.

Those thighs fell away, the sounds of her heavy breaths and the whirling air-conditioning flooding back. Breathing hard, I placed a reverent kiss to her center while thanking the fucking gods I had this chance. Even if it was just this one time with her, my only glimpse into her heaven, I was grateful.

And I knew, in that moment, no one would ever compare to her.

Rhyan Riggs had officially ruined me.

And I wouldn't change a fucking thing.

16

RHYAN

I was dead. As in "saw a bright light and Grandma Jubilee calling me home" dead.

Yet my heart still thundered in my chest, lungs working overtime to suck in enough oxygen to keep me conscious, and I was fairly certain heaven didn't have a yellowed ceiling like the one that hovered above. So maybe I didn't officially die. The way my body convulsed and my mind blanked from the most intense orgasm of my life—one of the few I'd ever had, actually—I was almost certain Charlie killed me for a few seconds.

Death by pleasure. What a way to go.

Feather-soft kisses peppered along my inner thigh down to my knee, drawing me back to the present and reminding me there was still a drop-dead-gorgeous man with a killer tongue between my spread legs.

"I think I saw heaven," I said out loud, immediately regretting the declaration.

He would no doubt think I was an idiot for saying that. *Could've been worse, I guess. I could've spouted off more STD facts.* Chewing on my lower lip, I squeezed my eyes shut, hoping that would stop the bombarding anxious thoughts, and tossed an arm over my eyes as a barrier for the upcoming critical words I knew would follow.

"Funny," he commented, his lips now whispering over my belly as he worked his way up my body. "I thought the same thing." Fingers clasped around my wrist to lift my forearm. I squeezed my lids tighter. "Baby, look at me."

I shook my head.

"Why?" he asked softly, brushing fingertips across one cheek, then the other.

The lack of accusation or annoyance in his tone had me peeking one eye open. Propped up on one arm, his head rested in his open palm, Charlie watched me, his features open and soft.

"Because," I rasped, "I'm expecting the worst."

"The worst?"

"Yeah, like how I smelled—"

"Like heaven."

I opened the other eye in shock. "Or tasted bad—"

"Like cherries," he said, closing his eyes in bliss. "And you know what my favorite part was of eating your delicious pussy like it was my last meal?"

"What?" I asked, apprehensive of his next words yet desperately needing to know.

"That I got to be the one between your thighs. I'm the one who made you cry out. I'm the lucky bastard on his knees worshipping your beautiful body the way it deserves." Not sure why, but tears built on my lower lids. Those honest words chased away all negative thoughts and worries. "Not sure if you've noticed, but I like you, Rhyan Riggs. All of you, not just this physical side we're exploring. You sharing a piece of yourself, being vulnerable, it makes me so fucking happy."

It was like he knew the exact words I needed to calm my anxious thoughts.

The mattress dipped beneath my elbows as I pushed up, pressing a kiss to his scruff-covered cheek.

"Thank you." I cleared my throat, hoping to get rid of the lump of

Chapter 16

emotions making my voice raspy. Slight movement lower drew my attention. I stared, lips parted, at his bobbing hard dick. A fresh wave of desire pulsed through my veins.

His head dipped, locks of dark hair falling forward as he followed my wide-eyed stare. "See? If my words didn't convince you of how much I enjoyed you, then there's your physical proof." Shoving off the bed, he sat up and raked a hand through his disheveled black hair. "I'll throw some pants on."

I whipped my hand out, fingers wrapping around his wrist, keeping him close. He turned, flicking confused glances between me and where I restrained him.

"No," I said, swallowing hard to quell the tremble in my voice. "I want to help."

"Help?" It sounded like a purr. "Help how, baby?"

"What can I... what do you want?"

A devilish smirk grew on his face. Immediately, I knew I was in the best, most amazing trouble.

Cupping my chin in a tight grasp, he brushed the pad of his thumb along my lower lip. In a daring, not at all like me move, I flicked out my tongue, licking the tip of his thumb. Taking the opening, he surged forward, pressing inside to the last knuckle.

The comforter gathered beneath him as he twisted to kneel, one knee on either side of my waist. With a quick flick, he dislodged my grip around his wrist and now held mine. He guided my hand lower, eyes trained on me as if watching for any signs of hesitation. Which he wouldn't find. Sure, I wasn't that great at any of this, but for the first time ever, I wanted to touch, to feel, to explore. Because I *wanted* it for myself, not out of duty or pressure.

A quick hiss followed by a low, chest-rumbling groan bolstered my confidence when my fingers wrapped around his thick, silky length.

"Tighter, like this," he instructed, moving his hand to cover mine. His longer fingers squeezed so hard my own knuckles popped. "Holy fuck, just like that. But we're missing something." Pulling my hand away, he dropped it between my own thighs. "Coat your hand," he commanded.

A shiver of excitement raced through me, my belly flipping and twisting at the way he lorded over me with a steamy possessive glint in his hooded gaze.

Not looking away, too consumed by the fire behind his bright blue eyes, I pressed my open palm directly against my center, slicking it with my pleasure. A small gasp escaped around his slowly thrusting thumb. Pleasure tingled, a new rush of desire making liquid leak onto the heel of my palm pressing against my overly sensitive bundle of nerves. A wicked smile split Charlie's face.

"I think you need some help." Reaching between us, he thrust two fingers into my center. Air swept along my sweaty back when it arched off the bed from the sudden amazing intrusion. "Fuck, you're drenched for me again. I fucking love it."

I nodded, unable to talk around the thumb still pumping in and out between my lips.

My muscles trembled with the need to yank him down, to seal our bodies together, quelling the ache once again building. But I knew through the lust fog that going that far tonight would be a mistake.

Shifting back, his thumb popped free. He wiped my saliva along my lower lip while he bit his, watching the way he coated my lips. Abs tensing, I curled forward, guiding my greedy mouth toward his twitching cock.

"Baby, you don't have to do this." With one hand still between my legs, he cupped my cheek with the other. "I'm just as happy with your hands on me."

I knew that was a lie. What guy wanted a hand job over what I wanted to do?

Not a one.

Flicking the tip of my tongue, I danced it along the swollen head, licking up the bead of precum from his weeping slit. His hips jerked forward, barely pressing the swollen head between my parted lips.

"I'm not good at this, but I want to," I shamefully admitted.

Chapter 16

The hand once cupping my cheek slipped in my hair, tightening so I was completely at his mercy.

Blue eyes glittered, and flashes of silver rolled between his lips as he drank his fill of me.

"Do you want me to teach you, baby?" His voice was deep, raspy, full of want.

I whimpered when another finger slipped inside me, joining the previous two. His hips flexed, tipping him forward, pressing himself an inch inside my mouth.

I nodded with pleading eyes.

Fuck, when was the last time I was this turned on by the idea of pleasuring someone? I wanted him to explode the way I did. I wanted me to cause that insane bliss.

"Good girl," he praised. "Open wider and relax your jaw so I can fuck that smart mouth of yours."

I couldn't help it. A pleasure-filled groan rumbled up my throat. Charlie tossed his head back with a grunt as he rocked deeper between my lips. My abs trembled with the work it took to hold my position. As if sensing my strain, he pulled himself free from my mouth and slipped those fingers from my center. I cried out, missing every inch of him.

"Come here, baby," he directed, now standing at the side of the bed, his cock fisted in a tight grip. I hesitated. He tsked. "If you make me wait, you'll be punished." My eyes flared wide, and more wetness dripped from between my thighs. He studied my center like he was committing every quiver to memory. "I think you like that idea."

In a dick trance—was that a thing?—I crawled on all fours, the bed dipping and shifting beneath my weight.

"Hmm, I like you like that. Open up, baby. I'm about to explode just seeing you on your hands and knees, those lips of yours begging to take my cock."

With a needy whimper, I parted my lips, leaning forward as he thrust into my willing mouth. Throaty groans mixed with sweet praises helped me relax, taking him deeper down my throat.

"That's it, baby. Holy fuck, your mouth is pure heaven. Just like that. Relax your throat. Yes," he hissed. "Good girl, taking me fucking deep. I love being inside you, whether it's my dick fucking your throat or my fingers pounding into that perfect pussy."

Starting at my nape, he slid his hand down the length of my spine, sprouting fire in his wake. Two fingers trailed along my backside, continuing until he brushed against my opening. Desperation mounted, the need to be filled rocking my hips back onto his digits.

"That's it," he grunted as he thrust deep, tapping the back of my throat. I gagged, tears stinging my wide eyes. "Swallow my dick, baby. I'm so fucking close."

And so was I. Two fingers speared into me, curling to tickle a certain spot that made my legs tremble. I almost cried out when his fingers disappeared, only to moan when they slipped forward, pressing to my swollen clit, his thumb inside, filling me once again.

"If you don't want me to come in your mouth, I need you to pull back."

I didn't move. Instead, I doubled my efforts, licking and sucking, taking him as deep as I could, past my gag reflex, needing him to explode—all because of me. His grip in my hair held me steady as his thrusts quickened, turning erratic. My lower belly quivered, once again on the edge of orgasm as his fingers flicked and teased.

"Fucking hell," he hissed through a tight jaw, my only warning before his release shot down my throat.

Swallowing fast, I took everything he gave. Still hard, leaking cum along my tongue, he pulled out and carefully flipped me to my back. The room spun, my clouded thoughts struggling to keep up with the sudden turn of events. A tight grip wrapped around both ankles, and then I was sliding against the comforter, a gasp lodged in my throat. When my ass was hanging off the edge of the bed, Charlie bent both legs, pushing them until my knees were pressed to my shoulders.

"What—" His lips sealing around my clit cut me off. With a hard suck and not-so-soft bite, he thrust his fingers inside, shooting me over the edge.

This time I couldn't scream, my voice silent as I clutched the comforter in a death grip, riding out the second most intense orgasm

Chapter 16

ever. Tears leaked from the corners of my eyes, copper coating my tongue from where I bit too hard on my lips at some point.

The hold on my thighs relaxed, followed by a hot, heavy pressure sealing to my stomach and chest. Peering down through hazy vision, I smiled at the man collapsed between my thighs, head resting just below my breasts. His slick skin shimmered in the dim light with each of his deep breaths.

A half groan, half sigh brushed along my skin as I trailed a single finger down his spine. But as the silence stretched, my anxious mind whirled with the what-ifs.

"Whatever you're thinking, don't," Charlie grumbled before placing a kiss just above my belly button. His hard chin pressed between my breasts. A lazy smile made him look years younger. "There's nothing to be anxious about. Never with me, okay?"

I nodded to placate him. His brows dipped as if he knew I didn't believe him. In a flash, he was up and had me rolled on my side, and a sharp slap vibrated through the room.

The sting along my ass cheek registered half a second after his palm smacked against my skin.

"You spanked me," I shouted, scooting away from him in horror.

He just smirked and prowled across the bed, following my retreat. "I did. You were being a bad girl, not listening to me."

"I can't help it," I argued, but stopped myself from saying anything more.

"But that spanking did, didn't it?"

Pursing my lips, I tried to smother my smile. He was right. Now all I could focus on was the delicious burn on my skin and the look of victory in his blue eyes.

"Thought so." He chuckled. "Do you want to sleep or shower?"

I knew I should say sleep, that saying shower would make me a greedy, greedy woman. But I desperately wanted to say yes, to feel his hands roaming my body one more time before this night ended and reality settled back in with the rise of tomorrow's sun.

As if reading my mind, he hopped off the bed and bent forward, scooping me into his arms.

"That was my choice too," he admitted as he carried me bridal style in the bathroom's direction. "I'm not nearly done with you yet."

He clutched me to his chest, the air puffing out of my lungs at the too-tight hold, but I didn't say a word of complaint. I felt precious, cherished, held against him. Not a prize to be won, not an object to be used. Maybe this was the way real men treated women.

Or maybe it was just Charlie. Something told me the shy smiles, soft looks, and insight into his past weren't for everyone. Because he and I both found what we desperately wanted in each other.

To be seen.

EVEN AFTER SEVERAL orgasms and now snug against Charlie's side, my overactive mind pulled me from a light sleep. I stretched for the nightstand, fingertips brushing the edge of my phone until it scooted closer. Holding it a hairbreadth from my face, I squinted at the screen to make out the large numbers: 5:00 a.m. I sighed, tucking the device under my pillow and turning to stare at the ceiling.

Just because I had several heart-stopping orgasms didn't mean my anxiety would suddenly calm. However, it was dulled to an extent. I didn't wake festering over my performance or fixate on how Charlie would look at me in the morning light after last night's activities. No, he silenced those thoughts by telling me everything, exactly how he felt, clearing the air on anything I might fret over later.

No, it wasn't Charlie or anything we did just a couple hours prior. It was the damn confusing-as-hell case that pulled me awake, and after a few minutes of not falling back asleep, it eventually pulled me from the bed too. There were too many unanswered questions, and now, with the deadline, we were running out of time.

Tiptoeing, using my phone as a flashlight, I found my clothes and hastily pulled them on before sneaking out, softly closing the door behind me.

I blew out a hard breath. How in the hell did I already miss him?

Shoving my personal feelings aside, I hurried to shower, since the

Chapter 16

one I took with Charlie was not about hygiene, and flowed through my normal routine of getting ready for the day.

After double-checking the coffee shop's opening time on my phone, I picked up two to-go coffees and breakfast sandwiches and hurried back to the hotel. Grabbing my notepad from my room, I snuck back into Charlie's, hoping I was stealthy earlier and didn't wake him when I left.

A few sprinkles of coffee sloshed out of the lids, my balancing act precarious as I quietly closed the door. Despite all the things in my hands, I paused at the foot of the bed. Charlie was sprawled out on top, lightly snoring, arm stretched out wide toward the spot where I woke up.

For a few moments, I studied his exposed back, memorizing the lines of black ink and muscle.

A wistful sigh brushed past my lips. There was no doubt he was gorgeous physically, but that wasn't all. Charlie Bekham completely surprised me with his sweet soul hidden beneath his tough exterior.

Shaking my head, I forced my attention away from the naked man and sat in the upholstered armchair. Careful to not spill or drop anything, I set the food and coffee down on the desk, keeping my notebook, pen, and cell phone close.

I found through years of managing my anxiety that I could calm my swirling thoughts by writing them down. It was strange how it worked, but once it was on paper, it was as if my brain checked it off my worry list.

Tapping the end of the hotel pen against the armrest, I shifted through my rotating questions to determine what to list first.

Question one: How was he getting the bodies to the dump point on the bridge?

Dead weight was almost impossible to carry, even for a powerful man, and there were no abrasions on the bodies showing they were dragged. That meant the unsub was a very strong man, or he used something to cart them along the bridge, a dolly or wheelbarrow, maybe. But if he used either of those, a late-night visitor to the bridge would notice, risking his exposure. It had to be something unassuming that wouldn't raise a red flag if seen.

Shaking my head, I turned my focus back to writing all the questions down first, then solving them.

Question two: How is he subduing them without leaving a mark?

Question three: Why? What was his trigger?

The crinkle of paper filled the quiet as I flipped through the pages of notes, searching for the date the first victim was found. Seven months ago, but the coroner assumed she was in the water for a few weeks before being discovered. So what happened in the unsub's life, say, eight months ago to make him hate cheating women to the point of luring them in with a promise of a steamy affair, then killing them by essentially exploding their hearts?

The phone resting atop the side table vibrated, moving across the glass. With a mouthed curse, I dropped the pen and hurriedly reached for the phone to silence it before it woke Charlie.

Louisville ME: Found something you should see.

I blinked at the screen before texting back a quick reply that we'd come by later that morning. Turning my attention back to my notes, I jotted down a couple more thoughts before settling on an action plan for the day.

The top of the list was asking Charlie to run a search in Louisville for men thirty-five to fifty, recently divorced and with an ex-wife reported missing or who had a suspicious death. Then we'd narrow that down to anyone with medical knowledge and high income. Maybe that would turn up a good list of suspects.

There was another way, though I knew Charlie, Bryson, probably our asshole boss, and most definitely the assistant deputy director wouldn't be huge fans of this other, more dangerous idea. But if it got the job done, who cared if I was in harm's way?

Sneaking a peek toward the bed, ensuring Charlie was still fast asleep, I pulled the list of apps he wrote down as unknowns from the victim's phone. On my phone, I pulled up a new web page and typed in the first app on the list, then tapped the tiny magnify glass.

After a quick sip of coffee, I relaxed back in the oddly shaped

Chapter 16

chair and adjusted my glasses from where they'd slipped down the bridge of my nose. Several web pages populated down the screen, some articles on the app, others advertisements drawing more to their site. Tapping the first one listed, I toed off my shoes and tucked my long legs beneath me.

Fifteen minutes of research later, I was sucked in, clicking on every available website to learn more when a deep groan dragged my attention from the phone screen to the bed. Charlie's messy bedhead popped off the pillow, frowning at the empty spot beside him.

"Good morning," I said. His attention snapped my way. A look of relief washed over his sleepy features. "Sorry, I couldn't sleep." I tapped the pen's rounded plastic edge against my temple. "Too many things running around in here."

"Good things, I hope." He flopped back onto the bed and ran a hand through his hair, blinking at the ceiling.

"Dead things," I said and laughed when his nose scrunched. "The case. I had some thoughts I needed to write down before they drove me insane." Popping out of the chair, I moved to sit beside him and held out my notepad.

He squinted at my horrible writing and shook his head. Reaching out, he palmed the back of my head, pulling me down to the bed with him to press a gentle kiss to my forehead.

"Too early for profiling," he grumbled, releasing me.

"It's six thirty." I chuckled.

With a frustrated huff, he plopped his head back on the pillow and slapped a tattooed forearm across his eyes.

"Okay, okay, you win. It's profiling time. Tell me what that clever brain of yours discovered while I was busy getting my beauty sleep."

Biting my lower lip, I fought a smile as I tucked a stray lock of hair behind my ear and adjusted my glasses. I was almost certain he would hate this idea of mine, but even if he didn't like it, it might be our best chance at finding our unsub before he could kill again.

"Hear me out, okay? I have an idea...."

17

RHYAN

The constant ring of desk phones and general chatter around us faded to the background as I stared at the question I'd scratched out the moment we returned from the eye-opening meeting with the ME.

"Why a stun gun to subdue them?" I mused as I tapped the end of the pen against the table.

"Easy," Bryson offered with a shrug.

"Quiet and clean. Doesn't leave evidence behind like a stab wound or draw attention like gunfire." Charlie kept his focus on his laptop screen, partly because he was engrossed in the search parameters I gave him earlier, but mostly because he was pissed.

At me.

Charlie was not a fan of my plan to lure out the unsub. He'd leapt from the bed, gloriously naked, almost distracting me from his objections. Almost. I heard his reasons for forbidding me from moving forward with my idea. I just chose not to accept them. And that made him even pissier. Now we were both frustrated with the other. Just because he drew several orgasms from me with his talented fingers and tongue didn't make him my keeper, though I had to admit knowing he wasn't too happy with me soured my mood.

"What if that means he's smaller than we're thinking?" I said absentmindedly as I turned to face the murder board. "I've already questioned how he's getting the bodies down the bridge. Maybe he used something normal to cart the bodies to the center of the bridge because he wasn't strong enough to carry them on his own."

"The most recent victim's husband wasn't a strong, dominant man, which was why his wife stepped out on him."

I nodded, agreeing with Bryson. "More than likely that was the trigger. He found out his wife cheated on him because he couldn't or wouldn't perform in the bedroom, or the wife lost interest because of his size and presumed weakness. Which makes me wonder if he killed his wife first or later after he perfected his signature."

"So we've already interviewed him?" Bryson asked.

"No. He would've weighted down her body or buried it since we could trace her directly back to him." Glancing toward Charlie, I waited for him to offer any insight, but he remained silent, glaring at his screen while striking the keys on his keyboard like he wanted to push them into the table. "Agent Bekham?"

Those icy blue eyes flicked over the screen, zeroing in on me. "Huh? Sorry, in the zone here. I have the list narrowed down to the age range you gave me for men in the Louisville area and surrounding suburbs who filed for divorce or their spouses filed for divorce. I took out any same-sex marriages and anyone with a history of violence."

"Great, how many does that leave us?"

Leaning back, he ran a hand through his hair, tugging at the ends. "Way too fucking many to do anything with." His eyes narrowed when I opened my mouth to remind him of my brilliant plan. *Again.* "Don't even say it, Agent Riggs. It's not happening. It puts you in too much danger."

Pursing my lips to keep the comment of me outranking him from spilling out, I turned to face the clearly confused Bryson.

"What am I missing?" he asked, darting glances at me and Charlie.

"Rhyan here thinks—"

Chapter 17

"It's a good plan," I gritted out through clenched teeth.

"Yeah, if you have no problem risking your life," Charlie snapped back.

"Hello? We're in the FBI. Pretty sure that was in the fucking job description."

"We don't even know if they all met him on the same damn app."

"What do you want us to do, just sit on our asses waiting for another body to drop from the sky?" I shouted accusingly.

"Hey, guys," Bryson said quietly, tilting his head toward the now-quieted detective bullpen. "Might want to take your little lovers' quarrel outside unless you want everyone to know you two are not only fighting but together."

"Not a lovers' quarrel," Charlie growled as he stood. "It's one agent telling another—"

"One agent telling his superior, might I add." My grin turned sharp, like my words and tone.

"Oh, now you're tossing that on the table? Doesn't change a damn thing, Rhyan. You're not creating a profile on that damn cheaters app to lure out the unsub."

If this were a cartoon, smoke would be billowing out of my ears. "Agent Riggs," I corrected.

"Fine, Agent Riggs, my vote is no."

"It's not a bad idea."

The tip of my ponytail popped me in the face with how fast I whirled around. I thrust my hand across the table, pointing at Bryson like his statement justified my entire life's work.

"See?" I exclaimed.

"Bryson," Charlie warned. "Stay out of this."

"Listen," he said calmly and leaned toward the middle of the table, resting both forearms along the smooth surface. "I like you two. You're both damn good profilers and listened when I thought we had a case down here. But whatever is going on right now between you two isn't the best for the case, for these victims to find justice." Turning a pointed look to Charlie, he tilted his head my way. "Her plan is solid if we can get it to work. We know what clues to look for."

He held up a hand, ticking a finger up with every detail we knew the unsub preferred. "His approximate age. Getting her alone. Paying for everything. Meeting at that damn fancy hotel. Let's use that to our advantage to catch this son of a bitch." He slashed that hand through the air when Charlie attempted to cut him off. "Listen, I get it. You like her. There's not much to *not* like. But this is her job, man, and you have to let her do her job. If this works out, we'll protect her, together."

"Fuck." Charlie groaned and slouched into his chair, looking like someone kicked his puppy. "I don't fucking like it. We don't know where or when he's attacking his victims during his time with them. What if it's at a point where we can't get to her in time? Once that needle is in, air in her veins.... You heard the ME, there's no coming back from that."

"You're not giving me enough credit," I whispered.

"The way I see it, Agent Riggs"—I snarled at the way he hissed my name—"you're not giving our unsub enough credit. It can happen quick. It's not like this guy is holding them for days." Those blue eyes softened, pleading with me. "Give me a day to work through the list of potential suspects based on the parameters you gave me."

All the fight drained from me, leaving me physically and mentally exhausted. As much fun as last night was, I really could've used over two hours of sleep. "We only have two more days to identify this guy, Charlie."

"What do you mean, only two more days?" Bryson asked. "Are you guys leaving?"

"Our section chief called last night. He wants us to deliver the profile and report back to DC."

Bryson's face fell. "Even if we don't have the bastard in custody?"

I dipped my head, chin nearly resting on my chest. Pulling off my glasses, I massaged the bridge of my nose. "If we're moving forward with my plan, I need to create a profile on that app and search for viable targets to reach out to."

"Dates," Charlie said with a sneer. "Viable dates, hookups, affairs. That app is disgusting."

Chapter 17

"Couldn't agree more, but it's out there, and we know at least one of our victims used it, so let's use that knowledge to find this guy before we have to leave."

Too distracted by Charlie's frustration, my exhaustion, and the pressure of finding this guy sooner than later, I failed to check the screen when my phone rattled on the tabletop with an incoming call.

I tossed my glasses to the stack of files and answered the call, pressing the smooth glass to my ear.

"Agent—"

"What the actual hell, Rhyan!" Brian shouted. "You had me put on the no-fly list?"

I pulled the phone out an inch to save my eardrum as Brian continued to rage, rattling off every mistake or offense I'd done in the last few years. Slipping my black frames back on, I snuck a glance at the two men around me. By their flushed faces and tight features, they heard every word of Brian's tried-and-true derogatory claims as he spouted them from the other side of the country.

I winced at the sting from my now-bleeding lip. My shoulders rounded as I silently prayed for the floor to open up and swallow me whole.

"The hell?" I heard Bryson say over Brian's shouts. "Who the fuck is talking to her that way?"

"Her ex," Charlie responded. The chair flipped backward, smacking the concrete as he shoved back from the table. Pure fury radiated off him as he stalked closer.

"Ah hell no," Bryson snapped. He lunged across the table, beating Charlie, and plucked the phone from my hand.

I groaned and stood to lean across the table to get the phone back, but a muscular arm wrapped around my waist, holding me back.

"Hey, fuckstick," Bryson said, his tone all authority and malice. "Yeah, asshole, I'm talking to you. Who am I?" I tried to wiggle free from Charlie's hold, but he just sealed my back against his chest. "I'm the fucker who'll be teaching you some damn respect if you keep talking to a fucking woman that way. And believe me, you don't want me on your bad side. I spent years undercover infiltrating the Irish

Mafia. I know more killers who would gladly do me the favor of shutting your fucking mouth for good than you know people."

Holy hell. I stopped fighting Charlie, totally stunned at this version of Bryson. He'd transformed from this bulky nice guy to someone I was slightly afraid of. Hazel eyes blazing, square jaw clenched in anger, his deep voice an octave lower, making it rumble through the squad room—hell, every officer in the place now stared at Bryson with a sliver of fear in their tense posture.

"You're drooling," Charlie said against my ear and gave my ponytail a hard yank.

Swatting at his hand, I turned and stuck out my tongue. The flash of heat and returning smirk said my response had the opposite effect on him than what I intended.

"Please give me the phone back," I said to Bryson. "I need to end this shit show myself."

"If I hear one word I don't approve of, I'm sending a visitor with an appreciation for sharp things to your address, and believe me, if Rhyan here doesn't give it to me, I know someone who can find your exact location in a matter of seconds." Bryson shot Charlie a wink as he slowly extended his hand toward me.

Taking a deep, calming breath, I pressed the phone back to my hot ear. Silence from the other end had me thinking Brian hung up, but a quick check of the screen showed the call was still connected.

"It's over, Brian," I said with more strength than I felt with Bryson's and Charlie's full focus on me. "I left you. Deal with it. You clearly moved on based on the position I found you and your TA in at your office before I left." Charlie stroked a comforting hand down my spine, bolstering my confidence. "We're done. Do not call me again, and stop texting me. I'm not yours. I never was. I know my worth now." I shot an appreciative smile over my shoulder. "And you don't deserve any part of me."

"After everything I did for you, you're ending it like this, with some asshole threatening to kill me? Are you really that pathetic?"

I chewed on my lip, debating my response. Clearly, he wasn't understanding this.

"It doesn't matter what you think of me anymore. I don't believe your lies, and I will never, ever go back to the woman I was with you. Move on to your next casualty, Brian, because I'm done being your victim."

After hitting the red dot to end the call, I tossed the phone away. It clattered to the table.

Several long seconds passed with not a single word spoken. Slowly, the squad room's background noise picked back up with the free drama show done. Groaning into my hands, I debated the probability of sneaking out with no one noticing to worry about all this in peace.

A loud slam and rattle startled me, and I snapped my face up, heart racing.

Bryson's palms were still sealed on the edge of the table. "It's Friday, we made headway on the case, and I need a fucking drink." He stood, stretching his long arms high over his head. A few of the female officers turned their attention to watch, appreciation in their eyes. "Let's go."

I flicked my wrist, bringing my watch to life. "It's only three," I countered.

"Nah, your watch is still on DC time," he said with a smirk as he grabbed his jacket off the back of the chair. "Last one there buys the first round, and I'll warn you, I'm no cheap date. I like expensive IPA stuff."

"Figured you for a Guinness guy," Charlie said, clearly on board with leaving since he was shoving folders and his laptop into his backpack.

"Had enough of that stuff undercover." He pounded a fist against his chest. "Shit gives me heartburn now. Getting old sucks."

"So that was true?" I asked as I followed suit and began stuffing all the files scattered across the table into the side of my laptop bag.

"Worst three years of my life." Draping an arm across my shoulders, he guided me toward the elevator. "I'll tell you more about it over that drink you're about to buy me."

I glanced over my shoulder, finding Charlie a step behind, a small smile tugging at his lips.

Leaning toward Bryson, I whispered conspiringly. "Let's both win and make Charlie buy."

Bryson's smile grew, making him look younger than that angry, growly man who threatened my ex only moments earlier. "Sounds good, Agent Riggs. Though I highly doubt that man would've let you pay for anything anyway." He pushed a thick knuckle against the down arrow, calling the elevator.

"Damn straight," Charlie said behind us. "Unlike some of us, *Bryson*," he emphasized with a fake cough, "I was taught to always treat a lady."

"But," I dragged out, "what if that lady has a higher daily per diem than the both of you?" I turned, finding them exchanging a look.

"You're buying," they said in unison.

As I stepped into the elevator, my cheeks hurt from the wide smile that wouldn't fade. It was clear what they were doing, making me forget about that horrible phone call. And it was working. The two continued to exchange jabs back and forth as the elevator descended to the street level. Inhaling deep, I savored the lightness in my chest with the weight of Brian's potential calls and texts gone.

Free.

I felt free.

And I knew exactly what to do with that freedom.

I could finally let the real Rhyan Riggs take the reins. Would I still be an anxious mess? Probably, but a confident anxious mess.

Pulling out my phone, I typed a quick text to Olivia.

Me: Brian called. Another agent threatened his life. I told Brian we were over and hung up on him.

Me: And I feel good. Fantastic even. Wish you were close to celebrate.

Olivia: Please tell me you plan to celebrate by riding my backup husband, Charlie.

Me: Stop it. He is not your backup for anything.

Olivia: Is too. But I'll let you use him until I'm ready for him.

Me: You're nuts.

Olivia: No, you are if you don't scrape those cobwebs out of your lady bits with his dick.

Olivia: You said earlier that last night was amazing.

Olivia: Plus, you already shaved.

Me: We haven't even had the talk.

Olivia: Oh hell, sweet, sweet girl. This isn't high school. It's more of an in-the-moment agreement and quick prayer he has a condom handy. It's not a bullet-point slide show on your respective sexual history.

Me: It wasn't bullet-pointed...

Olivia: Liar.

Smiling at my phone, I hold back a laugh as we descend the few concrete steps to the sidewalk, Charlie's palm pressed on my lower back, guiding me toward our destination and moving me out of the way of pedestrians since I clearly wasn't watching where I was going.

"What are you smiling about?" Charlie asked.

"Olivia," I said, hitting the Home button to make the screen go blank.

"Oh, tell her I said hey."

His phone dinged in his jacket pocket. Pulling it out, he held out the screen. I jumped at the loud, booming laugh that erupted from him. His shoulder trembled against my own. "Seriously, your girl wants me to use my dick like a chimney sweep?"

"Oh fucking hell." I groaned and smacked the heel of my hand to my forehead. Pulling off my glasses, I rubbed at my eyes. "I'm going to kill her."

"And what's this about a presentation later?"

"Bryson, can you send some of your hooligan friends to my best friend's house in Seattle to forcefully remove her phone from her person?"

"Ah, come on." Charlie chuckled and snuck a hand around my waist, sealing my side to his. Pressing his lips into my hair, he whispered, "Will this presentation be done in the nude? If so, I suggest extending the meeting time and planning a hands-on demonstration."

"You're the worst," I said, shoving him off. Smiling, I walked through the door of a shady dive bar that Bryson held open.

"Actually, I'm the best if you're looking for exact quotes from previous—"

I smacked an arm to the middle of his chest, cutting him off. Only a few patrons dotted the small area. Their eyes followed us as we weaved around the low, dark wood tables toward the bar.

"It looks shady as fuck," Bryson said over his shoulder, "but it's the only bar in town that doesn't charge ridiculous prices."

At the bar, Charlie pulled out the stool putting me between him and Bryson and patted the top. After ordering a round of drinks from the surly bartender with a beard down to his belly button—Bryson, an IPA; me, the fruitiest cocktail they made; and Charlie, whiskey on the rocks—we settled into easy conversation about life and work.

It didn't take long for it to become clear that Bryson was adorably obsessed with his two-year-old daughter in the best possible way. Though any time the topic of her mom came up, he clammed up.

After my second caramel apple martini, I let curiosity get the best of me. "So what happened between you and Victoria's mom?" I asked.

Bryson's face fell, and sadness wafted off him in waves. Fuck, I hated myself for asking. I was the reason he went from happy to devastated in a blink.

He stared into the mirror behind the bar. "My wife—"

"Wife?" Charlie said, clearly shocked at this revelation.

"My wife, Victoria's mom, died in a car accident." The urge to wrap him in a bear hug, to chase away the devastation in his voice, was strong. "We met when I was an agent in training. She was the psychologist assigned to gauge our mental health." His sad smile tore my heart right open. "The moment I walked into her office, I knew she was the one for me. We dated, secretly." He shifted his gaze in the mirror, arching a brow at Charlie. "Then got married after she left the FBI. We were happy for years, her working at a children's mental hospital in Dallas, me working my way up the ranks. Then we found out she was pregnant. She was so fucking happy, couldn't wait to be a mom.

"She'd just gone back to work after maternity leave when one of her teenage patients began obsessing over her. I told her to quit, that it wasn't safe. She said she'd handle it, and she did, but we still fought about it. Victoria was six months old when it happened. Heather, my wife, and I had gotten into a huge fight because she'd been called in for an emergency at work, leaving me at home with a screaming, sick baby. My last words to my wife, the woman I fucking adored, were said in anger. I don't know if I'll ever—"

Maybe it was the alcohol or the agony in his voice, but I couldn't hold back a second longer. Leaning over, I wrapped my arms around his side and squeezed.

"I'm so sorry," I said, resting my head on his shoulder. "Whatever you said, she knew you didn't mean it. You guys say a lot of dumb shit when you're trying to be protective of the women in your lives. She knew that, I know."

"Hey," Charlie said as he peeled me off Bryson's side. "Stop hogging my girl."

"Your girl?" I said, spinning the stool to put Bryson at my back. I straddled Charlie's stool, one knee on each side.

"Do you disagree?" he asked, brow raised in question or challenge. I swallowed hard. At the slow shake of my head, he grinned. "Good." Sliding the open laptop along the bar, he positioned our glasses far away from his precious. "Now. Rhyan Riggs, are you ready to set up your cheater profile and lure out a sick fuck?"

"Yes, please," I said with an enthusiastic clap. "And just so you know, I agree with you on the risks. There are so many things that could go wrong. Believe me, I know. I've run through them all. The worst scenario ends up with the unsub chasing me down the stairwell, me falling and breaking my ankle, then being forced to watch, unable to escape, as he approaches with the needle of death in his hand. Or him taking me to the bridge and pushing me over, sending me plunging to my death." I wave off both their gaping looks. "Don't worry, I have a plan for that one. I'm a really excellent swimmer. It's the only beneficial side effect of anxiety—you're always prepared."

"What the...?" Bryson stammered. "Then why—"

"Because this could be our chance to wrap up the case before we have to head back to DC," I stated.

"I'm regretting my decision to support this idea," Bryson grumbled into his nearly empty pint glass.

"Too late. I know you guys will have my back." I pointed at the glowing screen, snarling at the picture of a black-painted door with a bold "Do not disturb" sign dangling from the handle. "What picture should we use for my profile?"

18

CHARLIE

There was a cool dampness in the air by the time the three of us walked out of the now-packed bar. Night had yet to completely blanket the sky in darkness. Pinks and oranges lingered, faintly coloring the horizon with what remained of the day's light. With Rhyan secured between us, we lazily walked along the busy sidewalk toward the station where our cars waited in the parking garage. Thankfully, we'd all slowed our drinking hours ago and each devoured heavy meals, even Rhyan, which made me happier than it should have.

The other two talked, joking about one of Rhyan's random fun facts, while I savored the normalcy of the moment. I glanced to the side, watching as she tossed her head back in laughter. The earlier phone call made a distinct difference in her demeanor—that and the bit of alcohol. She seemed lighter somehow, free of whatever weight had clung to her from that dipshit ex of hers.

Before I was ready for the peace of the walk to end, we were at the station's front steps.

Sighing, Rhyan looked at the doors and adjusted the strap of her laptop bag, which she refused to let me carry. "This was fun, guys. Thank you."

"For what?" Bryson said with a smirk around the toothpick he'd snagged from the bar on the way out.

"I know what you two were doing, offering a distraction from earlier."

"We got some good work done too," I added. "It only took us a few hours to make the most serial killer–friendly profile for you."

She laughed and shoved at my arm. I moved sideways, conceding a step. "That's because you kept adding all those qualities that I absolutely do not have."

I crossed my arms. "Like what?"

Rhyan chewed on her lip, eyes darting along the sidewalk. Snapping her fingers, she pointed at my face. "Health food lover."

"Well, he had to list that one," Bryson said, rocking back on his heels. "No one would believe the shit you eat and still look like that."

"Like what?" she snipped, clearly not happy with us pointing out her unhealthy food choices for every damn meal.

Bryson looked at me with raised brows.

"Good enough to eat," I fill in for him.

Bryson barked out a boisterous laugh, covering his open mouth with a loose fist.

"Holy hell, you two are killing me with all this." He motioned between me and Rhyan. "Tension. I'm headed home. Good night. And don't do anything—"

"You wouldn't do," I finished for him and waved him off. "See you tomorrow."

"Hopefully we'll have a hit or two on my profile for us to consider as viable options in the morning," Rhyan said, optimism brightening her voice.

Bryson and I exchanged a knowing expression.

"Pretty sure you'll be shocked by the number of responses you get," I grumbled under my breath.

With another goodbye and a hard slap to my back, Bryson jogged up the steps. Rhyan watched with brows dipped as he disappeared through the glass door. A worm of jealousy snuck in, only to be squashed with her next words.

Chapter 18

"He's so sad," she said, catching me completely off guard. I just assumed she was staring at his ass like I did hers when she walked away. "I don't like seeing people like him, good people, sad."

"He's got a lot on his plate. Single dad, working a tough-as-hell, demanding job, and still mourning his wife. Though, I think he's on his way out of it, you know. He seemed happy with us tonight."

Her green eyes found mine, flicking between one eye and the other. "Do you think he'll ever be whole again? I can't imagine losing someone you'd spent so many years with, having a child together, and then one day they didn't come home."

"I think... someone like him can move on. He just has to find the right person who makes him take that step. I'm sure that's hard with a baby added to the equation. Dating is hard enough without one."

Her eyes narrowed. "This is getting really deep."

With a soft chuckle, I tossed an arm over her shoulders and turned us to face the direction of the hotel instead of the station doors. The beautiful evening begged me to walk back to the hotel, to cherish these last couple nights with Rhyan all to myself.

"What do you say about a little nighttime stroll instead of driving back?"

She tilted her face up to the cloudy sky and closed her eyes. "That would be great. I love this kind of spring weather. A bit of chill but not cold. It's eerie almost."

I searched the sky. "Yeah, looks like it might rain tomorrow. Maybe bring in actual spring weather for this city." I urged her forward, and we started toward the hotel. "Have you thought about what you'll wear if we do set a date with the potential unsub?"

She shrugged, moving my arm up and down with the slight movement. "Not really. I mean, I didn't pack any dresses, but I'm sure one of my suits would work."

"For a date?"

"Well, yeah. It's what I have."

I shook my head as we crossed the street. "If we get a hit that seems like our guy, then we'll have to figure something out. Don't get me wrong, you look sexy as hell in those suits, but they don't really say 'stepping out on my husband for a one-night stand.'"

She bumped her hip against mine. "Oh really? What does?"

"A little black or red dress."

Her petite nose scrunched. I had the sudden urge to kiss the tip like some lovesick fool. "Does that mean makeup too?" I nodded. "That will need to be on the shopping list too. I didn't bring any. Well, except for an expired tube of mascara that I can't seem to throw away since it still has some gunk in it."

Lowering my arm, I reached between us and interlaced our fingers. Maybe I was a lovesick fool, based on the soft sigh that escaped when her fingers tightened around my own. My emotions were moving fast, but at the same time, not fast enough. How I already felt so much for this woman was unusual, but I saw the signs and knew without any doubt I was falling for Rhyan Riggs. What that meant for when we returned to DC, I wasn't sure. But I sure as hell wouldn't waste our time together now worrying about it.

"You don't need it," I said after a few beats of silence, both of us lost in thought. "Your fair skin, paired with those green eyes and golden red hair, is enough to draw attention of every man and woman in the room."

As we passed under a streetlamp, I noticed the blush staining her cheeks. Tucking a lock of that beautiful hair that had slipped from her high ponytail behind her ear, she glanced up, catching me watching her.

"Thanks. Truth is, I never really got into all the makeup and girly stuff. Where I grew up in Kansas, it wasn't needed. None of the other girls did because you helped on the farm before school and after if you didn't play sports."

"Did you?" I asked, tugging her to the side to avoid a man in a suit paying attention to his phone instead of where he was going. I took a threatening step toward him for putting her in danger, but Rhyan pulled me back with a tug to my hand.

"Did I do what?"

"Play sports?"

She shot me a challenging glance. "You tell me, Mr. Profiler."

"Hmm." Pausing, I stepped back, stroking my chin as I gave her a slow once-over. "Track, for sure. You'd make an excellent runner with those long legs of yours." With a single finger, I gestured for her to turn. "And with your height, I'd say volleyball too. And cross-country."

A wide smile grew, making her cheeks bunch and eyes squint behind her glasses. "Hurdles in track, center for volleyball, and terrible at cross-country. I was always last."

"Why?"

"Because I hate running. But you forgot one: swimming. I only did one event, the 500-meter freestyle. I wasn't that great at that either, but it got me out of doing chores at home." Stepping off the curb, we crossed the street, me holding up a hand when a car tried to go before we were safely on the sidewalk once again. "What about you? Did sports fit in between all your international hacking and espionage?"

"Espionage is a stretch." We both reached for the door handle, but I swatted her hand away. Pulling the glass door open wide, I urged her inside with a hand on her lower back. The same one that wanted to slip just a little lower and grab a handful of that ass that had teased me all day in her tailor-fit slacks. "But no, no sports for me. Just computers, school, and hanging out with my hacker friends."

We didn't say another word, our shoes clicking along the tile floor of the hotel as we made our way to the elevators. Tension mounted between us, a live crackling energy as we waited side by side. All the built-up need from the day was set to explode if I didn't get my hands on her in the next thirty seconds. I needed to kiss her, touch her soft creamy skin like I needed my next breath to live.

The moment the elevator door closed, sealing us alone inside, I turned and prowled toward her, herding her into the corner. Red flushed her cheeks, her breasts pushed against the snug buttons of her dress shirt. With a tortured groan, I surged forward, sealing our lips together in a demanding kiss. The stress from the day faded instantly. Now all that mattered was that she was back in my arms.

Pulling back, I kept my lips a hairbreadth away, brushing against hers as I spoke.

"I've wanted to do that all fucking day."

"Is that all you've wanted to do?" she asked, her quick breaths fanning across my face.

"Do you want it to be all?"

The second the elevator dinged, I shoved off the smooth metal wall and hit the button for the highest floor. Turning back, I caged her in between my forearms, pressing against the elevator wall on either side of her head.

I watched her chest rise and fall in quick succession, her full tits desperate to come out and play. With nimble fingers, I unfastened the top button, then the next, until the full line of her beautiful cleavage was on display. With the tip of my middle finger, I traced the exposed curves of her breasts.

"Answer me, baby," I whispered in her ear before nipping at the lobe. "Do you want to hear how every time you bent over, all I could think about was that fine ass of yours up in the air while you deep-throated my cock? Or how every second I wasn't touching you was pure torture? Maybe you want to know all the dirty fantasies I created throughout the day of what I wanted to do to you tonight. Taking my time, making you scream my name with me so deep inside you'll feel me for weeks."

"Yes," she whimpered, visibly shaking with need beneath me. "Yes to all of it."

"Thank fuck." Reaching out, I hit the button for our floor once again and stepped to the middle of the elevator, shoving my hands into the pockets of my slacks. Seeing her flushed, painfully aroused, with her top scandalously unbuttoned had my dick throbbing against the zipper, ready to fulfill everything I just described.

"I'm not.... I want to, but I'm not on birth control." Her cheeks flooded a darker shade of red, turning to more embarrassment than the dusty pink of arousal. "Do you have a... anything?" She grimaced at the end.

Her innocence involving anything remotely tied to sex was cute.

Chapter 18

Putting her out of her misery, I smiled and nodded.

"All you have to worry about, Rhyan, is if this is something you really want." I watched as she chewed on the corner of her lip, processing my words. "If you say you're not ready, then I eat you all night like last night, and we fall asleep together again."

"You wouldn't be disappointed?"

My smile fell. "Fuck no. I still get to be with you, sleep next to you. Why in the hell would I be disappointed?"

"Because I'm being a prude," she mumbled under her breath.

In two steps, I was back in front of her, our bodies sealed together. I shuffled back to keep from grinding my hard length against her. "You're making the right choice for you, at your pace. What you do with your body does not, under any circumstance, make you a prude. Just like if you wanted to sleep with every guy who crosses your path wouldn't make you a slut. It's your body, your decision. No one else's."

I left out that I'd beat the shit out of anyone who touched her while she was mine until the day she realized she was too good for me and walked away.

My heart stuttered at that reminder. She would go at some point, leaving me behind, desperate for more of her in my life.

The slow of the elevator snapped me out of my dark inner thoughts. I had her off the wall, her hand wrapped in mine and our bags in the other, moving toward the door a second before it whooshed open. Her long legs kept up with my quick, determined pace with ease. She squeaked in surprise, slamming into my back when I came to an abrupt stop in front of her door instead of mine.

The flimsy key card wobbled in her shaking hands as she held it up to the scanner. I released her hand, her fingers slipping from mine when she stepped inside, not following.

"I won't rush this," I said, leaning against the doorframe, the picture of casual despite the overwhelming urge coursing through me to rip her clothes from her body and toss her on the bed. "We have time, baby. If you say wait, then we wait. I follow your lead."

One hand on the edge of the door, keeping it open, she used the other to pop open another button on her shirt, revealing the bottom of her sheer black bra. Yanking the ends of the shirt out of her slacks, she worked her way down until it hung open. I licked my lips at the small gap, revealing a creamy, firm stomach and a glimpse of her tits.

The sound of voices and a door shutting snapped my attention down the hall. A young couple stared at me, eyes wide, like they expected me to rob them or something.

Fucking tattoo stereotypes.

Without a word, I stepped closer, Rhyan retreating farther into the room. The door vibrated at my back; I needed the distance to not grab her and finish the job myself.

I tossed our laptop bags to the floor. Well, tossed hers, hoping to break the beast, and gently set mine down like one would a newborn. "Keep going," I commanded, rolling the smooth metal ball along my lower lip.

She hitched her chin toward me in a silent command for me to follow her lead. Her blazing green eyes tracked my fingers as I worked each button down my shirt.

"I love the tattoos on your hands," she said, shrugging off her shirt. It pooled around her black pumps.

"You should see the ones on my fingers disappear into your pussy when I finger-fuck you. It's erotic as fuck. Maybe next time I'll get a mirror."

Her lids fluttered closed, and a fresh rush of red rose along her fair chest. Reaching back, she unclasped her black lace bra and pulled the straps along her arms. My fingers dug for traction along the smooth wooden door to keep me from reaching out to palm her perfect breasts.

Tit for tat, I fisted the middle of my white undershirt and ripped it over my head, tossing it onto the pile of discarded clothes. Next came her belt and mine, both of us working in sync, stripping slowly as we visually devoured every newly exposed inch of skin of the other's body.

Those black pants that teased me all day puddled around her ankles. Careful to keep her balance, she stepped out of her heels and kicked off the pants and black lace panties. Using my toes, I flung off

Chapter 18

one shoe, then the other, pulling my pants and briefs down, taking my socks off with the smooth movement.

We stared, chests rising and falling, the scent of desire filling the air. I licked my lips, desperate to suck and bite her peaked nipples and press my face between her thighs.

"Take your hair down." A groan rumbled from my chest when her beautiful hair cascaded down around her fair, slim shoulders. "Now crawl on the bed, baby, with that perfect ass toward me."

With zero hesitation, she obeyed, her tits bouncing with each step. Gripping my throbbing dick, I squeezed until my knuckles popped as she crawled on the bed, that round ass begging for a bright red handprint.

Waves of red hair shifted when she snuck a glance behind her. And what a fucking sight it was with her fuckable lips parted, innocent eyes wide, practically begging for my cock.

I kept one hand wrapped around my eager dick, caressing her ass cheeks with the other. Pressing firm, I ran the heel of my palm up her spine, making her arch, shoving that ass higher. Her desperate moan filled the room.

Pumping my hand, I pinched my swollen head at the same time I trailed a single finger between her cheeks, caressing over her tight hole, only lingering for a moment. My interest piqued when she didn't shy away from the touch.

"Have you ever played back here, baby?"

I swear her entire body flushed crimson.

"No," she whispered. "But I've wanted to."

"Good girl. Such a good, innocent girl," I purred as I dipped my hand lower into her drenched center. Without warning, I thrust three fingers into her tight pussy, my hand tightening when she squeezed around my digits.

"Fuck," I said, leaning closer to plant one kiss on each cheek. "You smell fucking amazing. I can't wait to bury my cock inside you, feel you stretch around me." I released my dick to smack a palm hard across her ass while I pinched her swollen clit at the same time. Her back arched, head falling forward. Soft begs for more filled the room.

Fucking gladly.

Reaching back, my palm sailed through the air before spanking the other cheek, then went back to the first, smacking right where my reddening handprint was already forming. With a quiet whimper, she thrust back, pushing my fingers deeper.

Palming her now flaming ass, I squeezed a tight handful. "What do you want, baby? You're in charge."

Well, kind of. I smirked to myself. Once she laid down her limits, then I would be back in the driver seat. I knew I could open her eyes to how amazing fucking could be with the right partner and mutual trust.

"You," she said with a moan. Sliding her knees wider, she opened herself up more for me. "I want it all. All of you."

I almost exploded all over her ass. Groaning, I pulled away to retrieve a condom from my wallet. Ripping it open, I took my time rolling the rubber down, loving the way she peeked over the rim of her cockeyed glasses to watch.

Behind her once again, I curled over her back, sealing our bodies together, my cock bobbing between us. Knocking her knees wider with my own, I positioned myself between her slick slit and rolled my hips, easily sliding up to hit her swollen nub.

An evil chuckle vibrated my chest at her pitiful whimper. Reaching around, I palmed her tit, pinching and twisting her hard nipple until those whimpers turned to curses.

"Charlie," she begged. "Please."

"Please what, baby?" Giving each nipple a hard tug, I nipped at her shoulder hard enough to leave small indentions.

"Fuck me, please," she cried. "I need it. I need you, please." Her words ended on a sob.

Pulling back, I positioned myself just outside her entrance and pushed in an inch. Groaning against her skin, I fought the urge to shove all the way in, to feel her tight pussy strangle my dick. Knees on the bed, I peeled myself off her back and gripped her hips, holding her steady to push deeper.

My jaw ached from how tight I clenched my teeth, thigh muscles

Chapter 18

trembling with restraint as I slowly pushed forward until I was fully seated inside her. Flexing my fingers, I adjusted my grip to keep from holding on too tight and leaving marks. The bed squeaked as I rocked back and forth, pulsing small strokes along her sensitive walls.

"Harder," she cried and thrust her hips backward. I cursed under my breath to keep from coming that instant.

Stroking loving fingers up her back, I wrapped her golden red hair around my fist and tugged. Her back arched, face tipped to the ceiling. I stared at her parted lips and hooded eyes.

"As you wish, baby. Hold on." I watched with wicked delight as she gathered the comforter beneath her curled fingers to do as instructed.

Pulling out to the swollen head, I waited for her to relax before slamming home. The bed knocked against the wall as I tightened my grip on her hair, letting it slip between my fingers as I repeated the demanding thrusts. Sweat covered every inch of our skin, beads gathering along my spine and slowly sliding down. Rhyan's sweet moans, my grunts, and the slap of our skin flooded the room.

Squeezing my eyes shut, I focused on the places that made her clench around me, hitting them harder with each thrust. At the first quiver, I quickened my pace, knowing she was close, which was good because I was half a second from exploding. With a strangled cry, she slammed her hips backward, shoving me deeper and strangling my dick with her sweet pussy as she convulsed.

Reaching between her thighs, I flicked her swollen clit, making her cry out again, this time more of a sob as she fell into her second orgasm. My finger slick with her release, I delicately caressed her tight hole. Intense heat shot through me when she moved back, urging the tip of my finger inside.

"Dirty girl. My dirty, beautiful girl," I praised. Releasing her hair, I pressed on her swollen bundle of nerves and drew slow, teasing circles. "One more, baby." My balls slapped against her ass as I slammed into her. "Come with me, baby. I'm so fucking close," I said through clenched teeth, desperately trying to hold off until I could feel her tighten around me again.

"Fuck," she cried. Her arms gave out, sending her face-first to the white comforter.

With a curse of my own, I slammed in as deep as possible, my muscles tensing and releasing as I tipped over into bliss. Falling forward, I covered her, catching some of my weight to keep us from collapsing onto the bed.

"Holy hell." Her words were muffled, lips smooshed into the bedding.

My thoughts exactly.

Even completely blissed out, a nagging thought wormed its way inside.

Now that I've had her, how in the hell will I ever let her go?

19

RHYAN

It was either the rain pelting the window, the occasional rumble of thunder vibrating through the hotel room, or my always-active mind that drew me from a deep, sated sleep. Groggy from too little sleep, I rolled to my side, slipping out of Charlie's arm around my waist to check the time.

Four in the morning.

Sighing through my nose, I wiggled against the cheap sheets and blinked into the dark, staring at the ceiling as thoughts of Charlie and the case bombarded my now very awake brain. Gaining another couple hours of sleep was no longer in the cards, it seemed.

My hair slid along the pillowcase as I turned toward the side table where my phone and glasses rested. I could check if there were hits on the profile we made, but that didn't seem right, flipping through men interested in hooking up with me—even if it wasn't real on my end—with Charlie sleeping beside me.

Rolling my head in the opposite direction, I stared at Charlie's blurry profile. Gone were the faint wrinkles that almost always lined his brow. The lips normally pulled in a cocky smirk were slightly parted, jaw soft. A few locks of longer dark hair covered one eye and his forehead.

Without thinking, I reached out, fingers faintly brushing his forehead to clear the view of his full face. The silky strands slipped along my skin, falling right back across his face. Running two fingers through his amazing hair, I smiled into the dark.

Last night was beyond incredible. From the fun we had at the bar, the simple conversation on the walk home, and, of course, everything that happened after in my hotel room. Charlie was like my missing puzzle piece, pairing with my quirks perfectly. Even though I'd only had a handful of insignificant relationships, my gut told me this was different—a whole new level of intimacy that had nothing to do with the amazing sex.

Sure, *that* was incredible. I did not know sex could be that… explosive. But with Charlie, it felt right. I felt free because of trust. I loved the way he focused on me first, never putting his own pleasure above mine, unlike—

No, I would not ruin this peaceful moment thinking about Brian.

With a single finger along the column of his neck, I traced along a black ink design covering his exposed shoulder. How could this anomaly of a man even exist? Physically perfect, an amazing personality, and smart as hell? It didn't seem real, but he was. There hadn't been a single hint of deception from him since he picked me up in front of my apartment a few days ago.

A few days ago.

How did I go from a secret crush, daydreaming about him from across the room, to sleeping beside him and never wanting to let him go?

My fingers continued to explore down his arm, memorizing every curve and dip of muscle along his bicep.

What would happen when we got home? Would he want us to part ways, be fuck buddies, never see me again? Any of those options would shatter the part of my heart that had been repaired because of him. But if that was what he wanted, then I wouldn't cling to him. I'd have to let him go.

Tears filled my eyes, a single drop escaping the corner and dripping onto the pillow.

Chapter 19

He was sneaky, burrowing his way into my heart with his easy smiles, jokes, and encouragement. I wouldn't change a thing, even if this wasn't a long-term thing for him. He changed me these last few days, in the best way possible. Sure, I was still an anxious ball of energy, worked too much, and struggled with confidence away from being Agent Riggs, but I was better. A thousand times better than that woman who stood waiting for him at my apartment thirty minutes early, with anxiety running so high I almost made myself sick.

More smiles had bunched my cheeks, making them ache by the end of the day, in the past few days than the past few years combined. Usually Olivia drew me out of my head, pushing my past to the background for those glorious minutes we spent on the phone, and it seemed Charlie could do the same.

"Hey, baby." My fingers stilled at his low, raspy voice. His arm around my waist tightened, scooting me an inch closer against his naked body. A soft sigh brushed past my lips, that added physical touch calming a part of me. "Why are you awake?"

"Thinking," I whispered, going back to my exploring, this time mapping out the ink on his chest.

"I think that's a common thing for you. Want to talk about it?" Long black lashes fanned as he slowly blinked, turning on his side to face me. His brow furrowed at whatever he saw in my expression. The hand along my stomach slid upward to cup my face, swiping the trail of tears along my nose and cheek. "Why are you crying?" The mattress shifted, his elbow digging into the bed. His eyes searched mine as he hovered over me. "Fuck, are you regretting—"

Straining my neck, I lifted off the pillow, pressing a gentle kiss to his moving lips, cutting him off. I fell back, a soft puff releasing from the pillow as it cradled my head.

"Not that, for sure." I offered him a weak smile, chewing on the corner of my lower lip. With his hand still cupping my face, his thumb pulled my lip from between my teeth. "It's nothing."

"Obviously it's not nothing. Talk to me, Rhyan. That's the only way we'll work. I don't want you to worry. I'm your safe zone. You'll always know where you stand with me. All you have to do is ask."

Swallowing the lump of emotions in my throat, I nodded.

"Okay. I've been thinking about where we'll go from this. What will happen between us once we get back to reality?"

I searched his eyes in the dark, wishing I could turn on a light to read his features.

"What do you want to happen?" he asked, hesitation slowing his words.

"I don't know." Even in the dark, there was no missing his slight wince. "No, that's not what I mean." I grabbed at his side and squeezed. "I know what I want—you and me together. But technically I'm a senior agent, for one, and two, I don't want to hold you back if I'm not what you want long term. If you want this to be a fling—"

"Do *you* want this to be a fling?"

"No," I breathed, the single word barely audible. "Not at all."

He nodded, slipping his hand into my hair. Rolling to his back, he pulled me with him, tucking my face beneath his chin. Heat seeped from his bare skin, warming my cheek, his natural masculine scent a calming balm to my overactive thoughts.

"This is what I want. I'll lay it out there so you don't have to question or worry about where I stand. I like you, Rhyan, every quirky, beautiful part of you. I'd be a fool to not give everything to ensure this, what we have building, keeps heading down the path we're on. This isn't a fling for me, not even close. I'm not asking you to be my forever, but I would like the chance to figure out if that's where we're heading. I'm not ready to give up on the possibility of the most real thing I've had with someone."

Chewing on my lip, I twirled the end of my hair between two flicking fingers.

"So you want to date me?" I asked tentatively.

"I want anything you're willing to give. In my mind, you're my girl until you tell me otherwise. Whatever you need or want, that's what I'll do."

"Why?" I blurted.

"If you have to ask that question, you haven't been listening to me.

Chapter 19

You're amazing, Rhyan, all of you. Even if you told me to hit the road, to leave you alone, a part of me would always be yours."

Pulling away from his neck, I arched up to seal my lips to his, the only way I could convey the swell of emotions his words evoked. The scruff covering his jaw scraped beneath my palm when I cupped his face.

Despite the multiple rounds earlier, a throbbing ache bloomed in my lower belly, inching me closer to his naked body. Running a hand down my arm, to my thigh, he slid backward to grab a handful of my ass. A soft moan of approval tickled up my throat. Holding him in place, I deepened the kiss, desperate for more. His hand engulfing the width of my thigh, he hooked the leg over his hip, my damp center grinding against him.

"We need a condom," he murmured against my lips. "Hold on."

At my pitiful whimper, he patted my ass and rolled toward the nightstand, plucking the last foil packet off the top. While he ripped it open, I bravely reached beneath the tangle of sheet, wrapping my fingers around his already rock-hard length, squeezing hard like he'd shown me, a barked curse rattled through the quiet.

After he was covered, he rolled toward me and replaced my thigh, hooking it back over his hip.

"You're amazing, Rhyan Riggs," he said as he kissed down my neck. "No matter what happens in the future with us, know that's my fun fact about you."

Holding on to my shoulder, he rolled to his back, bringing me with him until I sat straddling his hips. With both hands, he reverently cradled my face, urging me lower until our lips touched.

His tongue slipped inside, teasing my own with the metal bar, reminding me of what it could do elsewhere. The sheets slipped beneath my knees as I lowered until my needy center pressed against his long cock. Back and forth I rocked, driving my need higher and higher while he held my face and devoured my mouth.

Lifting my hips, I grabbed his length and positioned him outside my entrance before slowly lowering. Charlie groaned into my mouth, his grip tightening around my face as if he were afraid I might disappear. Our breaths mingled as I raised and lowered, each time sinking a little deeper.

Up and up the pressure in my core wound, building with tingling tension. Chasing my release, I increased my pace, his hips slamming upward to meet mine. With a sharp nip to my lip, he pulled away to press his forehead against my own, inhaling ragged gulps of air. The temperature in the room spiked. Sweat coated my bare skin beneath the weight of the covers.

"I didn't know," I said, eyes squeezed shut, "that it could be amazing like this."

"It's you. Only with you. I'll never have enough."

"I'm close," I whimpered, riding him harder and faster, thigh muscles burning to push me over that edge.

His hands slipped over my shoulders, running along my spine to grip my hips in a bruising hold. With ease, he lifted me, taking on most of the work, and slamming me back down, meeting me halfway with his thrusts.

It was too much, the truths we expressed and the feel of him. I shot over the edge, crying out as spasms racked my spent body.

Gripping his shoulders, I dug my nails into his slick skin as I cursed in his ear. At the same time, he groaned his own release, thrusts turning erratic before finally slowing. Releasing my weight, I fell on top of him, his chest heaving me up and down with every labored breath. The smooth, comforting cadence, plus the soul-altering orgasm, had my lids drooping, suddenly too heavy to keep open.

I must have fallen asleep, plastered on top of him. He shifted me to the side, slowly rolling me off him and slipped out of the too warm bed.

Disappointment filled my stomach only for it all to vanish when the bed dipped again, the covers fluffing amazing cool air into the sheets, and a heavy arm wrapped around my waist. With a happy sigh, I sank deeper into the pillow and fell asleep once more—happy and calm.

Because of him.

Chapter 19

"Thanks for meeting me here," Bryson said behind the fist covering his wide yawn. Dark, puffy circles sat beneath his bloodshot hazel eyes. Beyond the opened pale blue door, the sound of cartoons and the scent of baby powder drifted out to the porch, where Charlie and I stood side by side.

"Of course. It is Saturday," I said as I stepped into his home, Charlie following. A tiny dirty-blonde head of curls popped over the side of the couch, wide innocent eyes tracking my every movement as we entered the living room area. "Is it okay to discuss this with your daughter here?" I gave her a tiny two-finger wave. Her returning wide smile had one blooming on my face.

"Yeah, when her cartoons are on, that's all she focuses on. But let's keep the gory details vague just in case." He scrubbed a hand down his face. "Vic was up all night, just wanting to hang out. I might be sleepwalking. You two want some coffee? I can start a new pot. I already finished what I made earlier."

"I can get some going for us all. Looks like you might need a few more cups too," Charlie said, pointing a finger toward the back of the house. "Kitchen that way?"

Bryson's features relaxed. "Yeah, through the living room. Thanks, brother."

I watched Charlie's fine ass flexing in his dark-wash jeans as he strode across the room.

"Oh hell, Rhyan. You've got it as bad as he does," Bryson said as he moved into the living room, rounded the couch, and fell onto the cushion next to his daughter. She giggled and squealed when he picked her up, tossing her a foot into the air, curls floating around her sweet, innocent face with each toss. "I wonder if I'll ever have that again."

Setting my bag down, I settled into a comfortable low-back leather chair. The living room was cute, not cluttered, but warm and inviting. "You'll find it again. If you've loved once, you can love again, right?"

He offered a sad smile in return. "Maybe. But I don't really try. I'm working or here with her. Being a working single dad is the toughest job I've ever had."

"Do you have help?"

"Thankfully, my late wife had good life insurance. I'm using that to help pay for a full-time nanny, but the one we've had for the past year just moved to New York. Her last day was yesterday." He set Victoria down on the couch beside him and tucked her against his side. "Now I have to add interviewing to my to-do list next week."

I studied the two for a minute. "I wish I could help."

His dark eyes met mine. "You are already. Seeing you two, hell, maybe it's what I need to see to remind me this isn't all that's out there. That I should try, you know, to find that light."

Charlie strode through the open archway, hands stuffed into his jeans pockets. He glanced between the three of us before plopping down beside Victoria.

Apparently, Charlie's charm worked on women of all ages. Wiggling out of her dad's hold, the little girl crawled across the couch and climbed onto Charlie's lap. Without a single beat of hesitation, he wrapped an arm around her tiny waist, pulling her against his chest.

Bryson's features morphed into a mix of humor and relief. Leaning forward, he grabbed the remote off the wooden coffee table and flicked the channel to a new show. The little girl squealed, babbling something, and shifted, getting more comfortable in Charlie's hold.

Not missing a beat, as if having a tiny squirming human in his lap was an everyday thing, Charlie began explaining to Bryson the hits on my profile, but I couldn't focus on anything other than the adorable scene. Charlie's knees popped up and down in a quick cadence while his fingers played with the tiny one desperate to explore him. A swell of unfamiliar emotions filled my chest, making me sad and happy all at once. Kids were always something I pictured in my life, but lately I'd started to think being a mother wasn't in my future after wasting so much time with Brian.

Chapter 19

"Right, Rhyan?"

I shook my head, reluctantly tearing my unfocused gaze away from where it slipped to the floor. I blinked at Bryson, confused, clearly missing a large part of their conversation.

"What?" I said, clearing my throat. The bubbling and gurgling of the coffee in the next room had me abruptly standing before Bryson could clarify. "I'll go get the coffee." Avoiding their curious gazes, I hurried across the small room for the kitchen.

I waited in front of the almost finished coffee machine, gripping the tiled counter edge. My thick ponytail slid over my shoulder as I tilted my head. Eyes sealed shut, I inhaled slowly, shoving down the bitter loneliness and regret seeing Charlie with that sweet baby stirred up. Now was not the time to sulk over my missed opportunities or what could've been. There was a killer to catch. Not the time to open the Pandora's box of emotions I kept locked down tight.

A soft touch to my shoulder had me gasping. Whirling around, I stumbled back against the counter. Heart racing, I gaped at the frowning Charlie, still holding a babbling and handsy Victoria.

"You okay?" he asked. A wince pinched his features, his head tilting to the side when a tiny hand pulled on a section of hair.

"Yeah, all good. Why would you think something's wrong?" Chewing on the corner of my lip, I turned back to the coffee maker to fill the three mugs lined along the counter. Maybe he wouldn't sense the lie if I had my back to him.

Yeah... that made perfect sense. Besides the fact that Charlie was a damn good profiler and knew avoidance was a major red flag that someone was lying or hiding something.

A hand snaked around my waist, inching me back until I pressed against his chest. His lips brushed against the shell of my ear. A shiver trembled across my shoulders and slid down my spine.

"I know you're lying. But if you're not ready to tell me what's bothering you, that's okay. When you are, just know I'm here and eager to listen. Even if it's about that idiot ex." A smile tugged at my lips, noting he'd cleaned up his normal name-calling for the tiny ears in the room. "Or about me, the case, anything. I want to know all of you, Rhyan. That includes whatever affected you in the living room."

"It's stupid," I whispered.

"I assure you it's not. But like I said, you tell me when you're ready. Just because I know every dip and curve of your body." His hand squeezed my hip for emphasis. "Know how you taste inside and out." Heat bloomed beneath my skin. "And care about you more than I have anything in a long time, that doesn't mean I've gained your trust. But just know when you're ready, I want all of you. Even the parts of your mind you think are best left silent and covered. Those are the parts I want the most, the ones you don't let anyone else see. I want to be that person for you. The one you trust with your soul, not just your beautiful body."

His warmth vanished, and the arm secured around me slipped away. A single tear escaped from the corner of one eye. For several seconds, I blinked at the dark liquid in the mugs, trying to make sense of his words and the jumbled mix of emotions he stirred up.

Once I was certain I had myself under control, I grabbed two mugs in one hand and one in the other and forced a fake smile as I made my way back to the two men and Victoria. I avoided their curious glances as I set two mugs on the coffee table. Their conversation picked back up, discussing various aspects of the case as I settled in the chair.

"So, lots of potential candidates, which we knew would happen. Rhyan?" I hummed into the mug, responding to Bryson, the steam fogging my glasses. I shot a middle finger to the chuckling Charlie. "Which one are you leaning toward?"

Cupping my palms around the hot ceramic, I leaned forward, resting both elbows atop my jean-clad thighs. "There are two, but the verbiage of one makes me lean more toward him. He made himself out to be the perfect candidate, stating he was good at anything the other person would want to try." Raising the mug, I took a sip, letting the warmth soak away the chill that settled over me after Charlie walked away. "He even has five stars for performance. His profile picture is what you'd think a real-life Ken doll would look like. He's the perfect lure for desperate, vulnerable, neglected women."

I dared a glance up and found Charlie frowning at the empty fireplace.

"He's not happy about it," I said to Bryson, with a small head tilt toward Charlie.

"Well, of course he's not," Bryson said with a humorless laugh. "No man wants the woman he loves in a dangerous situation."

The mug froze halfway to my lips. I blinked at Charlie, waiting for him to correct Bryson on his choice of words.

Love.

That was a big word.

Sure, I wanted him. The thought of saying goodbye made my heart ache and my stomach sick, and I'd somehow already started to expect him to always be a part of my life.

But that wasn't love.

Love came after years together. Love was fought for through give and take, fights and makeups. Infatuation, lust, attraction—all those things fit for me and Charlie, but love? That wasn't possible, not yet.

Right?

"He wanted to meet her tonight." Placing a kiss to the top of Victoria's head, Charlie set her on the couch and shoved off the armrest to stand. Pacing in front of the small fireplace, he raked a hand through his black hair. "It's another point in his corner to him being our unsub."

"Tonight," Bryson exclaimed. He frantically glanced around the room. "That's not enough time to get the needed surveillance equipment to monitor her, the manpower stationed outside the hotel, hell, a babysitter for Vic."

"We agree," I said. "That's why we pushed it to tomorrow night."

"Tomorrow night at nine," Charlie grumbled, now facing the wall. "I need everyone you can spare on this. From the local FBI office to the Louisville police force." Strained eyes found me when he turned. "Nothing can happen to her."

"It won't. We won't allow it. She'll be safe the entire time."

I concealed my grimace behind my mug, taking a long sip of coffee.

That was a lie. Bryson knew it. Charlie knew it. I knew it.

He couldn't promise my safety.

None of us could.

20

RHYAN

Shopping bags clutched in both his hands, I followed behind Charlie, ducking under the restaurant's awning to avoid the spitting rain. Moving the bags into one hand, he opened the glass door, waiting for me to walk inside first. Silverware clattering against plates, boisterous laughter, and delectable scents of freshly baked bread assaulted me the moment I stepped over the threshold. My stomach grumbled in response to the savory smells and yummy-looking dishes on other patrons' tables.

The young woman at the hostess stand didn't bother to glance up from her phone when we approached until Charlie cleared his throat, catching her attention. Her bored stare flared to interest when she swept an appreciative eye over him. He *did* look edible with his snug T-shirt that showed off both full tattoo sleeves and dark-wash jeans. Women had been gaping at him all day, much to my chagrin.

With more seduction than kindness, the hostess batted her lashes, voice purring when she asked how she could be of service.

No lie.

Of service.

I rolled my eyes and stepped between Charlie and the woman, blocking her view and forcing her attention on me. A deep chuckle sounded at my back before two fingers snuck around my shoulder at the same time he requested a booth. Leaning to get a different angle to see him, the hostess grabbed two menus and rolls of silverware, nearly running into the wall when she turned to guide us into the restaurant.

Annoyance mixed with jealousy churned in my gut as we followed her sashaying ass toward our table. I glanced over my shoulder, expecting Charlie's eyes to be on her perky backside, but found them on mine instead. Knowing he was caught, he shot me a wink and flicked that tongue ring of his. Biting my lip, I turned back just in time to narrowly miss running into another patron's chair.

Ever since we left Bryson's house earlier in the day, Charlie had been distracted. Some of it because of the various details we needed to coordinate to ensure tomorrow night went smoothly and safely, but for the most part, it felt like his dampened mood was from something else altogether.

At the booth, I scooted along the firm red leather bench seat, Charlie placing the bags down and shoving them toward the wall before sliding in to sit across from me. His smile was tight when the hostess lingered for several seconds longer than necessary. I shifted in the booth, avoiding the awkwardness that was blooming by grabbing the menu and pretending to read the words I couldn't seem to focus on.

What if he was regretting last night because today he was having to focus on me and not someone like the hostess? Especially after Bryson's false accusation that Charlie loved me. Maybe that was what had him distracted and withdrawn all day. He thought I took Bryson's words to heart. I sank deeper into the seat at that revelation.

"Whatever you're thinking, stop," Charlie said. I looked over the top of the menu, finding us alone, the creepy stalker nowhere in sight.

"You don't know what I'm thinking," I grumbled and laid the heavy menu down. Clasping my hands, I rested both on top of the table.

"You're working something up in that busy little head of yours because I haven't been myself all day." Pursing my lips, I refused to give him any sign of agreement. "You could always just ask me instead of creating worst-case scenarios."

Our server appeared at that moment, asking for our drink orders. Charlie ordered a double whiskey on the rocks, and I got a water. I'd just gotten rid of the slight headache from yesterday's sugary drinks; I didn't want another one tomorrow when I needed to be at the top of my game mentally and physically.

After he left, I searched the restaurant for anything to steer the conversation away from us. My eyes landed on the bags at Charlie's side.

"I'm glad I chose the simple black dress," I said, hoping he didn't catch on to my deflection. "It's pretty but still something I'll feel comfortable in. Plus, I already have shoes that will go with it." I caught his knowing grin out of the corner of my eye, but I kept plowing forward, completely okay with staying on the avoidance train. "The lady at the makeup place was super nice. I never thought about that shade of red for my lips. Always thought it would wash me out because of my hair color, you know?"

"No, I don't know." The humor in his tone stilled my busy fingers where they fiddled with the edge of the menu. "Rhyan, just ask me. I think my answer will surprise you."

I shook my head. "No, it won't. I know how this goes. You heard what Bryson said earlier, and now you're freaking out that I believed him. Now you'll pull away so I don't get too invested in this—"

My heart dropped into my stomach, the next words catching in my throat when he slid out of the booth. Blinking up to where he stood hovering over the end of the table like a beautiful fallen angel, I fought the urge to grab his hand and beg him not to go.

This was it. This was when he realized I was too much of a head case to be with.

The firm seat beneath me bounced, drawing my panicked focus to where he now sat beside me, scooting closer. Tossing an arm over the back of the booth, he reached across the table and slid his water glass to sit beside mine.

"Ask me."

"What are you doing?"

"Sitting beside the most beautiful woman in the restaurant so other fuckers in here know she's mine. Now if I could only convince her of that, my life would be much easier."

"I know you don't love me," I said in a rush. "I didn't put weight into what Bryson said."

"Is that what was bothering you?"

"Is that what was bothering you?" I questioned in return.

"You first."

Grumbling under my breath, I let my head fall forward, my glasses slipping down the bridge of my nose.

"You've been distracted," I offered with a shrug. "I just figured you were dwelling on his comment like I was."

His heavy arm dropped from the top of the booth to drape over my shoulders.

"Hey, look at me." When I shook my head, he pinched my chin between two fingers, forcing me to turn and face him head-on. "I have been distracted," he said, blue eyes looking between mine, "because tomorrow night, the one woman I'm quickly falling for is going on a date, not only with another man in a dress that nearly made my dick rip through my jeans from how hard it made me but a potential fucking serial killer. So yeah, I'm a little distracted. I've never had a personal interest in the agent going in undercover, and I'm not sure how to handle it. Everything tells me to demand you stay back and we find another agent to take your spot."

"But I know what to look—"

"But you know what to look for," he finished for me. "You're great at what you do, but that doesn't mean I have to like that. I'm putting you in harm's way. Just cut me some slack, okay? This is...." He looked toward the busy restaurant as if searching for the right words. "Uncharted territory. I'm not upset about what Bryson said. I'm completely engrossed in the details to ensure my girl goes to work tomorrow and makes it back to me at the end."

I opened my mouth to respond even though I had no clue what to say, but he kept me from stumbling over my words by pulling me forward for a quick kiss.

"Now," he said, moving back and dropping his hold on my chin before blindly reaching for the highball glass that appeared at some point during his captivating speech. "Let's talk about my expectations."

I watched his throat work as he sipped the light brown liquor.

"Expectations. Right. Okay, yeah… expectations for what again?"

He smiled, the smooth edge of the glass pressed to his lower lip.

"You will not put yourself in additional danger by doing something stupid."

I huffed and crossed my arms, faking annoyance. But in reality, I loved him taking a vested interest in my well-being. Sure, it was a little on the possessive side, but it was hot and made me feel valued.

"I'm not an idiot," I grumbled.

"If you think something feels off, you walk away." Something heated flared behind his blue eyes. "Do not push your limits beyond what you're comfortable with. At any time, you can tap out and we'll walk away from it all. You will stay in communication with us at all times." I nodded with a "Duh" look on my face. "You will wear a tracker—that is nonnegotiable—on your body and in your purse. And that dress you bought?" He leaned in closer, brushing his lips to mine. "I'll be the one to take it off you tomorrow night."

I nodded, eyes wide.

"Are we clear, Agent Riggs?"

"Crystal," I somehow got out despite my mind going haywire. "Don't be dumb, be safe, and you're my reward after for not getting hurt or dying."

"Exactly."

Wow.

The server walked up asking for our orders, breaking the intense moment. While Charlie ordered for us both, I held an unfocused stare on the clean white napkin draped across my lap, processing his words repeatedly.

Brian always offered a compliment with a degrading one immediately following, making me feel like I was never quite good enough for him, or anyone. And now here was Charlie, who made me feel... enough. More than enough, special and valued. He wanted to protect me yet wasn't holding me back.

"I'm enough," I whispered to myself, hoping if Charlie believed it and I said it out loud, maybe one day soon I'd believe it too.

"More than." Turning, I smiled at the man smirking down at me. "Just calling it like it is, baby. And just so you know, I won't stop until there's zero hint of hesitation or question in that statement."

"Okay. It might take a while, though."

His smile grew wider, cheeks bunching and fine lines bursting from the corners of both eyes. "That's fine, baby. I'm not going anywhere."

FEET TUCKED UNDER ME, I sat crammed in the small armchair in Charlie's room, staring at my notes on the case. Over and over, I read through my questions and subsequent answers, but it didn't feel right. There was something big I was missing, but what that important piece of the serial killer puzzle was, I had no idea.

Across from where I sat, the click clack of keys and frequent grumbles and curses made me smirk despite my rising frustration with the case. Chewing on the end of the pen I watched Charlie as he worked.

The parameters I provided yesterday to compile a basic list of suspects delivered too many names to efficiently search through. Add in the fact that the name of the person I was to meet tomorrow night was clearly made up, so not a single blip of information was found—legally, anyway, unless we got a warrant for the app's subscribers—and Charlie was beyond frustrated and headed toward pissed off.

"Do you think there's something off about the profile?" I asked, closely monitoring his face to read his reaction.

"Off how?" he tossed over his shoulder, never looking away from the laptop screen. "Too many fucking divorced men in this town," he grumbled.

"Did you add in the medical knowledge?"

"Yep. Added in everything, including EMTs and techs, plus the higher income bracket, but there are still a lot of names to filter through. I need more parameters besides what we've already profiled."

"I don't know what else to add," I admit. "But I guess it doesn't matter since everything is all set for tomorrow night."

"Tonight," he corrected.

I checked my watch. One in the morning. He was right.

My date with a serial killer is tonight.

I swallowed to push down the nerves, making my stomach queasy. "Right. Tonight."

"But if this guy isn't our unsub, then we'll still need this list. A more narrowed-down list, but still it'll make me feel better leaving Bryson with something tangible to use when we're gone."

My lips dipped into a frown. "I can't believe we have to leave."

And we did. The phone call from the section chief after dinner confirmed he still wanted us back in DC on Monday. That meant tomorrow—or today, rather—was our last chance to catch this guy.

Groaning at the ache building behind my eyes, I pulled off my glasses and rubbed at the bridge of my nose.

"Let's think about something else for a while. Maybe we'll have an epiphany or something."

"Good idea." Swiveling the chair around, he leaned back, interlacing his fingers behind his head. I knew what was coming before a single word exited his lips. He'd hinted around it all day, and now it seemed I just gave him an opening to ask. "What were you thinking about this morning? At Bryson's house?"

Turning, I looked beyond the water droplets dotting the window into the dark night sky.

"Do you want kids?" I shook my head, realizing how he might take that question. "Not now, not with me. I'm not asking you to knock me up. It's just... did you ever see yourself at this point in your life with a family?"

When his answer didn't come, I shifted back around to face him, finding his full attention locked on me.

"Yes."

I nodded. "Me too. Even with everything we see in the world, all the bad, I see the good too you know."

"So why haven't you?"

"Brian didn't want kids, and honestly, I knew deep down I would never want kids around that kind of toxic relationship. But now I feel like I've lost my chance. I wasted so much time in a relationship that would only be as deep as he allowed it. Seeing Bryson doing the single dad thing, watching that sweet little girl in your lap, just tugged on something." I pressed the heel of my palm to my chest. "Something I'd forgotten I wanted, and now I'm afraid it's too late or maybe not even in the cards because of the career I love."

"I want to be a foster dad."

"Want," I repeated, brows high on my forehead. "As in you've tried recently?"

He nodded. "But being a bachelor and with the travel, no agency will approve my application."

"I'm sorry," I whisper. "Because of the way you grew up?"

He shifted in his seat, rolling the chair closer. "I want to be a positive influence and support for a kid. The one adult they know is on their side. I want that child who feels alone even in a crowded high school to know they have somewhere they belong and are wanted."

"Charlie." My voice caught on the tears lodged in my throat.

"It could change the course of their lives. Just one positive influence. But finding someone who wants to do that with you, to take on the challenge of letting a teenager into your home only to repeat the process once they graduate and move on, is a fool's dream. It fucking sucks that as much as I want to be that person for someone, our government says that's not enough."

My feet tingled with the rush of blood when I placed them on the floor and launched myself across the small space between us.

Chapter 20

Surprise widened his eyes, but he recovered quickly enough to catch me and keep us from toppling backward.

"You're an incredible human being," I said against his neck. "The world would be a better place if there were more of you in it."

His muscular arms encircled my back, holding me tight against him. "But then we'd be out of a job," he teased.

"Totally worth it."

His hold didn't loosen, and neither did mine, both of us content holding the other. We stayed like that, locked together, long enough for the toll of the last few days to rush forward, stealing my last reserves of energy. My lids drifted shut, the feeling of comfort and safety calming my mind and soothing my nerves.

"We'll figure out a way to make this work," I heard him whisper in my hair as I drifted into that limbo between awake and asleep.

The world tilted, the fact that he was carrying me barely registering. A soft surface molded beneath my side and head. Forcing my eyes open to fight back the sudden sweep of exhaustion, I blinked up at Charlie.

He cupped my face, brushing his thumb along my cheekbone. "Now that I've found this, know that this kind of happy exists, I'm never letting you go."

"Good," I whispered before my lids fluttered closed, my calm mind floating easily into sleep.

21

CHARLIE

"And there's another." Rhyan pointed down the narrow alley that ran behind the hotel halfway down from where we stood.

"That's six blind spots," I said, my tense jaw making the words harsher than I intended. Tipping back the black umbrella, Rhyan studied me. "I don't like this one fucking bit."

Chewing on the corner of her lip, she turned back down the alley. "Yeah, you've said that a lot today." Stepping deeper into the alley, I followed closely behind her. "It is what it is, though. Everything is in place. How were we to know the outside of this place would be a security nightmare? We can only hope the inside is better."

Hope.

That word stoked my already blazing irritation at the situation. Without the warrant, we couldn't even get inside the hotel to be as close as possible. Instead, we were forced to be stuck outside, watching the numerous exits while Rhyan met with a potential serial killer.

"We need to call it off," I said through clenched teeth. "This isn't safe."

"It's fine," she snapped over her shoulder. "Stop making this personal. I'm a trained agent. We need a damn break in this case, and we created a situation to get it. End of story. You already put your conditions in place. Those will help keep me safe."

I swallowed down my irrational response. She was right. That didn't mean I had to like it, though.

For the last few hours, we'd walked in the steady drizzle, mapping out where we would need plain-clothed Louisville PD stationed while Bryson and I monitored the mic feed from a nondescript van parked along the street in front of the hotel. Rhyan shot down my offer to go in and monitor the situation from the bar. She said it would be too obvious and didn't want to risk spooking the unsub.

She was full of points that didn't fit my overprotective narrative.

Bryson rounded the brick corner, looking as frustrated as I felt.

"I caught one employee leaving. She said there's an employee entrance, plus the loading dock, kitchen entrance, and multiple other ways into the hotel for guests who would rather not be seen entering or leaving the establishment."

I pointed to Bryson and shot Rhyan a pointed look. "See?"

She rolled her eyes and walked away without looking back.

"I don't like it," Bryson said under his breath. "There are too many ways for this fucker to sneak her out right under our noses. We need more time to get a proper sting set up."

"We don't have time," I reminded him of what Rhyan had said multiple times today. "We leave tomorrow." Bryson started to argue, but I held up a hand. "She's right. We have to do this tonight. We only have a basic profile, one she thinks is still missing something, to leave you with. We need to take this one opportunity, no matter the risks. If it's not this guy, then maybe he's seen something in this sick circle that could lead us to the right guy. I don't enjoy being in this position, but it's one our section chief has put us in, unfortunately."

Bryson slipped his hands into the front pockets of his slacks and rocked back on his heels.

"You're thinking about this a lot more rationally than I would be."

Chapter 21

"I don't have a choice," I said, grimacing. "Agent Riggs is a hell of a force to go up against."

"Maybe you should just tie her to the bed," he said, tongue in cheek.

I tipped my face up to the mist, allowing it to soak my skin. "If I didn't think she'd fire my ass the second I untied her, I would." Wiping the dampness from my face, I groaned. "We'll do this right, the best way we can."

"We will."

"Nothing can go wrong."

"We'll be there for her." I nodded, agreeing with him. "And I'll be there for you." I tipped forward when his hand connected between my shoulders. "When you freak the fuck out in the van."

"When," not "if."

And damnit to hell if he wasn't fucking accurate about that.

I STARED at my interlaced fingers hovering between my spread knees. Everything was in place for the night's events; now all we had to do was set the sting in motion.

Shifting my attention, I eyed the closed bathroom door. Rhyan had been in there for over an hour now getting ready for her meeting—no way in hell would I call it a date. There was no doubt in my mind that she'd be a damn knockout all dolled up. Hell, she was without an ounce of makeup and her hair pulled back. My knuckles popped beneath my tightening grip, the anger at the whole situation riding me hard.

A squeak of hinges. I sucked in a breath, holding it as I made my way up her fantastic body. Even though I knew what to expect from being there when she bought the dress, I most definitely wasn't expecting my heart to lurch up my throat and my dick to swell at the sight of her in it tonight.

She was a goddess.

Golden red hair cascaded around her shoulders in soft waves, glasses gone, no longer hiding her brilliant green eyes that now popped from the dramatic eye makeup and bright red lips that highlighted her fair skin.

And then there was the dress that hugged her lean body, accentuating every soft curve and her trim waist. The deep V exposed the sides of her round breasts, just a teasing peek at the full mounds hidden beneath the black fabric.

Black heels made her long legs look sky high, reminding me of them wrapped around my waist, squeezing the air from my lungs as I pounded into her tight pussy.

"Charlie?"

"Hmm?" I said, unable to speak just yet. Fuck, she'd knocked me speechless with her beauty.

She smiled. "I asked, how do I look?" she said with a bit of laughter in her soft tone.

"Unpresentable for anyone to see but me," I said like a possessive caveman.

That easy smile fell. Her hands swiped down her hips.

Fuck. I said the wrong damn thing in jealousy.

"Come here." I crooked a finger until she stood between my spread knees. "I meant that as a compliment." With my thumb, I pulled her lip free from her teeth. "You're beautiful, too beautiful for me to want any other man out there to see. I'm a jealous asshole, I know, but doesn't change the fact that I want to keep you all to myself."

"So this is okay?"

I huffed and tugged her closer, pressing a kiss to her stomach. "You're perfection personified in every way, Rhyan Riggs. 'Okay' isn't even in the scope of words to describe how you look tonight."

The insistent need to take her before she left, to yank up that dress, rip off her panties, and pull her down on top of me, thrummed through my veins. My muscles quivered from my restraint.

"Okay." The shy smile that crept up her beautiful face squeezed my heart. How in the hell was I lucky enough to find myself here with her? "Everything all set on your end?"

"Yes. Bryson is waiting downstairs. That reminds me." I wheeled the chair back and stretched to grab the trackers. "This one goes on you."

She plucked the small device from my palm and held it high, inspecting each side. Features pinched in concentration, she dipped two fingers down the front of her dress, the tracker gone when she pulled them free. Cupping both breasts, she shifted them around, staring at her cleavage with the tip of her tongue caught between her teeth. Situated, she tugged at the dress's hem and held out a hand, palm up for the other tracker.

"That one," I said, tipping my hand over and depositing the device into her own, "goes in your purse. The one I'm currently jealous of"—I tapped a finger to where she hid the tracker, making her breast jiggle—"can never leave your person. Did you get the mic secured okay on your own?"

She nodded and pointed to the middle of her cleavage. "I connected it to the center of my bra. That should give you the clearest audio. Too bad we couldn't score a small camera because of the short notice."

My grip on her hip tightened, fingers digging into her soft flesh at the reminder. Bryson tried to locate a small enough camera that she could wear, giving us a visual of her every step, but the ones available were too big for tonight. Instead, I planned to do something my by-the-book girl wouldn't approve of.

I checked earlier in the day, and while the hotel's firewalls were decent, I was better. It would be easy to slip in undetected, hacking into their security feeds to give us a few options for watching over my girl. The short time we were in the hotel that day, I noticed several hidden cameras in the lobby; hopefully there would be some in the bar area where Rhyan planned to wait until the meeting time. It wasn't much, but still better than going in blind.

"Yeah, it's too bad, but we'll make it work." I stood and pulled her into a tight hold, sealing her front to my chest. "Promise me you'll be careful tonight."

"I promise I'll do everything by the book."

I believed her.

I just hoped it would be enough to keep her safe.

22

RHYAN

The heels of my stilettos clicked up the steps as I hurried toward The Black Rose's revolving doors, desperate to get out of the sudden downpour. Inside the elaborate lobby, cold air chilled my damp skin, causing goose bumps to sprout along my bare arms and legs.

There went my smooth legs.

Raking my fingers through my hair, I gave it a few shakes to dispel the water clinging to the strands.

"You good?" Charlie's voice shouted in my ear.

With a wince, I tugged at my earlobe to wiggle the earpiece loose. It stayed in better, deeper in my ear canal, but not only was it uncomfortable, the volume was unbearable. "Yes, if you'll stop yelling at me."

"This better?" he asked at a much more reasonable volume.

"Yes," I whispered. Smoothing my damp palms down the front of the dress, I inched the short hem back down my thighs. Taking a deep breath, I willed my nerves to settle. Curling my fingers into loose fists to stop their fidgeting, I surveyed the empty lobby.

There was a new sparkle to the room, somehow feeling more opulent. Or perhaps I saw it differently dressed like this instead of my normal smart suit. I loved my pantsuits, but the dress Charlie picked out was something special. The way he studied every inch of me when I stepped out of the hotel room's bathroom, like he wanted to devour me whole, made me thankful I listened to his wise advice to not wear the straitlaced agent outfit.

High above me, a massive crystal chandelier sparkled, shooting rainbows across the walls and ceiling from the soft light coming from the center. Ornate wallpaper covered the walls, and the white marble floors looked clean enough to eat off. Just like when Charlie and I found this place, the space was empty except me, though the heavy sensation of eyes watching me told me I wasn't really alone.

Pulling out my phone, I checked the messaging part of the app to see if my so-called date had reached out. Nothing since the last message instructing me to meet him at the hotel at nine, turn off my phone, and he'd get in touch regarding the room number.

It was only seven thirty.

The super earliness was all my fault. My need to be early was bad on a good day. Add in what rode on tonight, and I was eager to head toward the hotel at five this afternoon.

Early bird gets the serial killer.

That was what I told them when they questioned me about wanting to leave so early. They didn't find it nearly as funny as I did.

The click of my heels along the pristine floor sounded like a death toll. My fingers trembled, fumbling nervously with the latch on my clutch. I slipped my phone inside just as I stepped into the deserted bar. I slowed my steps to take in every detail.

Movement in my periphery. The bar wasn't as deserted as I initially thought. A bartender busied himself with drying glasses, keeping his eyes downcast as I approached the long bar. Setting my clutch down, I folded both hands on top of the lacquered top and smiled.

"Can I see a menu please?" I asked quietly, but my question seemed to echo in the large empty area. I winced and tucked my busy fingers beneath the bar top. Chewing on the corner of my lip, I checked over each shoulder as he placed a thick leather-bound booklet on the bar top.

"You should order champagne, the good stuff," Charlie said in my ear.

I rubbed the side of my head against my shoulder to quell the itch the vibrations caused. This, going undercover, was not my forte. Give me clues, evidence, and a murder board all day, every day over this. But what I was good at didn't work for this case, so this had to.

"And why champagne?" I muttered loud enough for the two listening in to hear.

"Because this is your one night out on the town. You're celebrating the upcoming fuck-fest—"

"Stop it," I said, laughing. When I caught the bartender staring like I was a crazy person, I covered the laugh with a cough. "But it sounds good." Pushing the book toward the bartender's side of the bar, I smiled. "Champagne. The good stuff."

"Atta girl. Spend the taxpayer money on the good shit."

"Lucky her," Bryson snarked. "She gets good booze, and we get McDonald's."

I groaned, my stomach rumbling. Casting a quick glance to the bartender I waited to respond until he was farther down the bar helping a newcomer. "That's my favorite. Did you get a drink, with their thick straws?"

"She likes everything thick," Charlie said.

"Hey-o."

"You two realize I'm listening in to all this, right? Not just when you're talking directly to me."

The other side of the line went silent. Apparently, they'd forgotten to press the mute button earlier.

Shaking my head, I shot a thank-you smile to the bartender, who had yet to meet my eyes. I supposed if you were doing something bad, aka meeting up with someone to cheat on your spouse, anonymity was great, but for me it felt dismissive, lonely even.

Tiny dancing bubbles exploded in my mouth, the crisp, dry liquid coating my tongue with flavors I didn't know existed in alcohol.

Taking another long swallow, I studied my reflection in the golden-veined mirrors behind the bar. There was a flush to my face I hadn't seen in my reflection in years and a sparkle in my eyes that I assumed was gone forever after years with Brian.

Happy. I looked happy. I wasn't even smiling, but there was a light in me that only truly happy people radiated.

Charlie did that to me. Made me this.

"Looks like you're about to have company," Charlie said cryptically.

"Thank... wait a second," I whispered into the champagne flute. Setting it on the bar, I swiveled around on the stool to scour the corners and molding for cameras. I spotted one farther down the bar, but its view of where I sat was clear. "You hacked into their system."

"Can't prove it." I chuckled at the cockiness in his tone. "We needed eyes on you as well as ears, so I made it happen. Nothing too illegal." I wanted him to emphasize on the *too* part, but just as he'd indicated, a presence drew closer, dragging my attention away from my hacker boyfriend.

Boyfriend.

Whoa.

That's a big step from... well, whatever we were on the drive to Louisville.

"You're either here very early or haven't left yet."

Turning back around to face the bar, I kept my smile pleasant as I turned to the woman now occupying the barstool beside me. Bright, warm eyes immediately put me at ease. Add in the calm smile and the nerves she'd initially incited fell away.

"Very early," I said with a deprecating huff. "Story of my life."

"Remember your cover," Bryson muttered in my ear.

The cover wasn't anything in-depth; I just needed to play up the fact that I was there to cheat on my husband. Which really sucked, making me feel all icky inside, even if it was a lie.

"Guess I'm excited," I tagged on after a long pause. "This is my first time doing this."

The woman nodded, her smile changing to something more

sympathetic and... optimistic, maybe making her appear less genuine and more haggard. The lines on her face were more pronounced, deep wrinkles fanning out from the corners of her eyes that hadn't been there before.

"Trouble at home?" she asked into her nearly empty highball glass before finishing the last few amber drops. She slid it across the bar and motioned for another. When she caught my calculating gaze, she lifted a shoulder. "Trouble at home brings us all here. Makes others look elsewhere for the passion or comfort they no longer get from their spouse."

I nodded but took a drink of champagne instead of responding.

"You don't look like the typical first-timer," she said, turning on the stool, fresh drink in her hand.

"What makes you say that?" I asked, now worried I wouldn't be able to pull this sting off after all. Shit, what if it was my dress? Too conservative maybe? Knew I should've gone for the more revealing one, but Charlie said it wouldn't cover the wire. Which was a lie, but I let him win that one. "Is it the dress?" I asked in a rush. Charlie and Bryson both whispered in my ear to calm down. "It's too conservative, isn't it?"

She reached out and rested her hand on my shoulder. "No, the dress is perfect. It's just you're too...." She leaned back to study me from the new angle. "Happy. Yeah, that's it. Most of the first-timers are more nervous than happy to be here."

"Oh, yeah, right," I stammered. Taking a drink, I gave myself a few seconds' reprieve to come up with a viable answer. Good thing I had a backlog of memories from a terrible relationship to shuffle through for inspiration. "I guess things have been so bad with my husband that the thought of sex outside the missionary position makes me happy. After feeling alone for so long in a committed relationship, I don't feel bad doing this if it will give me something to look forward to, you know? Yeah, it's"—I glanced around the bar, checking for listening ears, but found none—"technically cheating, but is it really when the other person isn't giving you what you need?"

"Should you be concerned that Rhyan just came up with a great backstory on the fly?" Bryson said.

"Fuck off, man," Charlie replied. "She's not talking about me. Isn't that right, baby?"

Knowing he could see me, all I could do was nod so the woman beside me didn't think I was a lunatic for talking to myself.

"Some see it as the victimless crime," she said, now staring into her drink like it held all the answers in the world. "But that's a lie they tell themselves. There are victims." I wanted to tell her that hell yes, there were victims, and a couple were in the Louisville morgue right now, but I bit my tongue. "The ones who didn't know they were failing in an area and thought things were fine only to one day find out they weren't."

Whoa, sounds like this woman hurt someone she still cares about with her affair-ing life.

Affair-ing. Can I turn the word into a verb by just adding an -ing?

Sure. It works in this case.

Pun intended.

"They should've laughed more," I said randomly.

"Excuse me?" my new, slightly drunk friend said.

"They've proven that laughter can lead to more intimacy and closeness between partners. So if people are unhappy, they should laugh more."

"Did you try that with your husband before deciding an affair was the best course of action?"

Is that anger and resentment in her tone?

That made little sense.

"Yeah, I tried a lot of things," I said, staring at my empty glass. The woman motioned for the bartender, who returned with a full flute for me and another full glass for her. "Laughter, therapy—for me, of course, because he'd never go—being in the way, staying out of the way...." My hands trembled slightly when I raised the glass to my lips. "It was never enough. I was never enough, I guess."

"Was? Aren't you still married?"

Shit.

Chapter 22

"On paper, yeah. I guess I've already moved on in my mind."

"Why not just get a divorce, then?"

"She's quite nosy," Bryson said on the radio. "We should run a background on her."

"Because she's nosy?" Charlie said skeptically.

"Yeah, seems off for a hotel that caters to those who don't want their business known. Wouldn't all guests and patrons want to keep their private lives to themselves?"

"Okay, I'll take a still picture the next time she turns this way and run facial recognition. Though if anyone asks where I got her picture...."

"I'll say you were in the corner behind a plant or something, not that you hacked past their three layers of firewalls."

"Four." Charlie scoffed. "It's why it took me the full five minutes to gain access."

"Please stop," I said—out loud, unfortunately.

The woman winced. "Sorry, I was just—"

"Sorry, not you," I said and pointed to my head. "Anxious brain, always working overtime." With an awkward laugh, I downed the rest of the champagne. In a blink, another full flute was in its place. "I shouldn't have this third one."

"Agreed," the two men said in my ear.

"It helps," she said with a half-smile. "Takes away the nerves of what's coming."

"Nerves?" I asked, suddenly very interested. "Are you saying you've been in a dangerous situation doing this before?"

Maybe she'd been with our unsub, felt something off, and left.

"I've done this a few times, but the unknowns of the night always make me jittery. Excitedly." Her hazel eyes turned to me. "Did you get the hotel room, or did he?"

"He did."

She nodded like that was a good thing. "Good, make them take on the expense. Makes it harder for your spouse to trace later if he gets suspicious. If he can't track you to here, then you can keep him in the dark longer."

"The parking," I said, a light bulb blazing brightly in my mind.

"Oh no, you didn't park here, did you?" she asked, slightly disappointed. "Rookie mistake."

"No, I didn't park here. Down the street, there are several pay-by-the-hour cash lots."

That was a lie. I rode here with Charlie and Bryson, but since our other victims had parked in the various cash lots, I used that bit of knowledge from the case files to keep up with my cover.

The woman nodded. "Yep, it's where a lot of us park who don't want to be tied to this place."

It was all coming together now. Our unsub knew if he paid for the room, his victim wouldn't park here to reduce risk of the affair being discovered.

"Running facial recognition on the photos Bryson's taking of the men entering the hotel through the front door," Charlie said over the line. "I'll cross-check them with the names on the list we compiled based on the profile."

The clink of ice against glass shifted my attention back to the woman beside me.

"Well, that's enough for me, or I won't be on my game." The empty tumbler slid easily along the bar. "Thanks for the chat. Good luck tonight. Hopefully we both get what we want."

"Yeah, bye."

Eyeing the half-empty champagne flute I didn't remember drinking, I watched the bubbles dance.

"You okay, Rhyan?" Bryson asked.

"Yeah, just floaty."

"That's not good." I rolled my eyes at Charlie's panicked tone.

"We should pull her."

"I'll go in and—"

"Guys, it's fine," I whispered, cutting Charlie's overreaction off before he stormed through the doors and carried me out of here over his shoulder. My stomach quivered, loving that idea if future lives didn't rest on me sticking around. "I still have an hour before I meet my mystery date—"

Chapter 22

"It's not a date," Charlie corrected.

"Fine." I sighed and went to adjust my glasses, only there was nothing there. Though I preferred my glasses over contacts, I always brought some along just in case. Which for this case my anxiety-induced over-preparedness paid off. "Mystery person. I'll be fine."

"Did you eat today?" Charlie questioned with a frustrated growl.

"Yeah, sure..." I drawled, clearly lying. I was too nervous all day to get anything down. Even now, the thought of food sounded more repulsive than satisfying.

"Rhyan," Charlie warned. "What am I going to do with you?"

"I'm sure you can get creative," Bryson said, his laugh making my own lips twitch upward.

"Damn straight."

"What's with the tongue ring, by the way?" Bryson asked, clearly no longer talking to me. "Did you lose a bet or something?"

"Hey," I chided. "I like it."

"Yeah, you do," Charlie said with a purr. "And there's the answer to your dumbass question."

"Sorry I asked," Bryson grumbled. "Did it hurt?"

"Thinking about getting one?"

"Not soon. Wouldn't have a need for it. It's hard dating as a single dad who works ninety hours a week."

On and on the two talked, providing the distraction I desperately needed with their random conversation and banter.

Pressing the tips of two fingers against the base of the champagne flute, I pushed it toward the other side of the bar to keep me from absentmindedly finishing the delicious liquid.

I needed to be on point. No more drinking.

I had a date with a serial killer, after all.

23

CHARLIE

Thick drops of rain smacked the vehicle in erratic repetitions along the windshield and roof. Each loud *thunk* spiked my already high impatience. No matter how hard I tried to ignore it, the inconsistent noise filtered through. With a string of curses, I slammed a fist to the roof as if that would do anything to stop the pitter-patter of rain along the metal.

"You need to settle down," Bryson chastised from behind the digital camera. A heavy telephoto lens jutted toward the windshield, capturing an up-close image of every pedestrian who walked past The Black Rose. With the quick click of the shutter, several pictures appeared on the laptop screen, automatically uploaded from the digital camera.

"It's the damn rain," I grumbled, the words almost lost under my pounding fingers nailing the keys. After uploading the new pictures into the facial recognition software, I checked the results on the previous few that were processing. "The last two you sent triggered results, but their names aren't on the list I compiled from Rhyan's search parameters. Running this new picture now."

"It's not just the rain that has your panties up your ass, and you know it. Let's talk about something else to distract you."

"That's the last thing I need right now, to be distracted while she's in there without me."

Bryson pulled the camera away from his face to shoot a pointed look to another screen, where the security feed from inside the hotel was streaming.

"I mean without me in there, protecting her." Bryson snorted and shook his head. "What?"

"Have you ever dated a strong, independent, smart woman before?" My lips parted, ready to defend myself, until I couldn't come up with one name. I snapped my mouth shut. "I'll tell you this, because I have some experience in the area. My wife was brilliant, independent, and all around the best woman I've ever met and probably ever will." A wash of sadness took over his features. *Fuck, now I know what Rhyan meant about not wanting to see a good man like Bryson so fucking sad.* "They don't need your protection, but when you've earned their trust and respect, they want it."

"You're not making any sense."

"Women like my wife and Rhyan don't need us, and that's what makes them attractive to men like us. We want a woman to *want* us, not need us. If you go in there dick out, cape on, you'll scare her off."

"That description scared *me* off."

"I'm being serious, man."

"Me too. Can you imagine my dick wearing a cape? Talk about awkward."

He cut me a look full of irritation, but we both ended up chuckling.

"All I'm saying is let Rhyan come to you. When she does, when she sets aside that strength that has gotten her this far in life and leans on you, it's fucking amazing. But you can't rush it. You'll lose her respect and a slice of her own confidence if you do."

"You got another one," I said and hitched my chin to the man heading down the sidewalk hidden beneath an umbrella.

"This is when I hate the rain. I only have two seconds between them shaking out the umbrella and entering the hotel to take the shot." Another series of clicks, and several new photos populated on the screen. "She's holding her own in there, though. That other woman at the bar had no concept of personal space."

I nodded in agreement. Flicking back to the still shot I captured of the mystery over-talker, I checked the facial recognition for any hits, but nothing had populated—yet. Unless this woman lived under a rock since the digital age and didn't have a single ID with a photo, the search *would* find something, though it might take a while.

"So, dating as a single dad," I said to transition the conversation away from me and Rhyan. What he said made sense, especially since he spoke from experience, but that didn't mean I liked it. I wanted to take care of Rhyan, wanted to be her protector and make sure she never had to worry about being hurt again. This was new—well, slightly new. I felt some of the overpowering need to protect a while back in Texas when my friend's girlfriend went missing and was in the hands of a killer.

"It's nonexistent," he grumbled, answering my previous question, and leaned back against the cheap paneled van's driver seat. "Though I'll admit I put a lot of blame on Vic and my job, though that's not the real reason I'm a fucking monk these days."

"What is the real reason, then?"

"I haven't dated a woman in what, a decade? I don't even know where to start. I'm not signing up for some dating site—I've seen too many of those go wrong to trust a stranger—but all my friends are married and at that stage where they don't have any single friends left to set me up with." Twisting in the seat, he faced the back, where I was busy monitoring the searches, facial recognition, and hotel feed. "On top of all that, I know Heather was it for me. I'll never find another woman like her. She brought out the best in me, catered to my protective instincts, and loved me for all my faults."

The tightness in his voice had me darting a look away from the screens.

"It's not fair to date when all I'd be doing is comparing the women to her."

"What about Victoria?" I asked.

"What about her?"

"Do you think she's missing out by not having a strong, independent woman in her life, someone like her mom?"

"I'm doing the best I can," he snapped.

"Not saying you're not, but you're looking at this from just your perspective. It's not just you anymore, Bryson. You have that sweet little thing at home you need to consider too. Sure, you might be okay with being alone and savoring the memories of your wife, but is your daughter?"

Silence filled the van, Bryson's eyes taking on an unfocused look.

"You could always bring the women to you," I said, drawing out the words.

Bryson twisted back around to face out the windshield and sighed. "I'm not kidnapping women and holding them in my basement."

"What?" I barked with a laugh.

He shot a smirk over his shoulder. "Kidding."

"You're looking for a nanny now, right?" He nodded. "Well, find a nanny who fits for what you *and* Victoria need."

"I'm not screwing the woman I hire to take care of my daughter."

"Why not? If she's willing and your type, it's a 'two birds, one stone' type thing."

"How in the hell did you win over Rhyan with that kind of shit in your brain?" I stuck out my tongue and wiggled the steel bar at him. "Remind me to put piercings down as another quality to watch out for when Victoria dates."

"Another? You have a list going? She's three."

"The shit we've seen? Hell yes, I have a list going. And it's a long one already. Hell, I might send her to a convent somewhere from twelve to forty."

A ding from the computer halted our conversation, and I read through the results that populated on one of the hotel guests' pictures Bryson took.

"Another dead end. This guy is still married, upper middle class, and no medical education. Fuck," I shouted. Wrapping my hands around the screen, I gave it a hard shake, hoping that would change the results. "We're getting fucking nowhere fast while she's in there in the damn lion's den."

"With a gun."

"Right," I growled, my full attention now on Bryson. "Doesn't change the fact that she's in there alone."

He nodded. "What's up with this ex of hers? I already wanted to kick his ass based on the phone call, but after hearing her earlier, she's been through some shit, hasn't she?"

"Her ex is a narcissistic asshole who made her think she wasn't worth anything without him, fucking tool."

"Hold up," Bryson said, resettling in the seat and lifting the camera to his face. "This guy seems like a baller. I think he has an entourage."

The cloth seat bent beneath my tight grip. Using it as leverage, I craned my neck to look in the direction he had the camera pointed.

"Get an excellent shot," I whispered.

"No shit," he snapped.

Smirking, I eased back into my half of the van and waited for the pictures to come through.

"Could be a rock star," I mused. "Or some political figure. That hotel would cater well to those fuckers."

I checked the time on the screen: 8:00 p.m. One hour before Rhyan would head upstairs to meet our potential unsub, or just a creeper who enjoyed cheating on his spouse. Neither was an ideal scenario, but Bryson was right about one thing: I had to let Rhyan do her thing, to not squash that confidence she had in spades as Agent Riggs. The other side of her, the woman Rhyan Riggs, grew stronger every day. I smiled at the screen as the pictures filtered through. It had only been a few days, but we'd both changed, for the better, because of the other's influence.

"Or a judge," Bryson said and fell back in the seat. "No wonder he wouldn't sign the warrant for access to the hotel's guest list. The motherfucker is a regular guest, no fucking doubt in my mind."

I leaned closer to the screen, squinting at the hazy picture. "Huh, didn't see that coming. Think he's the one meeting with

Rhyan?" I flipped to the next picture. "Never mind, I have my answer." Turning the screen to the front seat, where Bryson was about to fall out of it to see the grainy blown-up picture, I tapped the middle of the picture. "He's holding hands with this one. The other must be his bodyguard. Who knows? Maybe this hotel plays for the sexually adventurous too and they're meeting their third here."

"You ever done that?"

I smirked at the screen and raised both brows. "Is that an offer?"

"Fuck, what?"

"Kidding. And don't ask questions you're not ready to hear the answers to."

"Holy fuck, you're so—"

"Fucking amazing?" I cut in, turning to drape an arm over the back of my chair, daring him to correct me.

"Busy."

Tipping my head back, I laughed at the metal roof, the sound bouncing off the small enclosed space. "It is a lot of work, especially when—"

"Just stop," Bryson grumbled. "I can't tell you how long it's been since I got laid. Just hearing about your escapades might have me blowing in my pants."

"That's a sad state, man."

"Don't I fucking know it."

"I'm telling you the nanny idea works."

"I'm not fucking the nanny." He laughed. "They're all either old, married, or way too young for me. Though...." He shook his head.

"What?"

"Nothing."

"Nope. You can't say 'nothing' now." I reached forward and shook his seat. "Who is she?"

"Someone completely off-limits."

"Not legal?"

"What the hell? Of course she's legal."

"Not into guys?"

"You're a messed-up motherfucker, you know that? She's my best friend's little sister."

I blinked, not having a good response for that reason to stay away. "So?"

"So," he exclaimed, running a hand over his short-cropped hair, "she's sweet, and innocent, and too damn young for me."

"How old?"

"Twenty-seven, and in a relationship. Well, at least she was the last time we talked."

"And when was that?"

He released a heavy breath. "I don't know, three months ago? Six maybe? All time runs together when you're a single parent just trying to survive."

"Hey, guys?" Rhyan said over the line.

My stomach dropped until I saw the mute button was still engaged. We could hear her, but she couldn't hear us.

Tapping a few keys, I opened up the line once again.

"We're here. Something wrong?" I sat up straight in my chair and narrowed my focus on the camera feed from the bar. She sat on the same stool, same half a glass of champagne sitting in front of her. "You see something?"

"I'm bored." She laughed. "Keep entertaining me. You guys left me."

"Sorry, I had some stuff to work through," Bryson said with a wink my way. "We're good now."

"Bryson has a crush on a twenty-seven year old," I said, smirking at the screen. "He's debating getting a tongue ring just for her."

"You're a bastard, you know that?" Bryson grumbled as he snapped an arm out, fingers grabbing for me. I leaned just out of his reach. "I don't have a crush on her."

"Pretty sure I saw heart shapes float over your eyes when you mentioned Bethany."

"The hell? Her name is Tinley, not Bethany."

"Oh snap," Rhyan said, clearly trying to hide her laughter. "You just fell for the oldest profiler trick in the book."

In the rearview mirror, a contemplative look flashed across his face before morphing into a frown. "I hate you, Charlie."

"Not possible. I'm a lovable fucker."

"You got the fucker part right."

A soft giggle floated through the feed.

"I do love to fuck her."

"Oh my," Rhyan gasped.

"That's what she said," Bryson said with a rumbling laugh.

An alarm on one of the laptops snapped my attention to the computer behind me. Twisting around, I tapped the keyboard, bringing up the alert. It took the first line of text to register the words, reminding me of this secret, mostly illegal search I'd set up earlier. Adrenaline shot through my veins, my heart thundering against my ribs. Ditching the chair, I kneeled in front of the laptop, scrolling down the list of names.

"What's going on in there?" Rhyan asked.

"Don't be mad," I said offhandedly, too focused on the results coming across my screen to think of a better reply to prepare her for this information bomb.

"That's never a good way to start things," she said wearily.

"Since I was already toeing the legal line by hacking the hotel's security feed—"

"Not toeing. You stepped right over that line."

"Semantics. Anyway, I just thought, 'Hey, if I get fired for that, might as well make a big splash, you know?'"

"No," both of them said in response.

"You two are the worst. I hacked into the Affair Me servers." I winced, knowing the hell that was about to break loose. A whispered string of curses filled my ear. "Did I hear you say, 'Fucking brilliant'? Yeah, I thought so too. Anyway, I narrowed my search to only the asshole you're meeting with tonight. Figured that would save my ass if I get caught."

"If?" Bryson questioned.

"I don't leave fucking breadcrumbs. I'll be in and out before anyone notices the line of code I snuck into—"

Chapter 23

Bryson held up a hand. "Just stop. You're way over both our heads."

"Agreed," Rhyan agreed. "What did you find in your illegal search?"

"The guy you're meeting with tonight is on the list of names I compiled from our profile."

The silence from both of them made me smile.

"See? Fucking brilliant. If you see anything suspicious, anything that feels off when you get inside that hotel room, you fucking take him down and alert us."

"We have to keep this quiet," she said under her breath. "If I think this is our guy, send up two of the undercover cops and have them take him out one of the employee exits. That way if I'm wrong, we don't alert the real unsub that we've identified his hunting ground."

"Smart," I said as I continued digging into Christopher Wilks's online history. "Looks like he's going through a nasty divorce, went to school pre-med but ended up taking a pharmaceutical sales role and has grown through the ranks. Mid-forties. I'll dig into his medical—"

"No," Rhyan shouted, followed by a mumbled apology. "That's crossing the line, Charlie. That's medical records. There are very clear laws and repercussions for anyone who breaks them. I like you, but conjugal visits will not happen."

Chuckling to myself, I put a pause on the medical history search and turned back to his background, hoping to find more information to use as evidence and possibly save Rhyan from ever stepping a foot into that hotel room alone.

"He lives and works downtown, close to the bridge."

Her voice was muffled as she talked to the bartender who approached. "It's time. The bartender just slipped me a note with a room number on it. Sneaky little place, isn't it?"

I sucked in a breath, my fingers frozen, hovering over the keyboard. I flicked a glance at the clock. "I still have fifteen minutes—"

"Charlie, I know what you're doing, and I'm thankful. I really am," she whispered under her breath. "But we all know I need to do this.

Hopefully he'll show his hand the moment I walk in, and boom, we're done."

The ding of an incoming alert sounded at the computer behind me running the facial recognition software, but all my focus was drilled on the screen showing Rhyan paying the bartender and sliding off her stool.

"You'll still be early," Bryson said, watching the monitor, then me.

"It's who I am, fake date or not. I'm early to everything in life."

"Lucky Charlie," Bryson offered, voice tight.

I huffed a forced laugh, appreciating his attempt to ease my rising stress.

The moment she moved out of the bar, I switched the feed to the camera in the lobby. With her head held high, she walked with an air of confidence across the expansive lobby. A few men completely ignored the women they were with to watch her.

My hands curled into tight fists, my blunt nails digging into my palms. High and higher, my anger and frustration at being stuck in this fucking van rose. Heat built beneath my skin, my entire body trembling. With a roar, I slammed a fist to the side of the van, careful to stay far away from my precious computers.

Metal groaned. Pain immediately bloomed. I hissed a curse, cradling my now red and swollen hand with the other.

Terrible idea.

"What the hell was that?" Rhyan asked, alarm in her tone as she waited for the elevator.

"Nothing," I grunted, sucking down gulps of air to keep my bellows of pain contained. "Be careful, Agent Riggs."

"I always am, Agent Bekham. Don't forget, I've already thought of eighty different ways out of this if things go south. No matter the scenario, I have a backup plan. Yay, anxiety."

The ding of the arriving elevator stopped my heart, taking my full focus off my possibly broken hand. On the screen, I watched her slip inside. Her green eyes scanned the hallway ceiling. The moment she found the camera hidden in the molding, she offered a sad smile and a small wave just before the gold doors swooshed closed, cutting off my view.

Lungs tight, I pressed both hands to the edge of the makeshift table, my head dropping forward as I attempted to catch my breath.

Something was off. The uneasy feeling had flared earlier while standing in the alley and then grew, pushing against my chest all day. And now... fuck, now dread filled every square inch, every cell, my panic and fear rising with every second she was inside that building.

She had to come out on the other side of this unscathed.

My future depended on it.

24

RHYAN

Hand still raised, fingers wiggling, I didn't drop the goodbye wave until the elevator jolted and began its ascent. Inhaling deep through my nose, chest blooming out, I relaxed against the gold-plated wall and pressed a hand to my chest. The rapid beat of my heart thundered against my palm, somehow driving my anxiety higher. The drinks from earlier churned in my stomach, threatening to creep up, but I shoved it down with a hard swallow.

I can do this.

Saving lives, catching the bad guy, and moving on to the next was my job, even if this aspect of the job was new.

Sweeping my gaze from the floor to the doors, I stared at my fuzzy reflection.

I looked the part of a woman ready for fun. Now it was time to play the part.

Walk in that room with a potential killer, give my best performance, and quickly decipher if this is our guy.

Easy.

Right.

The elevator slowed. The ding of my arrival on my floor had my shoulders rising to my ears. Sucking in a deep breath, I steadied my nerves for what was to come. The coolness of the metal wall seeped into my sweaty palms. They slipped against the smooth surface when I shoved off and stepped toward the now-open door, only for my trembling legs to give out under my weight.

With a surprised gasp, I stumbled forward, catching myself on the brass railing lining the elevator. Sucking down a lungful of air, I straightened, legs still trembling. Locking my knees to keep me from collapsing to the floor in a puddle, I smoothed both hands down the front of my dress. Warily, I attempted a small step, this time my legs bearing my weight.

The two doors pressed against my flattened palms, springing back open before they could smash my hands. Careful to keep my steps steady, I eased out into the hall. My hair shifted from side to side as I glanced each way down the hall. Coast clear, I stumbled forward, catching myself on the opposite wall.

The elevator doors whooshed closed behind me, sealing me to my fate.

Fingers trembling, I snapped open the envelope-style clutch, the badge and gun inside offering a sliver of relief. I wasn't a strong physical fighter, as in terrible. I always got my ass handed to me in various ongoing training sessions we were required to undergo as agents. Though I was one hell of a shot.

At the firing range.

Never once had I fired in the field, and I hopefully wouldn't break that streak tonight.

Straightening my spine, I rolled both shoulders up and back. I turned in a tight circle, searching for the sign that showed which way I should continue my shaky death walk.

This was it.

I wanted to turn around. To get in that elevator and race across the street to have Charlie wrap me in his protective arms. But I couldn't back out now. Too many things were in motion, and we needed to know if this guy was our unsub.

My entire body trembled with the first step down the way indicated for my room number, the second slightly more sure. Halfway down the hall, I was the epitome of a confident woman. Chin lifted, spine straight, strides long and smooth. This was who I needed to be for the next few hours.

At the end of the long hall, I slowed to a stop in front of a black-painted door. An ornate brass design decorated the outside, making me curious as to what luxury and indulgence waited on the other side. It was then I noticed there was no peephole. Odd for a hotel, but I figured that kept other guests from spying on the comings and goings of others. Smart, really.

A shaky breath pushed through my tight lips as I raised a hand. Time seemed to still, my hand hovering as if the world held a collective breath, waiting to find out what would happen next.

Breaking the spell, I rapped a single knuckle against the wooden door. The knock seemed to reverberate through my body, zapping every nerve seizing my lungs.

"You've got this, baby," Charlie said over the line. "We're here. You're not in this alone."

How he knew I needed his voice, those words of encouragement in that exact moment, I didn't know, but it worked. Just hearing him, knowing he was waiting close by, released the grip my fear had over my entire body.

A thump from the other side had me leaning closer, angling an ear, hoping to hear more. I didn't realize how close I'd leaned in until the door swung open.

Stumbling back a step, I gasped and instinctively went for the gun hidden in my purse, but I stopped before I showed my hand. Straightening, I forced a smile, hoping he couldn't see through my fake confidence. I took a moment to check out the man of the hour holding the door wide open.

Shiny black shoes freshly polished, black slacks that emphasized his muscular legs and thighs. A crisp white dress shirt, all buttons undone, showing off his defined pecs and—

"You're early." My gaze shot to his. Was that anger in his tone? "I'm not ready."

"I'm always early," I said in response. "Excited?"

"Was that a question or a statement, Rhyan?" Bryson asked, sounding just as tense as the man in front of me.

The man's lips pressed into a thin line as he stared me down. Not much taller than me, maybe an inch or two, but with the heels, we were eye level. Thick black hair, perfectly styled. Dark scruff covered his cheeks, giving him an edge, but something behind his stony stare made my heart hitch.

And not in a good way.

No, there was pent-up aggression lingering there, the same hidden anger.

Lies. So many lies hid behind his nearly black eyes.

Something wasn't right.

"Right, come on in. I'm almost ready. You will be punished for this, however."

"Yay."

Yep. I said, "Yay."

The man's frown deepened. Shit, I was fucking this up, and I wasn't even over the damn threshold.

"That's what I was hoping for," I added in what I hoped was a seductive tone.

The lines along his forehead eased as he nodded and stepped to the side, gesturing for me to enter.

To enter a strange man's hotel room.

Holy crap, this is really happening.

"All you have to say is your code word," Charlie's voice rumbled in my ear. "and we'll have two officers there in five seconds. They're waiting in the stairwell for our command."

My knees buckled with the first step toward my impending doom, but I caught myself before falling face-first. With an embarrassed chuckle, I slipped around the man and stepped into the room. Inside, I shifted to the right and sealed my back to the wall, keeping my clutch tight between both hands.

"Grab a drink. I'll only be a few minutes." With that, he disappeared behind another door, slamming it shut.

Releasing the breath I was holding, I shook out one hand, then the other to calm my frayed nerves. Now was not the time to freak out and clam up. This, me being alone, was a perfect opportunity to find the evidence needed to arrest the guy.

Rocking forward, I popped off the wall, forcing myself to move toward the wall of windows. A small fully stocked bar cart sat along the wall near a cozy sitting space, complete with two low-back chairs and a love seat centered before a TV, a large glass coffee table sitting in the middle.

Thick purple curtains hung along either side of the windows, tied back with a black sash, allowing the glittering lights of the city to shimmer through. Rain pattered against the tinted glass, barely making a sound.

Shifting to the bedroom area of this small efficiency-style hotel room, I swallowed hard, my wide eyes glued to the massive king-size bed. Thick, imposing posts stood sentry at each corner of the dark mahogany frame, the headboard and footboard made of the same stained wood. The smooth black duvet was folded back, revealing silk crimson sheets beneath.

It was what was on top of the sheets that had me gulping: black leather cuffs, secured to the bedposts by a thin cord.

"What's going on, Rhyan? We can basically hear you freaking out," Bryson said through the earpiece.

"Kinky cuffs," I whispered through my labored breaths. "On the bed."

"You won't let it get that far though, will you?" Charlie said with a snarl in his tone. "Don't let that derail you. Focus on finding evidence to get you out of there now."

Right. I nodded even though they couldn't see and tore my freaked-out gaze from the bondage equipment to the empty bedside table. Forcing my legs to work, I kept one eye on the still-closed door he'd disappeared behind while I tiptoed closer to the other side of the bed.

I trailed a fingertip along the silk duvet, shivering a little at the luxurious feel.

"I want silk sheets," I muttered under my breath, totally forgetting about the two listening.

"I can make that happen," Charlie purred.

"I was never a fan," Bryson cut in. "Too slippery, always fucked with my leverage."

"TMI, friend, TMI," Charlie said with a chuckle.

A small smile crept up my face despite my surroundings and nerves.

Easing around the footboard, I poked the black leather cuff with a single finger. Hard, sturdy leather with belt-type notches to secure the binding. The inside looked to be lined with fake fur to make it more comfortable for the one wearing it.

I turned in a slow circle, taking in the entire room, looking for... who the hell knew.

Frustrated, I blew out a breath and sat on the edge of the bed facing what I assumed was the bathroom, waiting for him to emerge. I swiped both clammy palms down my dress, the motion drawing my gaze to the bedside table near my knees.

I leaned forward, heart hammering, and reached for the gold-embossed handle, wrapping my fingers around the small knob. Glancing from the side table to the door, I eased the drawer open. Grimacing at the sound of something shifting inside, I held a breath, listening for any sign he'd heard the noise too.

Slowly, lower lip gripped between my teeth, I eased it open wide to peek inside.

All the blood drained from my face, my head turning dizzy as I gaped at the syringe resting in the drawer.

I swallowed hard, trying to find the words to alert Charlie and Bryson—hell, to alert anyone. But nothing came out. The room spun as I fought to remember how to breathe.

"Rhyan, what's going on?" Charlie asked, slightly panicked.

"Him," I wheezed at the same time the bathroom door swung open. "It's him."

The man, our unsub, looked from me to the opened bedside drawer. "What are you doing?" he roared and stormed closer, slamming the drawer shut.

Chapter 24

I lunged to the side with a pitiful cry when he grabbed for my hands.

Shouts vibrated from the earpiece, but I didn't understand a single word. Blood thundered in my ears, his grip tight around both my wrists.

"Get on the damn bed, now," he ordered an inch from my face. Minty fresh breath brushed across my hot cheeks. "You'll pay for being so damn nosy."

My red hair whipped from side to side from my violent head shake.

"I said get on the fucking bed," he shouted. With a hard shove, I slid along the silk sheets to the center of the bed.

"Stop," I shouted, twisting, stretching for my clutch lying near the foot of the bed.

"Don't worry, you'll like it. They always do." His scowl smoothed into a sinister grin. Near-black eyes raked a long look up and down my body. His brow lifted as I fumbled with the edge of my purse closure, fingertips sliding along the edge. With a laugh, he flung out a massive hand, knocking it away from my fingers. It landed on the floor with a loud thump.

"I will kill him if he touches you," Charlie roared in my ear. "Fuck this. I'm going up there."

The next second, a forceful pound vibrated the door. He paused, brows dipping. He considered the door, then me.

"Don't move. I'll deal with you in a second."

Hard fucking pass.

His open shirt billowed as he turned to investigate the interruption, and I forced my trembling body into action. Scurrying across the sheets on hands and knees, I slipped off the bed, my shoulder slamming to the hard floor.

Five feet were all that lay between me and the weapon lying hidden in my purse. Teeth sunk into my lower lip, I stretched an arm along the floor, the tip of a single finger grazed the smooth black leather.

One more inch.

"What in the hell are you—" He started toward me, a flash of concern overtaking the earlier anger. Another pounding knock cut him off, turning his attention back to the door. "For fuck's sake. Who the hell is it? If it's your husband, tonight is off, sweetheart."

With a grunt, I hauled myself that last inch, dragging my panic frozen lower half forward until I snatched the purse. With my shaking fingers, it took three tries to work the simple snap. A strangled whimper of relief scratched up my dry throat when my fingers wrapped around the grip of my Glock.

The door swung open.

Rolling to my back, arms extended, I aimed the barrel at the man's back as he inched into the room, hands raised in surrender. Two plain-clothed officers edged inside, both brandishing their guns as well.

"What the hell is this about?" The man's voice trembled as he eyed the two men. "You called the cops on me?" He shot a hateful glare over his shoulder, only for it to morph into shock when he took in my gun.

"I am the cops. FBI. Hands behind your head."

"FB... what the actual hell is going on here? All this is consensual—"

"They consented to their murder, did they?" Charlie's deep voice rumbled through the room seconds before he stormed inside. His eyes frantically searched until he found me on the floor.

"Murder? What the—"

"Read him his rights and then take him downtown for questioning," Charlie ordered the officers without taking his eyes off me. "We'll gather the evidence here and bring it to the station when we're done."

A round of "Yes, sirs" was lost to the man's frantic questions and pleas of not knowing what the hell was going on. Those shouts continued in the hall until the stairs' heavy metal door slammed shut, cutting him off.

"Rhyan," Charlie choked out daring a step closer. "You can lower the gun now, baby."

Chapter 24

I responded with a stiff nod but couldn't get my contracted muscles to obey.

Charlie's tight features softened. Keeping out of the line of fire should I accidentally pull the trigger, he shuffled around the room. His knees entered my periphery as he squatted beside my head. A firm hand wrapped around one wrist, while the other tipped the gun barrel down. He coaxed my grip free, and the gun slid easily out of my clasped hands.

Immediately, both arms plummeted to the ground, the muscles completely spent. A shoulder-shaking sob erupted from my throat. Slapping a hand over my lips, I tried to shove it down.

Charlie set the gun on the hotel room floor, stood without a word, and scooped me into his arms. The room swayed as he carried me to the small sitting area I'd admired a few minutes prior.

"Shh, baby, I got you. You're safe," he murmured in my ear.

"I'm turning off Rhyan's mic now," Bryson said in my ear. "I don't need to hear this. I'll join the two officers in escorting the suspect into custody. Good work tonight, Rhyan. Glad you're okay."

I nodded, my head popping Charlie's chin. Eager to be done with all the things on my body, I dipped a hand inside my dress. Plucking off the small mic hooked on the center of my bra, I shifted my fingers, digging into my bra for the tracker that had pressed uncomfortably into my skin since I placed it there earlier.

Charlie took both from me, tucking the small devices away somewhere I couldn't see.

"You okay?" he asked, smoothing a hand over my head.

"Yeah," I croaked. "Just in shock, I think."

"Did he...?" His hold tightened around me.

"No, just—" I shifted to search his tight blue eyes. "It doesn't matter. I'm fine, just shaken up." Closing both eyes, I inhaled through my nose and blew it out slowly. "Let's gather the cuffs in case our victims' DNA can be found on them. The insides are lined with faux fur. There's no way to clean those and remove all trace evidence."

Opening my lids, I offered Charlie a weak grin.

"I'm good now." Remembering we were on the job, I tapped his forearm until his hold loosened enough for me to slip off his lap. Standing, I smoothed the slightly wrinkled dress down my thighs and wiped my face of the few rogue tears. "The syringe I saw is in the nightstand. Did you bring an evidence baggie?"

A lock of dark hair shifted across his forehead with a slight head shake. "I'll go down and grab some."

"We need various sizes," I said as he walked to the door. "And gloves too, please. I'll hang out here until you get back."

He paused at the closed door, brows furrowed as he took me in. "You'll be all right alone?"

I knelt to the floor, knees popping, to retrieve my discarded gun. Slipping it back into my purse, I patted the side with a smirk.

"I'll be fine. Go, so we can get this done sooner than later. I'd like to be out of here before midnight."

With a final concerned glance, he disappeared around the doorframe.

Blowing out a heavy breath, I spun in a slow circle, taking in the room for the second time that night.

I did it. We did it. Now all we had to do was gather the incriminating evidence and be done.

The corners of my lips dipped, and a shiver of unease slipped down my spine.

The evidence pointed to him being our unsub. Even his background fit with our profile. But if we caught him, then why was there a nagging sense that we were still missing something in this frustrating case?

Something big.

25

RHYAN

An hour into evidence collecting, I ditched the heels, moving around the room barefoot while depositing various items into clear bags. After hour two, I commandeered a hair tie from a female officer, securing my long hair into a messy bun. Now approaching hour three, I was exhausted and over it. Though lingering jitters from the night's events had my fingers trembling, making the bags annoying as hell to secure.

Eyes dry, contacts burning, and seeing double from exhaustion, it was enough for me to finally tap out.

"Would you be okay with finishing up here?" I asked the officer assisting Charlie and me with carrying the filled bags to the van where another officer waited, securing the evidence for transport to the station.

"Got a hot date?" she joked, not looking up from where she wrote on the baggie in her hand.

A tingling sensation tickled my fingertips. I shook them out to get the feeling back. "No, I just.... Tonight was a lot, and I need to walk it off. Clear my head, you know?"

Maybe figure out why the hell all this felt so wrong.

"In those things?" She peeked over the clear plastic and eyed my discarded heels.

"I'm used to it." Tossing the Sharpie to the bed, I stripped off the black latex gloves, shoving them into the trash bag by the door. Conforming cool leather molded around my feet as I slipped on one heel, then the other. "I buy those insoles that help cushion the balls of your feel. When Charlie comes back from the van, tell him I'll meet him at the station after I change into something more appropriate."

"Will do. Be safe."

I raised my heavy clutch in a goodbye wave.

"Thanks for your help tonight. Have a good one."

At the elevator, I pressed the Down button and waited. At the same time the ding signaling the elevator's arrival pierced the quiet, Charlie appeared at the end of the hall, having come up the stairwell.

"Where are you going?" he asked, long strides quickly closing the distance between us.

"I need some fresh air." The doors whooshed open. When I stepped inside, the feeling of déjà vu engulfed me, making my tired head spin. "And to change out of this getup."

A hand thrust against the door as it slowly closed, shoving it back open. "Want me to come with you?"

"No, but thank you. I just need a few minutes to myself. I think the fresh night air, now that it's done raining, will be exactly what I need to calm down."

"It's midnight."

Leaning forward, I placed a soft kiss on his dark scruff-covered cheek.

"I won't turn into a pumpkin."

"I'm more worried about you walking the streets at this hour alone than you turning into a vegetable."

I smiled slightly. "Fun fact, they're actually a fruit."

"Stop distracting me."

"I'm fine, Charlie. I've walked downtown streets at this hour or later before and have been okay so far. We have our guy in custody, I'm carrying, and I'm only walking a few blocks to the hotel."

Chapter 25

An alarm squealed from the door being held open.

I gave Charlie a soft two-finger push against his chest, and he retreated a step, his hand slipping from the door.

"You have your phone?"

"Yes, Dad."

That concerned expression morphed into something heated.

"If you're into daddy play, we'll have to explore that later, baby."

A wide smile split my face. "Can't wait."

The doors slid shut, the alarm silencing, though the high-pitched sound still seemed to reverberate in my ears. Slouching back against the elevator, I grinned at the ceiling.

Daddy play. Not sure what that was, but with Charlie, I would no doubt love every second. A few bantered words and the stress of the night receded, all worried thoughts on the case gone for now.

Striding through the empty lobby, I shoved through the revolving doors. A chill swept across my exposed skin, and a shiver raked down my spine. Keeping my purse clutched in one hand, I used the other to chafe up and down the opposite arm.

Maybe this wasn't a great idea after all. Not because I was scared, but the temperature had dropped several degrees with the storm. Mid-fifties with the air damp from the earlier rain in this part of the country felt colder than the actual temperature.

Though the streets and sidewalks were empty, tempting me with the peace and space I desperately needed. Carefully walking down the steps, I tipped my face toward the gray clouds, studying how they covered the tops of the taller downtown buildings.

With a sigh, the tightness in my chest finally loosened, and for the first time in hours, I took a full, deep breath.

Sticking to the streets with the most functioning streetlamps, I took a right at an intersection instead of heading straight, the most direct route to the hotel. Sure, my feet hurt, and I barely had any energy left, but I wasn't ready for the reprieve from life's stress to be over. Not ready to change into my Supervisory Special Agent Riggs persona and question the suspect. Which was odd. Normally I was chomping at the bit to dig deeper into the suspect.

This time, though I wasn't sure why, that confidence I normally felt at this point in the case wasn't there.

Pausing at the next intersection, I checked each direction to cross the abandoned street, but something halfway between where I stood and the next block snagged my attention. Squinting, thinking that could help me see farther—it did not—I took in the flickering pay-by-the-hour parking lot sign. Just past that, beneath a dim streetlamp, sat a late-model van parked along the curb with the hood propped up and a figure leaning against the side, partially hidden in the shadows.

Ignoring the person while also keeping a watchful eye out, I'd just started to cross the street when the person moved, the yellowed overhead light illuminating the slight frame.

A woman.

A woman in a familiar dress.

Only when recognition flickered did I really process the parking lot. The nosy woman at the bar told me she parked near one, just like I told her I did, sticking to my cover.

A curse sounded down the street. I paused halfway in the middle of the intersection, angling her way.

"Hey," she yelled, hands cupped around her lips. "Do you have a phone I can borrow to call a tow truck?"

I hesitated.

"Please," she begged. "I need to make it home before my kids wake up."

Oh hell. Every instinct told me to keep walking, but my heart couldn't leave her there alone, stranded. If I left, there was no doubt in my mind I'd be back here in thirty minutes anyway. Women didn't leave other women stranded, right?

Groaning, mind already made up despite the risks, I strode her way, digging through my purse to find the phone, hoping to make this encounter short and sweet. With each step, the weight of tonight's events and zero sleep the previous night seemed to slow down my feet, my thoughts dragging with them. A long soak in a steaming hot bath sounded perfect before heading to the station. And I'd remove all the makeup that felt sticky from the damp air.

Chapter 25

"Oh my goodness. Thank you so much," the woman said, relief clear in her voice. "I've been waiting for you to walk by for a while."

I paused midstep at her odd choice of words. The edge of the phone dug painfully into my palm. "For me?"

She sliced a hand through the air and rolled her eyes to the gloomy sky. "Sorry, that sounded creepy. I meant anyone with a phone." Her glassy eyes flicked between my face and the phone. "Can I use it?" I held it out between us, stretching far to not close the significant gap. "Oh wow, you already put in your password and pulled up a list of local tow companies."

"I hoped to make this quick for the both of us." Rubbing a hand down my arm, I looked both ways along the sidewalk. "I need to get back."

"Will your husband be waiting up?" she asked, a harsh edge in her voice as she stared at my phone, fingers clutching the sides instead of scrolling through the list of towing companies I'd kindly pulled up for her. "The waiting and suspecting, but deep down knowing what's going on, is the worst. Though not having a fucking clue, then someone telling you your spouse is a damn lying asshole isn't great either."

I swallowed hard, retreating a step. Something was off with this woman.

"Oh, this one looks nice and safe," she muttered to herself and pressed the screen. She held it to her ear and smiled. "It's ringing."

I offered a stiff nod. Fuck, now she had my phone hostage, though the device wasn't worth that much. While she spoke to the person on the other end of the line, I took the opportunity to memorize every detail of the van. Late-model Ford, burnt red with rust spots and a spare tire on the front passenger side.

Shifting to change the angle of the overhead light, I gagged at the layers of trash covering the dash. A blue handicap sign hung from the rearview, standing out among the fast food bags and cups.

"It's for work." I startled, not realizing she was paying close attention to me while on the phone. "The dispatcher said the truck is on its way. Oh, I bet they'll want my insurance information when they get here." Phone still clutched in her tight grip, she turned, putting her back to me, and tugged open the sliding door.

Some of my suspicion drained as she turned, putting her back to me and rummaged through the trash that littered the back, which was worse than the dash. Shifting on my feet, I waited, releasing a sigh when she straightened and turned. Her wide, slightly manic grin sent a rush of energy through my veins. Ready to ditch the crazy lady, I grabbed for my phone that she held out between us.

No. Not my phone.

Hand already in motion, it was too late to correct my mistake. Too late to call out for help or reach for the gun nestled safely in my purse.

The first bolt of electricity zapped up my arm, my palm burning from the Taser prongs. Shocks raced through my body, making every muscle twitch and tighten to the point of pain. Shaking uncontrollably, my eyes rolled back just as my knees gave out. A lean arm wrapped around my waist, keeping me from plummeting to the sidewalk.

A heavy grunt brushed past my ear as my limp body was hauled without my consent. My hands and arms flopped uncontrollably from the aftershocks, though I forced my lids open just as she tossed the upper half of my body onto the van's floorboard. With little care, she shoved the rest of my torso and legs into the van, climbing in to hover over where I lay.

Neck bent at an odd angle, arms and legs jutting every which way, I couldn't move.

"Help," I whispered, though it was meant to be a shout.

"Strong one, aren't you?" she grumbled.

Another bolt of electricity radiated from my thigh, this one stronger and longer. Flopping among the trash, my temple clipped the hard base of the captain's chair. I would've cried out in pain, but my jaw clenched too tight to get anything but a muffled scream out.

"You're getting everything you deserve," she said, words hissed in undiluted anger.

Chapter 25

A grind of metal and the entire van rocked, followed by the slam of the sliding door.

Thoughts jumbled, tears freely leaking down my face, I fought to regain control over my body. I didn't deserve this. I wanted to shout at the woman, but I couldn't get my lips to move.

Still twitching, I frantically ran through the various plans I'd generated in case something went wrong during the earlier sting. Though I didn't expect this exact scenario, surely one of my other ideas could work. Though the one thing I needed was the one thing I was quickly running out of.

Time.

I needed as much time as possible, allowing Charlie and Bryson to realize I was gone and search for me. I needed to be compliant like a good little victim to figure out what in the hell this lady was after. Why was she waiting for me specifically? Why talk to me at the bar?

Shit. Where's my purse? It has my gun, badge, handcuffs....

Still unable to move, I couldn't wipe away the tears blurring my vision.

Okay, new plan. Find out what in the actual fuck is going on and go from there.

Clear as mud plan. Perfect.

All the boys needed was enough time to track down this lunatic and save me. I would do all I could to give them that.

For Charlie.

For me.

For us.

Resting back, a plastic bottle slipping beneath my head, I conserved what little energy remained in my exhausted body. Still my muscles tensed and strained, making me weaker by the second.

Now to focus on an actual plan with multiple options for survival.

I would survive.

Because *that* was what I deserved.

Trash and empty plastic liquor bottles shifted beneath my prone body with the movement of the van. Light filtered in from the open driver door, illuminating the back, followed by a hard slam.

Compliant was the plan until I came up with a better one. Pretending to pass out, I strained to understand her grumbling in the front seat. Hopefully that would give me a clue as to why she took me and what she wanted.

"...all her fault. Never should've tempted another wife's... deserves it for causing it all...."

Well, shit.

I knew there was something off with our profile.

The fucking gender.

Hell. This complicated matters and also gave me an edge. I knew our unsub. I could use this to my advantage to stay alive longer. Clearly *she* was our killer. Yay me, I'd find out firsthand why she killed those women. What would happen if she found out I wasn't like them, that I was just the woman out on a sting to catch... well, her?

I stilled, breath burning in my lungs, when her words shifted from her earlier ranting.

"...heavy-as-hell purse. What's she got in there?"

Shit. Shit. Shit.

If she found my badge or gun, there was a good chance I wouldn't make it out of this alive. An unraveling vigilante killer with a gun was not ideal. And bonus, this was absolutely not one of the hundreds of outcomes I'd plotted an escape from.

I should've dug deeper into why the profile felt off this entire time.

A woman. Now it all made sense.

"What the...?"

I swallowed, knowing what was coming, and squeezed my eyes shut. A tight grip on my shoulder rolled me to my back, pain flaring from the litter digging into my spine. But that wasn't what made me gasp, or my heart stutter. No, that would be the gun—*my* gun—pointed between my brows and the very angry-looking killer who held it in one hand and my badge in the other.

"I'll ask the questions," she said with a sneer, sneaking a peek at my badge, "Agent Riggs, and you're going to answer them."

Chapter 25

"Okay, sure," I croaked.

"First, take off the dress."

"What?" I exclaimed, subconsciously reaching up to cross an arm over my chest.

She flicked the gun down my body. "Need to make sure you're not wearing a wire. I've seen those crime shows." Leaning back, she scanned the streets as if expecting a swarm of Suburbans with flashing lights to descend on us. Which would be amazing for me. "Take it off."

When I still failed to move, she tossed the badge to the passenger seat with a frustrated curse and picked up the Taser.

"No." But my plea fell on deaf ears.

She lunged forward, jabbing the metal prongs into my exposed thigh. My scream would've been loud enough for all of Louisville to hear, except my jaw snapped shut and locked in place as bolts of electricity raced through my body. I flopped along the floorboard, sending the trash and bottles scattering.

Before I could regain authority over my muscles, one arm was wrenched up over my head, a thin metal band snapping and tightening over my wrist, then the other. She resituated in the driver seat, a confident smirk on her face, inspecting my restrained hands.

I knew what had happened, but a sliver of hope that she made a mistake had me yanking against the steel cuffs. My fucking cuffs. The thin metal dug in, cutting into the soft flesh.

Tipping back, I studied the side handle along the door she'd looped the cuffs through for any weakness.

None.

This just kept getting better and better.

Way to go, Agent Riggs. You allowed a serial killer to use your own agency-issued equipment against you.

If my damn anxiety hadn't driven me to be overly prepared for the earlier sting, I wouldn't be cuffed to the damn van.

With my hands secured with my own cuffs—if I lived through this, I was almost positive I'd never, ever live the mistake down—I was at her mercy as she explored up and down my torso, fingers slipping inside my dress. The sense of utter violation as she continued to search for a wire engulfed me.

"First question. Why were you really at the hotel bar tonight?" she asked, seemingly satisfied after her thorough inspection that I wasn't wearing a wire.

"I wasn't there to cheat," I said, avoiding the pointed question. "I've been cheated on. There's no way I could do that to someone else."

"Do what?" she demanded, wiggling the gun in my face.

Ugh, why are serial killers so fucking chatty? Good thing my statement of being cheated on wasn't a lie. I had the experience, the feelings to fall back on for her demand.

"The anguish when that trust snaps, shattering into a thousand shards, never to be repaired the same way again. Much like your heart when you catch him in his office with his younger, hotter TA sprawled out on top of the desk, his head buried between her legs."

Vision a little blurry, I stared at her, waiting for the rebuttal, for the next question, but it never came. Apparently I'd stunned her into silence with the honesty in my response. I wished it was all a lie, that saying those words out loud didn't rip open the still-fresh scar my bastard of an ex left over my heart. The scar that was slowly healing under Charlie's touches and smiles.

"Then why were you there if...? Oh. You were there to find me," she mumbled. "The FBI... fuck," she screamed, slamming a hand against the headrest. "They know."

I swallowed hard, keeping one eye on the gun and one on her crumbling features.

This was not good.

Not good at all.

She was past unraveling. Now her knowing we were looking for her tonight meant this would end up differently than how she'd originally planned with just me dead. And I knew it. Knew it the second that fear and worry vanished from her haggard features and a cold, emotionless mask slipped into place.

Tonight was the night she'd enact her endgame.

Chapter 25

And I was coming along for the ride.

I opened my mouth, inhaling a lungful of air to scream my head off, but another jolt of electricity seared through my veins, making me flail along the van floor. When I could focus, I whimpered at the syringe in her hand.

"Sorry, sorry. I won't make a sound, I promise. Just not that," I begged. "Tell me why. Tell me why those women. Tell me who hurt you."

The stretch of her arm paused, the tip of the needle only inches from my thigh.

"Tell me your story," I pleaded. "I want to know."

Sad eyes flicked to mine. "My story?"

"Don't you want one person to know why? Explain why the needle, why the bridge, why these women."

I knew her answer before she did. They all wanted to talk, to relive the murders or push the blame of their actions onto the one who hurt them, starting the killing spree. It wasn't a made-up monologue like they showed in the movies. No, this was cathartic for the killer. A cleansing of their soul of the incident that forced them to this point. Most of the killers I'd caught weren't true psychopaths, just wounded, angry, misguided humans who'd found the wrong way to vent.

Okay, the really wrong way to vent.

Did I need to know? Not really. I already knew. It was all in the profile, minus the gender mix-up. But her venting, divulging everything she'd done and why, was one minute longer I was alive and a minute more for Charlie to save me.

He would, because if she had my gun, badge, and the damn cuffs, that meant the second tracker Charlie demanded I carry was in the van with me.

He'd find me.

Now it was my job to make sure that when he did, it wasn't too late.

26

CHARLIE

"Holy fuck, this is a lot of fucking evidence. Is this the last of it?" I asked the plain-clothed crime scene tech as she deposited another clear bag in the van.

"Yes, sir. We're all done. Good timing too. The hotel manager stopped me on the last run up to the fifth floor and asked what was going on."

I grimaced. "Sure as hell hope that doesn't come back to bite us in the ass."

"We trapped a killer, one who preyed on the hotel's clients. Tonight was a win for all of us. I'm sure they'll see that and waive any lawsuits."

Highly doubtful, but I offered a reluctant nod to appease her. She was right. I should have been fucking ecstatic that the plan worked, but instead, I was emotionally and physically drained. Which didn't make a bit of sense. Usually this stage of the investigation, catching the unsub, thrilled me to no end, wiring me for days before I crashed.

But this time, it was different, and I had no damn clue why.

Reaching forward, I grabbed the handle of the back door and pulled it closed, sealing myself inside. Alone in the surveillance van, I scanned the bags of evidence we collected and sighed. Hands on my hips, I waited for the cause for my unease to snag my attention.

I was so damn tired.

Sighing I shifted through the bags, locating the one with the syringe. The thin plastic bunched between my fingers as I drew it closer, turning it one way, then the other, inspecting it from all angles.

"Huh," I said when the overhead dome light highlighted something none of us noticed upstairs.

Liquid.

There wasn't much, but where the rubber end of the plunger met the plastic base, miniscule drops of liquid collected.

That was odd, and out of place considering our unsub killed his victims by air injection.

Swiping my phone off the floor, I tapped Bryson's number and put the call on speaker.

"You almost here with the evidence?" he asked in way of greeting. "This guy is putting on one hell of a show, saying—"

"Why did he have a syringe hidden in his room?" I asked, cutting him off. The sudden spike of adrenaline rattled my nerves. "I need that answered now, Bryson."

"Then let's go have a little chat with him." The clip of his shoes along the station floor was followed by the whoosh of a door opening. I heard furious male shouts, calling out that everyone was fired and he'd sue the department. Cracking my knuckles, I stared at the screen, waiting for Bryson to calm the fucker down. "What was the syringe for?"

"Syringe?"

"In your hotel room, side drawer. The empty syringe."

"Why do you want to know?" The defiance in his tone had my already swollen hand bunching into a tight fist, itching to punch something, but no need to replay a dumb mistake.

"Just answer the fucking question. We don't care about your affair, or your tiny-ass dick." I chuckled, smirking at the phone. *Bryson might be my new favorite friend.* "Why did you have a syringe—"

Chapter 26

"I'm a fucking diabetic, you asshole," the man roared through the phone.

My stomach dropped, my body going numb.

Oh fuck.

"Where is his insulin?" I barked at Bryson, who relayed my question to the suspect.

"It was in the back of the drawer in a black zipper pouch. I had just given myself an injection when that woman of yours knocked on the door. Should've known something was up. They never show up early," he grumbled at the end.

Like a madman on a mission, I rifled through the bags of evidence, looking for what he described. Toward the back, meaning some of the first evidence we collected, I found it. Pressing on the center of the bag, I felt for a vial shape.

"He's telling the truth," I said in disbelief, hands falling to my side. "I have his insulin here in the van. Fuck," I shouted. "It's not him."

"It's not?" Bryson questioned. "He's on the list you compiled. So what if he's a diabetic? Maybe that's why he uses empty syringes. It's on hand and easy to clean up. Don't doubt yourself just yet, man. Let's process everything before we jump to conclusions."

He was right, so why did it all feel so damn wrong?

"Yeah, okay, you're right. I'll head that way shortly. Is Rhyan there yet?"

"Thought she was with you?"

Dropping the evidence bags, I scrubbed a hand over my face to hopefully clear the fog coating my tired brain. "She left about an hour ago saying she was headed to the hotel to change, then would make her way to the station."

"Huh. Maybe she took a shower first."

"Maybe," I said, my stomach now twisted in a damn knot. "I'm going to try calling her. Text me if she shows up."

"You got it. I'm sure she's fine."

If he was sure, then why was there tension in his voice that wasn't there moments ago?

He felt it too.

Something was wrong.

But fucking what?

Ending the call, I pulled up her contact information and held the phone to my ear.

It didn't even ring, just went straight to voice mail.

Each ragged breath was harder to suck down than the previous as worry wrapped its icy claws around my lungs. Tapping the edge of the phone against my temple, I tried to align my frenzied thoughts. The computer screen to my left, the one that ran all the facial recognition earlier, flashed with an alert I'd ignored when Rhyan stepped into the elevator. Hell, I'd ignored a lot of alerts since then, my sole focus on monitoring the mic feed for any hint of her needing me.

Crouched to not slam my head on the roof, I pulled the chair close. The dark screen flared to life with a quick tap to the keyboard. Seven new matches populated while Rhyan was upstairs, and during the extensive time it took to gather all the evidence.

The first three hits were so far off the profile, I only spent a few seconds screening their files before moving on to the next. The fourth looked promising but missed the mark completely, seeing as his address was an hour away and he had no medical training.

Fifth and sixth were similar in that they matched bits and pieces of the profile but not well enough to urge me to dig deeper.

I almost clicked out of the seventh just because a woman didn't seem pertinent to the case, but then I remembered why we ran her face in the first place. Scooting closer to the screen, I scanned down her background, my stomach rolling with each line.

Janice Hardgrove. Forty-three, divorced a year ago, and based on the multiple restraining orders taken out by her ex-husband's new wife, it wasn't amicable. With a few quick taps, I dug deeper into the divorce proceedings.

Irreconcilable differences.

I stared at that line for an entire minute, wondering if it should also list infidelity.

Lost her job as an RN a few months after the divorce. Almost bankrupt now. My fingers flew across the keyboard, searching through her work history. Now she was an in-home healthcare worker, not as a nurse but as an aide.

I slumped back, rubbing my scruff-covered jaw as I stared at all the information in front of me.

Everything matched our profile, except the gender.

Were we that far off? Rhyan did mention, multiple times, that something bothered her about this case. Something she couldn't put her finger on. With the woman's face staring at me, it all made sense. Women killed neatly, so no one had to clean up after them, and a water burial....

"Shit." Almost falling out of my chair, I moved to the other screen, bringing my keyboard with me. The entire van shook as I pounded on the keys, entering the search for the trackers I'd forced Rhyan to wear.

One blinked close by—too close. Closing my eyes, I lifted my face to the roof and yelled a string of curses at my dumb ass for allowing Rhyan to remove the tracker from her body. Hopefully the other one was close, which also meant she had her gun.

Changing the search string to the other tracker, a new red dot blinked, this time not hovering over where our van sat along the street. The screen blurred. Heels of both palms pressed against my eye sockets, I rubbed and blinked to clear my vision.

No, it wasn't fuzzy because of my eyesight. The red dot was moving—fast. Too quickly for her to still be walking the downtown streets clearing her head, and nowhere near the hotel or police station. And if she was in a ride share to the station, why didn't she answer when I called?

"Something is wrong," I blurted when Bryson picked up my call.

"Calm the—"

"That woman at the bar, the one you told me to run a background on. I got the results back. She fits our profile. I think... I think she's our unsub, not the fucker you have in custody."

"A woman." My anger boiled at the doubt in his tone. "But you two profiled—"

"I know what we profiled," I roared into the phone. "We were wrong. I can feel it, and I think she has Rhyan."

"What do you mean, you think?" he hissed. "What the fuck, Charlie? Where is she?"

"I don't know. Her tracker is going all around the city, like she's driving without a clear destination. Fuck, fuck—"

"Send me the tracking information, and I'll have an agent at the local office monitor it while gathering the forces. I'll request a helicopter to follow as well."

"We don't have—"

"I can do it all on the way," he said over the ding in the background. "I'm coming to you. Study the hell out of the route, and see if you can predict where she'll go next until I get there. You hear me? I'll bring a suburban with Wi-Fi so you can keep the laptop pulled up."

"Yeah." Without a goodbye, I tossed the phone to the floor, not caring about anything but finding my girl.

The red dot wove through the downtown Louisville streets. At this hour, a lone car on the street would be simple to spot. I just had to predict where they were going to cut them off and not incite a high-speed chase, putting Rhyan's life in more danger.

The clock was ticking to find them before Janice hurt my Rhyan. Unless she already had.

A harsh breath whistled through my clenched teeth as I struggled to keep control.

There was zero proof Rhyan was in danger, or that the woman on my screen was our unsub. But that didn't matter to my knotted gut. For the first time since we started this damn case, everything fit. The profile made sense. Except now it was too late.

The woman I loved was possibly in the hands of an unraveling serial killer with anger issues.

Following the tracker on the screen, I tried to make sense of the route. Though if she held true to her signature, she would head for the bridge. We'd profiled that the bridge held some kind of significance to the unsub, which kept him—*her* going back to that location.

Chapter 26

So what was the best course of action? Catch up with this woman on the streets and confront her there, or wait at the bridge?

As I debated the pros and cons of both, the red blinking dot took a sharp turn. Tapping a key, I zoomed in on the map to see where the road led.

The river and the massive pedestrian bridge the most recent victim was dropped over, to be exact.

That was where we needed to confront Janice.

A thundering pounding rattled through the van. I jumped up from my crouched position, slamming my head against the low roof. With a curse, I pressed on the spot, hoping to quell the pain I knew would come as I crouch-walked to the back of the van.

A bulletproof vest with white-blocked FBI written across the front was shoved into my face the moment I swung the door open.

"Put that shit on," Bryson ordered. "You have your gun?"

The ripping of Velcro sounded louder than normal with the quiet streets. "Yes, and an extra clip."

"Where are they headed?" Bryson asked over his shoulder as he strode toward a black Suburban.

"The bridge," I shouted. "Let me grab the laptop—"

"Does she still have her mic? I muted it earlier, but—"

"Fucking thing is in my pocket, where it's useless."

"And her earpiece?"

While securing the final strap around my chest, I opened my mouth to tell him I had that too, then slammed it shut. "Holy fuck."

"Grab what equipment you need for the transmission. Once we get in range, we can talk to her, let her know we're coming."

In a rush, I gathered the needed equipment and sprinted across the empty street, arms full, to the already running Suburban.

"You said this thing has Wi-Fi, right?"

"Yep."

"Great. Head toward the bridge, I'll tell you where to go from there."

Hopefully one of the many escape plans Rhyan concocted in that brilliant brain of hers included this scenario.

Someone took the only woman I'd ever loved until Rhyan from me before I could say goodbye, and I sure as hell wouldn't let the same thing happen again.

I would get her back safely.

Or I would go down with her.

27

RHYAN

My muscles burned and my shoulders ached, pulling as we took yet another sharp turn. My legs slammed against the passenger seat for what felt like the thousandth time. Asking for her story might have prolonged my life, but holy hell, the woman was a terrible driver. Or maybe the erratic driving was from the fact that she was drunk. Apparently kidnapping and plotting murder needed to be done with a fifth of cheap whiskey in your system, and she continued drinking now.

The driver seat blocked my view of her, but the stench of the alcohol filled the van. That combined with my nerves, already empty stomach, and all the rolling around, and I'd swallowed down enough stomach acid to do major esophagus damage at this point in the night. Though that would only be an issue if I lived past the next few hours.

While she ranted and raged about her cheating ex and his whore of a new wife, tall downtown buildings flashing through the side window told me we hadn't gone that far. Piecing together the slurred words, I discovered her abandonment issues started long before her husband's affair. Early in her childhood, her father abandoned the family for his secretary, leaving her mother a single working parent.

So when it happened in her own marriage, well, that triggered the urge for revenge to escalate into killing.

Why she killed the women and not the men who consented to the affair was answered early in the drive. She blamed *them*. In her crazed way of thinking, the women tempted the men away from their spouses, which meant the women needed to be punished. They knew the men were married yet still sought them out, making them stray by exploiting their womanly ways.

Her words, not mine.

She didn't have high opinions of men, complaining that a simple wink or hip shake would throw a committed man off course. To her, all men were weak prey. The way she talked, it all made sense to her, and in her husband's case, maybe it was true. Maybe he was weak and fell victim to his secretary's advances, or maybe he lied to her and he was the one to instigate the relationship.

If I lived through this, I'd ask him. Then punch him in the balls for being the catalyst for all this.

There was no way for me to decipher how long we'd driven around, but hopefully long enough for Charlie to realize I wasn't at the hotel or police station.

Silence from the front seat for the first time in a while struck a fresh chord of fear.

"Why the bridge?" I asked. *Keep her talking.* If she was talking, then she wasn't killing me. Solid plan. "It must hold significance to you and your ex."

A slosh of liquid followed by a sharp turn like she corrected a swerve rocked me along the floorboard. I bit my tongue to keep from crying out.

"It was where he proposed. To me, not her. Where he told me he wanted to spend the rest of his life with me." Her high-pitched shriek in the enclosed area pierced my eardrums. "It's where it started." Her harsh breaths filled the van. "And it's where it will end."

Oh no. That did not sound good.

Think, Rhyan. Come on, anxiety, don't fail me now.

Though of course it didn't work that way. My anxiety helped

come up with hundreds of different scenarios that would never happen, but in the moment when I needed to think clearly, all I could do was fucking panic.

Like I was doing right then.

"It doesn't have to end," I said, tugging against the restraints. The metal dug deeper into my wrists. "We can get you help—"

Her responding laugh was harsh. "Help? Help for what? For murdering eight whores?"

Well, that was enlightening. Apparently, we'd missed a couple bodies she sent downriver.

"Yes. They have medical centers—"

The van swerved hard, taking a corner on two wheels. "I'm not insane." *Right. Sure, lady, whatever you say.* "I won't go to jail or sit on death row. There's no going back for me now."

"What about me?' I begged. "I'm innocent. I'm the victim, just like you."

The van slowed to a stop. Frantic, I scanned the windows, searching for landmarks, anything I recognized.

Trees strategically spaced apart.

Same with the overhead lights, different from the ones I noticed on the downtown streets during my fateful walk. These seemed more like ones you'd find in a parking lot.

Craning my neck for a different angle, I caught sight of an elaborate metal arch through the windshield.

The pedestrian bridge.

Heart racing, I jerked on the cuffs. A bottle rolled beside my feet as I dug my heels into the gritty floorboard, shoving my body back and back until my head collided with the sliding door. Pain radiated from the impact, though it was nothing compared to the slices now dripping blood down my forearms.

Tears flowed down my sticky cheeks.

This can't be it.

"If you can hear this, we're on our way. Hold on, baby."

I stilled, focusing everything on that voice in my head.

No, not my head. My ear.

The earpiece.

With a relieved sob, I slouched against the sliding door, the hard plastic digging into my upper back.

"You're right, you are a victim." The resigned tone sent chills down my spine. She turned in her seat, the lip of that damn plastic bottle pressed against her lips as she tipped it upward. "But so am I."

"Don't do this. I have someone waiting for me," I sobbed, the words barely audible around my tear-clogged throat.

"Then I'm saving you," she said, tossing the empty bottle to the passenger seat. "He'll just break you."

"No," I shouted. "He won't. He's not like that. He's not like them."

And Charlie wasn't. His hard exterior was just that, hiding a sweet, lonely man inside who I desperately wanted to call my own. I loved that man beneath the ink and piercings just as much as I lusted over the exterior. He was the complete package, and I'd just found him. Just had a sliver of what it was like to be wholly and truly loved.

And now this.

Through the tears, I saw her reach for something on the floor.

I didn't think, just acted on sheer will to live.

With a yell, I curled my legs in and kicked out between the driver and passenger seats. With the seat in my way, I couldn't aim, just kicked, hoping to connect with something vital. Both feet connected with her shoulder. The van rocked when she slammed against the dash.

The solid hit to my left shin registered half a second before the excruciating pain.

I screamed through gritted teeth, yanking my legs to the back of the van. A powerful throb bloomed from my left leg down to my toes.

"I'll need you to hold still for this."

I turned my watery gaze toward the sound of her voice.

Gun in one hand, syringe in the other.

Now I had a decision to make.

Die by gunshot or by my heart exploding.

Decisions, decisions.

"Janice Hardgrove," a male voice shouted outside the van. She paused, going deathly still. "We have you surrounded. Drop the weapon, and come out with your hands up."

"I can't see Rhyan," Charlie's voice said in my ear.

"Neither can I," Bryson shouted back.

"Tell everyone to hold their fire until we have eyes on her. We will not fire until we know she's not in range."

I struggled against the restraints to sit up, to show them my location. When that didn't work, I heaved both legs into the air, my ab muscles burning, and kicked, attempting to draw attention to the back seat.

"Are those feet?" Charlie questioned. "She's in the back. Maybe restrained. Shit, the gun is trained on her. Do not fire. I repeat, do not fire."

"At least you won't have to go through it all again," Janice said, dropping the syringe but keeping the gun pointed at my gut. "I'm saving you from that."

"No, Janice, no. You're not saving me. You're killing me!"

"A heart shattered twice by betrayal is no heart at all."

"Janice, please," I begged, hot tears leaking down my cheeks.

"You'll thank me for this. Maybe, maybe, all this was for us to find each other. So someone would never hurt again us."

That's it. No more nice profiler trying to keep the crazy woman from killing me. That, unfortunately, was inevitable, no matter what I said or did.

So, I snapped.

"You fucking lunatic," I screamed loud enough for all of Louisville, most importantly Charlie and Bryson, to hear. "This is not fated. Let me go."

"Is that Rhyan?" Bryson questioned in my ear. "It's muffled, but it sounds like a woman screaming."

"Something just happened. She sounds panicked."

"No shit, I'm panicked," I screamed even louder, hoping they could understand me. "She's going to fucking kill us both. Shoot. Shoot the insane lady in the driver seat."

Her eyes went wide.

Whoops.

Way to go, you idiot. Now she knew I had a direct line to what was going on outside the van of horrors.

Who would've thought that would be my biggest mistake of the night?

Not profiling the wrong gender for the unsub.

Not the handcuffs or the gun in the purse.

Not being a kind citizen and offering a phone to a fellow female in need.

Oh no. Those were minor to this one, because it spurred what happened next.

Keeping the gun trained on me, Janice shifted to face out the windshield. With a clunk, the old transmission shifted gears, followed by a roar from the revving of the small engine. The force slammed my upper body and legs against the seat bases, quickly followed by the van ramming into something, sending me rocketing forward to hit the front seats.

Pain and fear crested within me. Tilting to the side, I vomited what little was in my stomach onto the floorboard.

My body shook, bouncing as the van popped up and down like we were no longer on a flat road but off-roading.

"Rhyan," Charlie bellowed in my ear. "No!"

And with that, I knew, even before the van's front end tipped downward and the sensation of free-falling bubbled in my belly.

Before we smashed into something solid, flinging my body forward.

Before the dark water engulfed the windshield.

This was the end.

"Goodbye, Charlie," I whispered. "I'll always love you."

28

CHARLIE

I sprinted toward the sinking van.

Racing across the parking lot, Glock in hand, I followed the rubber tracks burned out along the pavement, hopped over the small barrier fence the van had crashed through, and raced down the grass-covered bank.

Nothing mattered except saving Rhyan.

Thankfully, the helicopter Bryson called in on the way to the river hovered overhead, its spotlight following the van as it bobbed, moving downstream with the current.

In a dead sprint, tennis shoes pounding against the earth, I didn't break stride when I hit the concrete barrier. The gun's rough grip dug into my palm as I tightened my hand to keep from losing it in the water. With both hands outstretched, I shoved off the edge of the barrier, leaping into the air and diving into the choppy brown water.

The abrupt change in temperature almost stole the air from my lungs. Popping above the surface, I gasped for breath. Treading water, arms slapping the surface, I twisted in every direction, searching over the lapping waves for the van.

Another splash sounded close, but I didn't have time to see who'd followed me into the river. Kicking hard, I lunged one arm over my head, then the other, propelling myself through the waves toward the shaky spotlight.

Bottom half of the van fully submerged, the helicopter's light highlighted a flash of dark hair in the back seat. Pushing my body to the limit, I swam to the passenger side door.

Terrified green eyes met mine through the glass.

"I'm here, Rhyan," I yelled, hoping she could hear me over the helicopter's whirling blades. "I'm getting—"

An inhuman screech from inside the van whipped my attention to movement in the front. Face bloody, the woman from the bar slowly raised a gun, pointing it toward the window.

"Duck," I screamed as I yanked my gun to the surface, finger already on the trigger and one in the chamber.

The moment Rhyan's head dipped below the surface, I fired.

Glass shattered, shards flying into my face. Lids squeezed shut to protect my eyes, I failed to see where the bullet hit. Pain exploded like a set of knives jammed into my left pec, thrusting me backward a foot with the impact. Quick breaths hissing through my clenched teeth, I forced my eyes open, gun still raised despite the searing pain from my chest. A lifeless body bobbed facedown in the water.

A desperate gasp of breath had me sucking in my own and swinging the barrel to the sound to find Rhyan, mouth open, gasping for air, hair covering her mouth and nose. Water gushed through the hole in the glass, quickly filling.

"Cuffed," she called out.

Oh shit.

I nearly sank with the panic that overtook every cell.

"Door or van?" I asked, reaching out to wipe the hair from the front of her face, the water now up to where she strained to keep her chin high.

"Door." Her face slipped beneath the water.

"No!" I bellowed. Sucking down a lungful of air, I plunged below the surface to search blindly for the door's outside handle. Smooth metal gave way to a lump. Numb fingers struggled with the lever. I tugged but nothing happened.

Locked.

I reached through the hole in the window, glass shards piercing my skin, slicing through muscle as I pressed forward. Hard plastic met my hand, the water making my movements slow and sloppy as I felt for the manual door lock along the top.

Kicking back to the surface, I gasped for breath while nudging the lock upward and tugging on the outside handle. With a roar, I focused all my energy and strength into wrenching the now-unlocked door open. Another set of hands appeared beside mine, gripping around the metal doorframe as I kicked beneath the surface, trying for more leverage.

"She's cuffed to the door," I yelled to Bryson as I watched Rhyan's pert little nose slip beneath the dark water's choppy surface. "We have to get it off its hinge to save her."

"One, two, three," he yelled back.

Muscles straining, pain sparked from my chest and arm as I pulled with all my strength. Feet pressed against the van's frame, I used the leverage to put all my weight into yanking the door toward us.

I roared in defeat when our first attempt only rocked the van deeper into the water.

"Again," I yelled through gritted teeth. "She's in there."

"I'll try a different angle below," Bryson yelled before taking three quick breaths and diving below the surface.

I felt the door shift, my only signal. Foot wedged against the van's frame, back to the sliding door, I shoved with everything I had left. The water lapped all around my face, my nose and mouth the only parts above the surface.

A creak followed by a snap, and the metal at my back lurched.

Reaching inside, I felt around for Rhyan, grabbing hold of the first touch of smooth icy skin. Finding her waist, I hauled her out of the van, the dislodged door dragging us both down to the river's dark depths. The air in my lungs sizzled, my brain demanding I breathe.

Kicking hard, I urged us inch by inch to the surface. Suddenly we rocketed toward the bright beam of light. Somehow the weight dragging her down lessened.

Bryson.

Our heads crested the surface, desperate gasps for air mirroring the other's.

Except Rhyan.

"Get her to shore," Bryson yelled, already using his one free arm to propel himself that direction, the other below the surface no doubt with a death grip on the van's sliding door that we literally ripped off the rails.

Flopping to my back, staring up at the quivering beam of light, I hauled Rhyan's limp body on top of my chest to keep her face above the water despite the weight trying to drag her under. One arm wrapped around her chest, hand around her throat to keep her face upright, I kicked through the water, the blinding spotlight following us as we trudged through the water toward shore.

Swimming against the current made the distance feel like miles, but still I kicked, using my free arm to move us toward the swarm of officers waiting by the retaining wall. At the edge, waves slapped against my face as arms and hands stretched down from above, grabbing for her.

"Handcuff keys," I said between gasps. A cramp seized my left thigh. Clenching my teeth, I yelled through the pain, forcing my other leg to work twice as hard to keep up above the surface "Hands."

A shout rang out above us. Bryson's exhausted eyes met mine before sliding to the still-limp woman in my arms.

"Hurry," he bellowed.

Seconds later, keys dangled before my eyes, and extra hands slipped below the surface. Someone shouted a quick countdown, and then grunts filled the air as they hauled the door and Bryson out of the water. Rhyan's arms lifted as the surrounding officers held the heavy metal steady the few feet above the surface, allowing another officer to finagle the key into the cuffs. The moment one metal ring released, the men lowered the heavy door, turning to reach beneath Rhyan.

Chapter 28

Her limp body, now weightless, rose higher and higher before vanishing over the edge of the retaining wall.

She was safe.

Muscles limp, energy depleted, I slipped lower in the water.

"Oh no you don't," I heard above me. "Help him out. I'll work on her."

Multiple hands gripped along both arms, fingers digging into the ragged, ripped flesh of my left. I cried out, unable to hold it back. The concrete edge scraped my lower back where the vest stopped as they hauled me from the water and deposited me on the grass.

My head lolled to the side at the sound of counting, finding a drenched Bryson hovering over Rhyan, his hands stacked on top of her chest.

My heart lurched at the sight, flooding my veins with fear-induced energy. With a groan, I pressed both palms to the thick grass, my left arm completely giving out. Using only my right arm, I crawled the few feet separating us. A warm stream of liquid trickled down my left forearm, staining the grass red in my wake.

"Rhyan," I croaked, throat raw. "Wake up, baby."

Finding the strength, I clambered to my knees, slamming into Bryson's side to stay upright. He tipped over, falling to the grass. Heel of my palm to her sternum, I whispered the count while saying a silent prayer with each push.

"Come on, Rhyan, wake up. Fight for me, baby," I pleaded. Pinching her nose, I covered her mouth with mine and pushed air from my lungs into hers. Going back to chest compressions, I studied that lifeless face, tears stinging my eyes. "Come on, wake up I have a fun fact for you. One you've never heard before. Come back to me—"

Her entire body shuddered. Water bubbled out of the corners of her parted lips. Hope soared in my heart. Her tangled hair caught between my fingers as I turned her head to the side, more water gushing from her.

"We need that damn ambulance," I roared inches from Rhyan's face, making her wince.

"Loud," she rasped between coughs. "Where...?"

"Agent Bekham." I tore my gaze away from her glassy, bloodshot eyes to the men standing just a foot away, a stretcher behind them.

I nodded and turned my face back to hers, forcing a smile. Darkness encroached, tunneling my vision.

"Fun fact, Supervisory Special Agent Riggs." The words slurred past my numb lips; the arm holding me upright trembled. "I love you."

"Agent," one of the EMTs urgently called.

"I'll be right behind you, baby." Leaning forward, I pressed a hard kiss to her forehead. But when I tried to sit back up, the world spun, and that trembling arm gave out completely. Aware enough to not fall forward, I pitched to the side, crumpling to the grass.

Chaos erupted above me.

"Where is all that blood coming from?" someone shouted.

Turning my head, I met Rhyan's terrified gaze. This time I knew the fear was for me, not her own life.

Smooth grass slipped beneath my arm as I shifted it inch by inch until the tip of my pinkie caressed her soft skin. The surrounding sounds dulled, growing hollow, like I was in a tube. My tunnel vision continued to narrow.

Before everything faded, I zeroed in on her lips—her moving lips.

Without sound, I strained to understand.

Then it clicked as she repeated the words over and over and over again.

"I love you too."

And that was all I needed to know.

She was one hell of a woman. She'd made it out of this mess alive, and she loved me too.

As I slipped into the awaiting oblivion, I felt my lips tweak upward, wanting to smile.

She loves me.

29

CHARLIE

The overpowering scent of disinfectant registered first, followed by an annoying squeak. Throat burning, thoughts lethargic, I fought my way back to consciousness to find the source of the irritating noise. I blinked slowly, urging my heavy lids to lift only for a bright light to blind my sensitive eyes. Peeking through thin slits, I focused on back-and-forth movement at the foot of my bed.

My hospital bed.

Fucking hell.

A groan rumbled up my raw throat. Instantly, the movement and squeaking ceased.

"Charlie? You awake, man?"

I nodded, forcing my eyes wide despite the discomfort. Bryson's ragged face peered down from the end of the bed, fists pressed to the mattress on either side of my feet.

"You look like shit," I rasped.

And that was putting it nicely. Patchy scruff covered his pallid cheeks, eyes bloodshot, with swollen purple bags beneath. Even his short hair looked disheveled, though I wasn't sure how that was possible. Gone were his jeans, T-shirt, and bulletproof vest that last were suctioned to his large frame, now replaced with a new set of clothes, though they appeared wrinkled and not so fresh.

"You're one to talk," he grumbled, rubbing at his jaw.

"Fucking hell," I complained when I shifted to sit up. A dull pain radiated from both arms. "How long was I out?"

"First, stop putting weight on that damn arm. The surgeon will kick your ass if you pop those stitches."

Stitches?

Surgeon?

What the hell?

"What the hell are you talking about? What stitches?"

Bryson tipped his face to the ceiling. "You were shot—"

"Faintly remember that happening. But I shot her back, so I call that a win."

That explained the soreness in my chest.

Thank you, Kevlar. Better a deep bruise than a gunshot wound.

"Not sure how in the hell you sliced up your arm, but—"

"Reaching through the shattered window to unlock the door." The instant I said the words, everything came flooding back. "Where is she?" The bed creaked and groaned as I shifted, glancing to the back corners of the room, searching for Rhyan.

"Settle down. Fuck, I'm calling a nurse to knock your ass out—"

"Don't you fucking dare."

"Then stop moving around." With a huff, he walked around the bed, digging between the mattress and the rail. "Here. The beds move up and down for terrible patients like yourself."

"I'm a great patient, and you haven't answered my question. Where. Is. Rhyan?"

It was hard to put force behind the words when lying in a damn hospital bed, using the remote to help me sit since I was a damn invalid.

"They removed the glass shards from your bicep before stitching you up. One hundred and ten stitches to repair all the damage. One gash was so damn deep the glass nicked your artery, which was why you lost blood so fast." *Huh. That sucks, but it all seems good now. Why won't he answer me about Rhyan?* "They got you into surgery the moment you arrived, where you stayed for three damn hours."

"What day is it?"

"It's 5:00 p.m., Monday."

Damn. "Why are you avoiding my question about Rhyan? I want to see her." Desperation leaked into my words. I gritted my teeth and shook my head. "Now, damnit."

"They brought her here for evaluation." His hazel eyes flicked to the side. My stomach twisted with worry. "There were trace amounts of water still in her lungs, so they hooked her up to IV antibiotics. At some point, she fractured her shin, so she's in a boot for a while. Plus a concussion, the slices on her wrist...."

"What aren't you telling me?" I gritted out, jaw locked tight as I shuffled on the bed to shift the pillow lower.

"We're in deep shit."

I stilled. "What do you mean, we're in deep shit?"

"Well, the guy we wrongly arrested wants to sue the Bureau and the Louisville PD, The Black Rose is threatening a lawsuit for running a sting inside their hotel without approval, you were shot with Rhyan's gun, and she was handcuffed to the van with her own handcuffs. It's a clusterfuck out there." He tilted his head toward the door. "And she's... hell, she's not taking it well."

My heart sank. "What does that mean?"

"It means she won't talk to anyone. She's nothing but despondent to me, the nurses, her friend who's called a million times."

"She's blaming herself," I stated. There was no question about it. Her overactive mind was playing tricks on her, making her think everything that went sideways was her fault. "I need to see her."

"Thought you'd say that," he muttered with a wide yawn. He picked up a stack of clothes from the cheap metal chair in the corner and tossed them to the foot of the bed. "Picked up some of your clothes from the hotel. But I sure as fuck am not dressing you."

My responding chuckle hurt like hell, turning it into more of a pain-filled groan. Damnit, being shot even with a vest on fucking hurt. I would be sore for weeks, though that was significantly better than having to rehab the shoulder.

"Get a nurse to help." As much as I didn't want the help, there was no way I could get dressed alone from the pain and damn wires and tubes. I called out to Bryson as he reached for the door handle. "What are we looking at, for disciplinary actions?"

His wide shoulders slumped.

Damn, that was not a good sign.

"Your boss and the assistant deputy director of the whole damn FBI are coming—" He checked his watch. "—any minute now. Get dressed. She'll need you at her side for this."

"Thank you," I called. He paused while reaching for the door handle and turned to look over his shoulder. "For... hell, for everything. I'll make sure you stay out of the line of fire in this battle. You helped save Rhyan. I'll take all the blame if I need to."

"I can hold my own—"

"You have a daughter to think about. Rhyan and I got us into this. We'll make sure ADD Garr knows that." Not sure how, but we would, or I would. If I could figure out a way to take all the blame, I'd play that card. ADD Garr was known as a hard-ass, strictly by the book type. "And thanks for the clothes."

"You're welcome. It was self-serving. I didn't want to see your pale ass when you fought your way to Rhyan's room despite the doctor's orders." One corner of his lips twitched upward. "I'll go get the nurse."

When the door closed, I pushed past the pain, bending the arm not wrapped in gauze and bandages. Slipping a hand beneath the scratchy-ass gown, I ripped off the first wire I touched, moving on to find the others. Equipment blared in warning, lights flashed, but I didn't stop until every sensor was disconnected.

A swarm of nurses stormed through the door, catching me before I could remove the port taped to the back of my hand.

"Mr. Bekham," one of the older women in sea-green scrubs chastised. "What do you think you're doing?"

"Going to see my girl," I stated while shifting to the edge of the bed. "You can either help me or get out of my way. She needs me, and I sure as hell won't lie here doing jack shit."

"You're recovering—"

"Yeah, I got the rundown from my friend. Which is it, helping or getting out of my way?"

Her thin lips pressed into a tight line, the other two nurses watching her reaction.

"You keep that IV in," she demanded, jamming a finger toward my hand. "The river water is nasty, and you gave those germs a direct line to your bloodstream. You'll both need antibiotics for at least another day."

Thank fuck. I relaxed, pausing all movement. Already, sweat slicked my skin from the pain and spent energy.

After dismissing the other two younger nurses, she stood at my bedside.

"This is a terrible idea."

"Yeah it is," I said, laughing, then groaning. "But it's the only option. I have to be with her."

She sighed and flipped the blankets back, the cold air a welcomed reprieve from the heat building beneath my skin.

"Stubborn-ass men," she said with a click of her tongue. "I'll help you sit up, but be prepared. All this movement will hurt."

I dipped my chin, already prepared for the pain and exhaustion to come.

As long as I got to see Rhyan, make her understand this wasn't her fault, then I'd take it all.

HOSPITAL ROOM DOORWAYS passed on either side as the nurse wheeled me down the busy hall. If anyone asked, I'd say she forced me into the wheelchair, though that was a stretch. It took little push from the nurse to get me to concede. I underestimated the energy it would take to get dressed around all the tubes, and how the full-body pain would drain even more.

But I did it, and now I got Rhyan as my reward.

We took a right down another long hall, turning into the second door on the left. My heart swelled, breath catching at the sight of her. Head turned to the side, Rhyan faced the single window, unfocused eyes open.

"Miss Riggs, you have a persistent visitor," the nurse murmured at my back as she wheeled me to Rhyan's bedside.

No response.

"Give us a second," I muttered over my shoulder, not taking my eyes off the woman I loved.

Purple-and-green bruises dotted her face, red hair sticking up and knotted, and her face was pale—too pale. Yet she still looked beautiful. Against the odds, she'd survived, worked her way from death's door to come back to me.

"Baby," I rasped the moment the nurse left. Grimacing through the pain blooming from my shoulder, I rested my arm atop the white blanket, nudging her fingers with my own. "Look at me."

"No." A single tear dripped from the corner of her eye, rolling down her bruised cheek.

"Yes."

"No."

"Rhyan," I growled. Hooking a finger through one of hers, I gave it a weak squeeze. "Look at me. Now."

Her hair rasped along the thin pillowcase. Sad, defeated, bloodshot green eyes locked on me. "I'm so sorry," she said in a rushed whisper. "I fucked everything up. It's all—"

"You're killing me here, Rhyan," I groaned. "I want to shut you up, but I can't get out of this fucking thing to kiss you."

The mention of my condition opened the floodgates. Her desolate sob rattled through the small room as streams of tears cascaded down her face. "You got hurt because of my incompetence." Turning, she went back to staring out the window. "I got the profile wrong, I helped arrest the wrong man, and then I put myself in the worst situation with the actual unsub."

"Stop." I pushed strength into my voice. "We worked the case together. I didn't catch the fact that our killer was a woman either. You stated from the beginning that something was off. Everything else was spot-on. And the arresting thing, well, you might not have jumped the gun in accusing him if I hadn't been desperate for you to get out of that damn room. I was the one who told you his real background matched our parameters and to react the moment you saw anything suspicious. That's on me, Rhyan." Green eyes cut to the side, watching me from the corners. "And the last part, well, I'd love to hear how you ended up with her."

"I was an idiot."

"Doubt that. Tell me."

By the time she was done explaining what happened from the moment she left the hotel to the ambulance ride here, the sun had set, the last of the day's bright rays piercing through the tinted window. With a sigh, she lay back, closing her eyes.

I should have left her alone, let her rest. Hell, I was fucking exhausted, but I couldn't. Not yet. I needed to know. Needed to know if she meant it.

"Rhyan," I whispered.

"It's okay, Charlie," she said, eyes squeezed shut. "I can forget what you said. It was the heat of the moment, you'd just saved me, and—"

"Do you want to forget it? Want me to not love you?" There was no hiding the pain in my low tone.

"No," she whispered, lids flying open. "Of course not. I... I want it to be true because...." She blew out a slow breath. "I need it to be true."

"Good."

"Good?"

"Because it is true. I fucking love you, Rhyan Riggs." I tried to stand to get on the damn bed and hold her while I ripped open my heart for this woman, but I only rose an inch before collapsing back down. *Okay, rain check on that holding part.* "You're the most amazing woman I've ever met, inside and out. The way your mind works fascinates me, and the shit that comes out of your mouth makes me laugh harder than I have in years."

"Really?"

"Yes, baby. I love you, and I will work every day we're together to ensure you never forget that."

"Really?"

I smirked. "This is once again where I'd shut you up with a kiss, but that will have to wait."

"You don't blame me?"

"Blame you for what?"

"For making a terrible decision, missing the profile, and—"

"No, Rhyan. You were trying to be a good person, helping a stranded woman in need. That damn woman took advantage of your kind heart. She knew the moment she met you at the bar that you'd stop for her. I'm willing to bet she sealed the deal by mentioning something about kids."

Rhyan's grimace was all the confirmation I needed.

"We've always said killers are the best profilers. It's how they know who and how to target their victims to get them to forgo all warning signs."

"Charlie—"

The door flew open, cutting her off. Two men in suits walked through, one smiling—Carter—and the other, ADD Garr, looking fucking pissed off at the world.

Fuck, I hated our section chief. Prick was gloating in the fact that we fucked up.

Rhyan stiffened, pulling her hand away from mine.

"Riggs, Bekham," the asshole said louder than necessary. "You're fired."

30

RHYAN

Instead of listening to our idiot section chief, I watched Assistant Deputy Director Garr.

And he watched me.

Charlie groaned as he tried to turn the wheelchair around to face the two intruders.

Without a word, Garr strode to Charlie's side and wheeled the chair in a tight circle, parking him back at my side but this time facing the door.

"Thanks," Charlie grumbled.

"There will be a formal review—"

"Review? So, then, how are we fired if there hasn't been a review?" I questioned, sweeping my gaze to the idiot.

His chest puffed out. "Based on the reports—"

"Whose reports? I haven't filed anything yet, and I know Agent Bekham just woke from surgery, so I know he hasn't filed his incident report yet either."

I took slight delight in the way his face flushed red. *Why in the hell did I wait so damn long to stand up to this man?* It needed to stop, now. I would not allow him to ruin Charlie's career or Bryson's because he was incompetent at his job and allowed personal feelings to trump facts.

Did I mess up? Yes.

Would I pay for those mistakes? Yes.

But firing me before an internal investigation? I think the fuck not.

"There are several parties ready to sue the Bureau because of your incompetence—"

"Carter," Garr barked. The other man flinched. "As we discussed on the plane, this is not your call. It is mine and the review board's. SSA Riggs has valid points against your claim of being fired." Turning on the heels of his polished shoes, he ripped the door open and pointed toward the hall. "As also discussed, you're not needed. Wait for me in the hall. Do not, I repeat, do not speak to anyone. If I find out you've said a word, I will fire your ass without an investigation."

Charlie sat up straighter, and if I wasn't mistaken, his shoulders shook with restrained laughter.

"But, sir—"

"Out," the ADD ordered. The door slammed shut behind the dismissed man. When Garr turned back around, he scrubbed a large hand over his face. "Fucking hell, that man is an idiot."

This time Charlie didn't hold back, and his bark of laughter somehow made my smile grow wider.

"You really should've taken that role, Rhyan. When you turned it down, you stuck me with that moron until I can dump his ass on another agency."

"Sorry," I said, relaxing back against the pillow, my energy draining. "I wasn't ready."

His gray brows flicked higher. "Are you saying you might be now?"

I nodded. "I am."

Garr's green eyes slid to Charlie. Only because I'd known the man my whole life did I notice him suppress a smile.

"Well, that's great to hear. Now, would either of you care to tell me

Chapter 30

what the hell really happened Sunday night and how my niece ended up in a serial killer's hands?"

"Your niece?" Charlie exclaimed.

Uncle Garr's smile finally broke free. "We keep it very hush-hush around Quantico so no one can claim favoritism."

Charlie twisted to stare me down. I held up both hands in surrender.

"I would've told you, but you never asked why I wanted to be an FBI agent." I tilted my head toward the man making his way to the other side of the hospital bed. His large hand grasped my fingers and squeezed. "Uncle Garr is my mother's brother. He wooed me at a very early age with his stories of hunting killers and saving lives. I always knew I wanted to grow up and be just like him."

"Brilliant, handsome, and a likable fucker." Uncle Garr laughed.

"Well, she surely is all that and more," Charlie said as he grabbed my other hand and squeezed. Uncle Garr tracked the movement. "Sir, I—"

"We'll figure *that*," he said with a pointed look at our interlaced fingers, "out later. For now, someone please tell me what the hell happened? Rhyan's mom and that insistent friend of hers won't stop calling demanding updates."

My loud laugh made both men grin. The throb in my head and dull ache from the fracture seemed less severe than just seconds ago.

"Okay," I said. "I'll start from the beginning. Agent Bennett brought a case to Agent Bekham's attention several days ago…"

It took a solid hour, Charlie adding in a few details here and there, to walk Uncle Garr through the last several days. I left out the intimate times between Charlie and me, of course, and that we were in love.

Yeah, in love. Together. My heart swelled to the point of bursting every time I repeated his earlier declaration.

Uncle Garr blew out a heavy breath through tight lips and scrubbed a hand over his weary features. "He's worse than I thought," he grumbled, staring at the door as if he could see through it to our asshole section chief just on the other side.

"I'm more concerned about his blatant dislike for Agent Bekham—"

"For fuck's sake, Rhy. Call him Charlie. Enough with the formalities."

I felt my face flush with heat. "His blatant dislike for Charlie. Charlie hasn't been with the unit long and has already made a positive impact. He started strong, brings a technical ability that none of the other agents have, and already has a firm grasp on profiling."

"Whoa," Uncle Garr said. "I know, Rhyan. You don't have to sell me on Bekham here. I'm the one who pushed his transfer through."

"You were?" Charlie said. His lids drooped. Fuck, he had to be exhausted from sitting up this whole time. We needed to wrap this up so he could get back in his bed, even though the thought of him leaving sent a burst of panic through my veins, my pulse racing.

"I was. I wanted to see what you could add to the cases with your technical ability, though I have to admit I've been slightly disappointed in the results."

"He's kept me on a tight leash," Charlie gritted out, the muscle along his jaw popping. "He made sure I knew I wasn't to use my capabilities. That's what our analysts at Quantico are for."

Uncle Garr muttered something under his breath. "Well, that explains that." Turning to face me, he brushed a knuckle down the side of my head. "You two need to rest. I'll take Carter back with me, then send the jet to pick you both up in three days. We'll discuss next steps then. Bekham." With a nod, he headed out the door.

Charlie and I sat in silence for several minutes after Uncle Garr left. Building lights flickered in the window, darkness having fully overtaken the sky. My own lids grew heavy.

"I'll never stop loving you," I whispered to Charlie. "No matter what happens, you're a part of me I never want to lose or forget. You make me a better *me* just by being near you." Not the most eloquent of words, but hey, I was half asleep already.

At the *whoosh* of the door, I forced my eyes open. An older, pissed-off-looking nurse strode into the room, beelining for Charlie.

"Mr. Bekham," she chastised. I couldn't help but smile. "You're hours past the time for you to be back in your bed."

"Bring one in here." His words were slurred, lids barely opening. "Not leaving. She loves me."

"I can't—"

"Bring his bed in here, please." My pathetic plea was annoying even to my own ears. "I don't want to sleep alone."

"It's against the rules," she stated, but the tilt in her voice hinted that she was considering our request.

"Story of his life," I said, smirking.

I must have drifted off to sleep for a minute, noises and hushed whispers pulling me back awake. Turning to the commotion, I blinked at the fuzzy scene as they helped Charlie into his own bed right next to my own.

Snuggling deeper beneath the thin covers, I sighed.

Protected and loved by the one and only Charlie Bekham.

I was one lucky woman.

EPILOGUE
RHYAN

Alone in the BSU conference room, I slipped the end of the pen inside the dumb boot. I rubbed it to quell the itch along my calf. The doctor here in DC wasn't sure exactly how much longer I'd need to wear the dumb thing. It all depended on me and following the doctor's orders for rest and keeping it elevated.

Damnit.

At that reminder, I cupped a hand beneath my knee and lifted the injured leg, resting the heel of the boot on the chair beside mine. I checked my watch. Fifteen more minutes until the meeting with Uncle Garr and Charlie started.

I'd already been sitting for the last five.

Being super early really was getting old, but I doubted I'd ever correct the behavior.

"Good morning, SSA Riggs." I bit my lip to keep my smile contained. Charlie's fingers brushed along my shoulders as he passed. A shiver of want raced down my spine, curling heated desire low in my belly.

Which was dumb considering what we did this morning before work.

Twice.

"Good morning." My gaze followed him around the room until he sat in the chair opposite me. "Any insight into what Garr found in his investigation?"

"None." All good humor vanished, his lips tightening into a tight line. "You?"

"Nope." I popped the *p*.

"Did you eat this morning?"

Be still my happy heart. This man.

A content sigh lifted my chest.

"Yes. I ate this morning."

"As did I," he purred, leaning forward to rest both forearms on the conference table. "I love eating you before work. Makes the day so much better."

Heat blasted beneath my cheeks. I pressed the tips of my fingers to the hot skin to soothe the burn.

"Do you miss it?" he asked, acting nervous. I raised a brow in question. "The tongue ring."

Oh. That. They removed it in pre-op without his consent since he was nearly dead from blood loss.

"Honestly? It was fun, yeah, but I don't miss it, per se. If you want to get it done again, go for it. If not, I still love what you do with your tongue without it."

"Yeah you do, baby. I'll think about it, though—"

"Great, you're both here. Let's get started." The door slammed shut behind Uncle Garr. Charlie snapped his lips together and swiveled the chair to face the man now commanding the room. "First things first. Welcome back. You both look a hell of a lot better than you did last week in that damn hospital."

"Thank you," Charlie and I said at the same time.

I swallowed hard, throat suddenly parched. As if he read my mind, Charlie pulled a water bottle from the bag sitting in the chair beside him and rolled it across the table.

"You will both be happy to know we have convinced the two parties threatening lawsuits against the Bureau to drop the suits."

"Really?" I exclaimed, a dribble of water escaping my moving lips. "How?" I asked, using the back of my hand to clean up my face.

"Well, the hotel had a choice to either follow through with their suit and we would release to the press that a serial killer used their hotel as a hunting ground, putting their reputation at stake, or retract the suit and we'd keep their name out of the press releases. And the suspect you arrested, well, that took care of itself. The board of the Affair Me app caught wind that they were mentioned in his suit and reached out to him directly. Apparently, he enjoyed reaping the rewards of his status with them versus suing us and the Louisville PD."

He turned a pointed look at Charlie.

Nerves running high, my hands shook. Pulling them off the table, I tucked them underneath, wringing my fingers.

"If I gave you carte blanche data access for cases, yours and others, what would you say?"

"Thank fuck?"

We all laughed.

"I assumed as much." Turning to me, his features softened. "SSA Riggs. While visiting in Louisville, you stated you were ready to take the next step and directly manage a team. Does that still stand?"

"Yes, sir."

"Great. You will build your own team from scratch. I have a stack of agents I approve of, but the team will be yours to choose." My jaw fell open. "We've wanted to add a BSU division down in Texas for a while now but didn't have anyone we trusted to build a successful team."

"Texas?" Charlie questioned, shooting a wary glance my way.

"Dallas, to be exact."

"Wow, that's...." I chewed on my lip.

"Agent Bekham, we would like you to assist SSA Riggs." My heart soared. I whipped my face to Uncle Garr. "You will be based at the Dallas office but mobile if needed for certain cases. This means you will roll up directly under the Technical Unit, which is a side branch of the BSU."

I read between the lines.

That meant he wouldn't report directly to me.

Meaning....

My smile grew wider, cheeks burning.

"Do you both understand?"

"Move to Texas, build and manage a team of profilers, and maintain our relationship since Charlie won't be my direct report."

Uncle Garr grinned. "She gets her brains from our side of the family." He tilted his head toward me.

"Lucky me."

"Agreed. Now, if you two will excuse me, I now have the pleasure of breaking the news to Carter on your promotion. I'll announce the promotion and Bekham's shift in roles by the end of the week. We need you down in Dallas, starting the interview process while managing your current caseload, by the end of the month."

"That's in two weeks," I exclaimed. Instantly my mind whirled with the various lists I'd need to make for the team and the near cross-country move. "I—"

"Sounds great, sir," Charlie said, cutting me off. He stood and stretched out his hand. Uncle Garr gave it a hard shake. "Thank you for everything. I'll take good care of SSA Riggs and ensure she's all set for the move."

"I know you will. But just in case you forget, my best friend heads up the CIA. One wrong move and they will never find your body. Understood?"

I giggled when Charlie's face paled.

"Understood. Sir."

With a goodbye wave, Uncle Garr left, heading down the hall for Carter's office.

Oh, to be a fly on the wall when he learns of my promotion and Charlie's move.

"You good with this?" I whispered, now that the door was wide open.

"Very. You?"

"Very."

Twisting in the chair, I took a second for the full weight of the ten-minute conversation to crash into me, forcing an all-consuming panic, but it never came.

I cut a glance at Charlie, finding him smiling to himself. "Hey, Charlie," I said to gain his attention. "I have a fun fact for you."

He slid those tattooed hands into his pockets. "What's that?"

"I never had a chance of not falling for you."

His smile shifted to something soft and shy. "Crazy thing about that fun fact." He moved around the table, putting his back to the wall of windows and blocking his movement from the rest of the team as he stroked a knuckle along my cheek. "It's the same for me. So how about it, future Dallas Section Chief Riggs? Are you ready?"

"Ready for what?"

"For the best part of both our lives."

Hell yes I was.

With him at my side, us together, I could do anything. That included the thing I'd wanted most since leaving Seattle.

To finally live.

And what a fun fact that was.

Keep reading for a bonus epilogue!

Did you love the adorable Bryson Bennett? Preorder his book, Mine to Hold. Coming April 2022.

Love the Protection Series? Check out my SEALs and CIA Series, an interconnected standalone SEAL romantic suspense series.
Covert Affair, Book 1.

BONUS EPILOGUE
RHYAN

I swiped both sweaty palms down the front of my jeans. Grabbing my cell from the coffee table I checked for any missed messages for the hundredth time in the last few minutes.

Where was he?

My overactive mind began creating the worst possible scenarios, with Charlie having changed his mind about us and moving to Texas at the top of the possibility list. My grip tightened around the thin metal as I lounged back against my couch.

I scanned the living room hoping to find anything to distract me from overthinking Charlie's lateness and lack of communication. Stacks and stacks of boxes lined the bare walls. Everything I owned stuffed within waiting for the movers to arrive later in the week to haul them down to Texas.

Charlie and I planned to leave early, deciding to take a slower more scenic route to Dallas. With several stops along the way in small towns, I was looking forward to having the one on one time with him.

Though now I was questioning if he felt the same.

A sharp chirp had me bolting upward, perched on the edge of the couch with my back ramrod straight.

Charlie: Meet me outside.

My heart hammered as I swallowed hard.

Fuck, this couldn't be good.

Standing on trembling knees I sucked in a fortifying breath hoping to rally some of semblance of strength. If he decided he wanted out, that we weren't each other's forever it would shatter me. But I wouldn't make him stick by my side. If he didn't want me anymore I'd let him go, no matter what it did to me.

The wooden handrail slipped beneath my damp palm as I descended my apartment stairs.

At the bottom I paused, staring out the glass door at the sexiest man alive who stood just on the other side.

My stomach churned as tears welled. Raising my chin, I moved to the front door and pulled it open. Charlie looked up from his cell phone, his pursed lips immediately softening and turning upward to a sly smile.

Fuck I was going to miss that smile.

And those lips.

And that amazing tongue.

And fingers…

Okay I was going to miss everything about this man when he dropped me like yesterday's news. I loved him, really loved him. From his soft gooey heart and soul to the bad boy exterior he showed the world.

"Are you ready?" he asked. Lifting his sunglasses up to his forehead, his smile fell to a frown as he scanned my face. "Are you okay?"

"Just do it," I rushed. Holding up both palms I backed up a step needing more distance between us.

"Do what?"

"Break up with me."

His dark brows shot up his forehead. "Break up with you?"

"Yes?" Well hell. His reaction mixed with that tone, maybe I was wrong.

"Baby." Closing the distance between us he hooked an arm around my waist and held me close. Tipping my chin up I stared into those beautiful blue eyes searching for answers. "You're letting your mind take over again. I thought we discussed this."

"I just thought when you weren't on time-"

"Because your surprise took a little longer than expected."

I sucked in a breath. "Surprise?"

He nodded, a wide grin splitting his face. "You ready?"

"Yes?"

His chest rumbled with his laugh making a smile of my own curl the corners of my lips.

Loosening his hold, he slipped his hand into mine and interlaced our fingers. With a gentle tug, I followed him down the couple concrete steps and along the sidewalk. The bright afternoon sun blazed through the vibrant green leaves just blooming along the row of trees lining the street.

Was too busy relishing the fact I did in fact still have a boyfriend and the beautiful afternoon, I didn't notice he'd stopped until he tugged me back.

"So what do you think?"

My brows dripped. "Think about what?"

Charlie tilted his head. I glanced toward the street, still not understanding.

Then I saw it.

My free hand flew to my gaping mouth as I gasped.

"Charlie," I said on a forceful exhale. My mind swam as I stared at the mint condition, cherry red with a white racing stripe 1967 Chevy Camaro. "What is this?"

"It's yours."

I whirled around, the tip of my ponytail smacking my cheek. "What? How?"

The happiness radiating off him was palpable. "Me and your uncle decided you needed a *congrats on the promotion* present."

"This... this is too much."

He shrugged but kept on smiling. "Well the title is in your name, so if you don't like it...."

"I love it," I shouted then slammed both hands over my mouth. "But it's too much. I don't deserve—"

Charlie's hand lashed out, slipping behind my neck and pulling me closer. Those blue eyes bore into my own.

"You deserve everything, Rhyan Riggs. Everything. And some day, somehow I'm going to figure out a way for you to see that too."

"It's a car," I whispered.

"A fucking awesome car."

"You bought me a car."

"Me and your uncle. I can't take all the credit. Though I was the one who found it, negotiated the price, and picked it up in Vermont last night."

Turning to face the car I slowly shook my head at the beautiful classic. Just seeing it flooded my mind with many happy memories of dad and I working late into the night on the one he and I restored together.

"You remembered," I whispered.

"I did."

"Thank you." I turned and wrapped my arms around his neck. "Thank you. Thank you. Thank you."

"You're welcome, Rhyan. My bags are already in the trunk. Let's run up and grab yours, and we can start this cross-country trek like we planned."

I leaned to the side peering up and down the street. "Where's your Mustang?"

"I'm having it shipped so we could ride in your new beauty together. Is that all right?"

"Perfect."

Smiling like a fool helplessly in love, I leaned forward pressing my lips to his. Grabbing the dangling keys from his fingers I twisted to face the most outlandish yet thoughtful gift I'd ever received. A dull burn radiated from my bunched cheeks, from my wide smile.

Today was the start of a new life.

A life I was eager to live.

Preorder Bryson Bennett's book, Mine to Hold, coming April 2022.

Love the Protection Series? Try my SEALs and CIA Series, an interconnected Navy SEAL romantic suspense series. Start with book 1, Covert Affair.

Stay up to date on all my books by joining my newsletter.

ALSO BY KENNEDY L. MITCHELL

Standalone:

Finding Fate

Memories of Us

Protection Series: Interconnected Standalone

Mine to Protect

Mine to Save

Mine to Guard

Mine to Keep

Mine to Hold (Coming April 2022)

SEALs and CIA Series: Interconnected Standalone

Covert Affair

Covert Vengeance

More Than a Threat Series: A Bodyguard Romantic Suspense Connected Series

More Than a Threat

More Than a Risk

More Than a Hope

Power Play Series: A Protector Romantic Suspense Connected Series

Power Games

Power Twist

Power Switch

Power Surge

Power Term

MORE RANDOM FUN FACTS

I couldn't fit all the random fun facts I learned while researching Rhyan's character. Here are a few that I found interesting!

-When someone dies their sense of hearing is the last to go.
-The brain is sensitive to scarcity - the feeling that you're missing something you need
-If you inhale a pea it can sprout and grow in your lungs
-A hug longer than twenty seconds will release a chemical to make you trust the person your hugging
-Being lonely is bad for your health. Research shows fewer friends a person has the higher level of blood clotting protein: Fibnnogen
-Harvard Study shows having no friends could be as deadly as smoking.
-Children of identical twins are genetically siblings, not cousins.
-People who smell good appear more attractive
-Giraffes and humans have the same amount of neck bones.
-The human thigh bone is stronger than concrete.
-It takes up to four minutes to decide whether or not you like someone.
-Eating a banana can help fight depression.

-A super computer took 40 minutes to model one second of brain activity
-Sex slashes stress, it lowers blood pressure and calms you down.
-Honking of a car horns for a couple that just got married is an old superstition to insure great fertility.
-A pigs orgasm lasts for 30 minutes
-The sounds the Velociraptors make when communicating in Jurassic Park is the sound of tortoises when they have sex.

ABOUT THE AUTHOR

Kennedy L. Mitchell lives outside Dallas with her husband, son and two very large goldendoodles. She began writing in 2016 after a fight with her husband (You can read the fight almost verbatim in Falling for the Chance) and has no plans of stopping.

She would love to hear from you via any of the platforms below or her website www.kennedylmitchell.com You can also stay up to date on future releases through her newsletter or by joining her Facebook readers group - Kennedy's Book Boyfriend Support Group.

Thank you for reading.

ACKNOWLEDGMENTS

Thank you to every single reader who picked up this book and the others in this series. I LOVE that you chose to give me a chance. I've always loved the darker side of things, dealing with serial killers, murders, and such. Getting to mix it with my other interest, romance novels, is a dream come true. So thank you for loving this odd mix as much as me. Though my husband is quite worried about my dark little mind and wonders if he might turn up missing one day.

There is so much work that goes into writing a single novel. It's more than just sitting down and typing out words. The behind the scenes support is constant and instrumental for getting the story right. My three alpha readers, Chris, Em and Kristin, are there for me every step of the way. It's not only that I couldn't do this without them, I wouldn't want to.

One of the aspects I've loved in this author journey are all the relationships you make along the way. The women who make up my ARC team, my amazing ARC team, are some of those special relationships that I'll always cherish. Not only do they support me in posting, reading, commenting, and being a sounding board but they listen when I need outside advice. Truly I have the best group surrounding me.

And of course there is Dani with Wildfire. She single handedly turned my career around. If it weren't for her, well, this book or the last two wouldn't have happened. I know she's in my corner supporting me but she's also direct and focused on growing my career. I needed that desperately.

So thank you to everyone who's helped me in this journey and to all you readers who continue to read my words.